THE PROMISE OF SHADOWS

By Dan Rempala

THE PROMISE OF SHADOWS

PROLOGUE

June 27, 1877

Edgar Staley could scarcely say what sounded louder: the thunderous, earth-shaking crash that emanated from the direction of his sheep pasture, or the shrill, almost human screech his sheep unleashed when the thunder stopped. Before the rocking chair had a chance to lose its momentum, he grabbed the edge of the table and pulled himself to his feet. He raced across the room (as much as his weary body could "race" these days), lifted his rifle off of its rack over the door, and headed outside. The bang of the closing door reminded him what he was missing, and he stepped back through the doorway for a handful of bullets from the cabinet drawer. "Edgar?" his wife's creaky voice called from out by the clothesline on the north side of the house. "What in God's name is going on?"

"Don't know," he shouted as loud as he could, his sixty-eight-year-old lungs already begging for air, "but I'm gonna find out. You go on back inside." The wife's hearing wasn't so good these days, but Edgar still had enough voice that she must have heard him. He could picture Caroline's reaction: frown, hands on hips... as if any of this was somehow his doing. There was no way on God's green earth she would follow his instructions, but it might limit the shouting. In truth, he had already formed some suspicions about the source of the commotion. His sheep cried like that a few years back, when lightning struck one of the trees along the fence-line and landed on a few of his flock. They stood clustered together for protection from the elements, and while the middle of the cluster was the catbird seat when it came to cold weather and predators, it was the hardest spot to escape from when the danger came from on high. The falling tree broke the fence and crushed a pair of sheep flatter than a pancake. It crippled a few others, and half the flock escaped through the section of broken fence. It could have happened again. The crash almost sounded like thunder, except for two things: first, back in March, Edgar paid the Beckett brothers to cut down all the trees along the fence-line except for the smallest two, and second, the last time he checked, barely a splotch of fluffy whiteness marred the painfully blue sky.

Edgar was no longer a young man. Most of his hair had departed his scalp long ago, and his skin had gradually turned saggy and blotchy some years later, but cosmetic effects were nothing compared to the damage his respiratory system had endured. The short trip from the rocking chair to the outside stole most of the air from his body. He panted as he took the back off the rifle stock and shoved the bullets inside, and by the time his creaky joints carried him to the fence, he needed to stop to rest. The sun beat down as he propped the barrel of his rifle against the top fence board and manipulated the gate latch with his ten stubby digits. *Should have worn a hat,* he thought to himself. *God only knows how long this will take.*

White-yellow sheep bleated as they trotted toward him from over the rise. They came in ones and twos, no doubt expecting fresh water or an overdue sheering, as he pushed the gate open. They seemed healthy, but a little nervous, just like they got during a thunderstorm. Edgar pushed through them. A pair of clouds dotted the section of sky that he gazed upon, but the two of them combined scarcely could have squeezed out a drop of rain. The tall, thin tree on the near-left corner of the pasture still stood healthy and straight, its thin, angular leaves blowing in the light breeze. The other one stood in the far left corner. He could make out the top of the tree from over the rise, so it had not completely fallen over, but maybe there was... some other issue with it of which he was ignorant. Staley hiked up his britches and headed in that direction. After two steps, he could see that the problem was not in the far left corner, but in the middle of the pasture. That much became obvious the second the familiar smell of mutton hit his nostrils. Lines of smoke streamed from a charred hole in the side of the hill. If he didn't know any better, he would guess that some son-of-a-bitch had lit the fuse on a stick of dynamite and thrown it into the middle of his flock.

As Edger stalked up the hill, his left hand wrapped around the rifle barrel tight enough to turn his knuckles white. No, the years hadn't been kind, but he could still shoot straight enough to take care of any gutless sheep-killin'-son-of-a-bitch stupid enough to enter his line of sight. Every labored step conjured another mangled corpse on the horizon. A formerly white sheep lay to the left, with the remaining half of its body roasted the color of charcoal. The head and torso of a brown sheep lay fifteen yards further uphill than its lower half. A smell that would have been pleasant, savory even, under normal circumstances, when combined with these sights, became a thick, gut-churning stench. Edgar wrinkled his nose, took short breaths through his mouth, and stomped up the hill with a little more energy.

A black stretch of charred ground started about twenty feet from the back fence and continued into the middle of the hill until it became a wide furrow, the likes of which would take half a dozen full-grown men an entire day to dig. Resting at the head of this hunk of cleft ground sat a large, round rock the color of unfired clay. Its diameter could not have measured more than eighteen inches across, and assorted cracks and fissures covered its surface, through which, a dim, blue light shown.

Edgar had never seen anything like it. His eyes traced the trail of the rock backward, from its spot in the ground, through the section of broken fence, to the scorched tips of the head-high grass that grew beyond the far side of the sheep pasture. He repeated the procedure several times, but his muddled mind could not cough up an answer. No one had ever uttered the term "catapult," much less the term "meteorite," in his presence, so his brain had difficulty generating an explanation. "Cannonball" seemed like the closest approximation he could produce. Regardless of how the rock had arrived in his sheep pasture, the thing had damaged his property and his livestock, and any curiosity buzzing around in Edgar's mind was quickly washed away by a desire to get that thing as far away from his home as he could, as quickly as possible.

Edgar squatted down on his haunches far enough for his stiffened hip joints to pop and wiped the sweat from his slick brow with the back of his free hand. The unnatural blue light seemed to pulse from the hunk of rock. Edgar scowled as he re-gripped his rifle and rotated the barrel earthward. Poking the object with the tip of his rifle seemed like the perfectly natural, perfectly sane thing for a man in his situation to do. If anything moved, he would squeeze the trigger. The steel muzzle of the Spencer rifle crept forward.

He didn't have time to scream.

*   *   *

CHAPTER ONE

June 28, 1877:

The tapered end of the axe-head slammed into the top of the upright cylinder of log. The wood cried forth in a dull crunch as it split in half. A pair of slender hands reached down and plucked the uneven lengths of wood from the chopping stump and tossed them onto a pile to the right of the stump. The hands mechanically dropped another length of log into place, heaved the axe-head high into the air, then guided it on its crash earthward. *Pop.* Again, the wood split in one swing. There are two ways to accomplish such a feat: strength or skill. The slender hands and proportionally slender arms indicated the latter.

The boy swinging the axe paused for a moment to run the back of his grimy hand across the surface of his grimy forehead. Nothing quite like a Kansas June at high noon. The sweaty, dirty hairs of his head all hung down at roughly equal lengths like the brown tendrils of a mop. He had fragile, almost feminine cheekbones and his shoulders still shot upward at an almost forty-five degree angle to his neck, indicating that the brunt of puberty had yet to run its rugged course. He wore a pair of denim overalls with no shirt underneath, hardly an inch of which was not marred by a damp, dark blue stretch of sweat.

"Know what I saw the other day?" Emma Waits said from her spot on the fence. Emma was a robust country girl, every bit as hearty as the boy wielding the axe, but she dressed and sounded like something much more delicate. It was the voice that made the boy briefly turn from his work. Emma wore a white cotton dress and her dusty blonde hair remained in its perpetual state of curls, even when bound by a new, baby blue ribbon. She sat on the topmost of the three-board fence, her legs swaying playfully a couple feet above the ground. He didn't notice her approach, and he didn't ask her to continue, but she did anyway.

"Last night," she said, her hands bracing her atop the fence while her legs dangled freely below, "I was bored, so I went over to my Daddy's place."

Christopher Rutlage nodded as he balanced his log on the stump. Her father, James Waits, owned the Liberty Tavern, which along with the blacksmith's shop was one of the few prosperous businesses in town. Christopher had known Emma since they started school several years ago. She seemed to enjoy watching him work, for some reason, and even though he hated seeing her comfortably lounging on the fence while he wilted under the ninety-degree heat, it was better than chopping wood in solitary silence. The axe rose and fell with almost mechanical efficiency.

"There was some cowboys drivin' a herd up from Abilene to Kansas City and they was stoppin' at my Daddy's place, and he was busy, so he sent me lookin' for some pipe tobacco." A wince rippled across Christopher's face as he placed another log on the stump. Emma's father never asked her to do anything and took offense when anybody else did so, so Christopher knew to view whatever details that followed with a touch of skepticism. "He told me to look in this storage closet we got upstairs."

Christopher pictured the upstairs of the Liberty Tavern as the tip of his axe bit into another victim. This swing failed to make it through cleanly, so he needed to wrench the axe-head free and make a second attempt before adding it to the pile. *Must be getting tired.* He had only seen the upstairs from the ground floor. A balcony ran across the north side of the tavern common and opened into hallways on either end. Each hallway connected to a series of rooms, one of which housed the Waits family, the other of which housed another of Liberty's top-notch businesses: the town brothel. Only two women constituted the "brothel," but since Liberty stood over a day's hard ride from Kansas City, they received plenty of business from commuting cowboys.

"Well, there wasn't nuthin' but some old brooms and stuff in the closet, so I kept lookin' down the hallway." Her head lolled from side to side, but her eyes remained fixed on the ground. "I don't know what I was thinkin', but I went in the wrong room, where one of the girls was workin'. I ain't never seen them... doin' that before."

Christopher split the last log, the right half of which pin-wheeled to off the stump and clattered against the pile. He reached down, grabbed the remaining half, and flipped it onto the pile as he turned toward Emma and huffed out a breath of finality. "Your father find out?"

"Naw," she said, still looking in the direction of her dangling feet. "They was makin' so much noise, I don't even think they heard me open the door."

Christopher nodded absently as he squatted down and used his right arm to stack the chords of wood between his left forearm and his chest. He knew from experience that six pieces of wood (two rows of three) would fit comfortably into that space, and his free, right hand could hold a seventh piece. He could ask Emma to grab a piece or two and save himself a trip, but if she came home and James Waits found dirt under his daughter's fingernails, he might organize a lynch mob. Fully loaded, Christopher trudged the fifteen yards over to the side of the squat brown barn, walked around to the shaded side, where the nearly depleted stack of firewood sat. He let his armload clatter to the ground and proceeded to stack the wood so that the filthy old wood lay atop the freshly chopped pieces. With this accomplished, Christopher straightened his stiff back and brushed the flecks of wood off his damp overalls and his slick, bare chest. When he turned back toward the chopping stump, he nearly ran into Emma. She was an inch taller than he, so they stood nose to nose, and through the rise and fall of the girlish mounds barely inside her blouse, he could tell that she was breathing almost as hard as he was.

"You want me to show you what I saw?" she asked coyly.

A pleasant nausea swept over him, centered in the pit of his stomach. Emma's hot breath hit him in the face, synchronous with her heavy chest. He had known her since he was five years old. Their fathers were best friends. Yet, as the throbbing inside of Christopher Rutlage increased, and as he searched for a suitable answer to her question, he could not help but wonder how she ever could have been a little girl.

                        *   *   *

In the wake of the event, Christopher wasted no time contemplating its significance as he immediately re-entered his daily routine. He finished stacking the wood, said goodbye to Emma, and started across town, a few minutes late. The steady hum of empowerment remained with him as he strode down the main street of town. The Liberty, Kansas, of 1877 had only had one real "street," that is, a packed-earth path that was safe for wagon travel. This thirty-foot-wide thoroughfare traveled from the South, through the middle of town, split, circumscribed the church, reformed on the other side, and carried on out of town, in the direction of Kansas City. Otherwise, the narrow, irregularly spaced side-paths formed as a byproduct of the houses that had sprung up. These shabby dwellings were distinct from each other in the way that beaver dams are distinct, most only similar in the quality of their construction. A majority of the homeowners emigrated from the Eastern United States and beyond and had never built a house before.

Christopher remembered when the town was half its current size, but like the incident with Emma, he didn't really know how to feel about it.

The most solid and well-maintained buildings were the businesses. Harkness's Dry Goods Store stood on one corner of the church square, the Liberty Tavern on the opposite corner, conveniently close when some of the more ardent church-goes wanted to venture out and shout at the sinners. Half-a-dozen houses further down the street from Harkness's sat the blacksmith's shop, which shared a building with the Rutlage Family's living quarters. It was a stout building, built to last, because like his father once said, "Folks will always need blacksmiths." Regardless of where or how many houses sprouted out, the whitewashed church constituted the figurative center of town, its high steeple greeting the weary eyes of travelers as they rode across the sea of grass.

Christopher's thickly soled shoes nearly skimmed across the dirt as he walked in the direction of the church with his head held high. The sun still blazed away, high in the sky, and scarcely a breeze weft its way through his matted hair, but his every movement sung with vitality, as though through three-and-a-half minutes of passion, he had shed the shackles of boyhood and become a new, yet undefined entity. Since there were no boys his age in town, however, he had no audience to which to gloat.

Duty determined his direction of his travel, though, and Christopher's walk ended at the door of the last place (make that "second-to-last place") he could tell his tale: his father's blacksmith shop. He stood outside the weather-beaten sliding door, trying to remember why he had come. The familiar roar of fire and the clink of metal striking metal emanated from inside the shop. He took a deep breath and remembered his purpose: he was here because he'd finished chopping wood over at the Perkins' place. A second or two of concentration allowed the grin to slide from his face.

A familiar wave of dry heat hit Christopher as he slithered through the doorway. His eyes required a few seconds to adjust to the shadowy, red-glow of the chamber, before drawing forth the lean, wiry form of his father bent over the anvil. The grim man gracefully flipped a red-hot horseshoe back and forth with a pair of tongs and molded it with the musical clink of his well-placed hammer strikes. Christopher had entered this scene on countless occasions and witnessed the same man perform the same action each time. If his father didn't notice him at first, he would stand in the doorway and watch the master perform his craft. Mr. Rutlage was the only blacksmith in Liberty, but to hear the townsfolk tell it, he had every bit the skill of one of the cattle town smiths. Even if Lewis Rutlage seemed to take little pride in his work, Christopher envied him. *What it must be like to be good at something*, he would muse.

This trip to his father's shop held a surprise for Christopher. It appeared when he walked forward a few more paces and saw the coal black stallion standing in front of the enormous sliding door that led to Main Street, from whose foot the shoe must have been taken. The long, black mane, the single, diamond-shaped patch of white on its chest... only one horse in town fit its description, and it belonged to Deklan Lorenz, a man of whom the townspeople rarely spoke in voices above a whisper.

The instant Christopher recognized the horse, his legs stopped moving. Deklan Lorenz lived alone, miles out of town. In the few instances when fate took them in that direction, passing children feared even to look at the thicket of trees his house resided within. He was Liberty's own poltergeist: part town freak, part sub-human bogeyman. Christopher had seen him on more occasions than most people twice his age because the blacksmith's shop remained the only place in town that Lorenz had any use for. Even there, his sight was an anomaly. The thought of him lurking in the shadows left the fourteen-year-old boy frozen amid the suffocating heat.

Lorenz loomed over all but the tallest men and possessed a mysterious origin and a demon's face. Small patches of hair dotted a scalp so misshapen that phrenologists of the day would have had a hard time classifying him. Thankfully, he almost always wore a hat, but that could not protect observers from the rest of his face. His gray, scarred skin clung tightly to the bones of his face, and his beady, bloodshot eye stared out at a slightly different angle than his normal, gray-blue one. Worst of all, though, had to be the menacing, involuntary grimace that never left his face.

The rhythmic clinking stopped as Mr. Rutlage twisted his upper body toward his son, expectantly. After glancing about the shop and seeing no one but his father, Christopher coughed into his fist and asked, "Um, has Mr. Lorenz taken a walk or —"

Before he could complete his second hypotheses, the fire flared, sending its glow into the far corners of the room and revealing the black-clad hulk leaning against the shop's right-hand wall, next to where Mr. Rutlage's assorted tongs hung. *Of course he isn't walking around town,* Christopher chided himself, *men who look like that don't walk around town… not in daylight, anyway.* "What is it, Christopher?" his father demanded, his sweat-slicked, angular jaw tightening under the firelight. He acted like he didn't understand the nature of Christopher's problem, but that was impossible.

Christopher's gaze shifted to the dirt floor, where the toe of his shoe kicked the top half of a broken horseshoe nail a few inches forward. "I've - I've finished with the wood over at the Perkins' place."

Mr. Rutlage wrinkled his nose and used the back of his gloved hand to wipe away some of the sweat that had beaded up on his scalp under his thinning head of hair. "Yes, good," he said absently, his mind having already conjured another job. "Pick up a half a dozen eggs from the store and take them to your mother. She'll be starting supper soon."

He reached into one of the back pockets of his overalls and extended his closed fist. Christopher stepped forward with cupped hands in time to catch the assorted coins that his father let fall.

Christopher nodded, his eyes still locked onto the packed dirt floor. He turned to go, but something wouldn't let him. Maybe he wanted to provoke his father. Maybe he wanted to hear the sound of Lorenz's voice. Maybe he wanted to prove his bravery, urged on by the post-coital rush of hormones churning through him. Whatever the reason, Christopher twisted toward the corner of the shop and uttered the words that would change his life forever. "Hello, Mr. Lorenz," he said. The shadowy mound with the broad-brimmed hat shifted at the sound of his name. "I don't think we've ever spoken, I'm Christopher Rutlage."

Mr. Rutlage whipped his head around and nearly crushed his fingers under the weight of the falling hammer. Lorenz, though, did not bat a disfigured eye, even when the misguided tool struck the anvil at an awkward angle and uttered a clank several octaves too high. "We've spoken before, boy," he began in a voice that sounded more like a wolf's snarl than human speech. "You visited me at Dr. Ferguson's while I was recovering from my burns. You were small then. Maybe you don't remember."

Christopher opened his dry mouth to speak, but too many questions flooded his mind to decide on one. Why would he visit Deklan Lorenz at the doctor's office, or anywhere else, for that matter? And burns from what? A fool could see that something had burned the man severely, but to Christopher's knowledge, no one knew their origin. Christopher licked his cracked lips. Best to ask about the burns first. "Wha—"

"Christopher!" Mr. Rutlage barked. "Stop pestering Mr. Lorenz and get those eggs for dinner." His eyebrows dove toward the bridge of nose, and his face reddened so fast that Christopher wondered if the smoke filling the room had come from his father's ears. He squeezed the coins resting in his palm, and without hazarding another glance toward the corner, pushed his way into the relative cool of the Kansas afternoon.

*   *   *

Hours later, as the sun closed in on the horizon, the Rutlage family sat down to eat dinner. Each member occupied a side of the thick, rectangular, oaken table; children on the wide ends, parents on the narrow. Mother Rutlage hated spending money on candles, so dinnertime rotated along with the seasonal setting of the sun. That made for some hungry evenings during the summer. The family dined on scrambled eggs because, despite spending the majority of her day housebound, Mrs. Rutlage did not know how to cook much else. For dinner, it was often eggs. For breakfast, it was always... *always* oatmeal.

Lewis Rutlage sat at the head of the table, his face twisted into its standard scowl and his entire body streaked with more soot than a chimney sweep. His jaw moved with a labored rhythm as though he was masticating a mouthful of gravel. Agatha Rutlage sat at the other end, her gray hair pulled back painfully tight against her scalp, exposing her pale, frowning face. She always wore a scarf around her head when she set foot out of doors, and this made her face narrow as a cucumber. Her twig-like fingers looked barely capable of holding her fork. Christopher sat to his father's right, trying to look far more morose than he was, just to fit in. His five-year-old sister, Mary, sat across from him, all dark curls and bright eyes. She looked out of place, like a hummingbird flitting about amid a spiral of vultures.

The excitement and activity of the day left Christopher with a ravenous hunger, and he barely could wait to uncork his seemingly innocent question. He waited two or three solid minutes after his father finished saying grace, and squinted against the orange rays of the setting sun as he gauged his father's expression. Anything less than volatile would do. When he paused from chewing, Lewis Rutlage's mouth formed a line, not a snarl, so Christopher swallowed his forkful of eggs and asked, "What was Mr. Lorenz talking about earlier?"

After the words had left his lips, Mrs. Rutlage's wide eyes found her husband and her hand flew to her sternum in a delicate gesture of faintness. *Stupid, stupid, stupid*, a voice in Christopher's head chided. Lewis Rutlage swiveled his head around until his full glare fell with the weight of an oak tree on his teenage son. "You hear me good: I don't want you ever speaking to that man again," he growled, then shoved a helping of eggs into his mouth, as though the conversation were over.

Christopher bit his lip. Instinct told him to stay quiet. Instinct, though, is a constructed thing, not a manifestation of truth. A life lived inside these musty walls, breathing the same bitter air as his mother and father had forged Christopher's instinct, but even though it had saved him from a beating on occasion, he was fast learning not to bow to it indiscriminately, because a world existed out there beyond the wooden walls of his home. "Why?" he asked.

"Because he's dangerous," Father snapped, his eyelids expanding so far that Christopher could make out the red lines crisscrossing the exposed whites. He followed with a terse nod to drive his point home.

Christopher pressed on, like some hopeless variety of amnesiac unable to remember the result of past dinner table discussions. "But why did I visit him while he was recovering from being burned?"

"Don't talk back to your father!" Mother screeched, rising fully to her feet. The front two legs of her chair lifted off the ground for a second before thudding home. "He's trying to protect you, just as you always does, you stupid, willful boy!" She huffed through a pair of breaths. "You just think you can walk around town, talking to whoever you want, about whatever you want? You think you can just ruin the reputation your father has built over the years? This is no kind of game. That man has the mark of the Devil on him... and has worn it since the day that he killed his wife!"

Despite knowing next to nothing of the man, Christopher raised his eyebrows. "Then, why is he free?"

Mary's eyes darted from her brother, to her mother, then back. A look of whimsy clung to her face. Maybe she didn't know what was about to happen... or maybe she merely didn't understand how Christopher had become so foolish. Mary was used to the arguments, and for her, they still had an aura of unreality, if not amusement for her. After all, she had never felt the unique sensation of her father's leather belt flaying her back.

"The man that was sheriff at the time was a yella-bellied coward," Agatha Rutlage told her son. "If Sheriff Townsend had been here then, he woulda strung up that... that creature in the town square." She lowered herself into her seat, spent. "Lord, oh Lord, why don't they ever learn?" she muttered absently, her eyes cast in the direction of the pitched ceiling. "They shoulda learned like the ones that laughed at Your prophet Elisha..."

Christopher clenched his teeth and looked down at his plate. There was no way for him to extract any information from his mother without deciphering a series of obscure Biblical quotations. Sanity set in, though, and he clamped his lips closed and slinked back into his role of silent follower. He was lucky, extremely lucky to get away with nothing more than a verbal reprimand for his act of defiance. He only opened his mouth wide enough to slide forkfuls of eggs through, but even that he could have done without. In truth, his appetite had disappeared at the sound of his mother's keening.

The desire to solve the mystery of Deklan Lorenz, though, remained with Christopher throughout the meal, and only grew stronger as he cleared the table and deposited the dishes into the bucket of soapy water. His parents were not alone in viewing Lorenz as an agent of the devil; Christopher had always sensed a peripheral fear of Deklan Lorenz in some of the townsfolk, whether it came from the way their eyes scanned the shadows after mentioning his name, or the way posses, festivals, and church services never included him, and no one asked why. Naturally, Christopher had always assumed that there existed several well thought-out reasons for this blanket exclusion.

Behind him, Mr. Rutlage slammed the door on his way out to the barn. Across the room, Mrs. Rutlage sat in her rocking chair, churning back and forth at a spastic rate while she knitted something that might become a quilt in time for Christmas. *Perhaps… perhaps the reasons were not so sound*, Christopher considered as he wiped some soapsuds on his britches. After all, people were not always confined by rationality; two stellar examples slept only fifteen feet away. Mother's shrill ramblings had given him an idea, though, and as Christopher crossed the room to his loft, he privately resolved to devote the next day to speaking to as many people as he could about Lorenz, everyone in town, if need be. Everyone, that is, but the man himself. Christopher didn't know exactly what Lorenz was, but his father surely was right about one thing: Lorenz was a dangerous man.

*   *   *

Scrape.

Scraaaape.

The pencil-thin, metal file dragged through the bullet chamber in slow, sliding hisses. The lone figure leaned against the corner of a house and stared across the makeshift street, through the house's lone window, at the lone flickering candle. In the blue evening, his height and black clothing made him look like a distorted shadow.

Scraaape.

The teenage boy with stringy hair and stooped shoulders crossed in front of the window, then angled toward the far side of the house. He shambled when he moved, like he'd learned to walk when his whole body was a bruise.

Scrape.

The frail woman rocked back and forth as though powered by a steam engine, her hands looping and stabbing the knitting needles with equal fury. The little girl wasn't visible, but she was in there somewhere. Most parents didn't let their children out after dark; too many stories of Indian abductions in this area, confirmed or not… not to mention a certain bogeyman who lived a few miles from town.

The file poked into the next chamber. *Scraaaape.*

Over in the barn, the father rattled some things around, peppering the night with a few dull thuds for extra flavor. He would be coming out in a few minutes, huffing and puffing. He would wait until he'd crossed into the house before yelling anything, as though the sound of a shout or a punch could not permeate the thin, wooden walls.

Scraaape.

The man had sunk deep enough into the shadow to know that Lewis Rutlage would not see him. He was good at hiding. It was a talent, tempered by years of practice.

Scraaaape…

*   *   *

CHAPTER TWO

June 29, 1877:

The next afternoon, Christopher took a short break from sweeping his father's shop to meet with Emma. They rendezvoused at the Old Man Perkins' gigantic and often empty barn, but did not speak for the first few minutes of their encounter. In the sweat-soaked aftermath, Christopher propped himself up on his elbows from his position at the base of the haystack. "What do you know about Deklan Lorenz?" he asked.

"I dunno," Emma said as she buttoned the front of her blouse. Christopher had expected that answer, but he still asked, because he had to start somewhere. He gave Emma credit for not questioning the appropriateness of such a question in that context. Assorted pieces of telltale hay still poked from the curls of Emma's hair, so Christopher carefully brushed it out with his hand. Her head slightly tilted toward his hand, and she smiled warmly. "My Pa always said the guy kilt his own wife and kids."

Christopher nodded absently. Beyond "I don't know" or "what do you want to bother him for," that quickly became the standard answer he received from the townspeople that bothered to answer (Nicholas Gelman, with his beady eyes and leathery skin, continued to stride down Main Street without acknowledging Christopher). The basic story involved either the man killing his wife, his children, or both.

This is not to say that these responses lacked for variety. For instance, there was Ms. Dean. After Christopher carried her groceries to the front door of her house, the paunchy, wart-covered woman turned to give him a copper coin. Christopher raised his hand. "That's alright, ma'am. It's my pleasure."

Her nubby, yellow teeth sprang into view as her lips contorted into a smiled, and she placed the coin back into her reticule. "Well then, thank you again, Christopher," Ms. Dean said in a creaky voice that reminded him of his mother in her calmer moments, "and tell your parents 'hello' for me."

"Um, Mrs. Dean?" he said from her doorway. She needed a series of tiny steps to turn back toward him. "What do you know about Deklan Lorenz?" Her eyes slowly narrowed, so he added, "I mean, how did he get the way he is?"

Her pale, cracked lips pursed. "Well, some say he killed his wife, but I got a good memory and I been here since this town was a patch of grass on the prairie, and I don't remember nothing like that."

"Then why do people say that?"

She shook her head. "He might as well have. I'm not aware that he broke any of Man's Laws, but the fact that he wears the Scars of the Damned shows plain as day that he must have violated more than a few of God's Laws. That doomed his poor wife just as good as killing her." She stared at Christopher, her mouth forming a tiny "o," until he nodded and backed out of the doorway. He held out his snort of laughter until the door was closed.

Liberty harbored no atheists, at least to Christopher's knowledge, so everyone could be said to be "God-fearing" Christians. Within that generalization, though, there existed the subgroup that feared God in a more immediate sense, as if He was constantly preparing bolts of lightning to hurl earthward in the event something displeased him. Mrs. Dean belonged to this latter group.

While Christopher discounted her story as the ravings of a deluded zealot, he discounted the opinion of Mr. Harkness, purveyor of Liberty's general store, for a different reason. "That was before we moved here, so I don't know and I don't care," Harkness said, leaning on his countertop with his fists. He had Lewis Rutlage's tall, angular build, but his almost totally bald head and sharply pointed chin distinguished him from the granite-like visage of Christopher's father. "They should've hanged him from a tall tree a long time ago, though, along with the rest of the blacks and the Irish."

Christopher nodded automatically, wondering where the name "Harkness" originated from. "I see your point." Later, he asked a few people he encountered, people far more lucid than Mrs. Dean and less bigoted than Mr. Harkness, if Lorenz was of Irish descent, but no one knew even that. In all likelihood, Harkness probably did not know either, but he was a fussy, pragmatic man, and not one to take chances.

Walking out of Harkness's, Christopher slid around the squat, scowling form of Pat Zimmerman. He thought about saying something, but unlike Nicholas Gelman, who would glare at everyone, Zimmerman always seemed to save his sour expressions exclusively for Christopher. His eyes locked onto Christopher from either side of his hooked nose, until the door banged closed between them. Christopher stalked into the sun-bleached street with his hands in his pockets and his head down.

The impromptu interviews continued into the mid-afternoon. In most instances, the only way Christopher could get people to talk was by offering to do some small job for them and creating an obligation, as in the case of Mrs. Dean, or dangling it as a condition for his business, as with Mr. Harkness. Those who did talk gave information that wreaked of hearsay, with the year of the killings, the number of victims, and the murder weapon all seemingly drawn at random from a hat. Later in the day, while resting in the shade of an elm tree at the edge of the church square, an obvious thought dawned on Christopher: why not consult the one man who Lorenz mentioned by name?

Doc Ferguson's office stood on the other side of the square from where Christopher sat, two buildings beyond Harkness's store, so it took slightly over a minute to traverse the distance. When he arrived, he knocked on the door while pushing it open. The unmistakable smell of iodine hit his nostrils. "Dr. Ferguson?" Christopher called while leaning inside. He remained wary of visiting Doc Ferguson's office, especially during the hottest parts of summer. He always felt that the sweat and dirt clinging to him would contaminate the antiseptic environment that Doc Ferguson had obviously worked so hard to create.

Doc Ferguson leaned out from the doorway to his examining room, situated just off the waiting room. "Christopher?" late-middle-aged doctor asked, squinting behind his gold-rimmed spectacles. He was at least fifty but his hair had only started to turn grey. His strawberry blond curls hung down to the middle of his neck. Both corners of his mouth lifted into a smile, and Doc Ferguson's characteristic sparkle lit in his eye. "Christopher Rutlage. It is you! Come in, come in. I'm nearly finished with Mr. Staley. Just wait for me out in the front room."

Christopher nodded slightly as his eyes fell to the side of Doc Ferguson. It made him uncomfortable when people acted happy to see him; he just wasn't used to it. As the doctor turned back into his examination room, Christopher stepped inside the building and swiveled his head toward the unpainted, wooden chairs lining the walls of the spotless front room. Two chairs sat against the far wall, while the other two sat to the left of the door. Although her face was partially obscured by her white bonnet, Old Man Staley's wife occupied the seat in the near left corner of the room, her shifting hands wringing one another in the lap of her brown dress. Her ample breasts sagged so badly that they appeared to pull her into her pronounced slouch. Christopher sat down in the chair nearest hers and asked, "What's wrong with..." He paused, almost using the moniker, "Old Man Staley," then started over, "What's wrong with your husband, Mrs. Staley?" He had to speak at a rather loud volume, due to Mrs. Staley's hearing problems.

She flinched toward Christopher, as though the sound had startled her. It took her a moment of staring before she could nod in recognition. Her head bobbled back and forth, and she returned her worried gaze to the doorway to the examination room. "Oh, Edgar's feeling poorly. He hasn't slept in days and is having the pains all over. He's always had a spot of rheumatism this time of year, but it's never been so bad as this." She shook her head. "Poor Edgar." Her crimson-rimmed eyes betrayed a similar lack of sleep.

Christopher pressed his lips together and gave a solemn, silent nod. It wasn't like he could say anything that would relieve the worry, but he certainly did understand her distress. He'd met a handful of older individuals, but the Staley's were the oldest living couple Christopher had ever seen or heard of. If he ever saw one of them alone in town, they were always in the process of going to meet the other one. During a rare spat of conversation, Christopher's father once told him that the Staley's had been together for so long that when one of them met their Maker, the other would be soon to follow.

"Edgar," Doc Ferguson said from the examination room, "I have to be honest with you: these bumps on your forehead are something the likes of which I've never seen. When did you say you first noticed them?" A couple seconds of silence passed before Doc Ferguson repeated, "Edgar?"

"Huh?" Old Man Staley said, absently. "Oh, um, yes-yesterday, I believe." His voice sounded distant, like someone recovering from a long night of drinking.

"Well," Doc Ferguson continued, "they look like knots, particularly nasty knots, but they're too uniform to come from bruising."

Christopher leaned forward to the point that his backside lifted off the chair so that he could peer inside the examination room. Old Man Staley sat on the wooden examination table, his body unnaturally rigid. A single bump appeared in the same area over each one of Old Man Staley's glazed eyes, about an inch above the eyebrow. Every couple seconds, the elderly man twitched, enduring a series of full-body hiccups that threatened to send him off his perch at the edge of the sturdy table. He looked like Johan Hewitt, the time Johan spasmodically crept down the street, past Christopher's house and toward the Waits' tavern, his body in the grips of alcohol withdrawal.

Moments later, Doc Ferguson followed Old Man Staley to the door of the examination room and handed him a white envelope. "Mix this in with some hot water and drink it before you go to bed tonight, Edgar, and every night after until it's gone" Doc Ferguson said, forcing a professional smile. "It'll help you sleep." Staley closed his shaky fingers around the envelope, then dumbly shuffled over to the door to the outside, where his wife waited for him. She took his arm, gave a final glance in Doc Ferguson's direction with her tear-slicked eyes, and led Old Man Staley out the door.

After the door closed, Christopher turned toward Liberty's only medical practitioner and managed a sympathetic smile. Doc Ferguson blinked. As he exhaled, his shoulders sagged forward. "How are you, Christopher?" he asked, folding his arms and leaning against the doorway, wearily. "It's been a long time since you last paid a visit."

"I'm good," Christopher answered, nodding toward the departed couple. "What about Old Man Staley? Do you think he'll be okay?"

Doc Ferguson looked at his glossy, black shoe tops while formulating an answer, probably deciding whether or not Christopher was too old to lie to. When he looked up, he shook his head. "Honestly, I don't know," he admitted. "I'll do everything I can do to treat the symptoms, but that might be the extent of my effectiveness. Even if we were back East, and I had access to more equipment, I don't know what else I would do. Edgar's an old man, and unpredictable things start to happen to the body past a certain age." He looked out his front window, where he could see the Staley's gradually climbing into their wagon. "Those bumps on his forehead are what scare me the most. I've never seen anything like those." His light blue eyes found Christopher again and brightened. "So, how can I be of service?" he asked, clapping the young man the shoulder and forcing another smile.

Christopher stood looking up at the doctor for a moment, digging for the reason for his visit. "This may seem like a strange thing to ask," he said, finally, "but what do you know about Deklan Lorenz?"

Ferguson's expression shifted into a frown, and Christopher braced himself for yet another version of the man's atrocities. Instead, Doc Ferguson stepped back into his examination room, opened a drawer, and began to replace his medical instruments. "I really don't think that the man's life is any of your business, Christopher," he said, disappointment ringing in his voice. "I think after all he's been through, he deserves to be left in peace."

Christopher bit his lip and took a step backward. He suddenly felt like the town gossip- monger. "It's just that I heard that he'd killed his wife and kids, and —"

Doc Ferguson's head whipped around and revealed a pair of wide eyes hovering behind his rectangular spectacles. Christopher took another step back, unable to tell whether the expression bore anger or merely shock. He had crossed half of the waiting room before Doc Ferguson composed himself. The doctor shook his head and actually chuckled. "You heard what? That Deklan Lorenz had killed his family?"

Christopher nodded, confused.

"Who on earth did you hear this from?"

Christopher started to silently count the guilty parties on his fingers, then summed it up with, "Well, a lot of people."

Doc Ferguson chuckled again, mostly to himself. "Weeping Jesus on the cross..." He sat down in the examination room's lone chair, removed his spectacles, and massaged the bridge of his nose. Anticipating a speech, Christopher eased into the examination room, hopped up on the examination table and straightened himself into a rigid listening posture that he normally reserved for church services. "The only thing I know for a fact about Deklan's early years," Ferguson said, "is that he was close to one of John Brown's boys."

"John Brown?" Christopher repeated, his eyes narrowing. There weren't many famous people in that part of the world, but John Brown was one of them. "The same John Brown that killed all those people up in Pottawatomie?"

Doc Ferguson nodded. "The very same. Deklan and his wife moved to Liberty... let's see, about twelve years ago I guess it would be.... maybe thirteen. Handsome couple they were back then—"

"How'd he get his scars?" Christopher asked.

"I'm getting to that," Doc Ferguson assured the young man. "It would've been nine years ago as of last April, I believe, that the school house caught on fire—"

"I remember that," Christopher said with a sharp nod, eager to make any sort of progress.

"You should; you were one of the children Mr. Lorenz pulled out of the blaze that day." Christopher narrowed his eyes. He had started school a year early because his parents wanted him away from the shop as soon as possible. He was five years old when the school caught fire, so most of the details remained mired in the haze of time. All he could really remember were the heat, the light, the smoke, the crack of the ceiling's main support as it caved in. He didn't remember anything about a man in black, though. Doc Ferguson brandished a sophisticated sense of humor from time to time, and Christopher watched the good doctor closely, waiting for the punch line.

When Doc Ferguson was certain that his visitor would not interrupt him, he continued with the story. "He'd been riding by, as I recall, when he saw the smoke and all the people standing outside. The entire front half of the building had nearly collapsed, and the schoolmistress... her name escapes me right at this moment, but she ended up moving to Wichita a year or so later...she told him that there were still children inside. He didn't hesitate. He busted out the side window and saw several children passed out on the floor... from the smoke, I presume. He grabbed you and the Waits girl and took you outside."

Christopher sat listening, leaning forward so far that he had to shift his weight to keep from falling off the table. "Well, he managed to get you two out, despite being alone and having to face the smoke and flames, but when he went back in for the rest of the children, the roof collapsed on him." Doc Ferguson absently rubbed his right eye before finishing the thought. "Four children died, and Deklan was burned horribly before he managed to crawl out of the rubble. I have no idea how he survived, suffice it to say that Deklan Lorenz is made of sterner stuff than you and I."

Christopher's face wrinkled up in disgust. He felt a little dirty for believing the lies about Lorenz's past, even for a moment. Why did he even bother to seek information anywhere but here? He waited for Doc Ferguson to chide him, to call him the most gullible idiot in a town full of gullible idiots, but instead, Doc Ferguson's mouth curled into a sad, nostalgic smile. Christopher blinked hard. "So, he was a hero?"

"Yes, of course; that's what you call someone who saves children from a fire," Doc Ferguson agreed with a nod. "He still is, you know, whether the rest of the town admits it or not. Oh, Liberty loved him, but only for a few days. He received more flowers during the week I began treating him than I knew existed in the state of Kansas, and the women of the town made sure he never went with an empty belly once he was well enough to take down food. Things changed rather dramatically for Deklan once he was able to return home, but you probably already figured that part out."

Christopher rocked back and forth on the table. He had an idea, but was finished making assumptions for the day. "What happened?"

"Well," Doc Ferguson said, leaning against the back of his chair and setting his left ankle on his right knee, "gradually, the way he looked started rubbing people the wrong way, how he frightened children and such." His focus drifted for a second, but he blinked and got it back. "About a year after the accident, he couldn't even walk down the street without being stared at. Seemed like everybody forgot the real reason he looked the way he did, and how he saved you and Emma Waits. All those parents, though, the parents of the one's he couldn't get out, they never forgave him for not getting their kids out first."

The doctor folded his hands on top of his knee. "Me? I think more than a little of it had to do with guilt. See, those scars were a constant reminder to some people that they stood around, scratching their heads while children were dying. In some ways, the great man reminds the rest of us what we aren't... and if we drag him through the mud, it elevates us."

Christopher squinted, trying to follow the thread.

"Never mind," Doc Ferguson said, waving a hand. "At least one parent, Patrick Zimmerman, Lizzy Zimmerman's father, showed up at the schoolhouse, too, while Deklan was still pulling you kids out, even, but he never did anything but watch." He tilted his head to the left. "I don't blame Pat for being a coward; I don't know what I would've done. That makes his reaction worse, though, in my opinion: standing there, watching with your own eyes a man risking his life for someone else's children, then blaming him, for either not being fast enough or for not having the sense to leave someone else's child to die. In any case, I believe it was Zimmerman who started the rumor that Deklan lit the fire."

"What really did?" Christopher wondered aloud.

"Oh, it could've been a lot of things. There was a barn connected to the schoolhouse in those days, and it was a dry summer. Something could have knocked a lamp over, lit the hay, and the whole things could have gone up before anyone inside know what was going on. Another early theory was that it was lit by some locals with a vendetta against the schoolmistress, but that one always struck me as a little farfetched. The fact remains: I don't know. I don't know how it went up so fast that she wasn't able to get fifteen children out of a two-room building. None of it really matters, though. Eventually, since they didn't have anybody else to blame, some people, a few that hadn't even lost children in the fire, accepted that Deklan Lorenz was a child-killing arsonist that and that his appearance matched his evil heart. It... fit too well with what they wanted to believe."

Christopher shook his head. "That doesn't make sense. You said people were standing there. They know what happened."

"As you go through life, you'll find that people are both funny and tragic," Doc Ferguson said, holding up his palms in sequence, as if that helped explain it. His right eyebrow arched above the thin, gold glasses frame, and his eyes stayed on Christopher for a long moment, almost amused by his reaction. "The story didn't become part of the town folklore overnight, but it did happen. Deklan had his defenders, starting out, but it was a small town, and a lot of those people died or moved away. New people moved in who he scared the bejesus out of, and they were all too willing to believe the worst. The few defenders that remained... it wasn't worth it to them to get in an argument with their neighbors over some scarred-over phantom on the edge of town." He sighed, "And, though it shames me to admit it, I'm one of them; I didn't jump to Deklan's defense every time I heard a stray comment."

"It gets worse, though," he continued. "A couple years after the fire, Deklan's wife got kicked in the head by their plow horse. She was picking a rock from its hoof or some such routine activity... it was just a freak thing, really..." For the first time, Doc Ferguson's eyes took on a reddish tint. For a frontier doctor, though, tragedy is part of the trade. He merely paused, removed his spectacles and absently began to clean them, and continued with the story without shedding a tear. "Her skull was crushed. The swelling..." he shook his head. "She never made it through the night. Of course, this bitter little contingent of Liberty was quick to blame that one on Deklan as well."

"What? How could he get blamed?" Christopher asked, nearly shrieking with the moral indignation than only an adolescent can muster.

"Why not blame him at this point? It fits the story," the doctor said, replacing his spectacles and glancing at the shelves behind him. "He gets blamed for things all the time. Give them time, and they'll start blaming him for a bad harvest or the assassination of President Lincoln." Doc Ferguson paused and reached shelf behind his right shoulder, to the shelf where his pipe rested. "Such a shame about his wife, too. Such a lovely woman. Always defended him in public, you know."

He shook some tobacco into his pipe. "I remember once when Mrs. Zimmerman referred to Deklan as a... I think the words she used were, 'Demon Spawn,' or some such nonsense." He smirked. "Have to give her points for creativity, at least. They were over at Harkness's at the time, and Clarissa... that was Deklan's wife's name... Clarissa picked up her packages and calmly replied that nature would have to do more than give Deklan a few scars to keep him from being twice the man Pat Zimmerman is. Then she turned and walked out of the store." Doc Ferguson smirked. "'A few scars.' That's what she said," he told Christopher, shaking his head, a now lit pipe clutched between his teeth. "That's all they were to her, too. His whole face looked like a spent candle, but to her, they were a few little scars." He sucked on his pipe. When he spoke, a thick tendril of smoke trailed after the words. "Deklan was totally alone after she died, no way he could've found another wife, even if he wanted to. To be honest, I was afraid he might take his own life... but it hasn't happened yet."

They sat in silence for several seconds, enjoying the smell of pipe smoke mingled with iodine. Ferguson watched Christopher's face tighten up and stare at a spot on the floor. *What is he thinking?* Ferguson wondered. The only book his parents let him read was the Bible, so every person of mythical stature he knew probably came from it, and these figures were no doubt systematically contorted into becoming an enemy to young, free-thinking boys by his puritanical parents. The Rutlage Moses followed orders, just like the Rutlage Samson took his beatings in silence. Maybe Christopher never had a real hero. Ferguson sucked on the pipe stem again. He had books. Lots of books. Why didn't he ever offer to let Christopher read them? He smirked as the answer came to him: *because it's not worth getting into a fight with the neighbors.*

Christopher's eyes found the doctor. "That's not fair at all," he finally declared.

Doc Ferguson took another puff. "Not to spoil the surprise, but you'll find that life rarely is."

"Is that why Mr. Zimmerman doesn't like me? Because I survived?"

"Maybe. Pat doesn't need much of an excuse to dislike people. I've seen the McSorelys give you dirty looks, too, though... and the Gelmans. The Eberhardts probably would have to, had they not moved out to Fort Hayes." He folded his hands over his knee. "I doubt it's a conscious thing, in your case. If you asked them, they probably wouldn't say that was the reason. But that's the reason."

"I always thought it was because they had some ugly business with my father," Christopher said, mystified.

"Your father —" Ferguson began, then his eyes fell. When he started over, his voice was softer. "People respect your father; he embodies what a lot of them believe in. That's never been in question. Visibility. That's the issue. Lorenz, they could mostly forget about," Ferguson explained, pointing over Christopher's head. "He lived outside of town. They were lucky if they saw him once a year... and you might even say they got their revenge on him." He shook his head and sucked on his pipe. "You on the other hand... every time you stepped in to the street, you were a reminder of their lost children... and that never goes away. Emma, too, in all likelihood, even if being a girl made her more sympathetic."

Another bit of silence followed, Christopher again staring at the spot on the floor illuminated by the orange rays of the sun on its downward arc. A spark of recognition fired, and his head whipped toward the window. "Oh, god. It's almost sunset." He turned toward Doc Ferguson. "Thanks for everything, but I've got to get back to the house."

"My genuine pleasure," Doc Ferguson replied.

Christopher hopped off the table and took two steps toward the outside before stopping just past the door to the examination room. "Dr. Ferguson?" he asked, turning back.

"Yes, Christopher?" he said from his chair.

"Why did you laugh when I told you about Mr. Lorenz killing his family?" Christopher asked, resting his hand on the doorframe. "You weren't surprised, were you?"

"'*Allegedly* killing his family,'" he corrected. "You have to add that qualifier." The thought forced another smirk. "Yes, I was a bit surprised by the absurdity of saying he had killed his wife *and children*. You see: they didn't even have any children."

"They didn't?"

"No, Clarissa had... physical problems that wouldn't allow her to conceive." His eyebrows bobbed for an instant. "It seems ridiculous now, but once upon a time, women in town would remark... this was before the fire, of course... that a man as handsome as Deklan Lorenz deserved better than having to settle for a barren wife." Doc Ferguson's eyebrow bobbed again as he removed his pipe. "Fancy that," he said, sounding somehow amused and sad. Christopher left him like that.

                    *   *   *

Christopher's stomping feet left shoe tracks in the dust of Liberty's main street as he stalked back to the house, fuming. After he endured a phantom animosity for all his remembered years, Christopher's world suddenly made sense, but he did not like the sense that it made. The reason some of the townsfolk always made him feel unwelcome was because he was not welcome. They wanted him erased from existence for the sin of surviving, and he could do nothing to correct it. And what of the companion injustice visited upon Deklan Lorenz by those same ungrateful neighbors? How could people who supposedly worshipped a just God shun a hero and tell the worst sort of lies about him? The man lost his face saving lives, and they used this against him. Christopher's temper flared higher with each step. As his pulse thumped in his temple and an energy filled his stride to rival his recent moments of post-coital adrenaline, Christopher actually considered confronting his parents for lying to him. He had never confronted them before, about anything, but suddenly, it seemed like a good idea.

The rage built as he walked through the long shadow of the church with his hands contracted into fists. By the time he stepped up to the front door of his parents' house, however, the submission he associated with these familiar surroundings set in, and the palpable disgust drained from his body.

Staring at the latch key, reasons to avoid confrontation suddenly abounded. They might decide to hate Doc Ferguson. The scene would undoubtedly upset Mother. And there was ever-present fear of a severe beating. It would have all been worth it, though, if there were a chance that they would have admitted to perpetuating a lie, but that would never happen. His parents enjoyed finding reasons to hate people. It had to be someone different from them, someone that threatened their values. With Deklan, it was the way he looked. Even though his money was good enough for Father to take, both his parents had gone along with the popular notion long ago that Deklan Lorenz represented evil incarnate, and even a ridiculous, unfounded lie remained evidence enough for them. Anything else equated to heresy.

Facing the solid, impassive front door, realizing that he would not act out the fantasy of standing up to Father and Mother, Christopher did not know what he *would* do. *Some* sort of new venture seemed almost mandatory, but… Footsteps thudded across the wooden floor of the house, approaching the other side of the door. His pulse quickened again, this time out of fright, not rage. The door latch lifted, and in his fear-induced paralysis, Christopher merely watched. The door opened inward, and there stood Lewis Rutlage, glowering down at his son. His gray eyes refused to waiver or blink, and Christopher worried that the intensity of the gaze might burn a hole through the middle of his forehead. "Hello, son," he said, even though his lips hardly moved. The dead tone sent Christopher's stomach churning with a familiar dread. Nine times out of ten, when his father spoke, it was bad news for Christopher. When he used that tone, the probability jumped. The tone became more and more frequent with each passing year, as Christopher became more and more of a disappointment.

Though Christopher would have preferred to remain silent indefinitely, the unwavering gaze demanded that he say something in return. He mumbled something that might as well have resembled a coherent answer.

Satisfied, Mr. Rutlage continued. "Talked to Mr. Harkness today. Said you were over at his store, askin' everybody you could run down about that Lorenzen fella. That true?" Christopher had never met anyone better at extracting information that he already knew.

Christopher managed only a slight nod, not wanting to risk eye contact. He would have loved to ask why his father hated a man that had saved his only son from a fiery death, but his father rarely needed a good reason to hate. Maybe some of the families that lost a child in the fire looked at him like they looked at Christopher. Maybe that hurt business. Maybe he would have rather Lorenz minded his own business that day and kept on riding.

"At least do me the respect of lookin' at me when I'm talkin' to you, boy," Rutlage said sternly. When Christopher forced his chin upwards and achieved contact with his father's steely gray eyes, he could scarcely refrain from crying. He should be used to it by now, hardened like forged steel, but he wasn't. Despite his best efforts, he remained something more like porcelain. "Didn't I tell you to leave it be?"

Nodding might have broken eye contact, so he choked out a "Yes, sir."

Rutlage's over-sized blacksmiths hand slowly gravitated upwards, as though he might strike his son. Instead, the hand plastered back the loose strands of his gray, thinning hair. "Well, what do you reckon we should do about this?"

Christopher pulled his eyes away from the Medusa gaze to salvage any remaining dignity. "I reckon I should take a beatin'."

He nodded. "I reckon so, too." The job of announcing the predetermined punishment (there was only one) always fell to Christopher, as if it were his idea. Rutlage never failed to provide a nod of agreement, as if the boy's suggestion were a novel, yet excellent, thought: the one talent that his willful son possessed. In many ways, this exercise in sadism, the admission of an abuse-worthy mistake by a boy who did not truly believe he had committed a wrong, often proved worse than the beating.

His father propped the door open and allowed Christopher to pass in front of him while entering the house. The thick, black leather belt awaited him in the middle of the kitchen table, silent and menacing as a Biblical asp. The floorboards creaked under Christopher's shoes as he moved toward the short end of the table in slow motion.

Christopher knew he would endure an unexceptional beating that evening, nothing like the time he took some of Father's money and consequently passed out from the pain. Asking a few harassing questions would only entail a couple extra lashes with the belt. They wouldn't cause any lasting damage; he knew from experience that, after his father's belt tore through the pain threshold, his back would become numb with lacerations, which kept the extra lashes from hurting too badly.

Every corner of the house was empty and silent. Mother had left and taken Mary with her. She never watched the torture. By not watching, she could pretend to be ignorant of the beatings that took place in her kitchen, pretend that the bleeding welts crisscrossing her fourteen-year-old son's back came from another, more supernatural source. Stigmata, maybe. During the brief moments of coherent thought, clutching the table, gritting his teeth, wincing every few seconds, Christopher secretly believed that Mother wished she could participate in the whippings, but in the Rutlage household, beating the children remained a man's job.

"We are blessed with a good little town here, son," Lewis Rutlage said, his tone almost sympathetic. "Lot of good, God-fearing folks." Christopher unbuttoned his gray/white shirt and peeled it off before gripping the familiar edge of the table. He was surprised there were not finger-width indentations in the wood, where he squeezed with all his might for support... and to keep his hands from trembling. He clamped both his eyes shut, but he could still hear the quiet hiss as the uncoiled leather belt slid over surface of the table. Outside, crickets chirped, but they seemed miles away. Christopher set his jaw and awaited the initial blow.

Rutlage continued in his low, even tone. "The reason it's that way is because people obey the Commandments. They leave each other alone. Children honor their parents." He frowned as he wrung the buckled end of the belt in his fist. "You pull something like you did today... I just thank God we got you out of Kansas City before you became corrupted into some wicked little beast."

Christopher nodded silently. If they'd lived in Kansas City, he could have run away a long time ago, hopped a cattle train to St. Louis and disappeared. His father always stretched out the time between strikes as long as he could. That way, each one could sink in for several seconds and achieve the maximum amount of pain.

"You should be old enough to understand, but you obviously ain't yet," Rutlage said. The belt tapped the floor a couple times as he limbered up his swinging arm. "But believe me when I tell you this is for your own good." The air whistled as the belt cut through it, but Christopher had no time to wince. He heard the sharp crack and thought that the belt had missed him. A second later, the pain oozed in. The leather had bit into his left shoulder blade in a sharp burst. The first lash always hurt the worst. This time proved no exception. White spots filled his vision when he blinked away the gathering tears. "I can't have my own son championing the Enemy," Rutlage explained. Christopher had to wait several seconds before my right shoulder blade received the same treatment as his left. "I can't have my own son disobeying me."

From the second hit on, it would be a downhill run. Yes, the pain would steadily increase every time the belt flayed the already tender skin, but it was just a higher degree of the same kind of pain.

Christopher never bothered to count the lashes. What good would it have done? He could not argue that his father gave him too many, or he would have gotten another beating for violating the Fifth Commandment yet again. Instead, he just assumed that he would die clutching that table; that way, anything less served as a pleasant surprise. He also gave up on trying to make sense of the situation a long time ago. Usually, he focused on a single thought. The topic of that thought would change from beating to beating, but once the beating started, he had to concentrate on the one thing. If his attention wavered, his only thoughts would be of pain.

On this particular occasion, his thoughts stayed on Mary. She was a far more angelic child than he had ever been, but their father still slapped her on the bottom every once in a while. What would happen when she grew older? Would she receive a more "adult" punishment? Well, when she was older, Christopher would be older, too. Leaning

against the thick, wooden table, grimacing, Christopher promised that if
Father ever took the belt to Mary, he would kill the hateful old man.
Choke the life out of him, or dash his brains out with a rock. He made the
promise to himself, because he doubted that God was listening.

*   *   *

After the ordeal ended, Christopher struggled up the ladder to his
bed. Every time he raised his hands to reach for another rung of the
ladder, the skin of his back stretched or folded, and bolts of pain crackled
through him. Once in bed, he lay on his stomach, as not to bloody the
sheets or have them stick to the scabbed-over areas. After maybe an hour
of heavy breathing, Mary visited, as she tended to after her brother's
beatings. His loft stood just off the kitchen and, therefore, remained quite
visible from most spots in the house. On a couple of occasions, Mr.
Rutlage or his wife caught Mary visiting Christopher and yelled at her,
telling her, "Christopher needs time to think about what he done." This
time she waited until her father stalked out of the house and let the door
slam shut behind him before chancing a walk through the kitchen.

The routine was as simple as it was practiced. She would creep to
the edge of Christopher's bed and interrupt his attempts to keep from
sobbing. Father hated the sound of whimpering, and before Christopher
grew old enough to manage the pain, his crying would often summon the
elder Rutlage.

"Are you alright, Christopher?" Mary asked from the fifth of the
seven ladder rungs.

"I'm good," he replied, his facial muscles constricted. He knew
she would visit, so he had the foresight to position his head away from the
ladder.

"I'm sorry," she said.

Despite the inferno raging in the flesh of his back, half of
Christopher's mouth stretched into a smile. As if any of it were her fault.

The saved child agonizing over the sacrificed… after the events of today, he finally knew what that felt like. She reached her arms out to hug him, and he shifted over to meet her halfway. Again, careful not to get any blood on her or let her touch the tender expanse of his back. "Everything's going to be fine," he whispered.

She never asked why Father had beaten him. She knew better, and Christopher knew better than to try to explain it to her. The beatings were rarely justified, and he did not want entice her into doing something stupid, like asking their parents about some aspect of the incident or, God forbid, trying to defend him. Besides, Christopher had no wish to relive the incident. Reminders that your father hates you can hurt worse than a measly strip of leather.

Mary quietly tiptoed off to bed, leaving her brother ample time to repent. The idea that the fault lay with him, for something he did or something he was, would never leave him, and that applied to more than these father-son encounters. In his moments of failure and regret, somewhere in the back of his mind, a voice trying to make sense of things would insist that it was just like his father said: he had done something wrong, something he could correct or avoid if he just tried hard enough. That explanation at least gave him some feeling of control. If he worked hard, someday things would be better. Someday, Christopher Rutlage would be a worthy creature, someone who could make his own father smile with pride. The alternative was that his father just liked hitting him with a belt, and that left no possibility of a happy ending.

*   *   *

While Christopher lay on his stomach with his eyes clamped shut, one hundred yards away, Emma Waits lay on her back, atop her bedspread, with her eyes open. Her bare feet and calves slid over the surface of her quilt, restlessly peddling an invisible bicycle. She used to be able to fall asleep at normal times, like a normal person. Then she turned fifteen, and the early part of her night was filled with the sound of creaking hinges, shadows in the doorway, and a warm, hairy body that reeked of malted liquor crawling across the covers.

She knew what was happening to her was wrong, much worse than what she did with Christopher Rutlage. He should have known it, too. They worshipped in the same church, so he must have recognized his sin, but he kept showing up at her doorway every few nights. If it were every night, it wouldn't be as bad. At least then, she could wait, get it over with, and cry herself to sleep when he left. Some nights he didn't come, though, and she was lulled into thinking that he was tired of her body and he wouldn't come back.

Tonight was such a night. Every time the hallway floorboards sighed, she peered through the open crack of doorway and saw nothing but the hallway lamplight. Why couldn't Christopher come and take her away from all this? Why couldn't she be dead? Or him. Why couldn't he just die? It was a sin to wish that... it had to be. She must have done a lot of sinning to deserve this, though, if not in this life than in a previous one.

Something blocked the hallway light. The silhouette of a human body stood outside the doorway, then quietly pushed itself into her bedroom. Soon, it would be quietly pushing itself into her.

*   *   *

Chapter Three

June 30, 1877:

The next morning, Christopher contemplated suicide for the first time. While still sleeping, he absently rolled over onto his scabbed back, and the flare of pain jolted him awake. For several minutes, he stared at the slanted wooden ceiling as the rays of dawn crept across the floor from the shutterless east window. His spirits did not feel particularly low; no nausea permeated his guts and no lethargy clung to his brain. His body felt sore, like a horse had kicked him in the chest and then dragged his prone body over hot coals, but he had felt much worse on numerous occasions. He felt no conscious urge to die, either, as he waited to muster the courage and energy to rise from bed. The self-destructive desire must have lingered inside him somewhere, however, because that was the morning he walked away from town to visit Deklan Lorenz.

Christopher hurried through his morning chores as fast as his battered body would allow, especially when he was out of the sight of his parents. If either of them detected that he had finished his work early, they would merely assign extra tasks. Taking one of the horses out of town was not an option. Father would remain in the shop all day, but Mother would not overlook a missing horse, and she would immediately report it to Father. If his father found out, Christopher's life would be about as worthless as a bag of dirt. Instead, he calculated that if he spent that Friday morning working like the Devil to complete his chores, he would have enough time to walk out to Lorenz's house and back without making anyone too suspicious of his absence.

A few minutes before the church clock struck noon, Christopher finished scattering a bucket of feed onto the stretch of dirt that constituted the chicken coup, the last of his regular chores. That did not mean he had finished working for the day, but it bought him some time. He ran slightly behind on the mental timetable he had constructed, although not enough to cause any major changes in the plan. He strode out of town at a pace that was not quite a run but more than a walk. As the last of Liberty's houses drifted behind him and only the sea of grass stretched to the horizon, he remembered that Eastern Kansas's pancake-like topography failed to provide travelers with much shade from the mid-summer sun. He would have turned back to fetch a hat from his parents' house, but that would destroy what remained of his schedule. He just hoped it would not get too terribly hot that day. It did, of course, and in the ensuing days, Christopher came to curse his absent-mindedness every time he touched his sunburned nose.

Another dozen or so steps into the now thigh-high grass, and Christopher considered that he might lose his way. The distance he had to cover only amounted to a few miles, but he had not visited Lorenz's property in years. Curiosity drove the lone venture to the area: a young boy hoping to catch a glimpse of the town freak. The fear of getting lost did not involve the possibility of not finding his way back at all (he was not that inept). Rather, he worried about not getting back in time. He refused to allow the chance of another lashing stop his attempt to fulfill what he saw as a social obligation, but just the same, the puss-seeping welts lining his back stuck to his shirt every time the cloth shifted and readily reminded Christopher of a fate he preferred to avoid.

The oppressive heat radiated earthward and lingered there for a full hour of uneventful walking. His feet rose and fell with a regular, lockstep motion. From the outset, he had worried about encountering riders, either transient or local, who might divulge his day's adventure to his parents, but he found none to even avoid. Without the crackle of anticipation growing inside him, the walk might have been even more boring than the typical walk through rural Kansas. Christopher had no appreciation for the aesthetic qualities of nature, perhaps because at that stage in his life, he never saw any breathtaking scenes of natural beauty. He had spent his whole life on the plains, and while the flatness of the grass-choked landscape allowed one to see for miles, there were only more miles of grass to see.

There are more geographically diverse chunks of land in the United States than the one Liberty occupied. A few hills dotted the landscape around the town, as did a few more trees. This said, Deklan Lorenz somehow managed to find a spot to build a house that had both a decent elevation and considerable degree of foliage. Christopher could not have known this at the time, but even while a newlywed, Lorenz based his choice of living locality upon its tactical advantages. The elevation, however slight, combined with the vegetation that he and his wife planted, required that a potential attack upon his house come from close in.

Christopher paused at the rim of the tree cluster. The hanging shadows failed to frighten him to the degree that they had when he was a child, but they remained eerily long and silent. To a young Kansas boy, the light patch of trees might as well have been the densest sections of Appalachia. He walked down the only visible path through the overgrowth, trying to create as much noise as possible and not surprise the man. "Mr. Lorenz?" he called out in a hesitant voice. The words didn't feel right; you use the word "mister" when referring to someone that is part of society. Having only walked through something so close to a forest once before, Christopher found the experience unsettling. Every tree afforded a potential hiding place, and with every step, he expected to catch a bullet in the head. "Mr. Lorenz?" he called again.

The path angled sharply to the right, and Christopher caught sight of Lorenz's modestly sized house and even more modestly sized barn. The sturdy, single-story structures sat about a hundred feet from each other, and both would have seamlessly fit in with the typical architecture of Liberty. No one lingered on the house's front porch. No sound came from the darkened interior of the barn. A dozen softly clucking chickens milled around in the fenced-in area between the buildings, and a single, black horse with a white blaze silently used the far side of the fence to scratch its hindquarters awkwardly, but no humans showed themselves.

Christopher decided to check the barn first. He took one step and froze as a black and white milking cow shambled out from behind the barn, lolling its way across the fenced-in enclosure. One of the fence's top boards, near the barn, appeared broken. A lone replacement board lay on the ground beside the broken section, along with a hammer and paper sack of what he assumed were nails. It appeared as though someone had recently left the job.

Christopher cautiously approached the fence and peered over. The cold steel barrel of what had to be a pistol pressed against the base of his skull, forcing him to again freeze. "How can I help you, Mr. Rutlage?" a hoarse voice asked.

"I just wanted to talk with you," Christopher said, quickly, wondering if Lorenz would blast a bullet through his skull before he could offer an explanation. No one knew he had left town. Lorenz could bury Christopher's body in the back of his cow pasture and no one would be the wiser.

"Talk?" he said in his gravelly voice that belied problems with his throat. "I thought you might just want to stare at me like you and your little friends do when you come out here." Though not the warmest of statements, he did un-cock the gun, and as a further gesture of good will, even refrained from jamming it against the back of the teenager's skull. Christopher's lungs took these acts as signs that Lorenz no longer perceived him as a threat, and started to draw air again.

While Christopher's breathing began to normalize, Lorenz stuffed the barrel of his gun in his belt and returned to the work the intruder had interrupted, that of repairing the fence board. Lorenz wore a pair of brown britches and a dirty white pullover shirt. Such mundane clothing looked out of place on him. His normal, plain black attire resembled that of a priest, or a mourner at a funeral. Christopher had also never seen him without a hat before, and the scarred, wrinkled flesh covering the man's face continued several inches up his forehead, delving into his mass of stringy, black hair. Lorenz squatted down on his haunches and gingerly opened the paper bag with his right index finger. "So what is it you want to talk about?"

Christopher remained silent, staring at the other man, as if noticing his fascinatingly ugly features for the first time. *Great idea*, he thought when he realized what he was doing, *keep gawking at him until he shoots you in the face*. In the most professional tone he could muster, Christopher stammered, "I'm... I just wanted to thank you for saving my life, back when the... uh, the school house burned down."

Lorenz picked up his hammer and rubbed the metal head. He snorted. "Well, you're welcome. Is that all?"

Christopher's mouth remained horribly dry from the walk, but at that moment it somehow became even more parched, and his throat decided to pucker up so much so that breathing caused a succession of stings along the interior of his trachea. Despite the discomfort, he choked out the apology: "I'm sorry it cost you your face."

Lorenz expelled a short, mirthless laugh. "I'm not," he said, his response coming quickly, as if he'd been waiting to provide it for several years. "I've learned a lot more about this world since it happened, and the human garbage that lives in it." His bad, red eye rotated up to Christopher. At first, the boy thought Lorenz looked on him with disgust, but then realized that he always looked at people that way. It must be the lone expression his face could produce. "Why am I telling you this?" he wondered aloud. "You're just a stupid kid. Not exactly Liberty's favorite son, either, eh?"

Christopher could have walked away at that point. They had reached some degree of common ground, he spoke his peace, didn't get shot, allowed Lorenz to get in a not-so-subtle dig, and he could have walked back into town and back into his life without carrying the regret of unfinished deeds. Yet, he felt a need to reply to Lorenz's statement, even if his reply failed to make any sense. "Sir, I think it was a great thing you did, and, from what I understand of you, you are a great man. That's the reason I'm here."

"You're not here because I'm a 'great man,'" Lorenz replied. "You're here because somebody finally told you that your ass got pulled out of the fire. If that day taught you a damn thing, it should have taught you that life's arbitrary: we aren't rewarded or punished based on..." He shook his head and stood up. Even his casual moves looked fluid and graceful, unnaturally so for a man of his size. When he again spoke, his voice softened. "I shouldn't be saying all this out on you. You were... what? Six years old?" He wiped his hands on his britches. "You need something to drink, kid?"

Christopher nodded and followed him over to the well, making sure to maintain a comfortable distance between himself and his host. A bucket sat balanced on the stone rim of the well, and Lorenz offered a black metal ladle full of water to Christopher. The cool torrent of water slid down Christopher's raw throat, and he continued to dip and drink from the ladle until saturated, appreciative as only a truly parched man can be. After ingesting his third ladleful, Christopher pointed the handle toward his host. "Thanks," he said.

Lorenz took the ladle and unceremoniously dropped it back in the wooden bucket. "Look, kid, I still have work to do around here, a lot of work, so unless you need something, you better be heading back into town."

"Yeah, I suppose," Christopher said as he nodded, masking his disappointment well. "Thanks for the water, and I'm sorry if I bothered you."

Lorenz shrugged his broad shoulders and strode toward the damaged fence.

As Christopher walked back toward the path he had arrived by, Lorenz called over his shoulder, "Hey, kid, next time you decide to come out here, make sure to stay on the dirt path. I've got some nasty stuff in the brush. And for God's sake, bring some water with you...," the volume of his voice then dropped a bit as he added, "... if you decide to come out again."

"Sure thing," Christopher shouted to the man's back, "next time."

*   *   *

Christopher walked home from the Lorenz stead at a more leisurely pace than that which he departed from town. Thanks to the brevity of their discourse, more than enough daylight remained for him to return on time, and he had plenty to think about.

Even after meeting him... really meeting him, not merely exchanging formal greetings in front of a hostile parent in a dark, noisy blacksmith's shop... Christopher still did not know what to make of

Lorenz. He seemed actually threatened by a teenager's sudden appearance on his property, then bitter, then almost cordial.

Perhaps the man was every bit the lunatic everyone seemed to think him. The hermit's life, after all, had been known to push men beyond the brink of sanity. One could not consider shoving a gun into the back of a fourteen-year-old trespasser's head as behavior typical of a sane person. He didn't seem serious about pulling the trigger, though, so the act didn't quite measure up to insanity, either. Doc Ferguson had painted the picture of a distraught, but still virtuous man, so Christopher interpreted Lorenz's actions as those of someone who had not entertained guests for a very long time and did not know how to handle one suddenly appearing. It took a mile of walking through the grass for Christopher to decide that he knew nothing, and that he should keep an open mind about Lorenz.

The shadowy collection of buildings rose from the ground, miles ahead, like a series of irregular tombstones. Christopher wiped some dried spit from his lips with the back of his hand and silently wished he had taken some water with him from Lorenz's, even if it was in his two cupped hands. As he wiped the back of his hand on his trousers, the outline of a horse and rider approached from the direction of town.

Christopher froze. No trees or rocks to hide behind on his immediate left. The same went for his immediate right. The rider was galloping on a direct line toward him. He could always duck down in the waist-high grass, but that was liable to get a person shot for impersonating a Comanche, if anything. Instead, he continued to stroll, straight and easy. Living life under the accusing stare of his father had endowed him with the ability to come up with believable lies in a matter of seconds. He estimated himself close enough to town that he could claim to have gone on a short walk in the country. In that time and place, most considered recreational walking a time-wasting activity employed by the very old, the very lazy, or the very disturbed, but it still held some semblance of social acceptability about it, unlike, say, paying social calls to the demonically possessed.

As the lone rider grew closer, his outline became more familiar to Christopher's eyes. It was definitely a full-grown man. He knew that it was not his father, who rode rigid as one of the Riders of the Apocalypse. He continued down a mental checklist of people he would rather it not be. Not Waits. Not Harkness. Not Zimmerman. The rider continued riding directly toward Christopher, but the setting sun blasted its rays in his face and prevented him from making a positive identification until he stood in Doc Ferguson's shadow.

Doc Ferguson reigned in his chestnut brown horse, Dominic, rumored to be the fastest in all of Liberty, and stopped in front of Christopher. He seemed rather worked up, a rare state for him. "Christopher, I thought that was you," the doctor said. "What on earth are you doing out here?" Dominic let out an exasperated sigh, as if to emphasize the point.

Due to his years of conditioning, the temptation to lie struck Christopher, just to be on the safe side, but curiosity prompted him to seek Doc Ferguson's reaction to the truth. "I'm coming back from Mr. Lorenz's house," he said.

Ferguson's eyebrows rose in surprise, but he still looked preoccupied. "Well, good for you," he said, after recovering from the mild shock. "It's never too early to start thinking for yourself, you know. Just... don't let your father find out that I was party to any of this, if you would." The saddle leather creaked as his shifted in his seat.

Christopher shook his head and reached his hand behind him to gingerly pull his shirt away from the raw area of his back to which it had stuck. "Don't worry, sir; I... learned a long time ago not to give him any more information than necessary," he said.

Dr. Ferguson flinched away from Christopher and searched for something over by his right stirrup. Small town doctors examined everyone at some point. They recognized welts, and cuts, and bruises, and it didn't take a genius to deduce their sources. In a small town, though, and you learn to leave well enough alone. After all, a small town is like a tribe, and a man has to protect his own standing by any means possible.

"I'd better me going," he said with an awkwardness Christopher rarely saw in an adult speaker. More awkward than Lorenz, even. "The Staley's never showed up for their appointment today, and I figure, at their age, they need some checking up on."

They exchanged nods instead of farewells, and when Christopher watched Dr. Ferguson ride into the distance, it would be the last time he saw him as a free man. He did not know this at the time, of course; he had no idea what was going on out at the Staley ranch. Besides, he was too busy worrying about whether or not he would get back to town soon enough to feel Emma's gentle caress before either of them had to report for dinner.

          *   *   *

He found Emma sitting outside on the front steps of the Liberty Tavern, and they went for a walk. Though tired of walking, he endured the formality because a reward awaited him when they found a place with adequate privacy. Appropriately enough, such a place resided behind the schoolhouse.

Later, when he walked her home, neither made an effort to initiate conversation. Alone on the street in front of the great white building her family lived within, she leaned forward and planted a kiss on his cheek, then stood with her hands locked behind her, waiting for a reaction. *If her father sees you*, he told himself, *he will shoot you… many, many times*. Still, she looked as though she planned to stand there like an idiot until he did something. Christopher's mouth shifted into a fake, sheepish grin until she smiled back. "Bye," she said and fluttered her fingers at him, an affectation she must have seen performed by one of the women working at the tavern.

"Goodbye," he replied. His smile fell away the moment she turned her back and trotted up the steps into her father's tavern.

Christopher did not allow the issue of who was using who to bother him during his brisk jog home. How could he, with thoughts of Saturday filling his mind? Saturday, when his father rented him out as cheap manual labor for the entire day. When Mr. Rutlage could not find anyone to hire his son, he expected Christopher to walk around until he found work for himself. Sunday, after church services ended, Christopher almost always had the day off so that the Rutlage's could honor the Sabbath. This meant that either one or both days could present him with a chance to visit Mr. Lorenz's house. He didn't know what would happen when he did, but that was part of the rush: unlike almost every other aspect of his life, a jaunt to the Lorenz stead contained some mystery.

Christopher stepped through the front door of his parent's house a bit short of breath. His eyes locked onto the table to see if someone had already distributed the four place settings. Since the age of five, his parents had saddled him with that chore, and if Mother or Father had to do it, Christopher faced considerable trouble. No objects marred the flat surface of the table, and Christopher allowed himself to relax, slightly.

Mary sat playing with her jacks and rubber ball over in the corner. She heard her brother shut the front door, looked up, and gave him a smile without upsetting the rhythmic sound of the ball striking the wooden floor. He smiled back until Mother unleashed her most severe, thin-lipped scowl in his direction. She usually reserved the look for special occasions. Later, when he could read books other than the Bible, Christopher read the story of Jason and the Argonauts. In the section where Jason encountered the Harpies, he could not help but envision his mother's scowl from that evening etched onto the faces of each one of those winged beasts.

"Running a bit late, aren't we?" Mother asked in her voice that creaked like an unoiled door hinge.

"Sorry, Ma'am," Christopher said, trying his best to force his lips into a dejected frown. "Is Father home?"

"Of course he's home," she hissed. "He has the good sense to be home in time for dinner." While not late by any definition of the term, Christopher felt no urge to contradict his mother, and her sour, hard-eyed expression did not welcome contradiction. "He's out in the shop."

Christopher's feet slapped the floorboards as he walked across the kitchen area to the door connecting the house to the shop. His plodding pace normally conveyed the proper amount of mock shame. It was all about appearances… everything in his home, his town, his life… so that he could make it through one day and onto the next. He opened the door and called into the darkness and heat, "Father?"

All the fires were extinguished for the evening, but their aftermath would linger for almost an hour. Lewis Rutlage stood amid the low, lamplight of the blacksmith shop, stooped over, picking loose nails and bits of metal from the dirt floor. Every few seconds, they clanked against the bottom of a metal pail. "Yes, son?"

Christopher folded his hands in front of him and stood up as straight as he could. The mood of a formal inspection tended to accompany conversations with his father, and this one proved no exception. "Where am I to be working tomorrow?" he asked.

"No one came," Mr. Rutlage said wearily, in spite of the fact that the family did not need the extra money. Lewis always moaned about how much more prosperous and respectable he would have been if he had worked in Kansas City, were he not so concerned about his children growing up in a bastion of Christian morality. The truth, however, was that the steady traffic to Kansas City and Wichita had made the Rutlages one of the wealthier families in town. "You're going to have to find your own work." The words dragged out. Standing in the doorway, a thought occurred to Christopher for the first time: perhaps the sorrow clinging to his father's voice was genuine. Perhaps sending his son out to work for next to nothing was his father's version of atonement for his child surviving the schoolhouse fire.

He never allowed Christopher to keep a single cent of the money he made, but Lewis Rutlage still made it sound as though he did a gigantic favor by finding work for his son. It allowed for the building of some sorely needed character. A couple summers before, Christopher kept enough money from a job to buy myself some saltwater taffy from one of the jars under Harkness's front counter, but his father found out (probably from Mr. Harkness) and brought out the belt. That was the single worst beating Christopher had ever received and left him a quivering, unconscious mass of blood and ripped flesh. All for a few cents worth of candy. Since then, Christopher never considered doing it again.

Still, for once, the prospect of looking for work filled Christopher with such a sense of anticipation that he had to restrain his excitement or else he might have flung the door closed and performed some sort of makeshift dance. Instead, he solemnly nodded and turned back to the house so that he could set the table. During dinner, he forced himself to maintain the appearance of the whipped dog his parents expected. He could only hope that Mr. Lorenz had work for him to do and money or chickens with which to pay.

*   *   *

Until June 30, 1877, the bedroom of the Staley stead featured two dominant sounds: Edgar Staley snoring, and his wife tossing and turning atop their feather mattress. Edgar's nocturnal breathing habits remained nearly the only matter over which the couple conflicted since they married. He was Catholic. She was not. She converted. He drank. She didn't like it the way it made his breath stink or how ornery he became. He stopped. The snoring, though, persisted through prayer, medication, and position changes.

On the fateful night of June 30, though, things changed. Outside, the noises were common enough: laundry flapping on the clothesline. Wind rustling the leaves in the oak tree overhead. In the pasture, sheep bleated. A strange, chestnut brown horse hitched to the fence stood with its head bowed, breathing long, heavy breaths. The inside of the squat, cozy domicile, however, remained still as a coffin. The rough, guttural snort of air traveling from Edgar Staley's nasal passages failed to serve notice and disrupt the serenity of the night. His wife did not shift on the mattress or slide under the quilt, then over, then under again. In fact, no noise emanated from the house whatsoever...

...except for the clicking sounds.

*   *   *

CHAPTER FOUR

July 1, 1877:

The first rays of dawn crept through the window below Christopher's loft as he rolled out of bed. His bare feet touched the floor before Nells Donnelly's rooster began coughing out its morning welcome. *Water*, his sleep-clogged mind chanted as his thumbs slid his suspenders into place, *remember the water*. He lifted the strap of his circular, metal canteen from the nail beside the door on his way outside. A quick shake revealed that there was plenty of water inside to accommodate his trek, even if it would taste a little stale. He eased the door closed and hoped that he could let the town swallow him before his parents even knew he was awake.

The dull morning glow pressed through his squinting mole-eyes as Christopher pulled in a breath of dewy air. From the right, his father's voice called, unmarred by any early morning fatigue. "Where you goin' today?" Lewis Rutlage asked. The voice made Christopher freeze and urged him unsuccessfully to void his bowels. The voice's owner stood in the doorway to the shop, preparing to unlock it. His slow manner and gray, cragged features reminded Christopher of a drawing of a gargoyle he once saw in school.

Christopher relaxed his eyes so the panic would drain from them before turning to reply. "I might start on some of the farms east of town, see if they needed someone to pull weeds." His tongue snaked out and slid over the cracked skin of his lower lip. "I might head out to the Staley's farm. Old Man Staley's been feelin' ill, so they might need some help."

Rutlage nodded, silent and stiff. His silence conveyed that his son's decision-making ability did not violently upset him. To Christopher, his father's lack of reaction almost felt like a compliment. Part of Christopher thirsted for that feeling, but part of him resented it. Lewis still refused to let his son travel though the East Kansas summer on the back of a horse, however, so the Apocalypse was not upon them. Lewis returned his attention to the door and resumed his morning ritual.

Christopher's shoes struck the dusty street and carried him away from his father's shop at a leisurely pace, even though he felt like running. *The lie was a good one*, he decided, *especially the part about the Staley's*. The Staley's stead lay in the same general direction away from town that Lorenz lived, and if a random rider saw him going or coming this time, he readily could explain himself. Lies to his parents were delicate matters, and the closer they came to the appearance of the truth, the more opportunity he would have to save himself from a lashing. The delivery of the lie was adequate, even with the slight pause before he added the Staley angle. Something to work at, he supposed.

The canteen strap stretched around one of his shoulders, and the sound of sloshing water accompanied every step Christopher took toward Lorenz's property. The walk was a veritable romp compared to his journey the previous evening. He had water, he knew the route, the sun was still a squat orb clinging to the horizon, Lorenz probably wouldn't kill him, and, best of all, the fear of discovery did not loom over him like a trailing hawk.

Horace Langtree's dilapidated one-room shack was the last remaining building on the edge of Liberty. As Christopher strode past it, he released a sigh his lungs had clutched since the moment he turned his back to his father. He had escaped Liberty, and his feet glided over the earth. It had never felt so good to leave the town before; like church letting out on a balmy Sunday. The joys of recreational walking were steadily growing on Christopher, but there was more to it than that. Before a couple of days ago, life seemed very rigid, mundane, and predictable. For all he knew, the entire world was infested by the abusive and self-righteous, so there was nothing to escape to. It wasn't, though; at least not as thoroughly as he thought. There were people who had visited places and read more than one book. Equally as important was the finding that Christopher was not the flawed sinner living in a bastion of godliness. Discovering the pettiness of others helped him feel better about himself. Finding that the pettiness wasn't universal made him feel better about the future. There was a world outside. There was somewhere he could run to. There was hope.

His parents expected him to take over the shop eventually. Whenever that fate clanged away in his mind, however, he envisioned the sweaty, soot-streaked creature he was to become, and it was a twisted, hard man, caste and beaten into the image of his father. He shuddered so badly that he almost miss-stepped in the open prairie. Christopher's future occupation, though, did not reside among the handful of topics for debate in the Rutlage household. His mother and father generally expected Christopher to receive their assertions as one would the word of God, and not a kind, forgiving, New Testament-version of God, either. His taking over the shop, though, existed on an even higher plane of certainty. It was as an irrefutable fact: the sun would rise tomorrow, and he would someday receive his station as Liberty's blacksmith. Amen.

The grass grew taller as each of Christopher's steps carried him further and further from town. He had accepted his narrow, set future for a time, much as a child accepts the concept of his parents' infallibility. The prospect never appalled him, though, just as living his whole life in Liberty never appalled him, because he could never conceive of an alternative. Life consisted of living in that town and living in that house. Now, though, he felt unusually powerful: he could escape that fate, with nothing more than his falling feet to deliver him.

Perhaps it was his burgeoning physical relationship with Emma Waits, however straightforward and un-chivalrous his original motivation, that had empowered him and helped him question the workings of his life: he was a man now, after all, and men could make their own decisions. Learning the truth about Lorenz provided another revelation to fuel his questioning. Christopher's parents had lied to him about this principled man that fate had seen fit to curse. They were now not only capable of being wrong in fact, but also in principle. The facade surrounding them, so impenetrable days before, crumbled away with every step.

After walking close to a mile, Christopher unscrewed the cap of the canteen and took his first drink of the warm, day-old water. Realistically, he would have to steal a horse and run away to the city to escape his parents. Kansas City, probably... at least for starters. He doubted he could find any other cities in the region that were big enough to allow him to disappear. He didn't know what he would do when he got there, but he overheard conversations from travelers staying at the Waits' place and knew that the railroad and the cattle industries were always looking for workers. He would probably take Emma with him. A few days' time had diluted his initial passion, and while he probably didn't love her, a flimsy bond had grown between them over the years. They were the only survivors of the schoolhouse fire those many years ago. More than anything, she was a girl, a girl his age, so she would do.

Thoughts of escape continued to prey on his mind as he waded through the swaying sea of grass, his palms passing over the plant tips, but an ultimate decision still lingered in the distant future, or at least until the next beating. For the moment, the only sounds came from the wind sifting through the grass, the birds in the sky, and a canteen bouncing against his left hip. Christopher had time, to think of a way out and to enjoy myself.

*   *   *

Christopher's second appearance in two days on Lorenz's property met a much better reception than the first. He found Lorenz out behind the barn (the side opposite the fenced-in cow pasture), scattering handfuls of seed onto the ground of the chicken coup. A medium-sized metal bucket sat next to his foot. Only a dozen or so chickens populated the fenced in area, but a solitary man could easily subsist on half that number.

Lorenz wore his black, flat-brimmed hat that he wore to the shop the other day, and Christopher approached the man's back, but the older, larger man neither turned nor even paused from scattering the feed. "Back already, are you?" he called out, trying to sound menacing. "Just couldn't keep yourself away?" The tone failed to convince Christopher; if Lorenz had wished to inject the fear of God into his teenage visitor, creeping behind him again and shoving the cold steel barrel of a revolver against his skull would have sufficed.

"Good morning, Mr. Lorenz," Christopher called out casually as he approached the coup. Christopher waited for Lorenz to grunt some sort of answer before continuing, "Anything I can help you with today?"

Lorenz may have smiled at the question, even though his frozen expression made it impossible to tell. "No," he said gruffly. "I'm so used to doing all the work myself I'm not sure I'd trust a strange pair of hands working my property." He turned and dusted the chicken feed from his hands, his red eye peering at Christopher from over his right shoulder. "Don't tell me that's why you came all the way out here, to look for paying work?"

"No, I...," Christopher began, but the oddly set, red eye unsettled him. Even though a series of flaming-red arteries crisscrossed its surface, it might have looked semi-normal were it not imbedded within the twisted, angular monstrosity his face had become. The puffy cheekbone and the barely-functional eyelid made it bulge hideously from its socket.

When Christopher averted his eyes to the safe, unremarkable ground, he rediscovered his ability to speak. "Sort of," he admitted. "My father sent me out to find work today, and I just figured if you had work I could do, and could maybe pay me a little, then I could just spend the day out here."

"Your father, huh? That's mighty Christian of him." The words did not sound like a compliment. Lorenz dropped his chin instinctively so that his flat-brimmed, black hat could block Christopher's view of his face. "Why would you want to spend the entirety of this fine, summer day out here, with me?"

Christopher focused on the brim of the hat, where Lorenz's eyes would have been, and felt only a minimum of fear when he said, "Because I think you deserve better than the way you've been treated... and because you saved my life."

Lorenz stalked over to the gate, carrying the metal pale of chicken feed. When he set the bucket of feed back inside the barn, his massive shoulders sagged. He took a deep breath and straightened himself to his full, imposing height. "The way I've been treated?" he repeated in an exasperated tone. "Let me tell you a little bit about the way I've been treated: my wife was the only person in the world that I gave a good God Damn about, and when she left this earth, instead of the empty condolences I'd expected from the good people of Liberty, which would have been painful enough, all I got were unfounded accusations behind my back that I was the one who killed her."

Lorenz did not yell the words, but Christopher was used to yelling and shrillness; the low rumbling created a far more intense experience for Lorenz's lone listener than if he had screamed. Christopher could sense that something more than hate or sorrow smoldered inside the man's massive chest. Perhaps he had never spoken the words to another human being before (at least not a living one), and that fact that he was saying them to the son of one of his primary accusers seemed... significant.

"Killed her?" Lorenz continued. "Jesus, I wasn't capable of harming a hair on her head. She was everything to me, she was..." He stopped, not for want of control, but because he did not like the direction he moved toward. Those doors had sat locked for too many years. "All because I couldn't drag six kids out of a burning building at the same time... because I didn't look right, didn't look... human. And you being here for a day, holding a couple fence boards, is going to make up for that?"

Christopher could only blink once and stare, unaccustomed as he was to genuine outpourings of emotion. The effect was all vocal, too, because the frozen features of Lorenz's face were incapable of expression; sound that came from a pure, internal sorrow. Christopher had grown up enclosed by his parents' cold, brutal façades that towered above him like canyon walls. "Emotion" with them amounted to screaming about how badly he disappointed them that day, and that history failed to prepare him for this display. As for the rest of the town, Christopher was not Liberty's favorite son, and to him, most of its citizens projected little more than piety.

Lorenz looked down at the ground, absently rubbing the fingertips of his right hand with his thumb. Much as Christopher's physical relationship with Emma Waits gave him an instant version of love for the young country girl, the shockwaves of unfiltered emotion lingering in the quiet air left him convinced that Deklan Lorenz was the greatest man he had ever met. The delivery left Christopher stunned for several seconds, but also inspired him enough to give a respectable answer to a difficult question. He ignored the dryness in his mouth and throat and said, "I'd never forgive myself if I became part of the problem."

Lorenz turned, and again, his eerie eyes stared out from his warped face at the pristine youth in front of him. Every fiber of Christopher's body told him to turn away or else he might turn to stone, but he held his ground. Perhaps this absence of terror, more than anything spoken, led Lorenz to announce, "That's a good start. Let's get to work."

*   *   *

Christopher performed little actual work that day, unless one includes under the umbrella of "work" such menial tasks as fetching Lorenz water, holding boards in place while Lorenz drove nails through them, or brushing down his host's horse, Virgil. He spent over five hours out at Lorenz's home that morning, and along with noticing that Lorenz was among the worst carpenters in all of Liberty, most of his energy remained devoted to asking questions. Lorenz proved surprisingly candid with his answers.

Despite Christopher's best efforts to avoid the appearance of prying, there were a handful of questions that his host preferred to answer with, "I don't want to talk about it" or by ignoring the question altogether. Lorenz provided a good deal of detail about his life before he came to Liberty, though, and by the end of the day, Christopher probably knew more about him than any living person.

"My parents left Ireland when I was ten-years-old and came to America," Lorenz said. He stood with his back to Virgil's rump, the horse's back-right hoof pulled between the arch of Lorenz's legs. He dug the packed dirt out of the underside of the hoof with an L-shaped metal pick. His good eye stared up at Christopher, who leaned against the fence with his arms folded. "My father tried to set up an Irish Pub in Philadelphia." He snorted out a short laugh. "The business failed within a year, and we moved from Philadelphia to Lawrence, Kansas, when I was fourteen because some of my father's creditors were after him. People in those days... a lot of them could just keep going west until they just... disappeared." His visible eye rotated earthward. "My mother took ill and died on the way. We buried her in Illinois."

Christopher thought about the prospect of his own mother dying. Something told him that the thought should make him feel bad, but he didn't. He merely nodded. "Is 'Lorenz' an Irish name?"

"No, it's German," Lorenz replied, then continued. "Father's health also began to fail soon after we lay my mother to rest, but the old man held on and made a decent living tending bar in Lawrence for a couple years." A large chunk of packed dirt flipped out of the hoof and onto the ground. "He died when I was eighteen." The horse gave a shudder, but Lorenz held fast. "He was a good man, and I used up most of the money I had buying him a tombstone. If you're ever up at Lawrence, you could probably still find it, in the graveyard on the east side of town."

Christopher folded his arms across his chest. He felt rather useless, like Emma watching him chop wood. "John Brown was from Lawrence, wasn't he?"

Lorenz let the hoof drop to the ground and gingerly pulled himself erect. His eyes rotated to the corner of their sockets as he said, "What do you know about John Brown?"

Christopher swallowed the lump in his throat. "Not much." Whenever his parents referred to John Brown, they condemned the man as either the victim of demonic possession or a raving lunatic, and even though he knew that they had no room to talk and that their opinions were a product of their small minds, Christopher had no positive opinions of the man to compare this view to. He'd never met anyone that thought *well* of the late fanatic abolitionist, so Christopher did not know what to think, about the man or his cause. Brown's time had passed long before Christopher's began, and Christopher could not recollect Kansas ever catering to slavery. Most of the Negroes passing through town were on their way to Kansas City in connection with the cattle business. They seemed innocuous, but their presence never failed to engender derogatory comments from the townsfolk, even when the men couldn't hear them... especially when the men couldn't hear them.

Lorenz stood motionless beside his horse, clutching and releasing raspy breaths. "Come now. You're an intelligent boy. You must have an opinion."

Christopher bit his lip. "My parents thought he was possessed by the Devil."

Lorenz nodded and stepped over to clean Virgil's back-left hoof. "Old John may have been possessed, but it was the spirit of God, not Satan." He pulled the hoof between his legs. "I met John and his family right before my father died; one of his son's was just about my best friend in the world at the time. After my father died, they took me in, let me stay with them in Osawatomie." The dirt trapped in the hoof cracked and fell out in two hunks. "Old John and I were of one mind on the slavery issue, and he even let me come along on the raid on Pottawatomie."

Pottawatomie: the raid that left several slavers dead. It was one of the few events that put that region of the United States on the map. Christopher bit his lip. "Did you go to Harper's Ferry with him?" he asked.

"If I would've, I'd be dead," Deklan grunted. "No, after some people got killed during a raid into Missouri, we got into a big argument, John and I."

"Over what?"

"It was… complicated." Lorenz let Virgil set his foot down, stood up and ran the back of his hand across his forehead. "John was a more religious man than me, and the religious tend to see things as either all right or all wrong." Christopher nodded emphatically. "I didn't see killing as being necessary. John saw it as obligatory. Biblical justice and whatnot. He told me I didn't have the stomach for God's work and turned me out of his house."

"So you never saw him again?"

Lorenz shook his head.

"That must've been hard."

"He wasn't stupid," Lorenz said, his mighty shoulders shrugging. "He knew what he was doing. From what I know about the plan, it was suicide, but it did what it was supposed to: it started a necessary war that freed the slaves."

Christopher reached behind him and grabbed his left elbow with his right hand. "Do you wish you'd been there?"

"That's an interesting question." The remains of Lorenz's nose flinched. "In some ways," he said, hesitantly. "I do know this, though: it took an iron will to do what John did, to do the right thing, and I will admire him for that until the day that I die."

Christopher nodded without really thinking about the words. "I've heard some people say that it wasn't Brown's business to fight the Negro's fight."

Lorenz pulled the black leather bridle from off Virgil's face. "It's not something to be neutral to," he began, searching for the right words. "If you don't fight for black folks, you're condoning their oppression. And if that isn't enough, think about it: after all the poor colored people are used up and killed off, wouldn't it be safe to assume that they'd come after the poor white people next? You can bet Johnny Reb never thought about that one before he ran off to war."

Christopher did not bother to ask who "they" were, but the statement did spark a new question. "What did you do during the war?"

Lorenz stopped walking at the darkened entrance to the barn. He looked down at the bridle and rubbed the leather between his fingers. "Go get Virgil a bucket of water."

Christopher catapulted from the fence and nearly sprinted across the distance from the barn to the well and back to the barn again with Lorenz's black and gray retriever, Dante, scampering after him the entire distance. The gusto with which he performed the task came partly from his fear that he had asked the wrong question and partly out of the desire to do something useful. When he returned with the sloshing wooden bucket of water and set it down in front of Virgil, Lorenz emerged from the barn. Christopher could tell that Lorenz had gotten past the emotion of the question when he pointed toward the fence boards and said, "It's a miracle if I got a single one of 'em straight."

Christopher's eyes swept over the crooked, uneven fence and settled on the house. It couldn't have been more soundly built. "How come the house looks like it does?"

He laughed, which sounded more like a cough. "Because I just did what Clarissa told me to on those. She worked with her uncle for a couple years in a hardware store and never lost the touch."

Lorenz did not mention his wife again until an hour later, when he was hoeing the garden. He stood amid the knee-high rows of corn, looking even more gigantic next to the undersized plants. Christopher stood on the grass and watched. Dante lay in a patch of shade a few paces away, his head wearily resting between his front paws but his tail still pounding at the ground with a life of its own. The back of the barn stood to his right, the house beyond it. "When Clarissa and I first built this place, the garden was in front of the house," he said. "I moved it when the trees started to grow taller and cut off the sunlight."

"How did you and your wife meet?" Christopher asked.

Lorenz stopped chopping the dry dirt with the hoe and gazed up at the house. "A mutual friend in the east coast Abolitionist circles introduced us." He blinked, and that half-second of pause let him pull his eyes away from the monument to his marriage. He let the hoe fall to the ground and rested his hands on his knees. "Sometimes," he began, his voice soft, like a normal human's, "I'd come home late, from town, it would be dark and raining and I'd be soaked to the bone, and I could see her silhouette in the window, waiting in front of the candlelight." His voice quivered slightly, and the sound both fascinated and unnerved Christopher. He didn't know much about grief, and he wondered how long it took someone to get past a loss like that. For some reason, it never occurred to Christopher that Lorenz might be... unwell. "Sometimes, when I'm coming home from town and it's dark and the rain's falling, I'll still find myself looking up at the window, to see if she's there." He shook his head. "But by the time I get close enough, I realize I'm just alone and cold. Still do it, though. After all these years, I still do it."

He looked up, at his motionless guest. "C'mon," he said, his voice regaining its gruffness. "Let's get something to eat."

The inside of the house was as well-kept as the outside, and while his wife may have been responsible for the craftsmanship, Lorenz must have done a painstakingly thorough job of keeping it cleaned and organized. While Lorenz cut bread for sandwiches in the kitchen, Christopher drifted over to the doorway to the master bedroom. A framed photograph sat atop his dresser that had to have been of his wife. She had thick, brown hair in the photograph, which she wore tied back in a clasp. She also had dark eyes, but what stood out most were her delicate features. Most of the women Christopher had met growing up were from a heartier, thick-boned stock, but she looked exactly what he pictured East Coast women to look like. She was beautiful but fragile, thoughtful but happy, as though she never allowed sad thoughts to enter her mind. Looking at her, Christopher could not help but remember what Dr. Ferguson had said about Clarissa Lorenz's statement regarding the "few scars" on her husband's face not bothering her.

"What happened to the horse?" Christopher blurted out, then instinctively whipped his head over his shoulder. He expected Lorenz to ask, "What horse?" or at least demand that Christopher tell him how he found out, but he did not so much as pause from slicing the bread with his long, mirror-like knife.

"I thought about killing the damn thing," Lorenz explained, evenly. "Even went so far as to load the shotgun and walk out to where it was grazing." He looked up, out the window, perhaps toward the site of the would-be execution. "I couldn't do it, though: she loved that horse too damn much, and when I thought about how it was kind of all I had left of her…" He shook his head. "I put it down a couple years ago, due to bad health." He nodded with his mangled chin. "It had a good life."

Christopher stood in the doorway to the kitchen, marveling at how, upon meeting Lorenz and even after talking with him for a few minutes, the massive man struck him as being even colder than Christopher's own father. He rarely spoke unless spoken too, his answers were brief and monotone, and he constantly exuded an aura of disdain. Even when discussing a topic he obviously cared a great deal about, such as slavery, he spoke as if reciting from a script. Only when talking about his late wife, the seemingly absolute persona faltered. The wound had remained raw; when Lorenz spoke of her, his eyes became distant, and Christopher knew he was picturing her face. When this occurred, the voice softened, and the wretched face, ever so slightly, relaxed.

Lorenz loaded the sandwiches with salted beef and hard cheese using the same lockstep motion with which he assembled the crooked fence. It was time for him to shut down again, Christopher realized. Lorenz stayed alive by keeping the memory of his beloved close to his heart and the rest of the world at a distance. Not the healthiest way to live out one's years, but Lorenz must have recognized his future long ago. The accident that gave him his face all but guaranteed that he would never again marry, that a normal community would at best fear him, and at worst, hate him. Better to live in the past than face that kind of present.

*   *   *

As he prepared to leave that afternoon, Christopher forced himself to bring up the subject of payment. "I usually get paid in cash or chickens," he explained as they sat on the matching chairs that adorned the front porch.

"Well, you aren't getting my chickens," Lorenz said, flatly. "What do you normally make on a Saturday?"

Christopher's gaze shifted skyward, but a decent estimate eluded him. "It really changes from day to day, depending on the kind of work."

Lorenz nodded and reached into the pocket of his denim trousers. He produced a handful of coins, started to separate a few from the pile, then merely dumped the entire quantity into Christopher's cupped hands. It amounted to well over a dollar.

Christopher winced and looked up at his host. "It's all going to go back to my parents, y'know? I'll catch hell if I try to hide any and they find out."

Lorenz snorted out a breath. "You're a better son than your parents deserve," he grumbled, reaching forward to extract a few of the coins. His hand hovered over the pile, though, and ultimately retracted to his side. "Bury it in the ground if you have to," he offered, "I've got plenty."

"From where?" Christopher asked. He had seen the entire property, and all evidence pointed toward the fact that Lorenz subsisted independent from outside forces. He did not own enough livestock or produce enough crops to provide for even his meager needs.

"I don't want to talk about it today," Lorenz said, then sighed and added, "From the War." Then, he nodded in the general direction of town and went back inside.

*   *   *

The hammer struck the sizzling, bright orange metal with a clank. Lewis Rutlage bounced the hammerhead off the anvil to keep the rhythm, then struck it again, this time harder. He was making horseshoes, trying to, anyway. Some days, it seemed like no matter how hard you hit something, you just couldn't form it into what you wanted it to be. There was something appropriate about the thought, but Lewis wasn't one for non-religious symbolism and failed to pursue it.

The heat from the roaring fire caused dozens of tiny tributaries of sweat to trickle over his sooty, dirty arms. It felt like a legion of ants running over his skin. It was not a comfortable sensation, and even after twenty-odd years of blacksmithing, it still irritated him. The sweat and the dirt, though, had a character to it. At the end of the day, no one could look at Lewis Rutlage and say he hadn't put in a hard day's work.

He paused for a breath and stared at the dancing, crackling flames of the fire. The flame, too, was something that he admired about his work. It possessed a purity that few other substances could match. The blacksmith spends his whole life in front of the flame. Trying not to get burned. There was a symbol in that idea, too, and a religious one to boot, but the brief knock on the door of his shop interrupted the flow of his thoughts.

James Waits runty form stood in the open doorway, his gray hat tilted back to reveal his bushy eyebrows and pockmarked face. His lower lip jutted out and barely held onto his toothpick, as he stared sullenly at Lewis. "James," Lewis said, dropping the hot metal into a bucket of water. It unleashed the obligatory hiss as the steam raced toward the ceiling. He rubbed his hands on his apron, in case a handshake was forthcoming, but Waits' hands remained buried in the pockets of his trousers.

"Lewis," Waits returned, lifting a hand to scratch at the point where his patchy beard met his curly temple. "We've gotta talk. It's about your son…"

*   *   *

Chapter Five

July 2, 1877:

Christopher's feet barely touched the ground on the walk home from Lorenz's. Tomorrow would be a Sunday, and with any luck, after church services ended, the day belonged to him. He could repeat the entire day, if he wanted: the light work, conversation, and existential security that comes with the feeling of being free from judgment... this time without the painful formality of having to ask for payment. Secure... he never thought he would associate that term with spending an afternoon with Deklan Lorenz. It was true, though. It was like stepping into that thicket of trees and hearing Dante's distant bark transported him out of Kansas, out of his life, to a place far away. Trivial as it sounded, holding fence boards and fetching water for his new acquaintance had rapidly become more important to Christopher than any other activity, including his other newly discovered dalliance involving Emma Waits.

Christopher glided past the tufts of grass, ignoring the simmering heat of the day in favor of the mystery of Lorenz. There was nothing else in Liberty remotely like him, because Christopher didn't know what to expect. It helped that they shared the same cast of enemies, also known as "most of the town," but he was different, genuine, brave... well-traveled. He held so many secrets that every time Lorenz revealed a piece of his past, it only opened a room to another series of mysterious doors. Lorenz had lived what to Christopher seemed a grand life, in worlds that Christopher had barely heard of, and this filled him with a sense of adventure he had scarcely known in his fourteen years. The only reason he didn't run home was because it would have made the remains of the day that much longer.

Minutes after Christopher had returned to his father's house, Lewis Rutlage opened the front door, and his thudding foot heralded his arrival. Christopher lowered the one-page newspaper he had just started reading, and from his position at the table, he could see his father's cheekbones press so high that his eye sockets had become slits. Rutlage affirmed his son's speculation that something was drastically amiss by slamming the door closed behind him and savagely ripping the thick, leather gloves from his hands. The sound of the gauntlets slapping against the kitchen table ushered forth an aching in the scabbed-over areas of Christopher's back. He mainly felt disappointment; he had engineered his escape so flawlessly, and it seemed *far* too soon to start this again.

Never one to waste time on pleasantries, Rutlage scanned the room until he could lock his gaze onto Christopher's form. "James Waits told me something interesting today," he began, struggling to restrain himself until Christopher had formulated a defense that Lewis could smash through.

Christopher thought of a clever response, but kept it too himself. Instead, he gave a vague nod while gingerly setting the newspaper down on the table, slackening his features into a dumbfounded expression. Mother still lingered near the back door, but seemed oblivious to everything but her sweeping. Mary sat over by the washtub, playing with her cornhusk doll with the missing arm. She, too, continued with her activity as though nothing was amiss. For an instant, Christopher wondered if his father actually stood in the room or whether he was a figment conjured by a damaged brain.

The elder Rutlage strode over to where his son sat, placed his closed fists on his hips, and bent forward far enough so that his bony chin hovered inches from Christopher's nose. Traditionally, that gesture forced Christopher to look away. Lately, though, the tip of that pointy chin had started to resemble a target. If Christopher survived another couple years, he had no doubt that they were doomed to share a dramatic, violent confrontation. "Do you know what he told me?" Rutlage asked, his voice only a low rumble at this point, a pale imitation of the menacing vocalizations Deklan Lorenz could muster effortlessly.

"Looks like rain?" Christopher wanted to offer, but again decided that the satisfaction gained from uttering a clever remark would not compensate for a fatal beating. Instead, he silently shook his head.

"He said Emma said she wasn't a virgin anymore," he growled, his breath reeking of milk. "He made a special trip out to the shop tonight to tell me this, because he said he seen you two running around together so much lately." His entire body tensed up, and Christopher had no doubt that this dam of rage would soon break.

"Oh my," Christopher said, genuinely confused. He didn't know how, exactly, James Waits could know that, unless Emma just told her father... which seemed beyond unlikely. Given the gravity of the accusation, Christopher would have preferred to swear or take the Lord's name in vain, but that would have gotten him nowhere. Instead, he tensed his arms, ready to throw them in front of his face should his father attempt to punch him.

"I know you don't care what happens to your family." The senior Rutlage snorted in his son's face like a bull preparing to charge. "You've made it plain you don't care if they run us outta town, but don't you got nothin' to say for yourself?"

Still breathing steadily and keeping his eyes wide and innocent, Christopher said, "Father, I'm just as surprised as you. Emma and me, we's just friends. Only kissed her but once." He utilized the broken grammar in attempt to sound as naive as possible, a lame tactic, but it had proven surprisingly effective when dealing with his father in the past. This instance, however, became the exception.

"Liar!" Rutlage screamed. The volume and the accompanying spit flecks caused Christopher to cringe. The back door creaked closed, leaving Christopher and his father alone in the house. His mother had vanished with expert efficiency, taking Mary and his last vestige of hope with her. The likelihood of an impending beating increased exponentially with each passing second. The trick would be to get to his feet and distribute the abuse more evenly over his body; if Father blew up on him while Christopher was sitting, his face would sustain most of the damage. Otherwise, there was no running away, because there was nowhere to run to. "Where were you today?" Rutlage demanded.

Christopher froze for an instant, trying to re-assemble the lie in his head. As if answering the question by itself, his shaking right hand slid into his right pocket and removed most of the coins Lorenz had given him. While pushing the coins across the table to his father, Christopher swallowed to relieve the dryness in his mouth and thought for a moment that he had taken down his own tongue. Rutlage did not so much as glance at the money, his eyes still locked on his son's face, so Christopher announced, "There's the money I got from—"

"Answer me!" Rutlage screamed in a voice so shrill it might have sounded comical under different conditions. Surely the neighbors could hear. They wouldn't do anything, but if you're worried about the family's good name—"Where did you go today?"

Christopher's eyes widened, and his heart thudded against the inside of his ribcage. He had prepared for this question on the walk home, but suddenly could not remember the lie he had decided upon. His father opened his mouth, apparently on the verge of biting Christopher's entire head off, when the correct reply popped into his head. "I walked out to the Staley's place, did some work for them." The lie felt good the instant Christopher said it: they were old, Old Man Staley was sick, and old, sick people need help with chores.

Rutlage pulled back his head enough to allow Christopher some breathing room, but continued to eye his son like a wounded dog. "Staley's, eh?" he said, slowly mulling over the plausibility of the statement in the recesses of his thick skull. He finally looked down at the money. "Pay you good, did they?"

Christopher nodded, his heart cautiously returning to a normal rhythm. "There was... a lot to do."

Rutlage slid his right hand across the tabletop and, almost magnanimously, swept the coins into his left hand. He probably couldn't add up that amount in his head, but he still liked the sight of his money and stared at it for a while. He continued to stare at his open hand as he took a step toward the bedroom, then stopped. "Doc Ferguson'll be at the church service tomorrow, even if the Staley's aren't. I heard straight from Mrs. Braxton that Ferguson said he was goin' out to the Staley's yesterday, and I heard he wasn't in today either, so he was out there today, too, which means he'd have seen you." Christopher nodded with each logical leap. His father took another slow, plodding step away from the table. "If you're lyin' boy, I'll kill you." He continued into the bedroom, leaving Christopher to ponder whether his father intended "I'll kill you" as a figure of speech.

*   *   *

That night, Christopher lay in his loft, staring at the slanted wooden ceiling three feet above him. He'd lay in that position for a while, calculating his odds of surviving the next day. His safety totally depended on how his father phrased the question to Ferguson. If he asked, "Did you see my son yesterday?" the good doctor would probably decide that

Christopher had ventured somewhere he should not have and deny that he had seen anything, thereby condemning Christopher to the worst beating of his life. On the other hand, if Father asked something along the lines of, "Was Christopher at the Staley's yesterday?" Doc Ferguson would hopefully deduce that Christopher expected him to confirm his whereabouts and give a good lie.

The tension that festered between him and his father made that Sunday's church service even more interminable than the usual hours of torture in the hard, wooden pews. Reverend Skidmore droned on and on in his nauseating monotone as sunlight filtered in through the window behind him and heated the building to an almost unbearable temperature. The soft light gave him an almost angelic appearance up there on the raised platform in his white robe. The subject of the sermon, so far as Christopher could discern, had something to do with the various duties required of a good Christian. Lewis Rutlage would throw an ominous glare his son's way whenever the good reverend mentioned the duties a child must perform for his or her parents. Duties of the parents to not kill their children didn't make it into the sermon.

Christopher stared hard at the back of the pew in front of him, waiting for the service to end. His stomach churned away at a nauseating rate, and not just because of dozens of vintages of human sweat permeating the building; he had carefully scanned the face of everyone in that church, and Doc Ferguson's bespectacled face did not reside among them.

Christopher had felt better and better about his chances of eluding a beating as the morning progressed. After all, Doc Ferguson was an intelligent man, and any intelligent man could deduce Father's intentions and outwit him. This possibility completely eluded Christopher's father, of course, as did the possibility that Doc Ferguson, or any other adult in Liberty, could in any way detest him on a personal level. Granted, not many did, and many of those that did probably only hated him because his son had survived the schoolhouse fire and their child had not.

Looking around the church at the faces of the parishioners, Christopher could not imagine many of them thinking anything contrary to Father's public image as one of Liberty's most God-fearing citizens. They would stand correct if using the explicit definition of the term "God-fearing," because Lewis Rutlage certainly did fear the Almighty Creator, and if God had descended from Heaven and commanded that he stop beating his son, he would have without hesitation. Nothing short of such a miracle, however, would have been effective. Unfortunately, God never did get around to answering that particular prayer of Christopher's. Neither did the Son or the Holy Ghost. As a matter of fact, the entire Holy Trinity did not seem to have a clue where Liberty was at all.

After the service had finished, the stomping feet of the parishioners carried them out onto the dusty patch of ground in the middle of town to discuss the quality of the sermon in glowing terms. The elder Rutlage strode from one cluster of people to another, his chin tilted to an arrogant angle, asking if anyone knew the fate of the town doctor. Anyone looking on might have thought he had become quite concerned about Ol' Doc Ferguson. Little did they know that the underlying cause for his concern involved a sadistic urge to pound his son into a bloody mass. Unfortunately for Lewis, the Staley's were absent from the service as well, and they were his best chance at finding Ferguson. After a few minutes and a dozen questions, it appeared that that no one knew Doc Ferguson's location any better than Rutlage did.

Doc Ferguson proved rather hard to keep track of, even under normal circumstance. He was a widower, his children had all grown to adulthood and moved away, and he typically made an abundance of job-related house calls to outlying farms and even other towns. No one that

day appeared overly concerned about tracking him down until Lewis
Rutlage began his inquest.

It did not take long for Rutlage to coax his equally disturbed
friends, James Waits and Tom Harkness, into agreeing to ride out to the
Staley place with him for a neighborly visit. Christopher observed the
evolving situation from the shady side of the church, chewing on his
cracked lower lip and thinking, *This probably ruins any chance I have of
visiting Lorenz's today.* His father stalked over to where Christopher stood
using the long, loping strides that had become his signature. When he
stood about five feet away, he hooked a thumb over his shoulder, in the
general direction of the house, and said, "Saddle up the gray horse, son.
We're goin' out to Staley's and you're comin' along."

This decree may not have occurred specifically to give Waits an
opportunity to threaten Christopher, but it served that purpose.
Christopher saddled the gray horse and met the misanthropic posse over
at Harkness's store about one half hour after the church service ended,
giving everyone time to change out of his Sunday best. Waits took one
look at Christopher, snorted, and spat an amber streak of chewing tobacco
onto the ground. Harkness and the elder Rutlage had already mounted
up. Both men were similarly built and could have passed for brothers, the
only difference being that Harkness had lost most of his hair years before.
Waits looked like a troll next to them, his runtiness exacerbated by their
tall, lanky figures (Emma having inherited her robust size from her
mother). He tried to look evil and threatening to Christopher, his beady
eyes glaring out from under the brim of his derby, but next to the boy's
father, he only assumed the role of a lesser demon. "You better hope we
find that doctor, boy, 'cause if you wasn't where you said you was, you're
gonna be needin' one." He gave a little snicker.

Christopher glanced over at his father, as if expecting him to
defend his only son (if for no other reason than to keep the threats and

abuse within the family), but Lewis gave him no more than a passing glance, an ever-so-slight smile denting his lips. He never faked a smile, so Christopher had every reason to think he enjoyed watching his son squirm. The torture probably constituted another attempt to get Christopher to break down and be a good son, to be like him.

Christopher's eyes found the dusty ground. He couldn't do it. Even if he believed that his father was the man everyone thought he was, Christopher could not become that man. Even if you took out the aggression and cruelty, Lewis was far more pragmatic than Christopher ever would be. Christopher was a dreamer, and even though his was not a healthy environment for dreaming, he had no idea how to be otherwise. He prayed often, because there were few other options. Sometimes, he would pray that God would change him and make him something that would fit into this life better. He saw the way Waits and Harkness and others would defer to his father, how they valued and respected him, and part of Christopher wished that someday he would know the feeling of being respected. It was God that made him this way, after all; he had no choice in the matter.

That afternoon, Christopher rode upon the family's second riding horse, an animal that his father referred to as "the gray one." The Rutlages owned six horses in all, four for plowing and two for riding, which was more than most families in Liberty. One of Christopher's more enjoyable jobs involved caring for them.

The Rutlages obtained the Gray One from Waits, who in turn had procured him from a traveler who was shot to death in his tavern two years prior. Waits kept the horse and the man's other valuables for exactly one month, waiting for a relative of the man's to claim them, before he sold them off. Waits decided that the man staining the tavern's floorboards with all that spilled blood afforded him such a right; it may not have been strictly legal, but the wheels of justice turned slowly on the frontier. With three horses already cluttering his stable, Waits had no use for an additional mount, so he sold the Gray One to his friend, Lewis, for a mere five dollars. Rutlage had not charged Waits for any services since.

Lewis had no need for that many horses, either, especially the draft horses, since he owned no farm land. He liked to rent them around town, though, and they were always something of a status symbol for him. Despite complaining about how much he could have made without having to sacrifice to take care of his children, Lewis had accumulated considerable wealth and property over the years. He hadn't done anything with it, of course. Nor would he. He just liked to accumulate things to show how much God favored him. Christopher liked the Gray One well enough, so he didn't mind taking care of a sixth horse.

Waits needed two attempts to mount his undersized horse, but the moment he was securely in seated, Lewis Rutlage aimed his horse westward and led them out of town. The ride to the Staley stead took forever, as the draining weariness that clung to Christopher from the church service had yet to depart. Rather than ride in front and endure the stares of the three men in his back, he took the subordinate position and brought up the rear. The three adults made no effort to include him in any of their banal conversation, for which Christopher was grateful. He merely slumped in his saddle and let the deep drone of voices wash over him.

The synchronized thud of horse hooves striking packed earth constantly reminded Christopher that they were inching closer to the truth. His mind somersaulted in effort to come up with an escape route. He wasn't the world's greatest rider, so a direct flight was not possible. Besides, where would he go? However slim his chances of riding to safety and staying alive, he might as well try, because if his father found out that he had made love to Emma Waits, lied to his face, *and* visited Deklan Lorenz, his life wouldn't be worth spit. He could ride to Lorenz's house...

but what then? Ask Deklan to kill his father... and Waits... and Harkness?
All because of a teenage liaison?

The sullen quartet reached Old Man Staley's sheep farm before
Christopher could come up with a better plan than pointing his horse in a
random direction and digging his heels. The house and the land
surrounding it looked horribly under-kept, a drastic switch from the
showplace the Staley home had always been. The garden lay overgrown
and attacked by wildlife. Laundry blew across the pasture, and the sheets
that stayed on the line were caked with several-days-worth of filth. A thin
layer of grime coated the windows.

Mrs. Staley typically had little to do besides keep the place
looking nice, but at her advanced age, taking care of a sick husband must
have drained her time to the point where there was nothing to devote to
beautifying the landscape. Dr. Ferguson's horse stood right outside the
barn, hitched to a fence post. Foam lined its black lips. The reigns in
Christopher's sweaty hands felt a bit slippery, so he gripped them tighter.

The three pillars of Liberty commerce dismounted in front of the
house, while Christopher somehow tangled his foot in the stirrup and
narrowly avoided falling flat on his back. It was anxiety that made him
clumsy, and he had ample reason to worry: even if his father burst in on
Doc Ferguson attempting to revive a dying man, he would still demand to
know his son's whereabouts the previous day. When all four visitors
stood securely on their feet, the front door opened, and a figure that must
have been Old Man Staley emerged.

The figure stood with his hands shoved in his pants pockets.
Besides his normal attire, he wore a broad-brimmed, felt hat that
Christopher had never seen on Old Man Staley before. He had not visited
their house more than a handful of times, though, so perhaps, Old Man
Staley only wore it around the house. The hat's brim dipped at such a
drastic angle that, coupled with his head tilt, it made very little of his face

visible. To his amazement, Christopher's considerable fear for his three traveling companions ebbed away, replaced by a greater fear for the hitherto harmless visage of Old Man Staley.

"Can... I... help... you... boys... with any... thing?" he asked, twitching, just like he had done at Dr. Ferguson's office.

Harkness, traditionally the most outspoken of the group and, therefore, the leader, did his best to speak for everyone assembled. "Yeah, uh, hey, Edgar," he began, shoving his hands into the pockets of his own trousers. "We don't aim to bother you, it's just Doc Ferguson's gone missin' a couple days and some people in town were startin' to worry. So we figured..." he kicked the rock in front of his foot, obviously unsettled by the entire situation. Old Man Staley continued to twitch and stare until Harkness could not take it anymore. The shopkeeper turned and looked to his cohorts for support. Waits and the elder Rutlage silently gazed toward different sections of ground, so Harkness turned back and finished with, "We just figured we'd stop out and see how everything was goin'."

"Doin'... fine," Staley answered automatically.

During this brief exchange, Christopher scanned just about every inch of the landscape except for the bit where Old Man Staley stood. His eyes lingered on the fenced-in pasture where the Staley's let their sheep graze. Specifically, what caught his attention was a large patch of charred ground where no grass grew, as if Staley had burned a large pile of something out there. What in the hell would he have burned in the middle of his grazing pasture?

Christopher inched his way over to the fence while Harkness asked, "You mind if we speak to the doctor a minute? We got a couple questions for him."

"He's... tending... to... the...wife. She... can't... come... out," Old Man Staley explained, sounding like a telegraph cable. While he spoke, Christopher planted his hands on the topmost fence board and climbed to the second board. He craned his neck and peered toward the charred chunk of ground. A sizable hole sat in the middle of the patch of black earth. Behind him, Staley asked with audible concern, "What's... the... boy... doing?"

Before Christopher knew what was happening, his father had trotted up to the fence. As Christopher turned to regard him, Lewis swung his hand in an upward arc. His open fist struck Christopher in the side of the head and knocked him off the fence. Much as with the incident involving the stirrup, his foot become tangled among the fence boards, and Christopher fell on his head.

Christopher's right hand pressed against his right ear as he twisted toward his father. He could barely see Lewis's face because the afternoon sun was hovering behind him, but he saw lips moving. The ringing in his ears prevented most of the message from coming through. "Damn it— shame y— ?" Rutlage's words departed in a hiss and carried flecks of spit with them. "Now sh— respect."

Christopher struggled ineffectively to reach a standing position. Lewis had been holding on to that shot since the previous night, and he got his money's worth. The dizziness reminded Christopher of when he used to spin around in circles as a child. His free left hand groped for some variety of support, but it could only find air and clumps of grass. The ringing increased its volume as he righted himself, and by the time he stood, he winced and pressed harder against his ear. Neither action, however, prevented Harkness's words from coming through in a garbled slurry.

"Wel— gar," Harkness said, his hands still rooted to his pockets, "I guess- more—store—wife— better." Whatever he said must have been a complete concession, because he gave a wave in Old Man Staley's direction and the three men started back to their horses in an almost synchronized gate. Apparently, the elder Rutlage's scolding brought everyone back to his senses in time to implement Liberty's unofficial town motto of "Leave well enough alone" to the fullest. On the upside, in his haste to leave, Lewis neglected to ask Staley if Christopher had worked out there the previous day. Christopher, though, was too busy fighting vertigo and nausea to appreciate this fact.

The men had saddled up and begun to ride away before Christopher even staggered over to his horse. His dizziness tossed him back and forth with every step until his flailing hand smacked into one of his horse's stirrups. He needed several attempts to mount up, but ultimately threw himself over the animal's back. His face still bent into a mask of pain, Christopher glanced behind him and saw Staley standing outside his screen door, looking at him from under the brim of his hat. Nothing tangible was wrong with the picture, but even though the pain made it hard to focus, he could tell that everything intangible was badly amiss. It was all wrong. Old Man Staley didn't stand like that, he didn't stare like that, and he sure as hell didn't twitch like that. He looked at Christopher like he was deciding... something. Staley did not go back inside until his visitors had ridden out of sight, if then.

The gray horse did most of the work in getting Christopher caught up to the three adult riders. They bounced over the flat land, their garbled voiced barely making their way back to the injured boy. They certainly seemed content with the turn of events, riding high in the saddle. It was as though they already had forgotten about the bizarre scene they had just witnessed and their reason for making the trip in the first place and were ready to retake their positions as the three wealthiest, most well-respected men in the town.

Christopher felt horrible, like being deathly ill and beaten to a pulp at the same time, and sat slumped in the saddle, limply holding onto the reigns with his left hand and pressing against his ear with his right. After a couple minutes, the Gray One caught up with the rest of the pack enough to march in its shadow, but Christopher's nausea had worsened to the point where he had to ride slumped over in the event that he should vomit. The Gray One ignored the uneven weight shifting around on its back and kept pace like a good horse.

While Christopher worked to hold onto his most recent breakfast, his father and Waits looked back at the same time. Rutlage merely threw a brief, disinterested glance his son's way and returned his gaze to the flat, dry land in front of him, but Waits said something that Christopher could not hear above the constant buzzing. His mouth had warped into a sly smile that showcased his nubby, yellow teeth, so Christopher knew that the man was not enquiring as to how he felt. He doubted the message would be any easier to decipher the second time around, so he nodded lamely and hoped that it would suffice. It did, and Waits merely expelled a stream of tobacco juice onto the hunk of Kansas real estate to his left before facing forward. Waits must not have asked him, "Did you sleep with my daughter?"

When they eventually arrived back at the house, Christopher's father, as always, wordlessly dismounted and marched inside, leaving Christopher to unsaddle and unbridle the horses, brush them down, and put them back in the barn. This time, the task proved agonizing, but even so, he took his time so that he would not have to go into the house. What if the pain progressed to the point where Christopher cried in front of his father? What if his father ordered him to do something and he could not hear it? Neither were acceptable options.

He accomplished most of the work with his left hand so that he did not have to interrupt his right hand from its job of pressing against his ear. Unfortunately, Christopher eventually did finish with the horses, and shuffling up to the house, he gingerly brought his right hand away from the side of his head. The afternoon sun still hung in the sky, so plenty of light remained to see the thin smear of blood on his hand.

His father left him alone that night, mostly because Christopher walked a straight path from the front door to his bed after finishing with the horses. It was still early in the day, but in his condition, all he could have done was sit and wince his way through the suffering, anyway. The throbbing pain that flared every time blood pulsed through his cranium made sleeping equally difficult, but for lack of an alternative, he turned so that his bloody ear pointed upward and stuck with the plan until he succeeded.

Christopher's condition failed to worry him. He thought of his body as a fantastic machine. It had absorbed an astounding amount of abuse over the years and always recovered. If bed-rest failed to cure his ear, he would merely visit Doc Ferguson when he came back... if he came back. The doctor's safety wore on him more than his own. He said a silent prayer for the doctor's safe return. The man held a special place in Christopher's heart for being one of the few people in town that gave a damn about his well-being.

He had plenty of reasons to worry, too. The scene earlier that day at Old Man Staley's seemed too bizarre for belief. The way Old Man Staley (if that really was him) looked, moved, and spoke deeply disturbed Christopher, and though they would never have admitted it, it had disturbed his father and the other two men as well... they just refused to leave the shelter of their ignorance. Very little about Old Man Staley reminded him of the way people were supposed to behave.

What about that hole in the middle of Old Man Staley's sheep pasture? People generally don't start bonfires in the middle of their grazing land. And as for the hole, it looked like a large hunk of ground was missing, too much for a man of Edgar Staley's age to have moved. Something was out there, because Old Man Staley acted like he was hiding something, especially when he saw Christopher climbing the fence.

By the time he dropped off to sleep that evening, Christopher found himself no closer to solving the mystery than when he had started the internal analysis. He did know, however, that at least one answer lay in Old Man Staley's pasture, and one way or another, pain or no pain, Father or no Father, he would go have a look.

*   *   *

Doc Ferguson's mouth hung open, trying to force out a scream that would not come. A yellow-brown, sticky substance surrounded him, pressing against every exposed inch of skin, preventing him from so much as closing his eyes. The cool substance had seeped into each of his orifices, and kept him frozen there, his eyelids peeled back, his mouth hanging open, his muscles tensed.

He didn't know how he could still breathe, see, or even think encased in the chemical cocoon, but none of his remaining sensations provided any comfort. The scream could not escape. The substance filling his nasal cavities had no odor. The only images to see through the amber substance were the strange, man-sized shapes stiffly walking back and forth across the room. The only things to feel were the coolness touching every inch of his skin, and the churning in his stomach, the itching in his ears, and the headaches.

*   *   *

CHAPTER SIX

July 4, 1877:

The next day... Independence Day, appropriately... Christopher's brave vow from the night before became nothing more than a fond memory. His father made it clear that his services would be required in the shop all day long, so the only event to look forward to was the fireworks display at the town square that night.

When he first awoke, the screaming pain in his right ear had mercifully reduced itself to a dull ache. The ringing had stopped as well, but the downside was that he could no longer hear much of anything out of the injured ear. This discovery failed to send him into a panic, however, because his history or resilience. *What I have is some sort of bruise in my ear,* Christopher reasoned, *and bruises are temporary. I've dealt with them before, and I can deal with this.*

Around lunchtime, while Christopher crawled around on his hands and knees and picked metal shavings out of the earthen floor, Agatha Rutlage made a brief visit to the interior of the shop. After she left, her husband told Christopher to get cleaned up and sent him over to Harkness's Dry Goods to fetch some sugar. It proved a welcome respite from the filth and dreariness of the blacksmith shop, and even the intense heat of the summer day provided an indescribable relief compared to standing next to open flame.

Christopher's eyes focused on the few feet of ground immediately in front of him as he walked, but from the corner of his eye, he still detected Emma sitting on the front steps of Waits' tavern. She wore a rumpled, gray dress and looked as though she had been waiting there for quite some time. When she saw Christopher coming, she scrambled to her feet and trotted toward him. The thought of someone seeing the two of them together sent an involuntary shudder shooting down Christopher's spine, and his eyes darted in every available direction in search of anyone who might be watching them. He closed his eyes, picturing James Waits' leveling a rifle barrel at his head from the tavern's second story window. Hopefully she did not want to go have sex, because after all he had endured the previous couple days, Christopher honestly didn't know whether he could have declined. She stopped several steps in front of him, a respectful distance away.

"Hello," he said awkwardly, his eyes averted as he stood frozen in his tracks.

"Oh my God, Christopher," she began, earnestly. "I am *so* sorry about my father finding out. I didn't tell him a thing, I swear to you."

"That's all right," he assured her numbly, hoping that she had nothing else to say. He really didn't require an explanation because he wouldn't have known if she was lying to him; he wasn't much good at reading people. Also, he barely understood male physiology, so the workings of the female body were a complete mystery; she could have made up something about one of her eyes changing color, and he would have believed her. Hopefully, they would exchange a nod, and he could continue walking past her. *Go ahead*, his mind demanded, *give me a nod. Just one little nod.* Unfortunately, she had not finished.

"He just saw some spots on my underpants and just started yelling at me," she explained, running a hand through her long, blonde hair in a gesture of exasperation. "I told him he was wrong that they weren't anything, but he—"

"Emma," Christopher said through gritted teeth, "someone is bound to notice we're speaking with one another, and that can't be good."

"Yeah, I know, but—"

Despite his desire to be anywhere but standing there in the open street, conversing with her, a thought struck Christopher. "Emma," he asked, his features slackening, "how did your father see your underpants?"

Emma's eyes shifted to the right as she bit her lip. "Christopher, I can't talk about that right now. You're right; we'd better go." She leaned forward, as if to plant a kiss on his cheek, then must have remembered that such an act would have put both their lives in a great deal of peril. She quickly stepped back, smiled sheepishly, and nodded. "Um, good-bye," she said.

Christopher responded with an equally formal farewell, and they walked in opposite directions. Emma stopped near the steps of her father's tavern and looked back, sadly... longingly. Her eyes were wide with an emotion he knew well: fear. She wanted out of this town as badly as he did, because it would either kill her or force her to become something that she didn't want to be. Christopher saw her stop, but kept his head down and his feet moving. If he had looked up, she might have said something, and they might have done something that would have changed their lives forever. The moment passed, though, as such moments often did, and as Christopher plodded down the street, he felt as though one hundred pounds of chains followed in his wake.

It happened that James Waits saw the two teenagers conversing from the darkened interior of his tavern. The instant Emma walked back inside, he informed her that she would not be leaving the apartment for the remainder of the week. Christopher had scant time to consider her predicament that day, though, because his father worked him even harder after lunch than he had before it. He climbed into his bed early for the second straight night, dehydrated and sore from the day of hard labor. His entire body felt like a bruise. Missing the Independence Day celebration wasn't a big deal. He'd seen the centennial celebration the previous year, and there was no way this year could top that. The fireworks exploded outside the window below him, but he slept with his bad ear pointed toward the ceiling, and nothing roused him.

*   *   *

The next morning, Christopher's father had scheduled some deliveries to a few patrons. Delivery was one of those extra services Lewis offered that Christopher performed and did not collect a cent from. Lewis barely looked at his son when Christopher stopped by the shop to pick up the items he was to deliver. Neither a "Good morning," nor even a "How's the ear?" (which *still* did not work properly) passed his lips. "The deliveries you gotta make is over by the door," he said, twisting his rigid, soot-stained neck in the direction of the sliver of sunlight. He probably thought Christopher got off easy with a vicious slap to the head. After all, the ungrateful wretch embarrassed the elder Rutlage in front of his cohorts.

Christopher saddled the gray horse and went about performing the town deliveries first. There were a set of stakes for Mr. Torrance, a repaired gate latch for Mr. Wiley, and a wrapped something that may have been a weathervane for Mrs. McCann. When those were quickly completed, he sighed as he unfolded the scrap of paper that contained the remaining names on the list, the rural deliveries. The third and final name on the list, as fate should have it, belonged to Deklan Lorenz.

Christopher pushed his horse a bit hard in concluding the first two rural deliveries, but he wanted some extra time at Lorenz's before making an unscheduled stop at the Staley's. No one could ever mistake

Lewis Rutlage for the most alert man to ever come down the pike, but he always kept his son on a tight time schedule, and these deliveries were no exception. Christopher's only saving grace stemmed from the fact that it was normal for one of the people he delivered to provided him with a light lunch. It was an expected, neighborly gesture, what with the next-to-non-existent delivery fee, and he felt certain Lorenz would oblige.

When Christopher arrived at his house amid a chorus of canine barks, Lorenz came out onto his front porch, leaned against one of the middle posts, and crossed his arms. Although he stood in the shade, he still wore his broad, flat-brimmed hat, perhaps trying to cover as much of himself as possible. "Good day, delivery boy," he said with a nod.

"Hey..." Christopher said, giving an ambiguous wave. He didn't know how to address the man whom he visited. Were they friends? Neighbors? He didn't have many friends, so it was hard to tell. He tugged on the reigns until the gray horse eased to a halt. He dismounted and hitched his mount to one of the crooked fence posts. Deklan's dog scampered over to within a few feet of them and continued barking, but the Gray One hardly seemed to take notice and certainly did not let it interrupt his heaving sighs as he attempted to catch his breath. "You mind if I get my horse some water?" Christopher called toward the porch.

"If he doesn't mind dog slobber, you can just give him Dante's water bucket," Lorenz suggested, gesturing toward the wooden bucket that sat at the bottom step of the porch. "What's your horse's name?"

"The Gray One," Christopher thought about saying, but that would have sounded stupid. Instead, he said, "It doesn't really have a name."

"Names have power," Deklan informed him. "Everything should have one, especially a proud animal like this one." He gestured a gloved hand toward Christopher's nondescript, gray mount. "Why don't we call him... Thor?"

"Who's 'Thor'?" Christopher asked. He had certainly never met a person with such a name.

"In the Norse myths, he was the God of Thunder," Lorenz informed him. "Take my word for it: he would be honored to have such a fine name."

"Norse," another word he had never heard. He certainly was familiar with the edicts of the Christian religion, though. "Isn't that blasphemy?" Christopher asked.

Lorenz shrugged. "Maybe. No matter what his name is, though, he still has to drink out of a bucket with dog slobber in it."

Deciding that, at this point, Thor probably would be no more finicky about water sources than he would about names, Christopher bent over and slid the bucket over to where his horse could reach it. "I didn't know you took deliveries from us," he stated while walking up the porch steps. Lorenz's order sat wrapped in Christopher's left hand. It was something metal, obviously, about eight inches long, two inches wide, and two inches thick.

"This is the first one," Deklan replied, shrugging his broad shoulders again. "I figured you were competent enough to make it out here and I could save a trip into town."

Christopher's brow wrinkled in on itself. "But you must have ordered this at least a week ago. We'd never spoken before last Wednesday."

"No," he agreed, "but a conversation isn't always necessary. I knew who you were, and you struck me was being competent." He clapped his scarred, calloused hands together and motioned toward the package. "Let's have a look at 'em."

Christopher handed over Lorenz's order and watched the man peel away the cloth wrapping with a zeal contrary to the careful ease with which he normally carried himself. He removed five, eight-inch long, flat pieces of metal that tapered on one end into sharp, barbed points. "What are they?" Christopher asked.

Lorenz held one of his purchases up to the sliver of sunlight penetrating the leafy canopy, turning it in his hand to examine the sharpened edge. "Throwing knives," he informed his young guest with what might have been his version of a smile. "Whatever the man's other faults, your father is a fine craftsman."

"Throwing knives?" Christopher repeated. "Why would you need to throw a knife? Couldn't you just use a gun?"

Satisfied with the first, Lorenz raised a second of the blades up and let it glisten in the sunlight. "Fire arms are loud and clumsy weapons for desperate men. Besides, they aren't nearly as foolproof as people would have you believe: guns can malfunction, bullets can misfire."

"Yeah," Christopher conceded with a confident scoff, "but they're a lot more accurate."

Almost before Christopher could finish the sentence, Lorenz wheeled and flung the knife in an over-hand motion directly to the left of Christopher's head. The wind whistled in his good ear and he turned in time to see the blade imbed itself in Thor's water bucket, a target approximately thirty feet away, as if shot out of a cannon. Thor jerked his head up from drinking, surprised by the jolt, but just as quickly, he lowered his face into the bucket and resumed the quenching of his thirst.

Christopher blinked, his mind trying to catch up with what had just happened. At first, he had to bed down the alarm that Lorenz's movements had roused. *Relax*, he told himself, *he's not trying to kill you... or your horse... because if he was, you'd both be dead.* Only after he had drawn a couple breaths could Christopher begin to assess the event. The man's speed was uncanny. From the instant Lorenz lifted his weapon, his knife had struck its target before most men could have drawn a gun from its holster.

"C'mon inside," Lorenz casually offered while Christopher's gaze remained fixed on the impaled water bucket, "I'll fix you some lunch." It took a moment longer for the younger man to pull his eyes away and follow his host inside.

For lunch, Lorenz brought out the same heavily salted, corned beef and hard cheese they had eaten the other day. He seemed like the sort of man who could eat the same meal indefinitely, but Christopher didn't complain and consumed his sandwich quickly. "I can't stay long," he explained to his host. "Father expects me home in about an hour, and I still have to stop by Staley's." Lorenz nodded, probably assuming that the reference to Staley's involved another delivery. Christopher did not attempt to dissuade him from thinking that. In the face of anything else that he anticipated might befall him, Christopher did not wish to drag his new friend into a situation that might simply involve his stupid imagination playing tricks on him.

Christopher jammed the final hunk of sandwich into his mouth and kept chewing as he strode outside, over to where he had hitched Thor. After swallowing, he called behind him, "Thanks for the lunch."

Lorenz followed him outside, all the way over to Thor, and bent down to extract his throwing knife from the side of the wooden bucket. "Something wrong with your right ear?" he asked, wiggling the knife handle.

Christopher adjusted to his hearing loss so quickly in the few days since it happened that the question confused him for a moment. He nearly denied anything being wrong before remembering his condition. "How did you know?" he wondered aloud.

"You keep tilting your left side forward when I'm talking. You're doing it right now," Lorenz said, gesturing with the recently freed knife point.

"Huh," Christopher said, and noticed that Lorenz was right. He recoiled and decided to skirt the question as best he could. "Yeah, I, ah got hit in the head the other day." He shoved his left foot into the stirrup and swung his right leg over Thor's back, anticipating that Lorenz would let the subject drop.

"Your father?" Lorenz asked quietly from behind the protective brim of his black hat.

Christopher nodded, automatically, then the anger reflexively set in, and he stopped. Voices echoed through his head, telling him to be outraged. *How dare this stranger, who didn't even attend a proper church, make accusations about Father, one of the most well respected men in all of Liberty! How dare I confirm them!* The voices belonged to his father and mother, but by this point in his life, they had wormed their way into his brain and become his constant companions.

"My father is a good man," Christopher told Lorenz coldly. He didn't believe the words as he said them, but almost as if he'd been trained to say them, he couldn't stop them from coming out either, "and any punishment I receive is well deserved." His glistening eyes avoided Lorenz and pointed across the fenced in area, at the tree-lined backdrop. "And I don't think my family life is any of your business." That said, he turned Thor around and rode down the packed dirt trail. Lorenz might have said something, but he couldn't hear it.

By the time cluster of trees ended and the expanse of rolling Kansas countryside rose to meet Christopher, the anger stewing inside turned to relief. He knew. Lorenz knew the truth. Everyone knew, of course, but finally, someone had *admitted* that they knew what he had endured since he could remember. He didn't know at what point he started crying, but the warm tears sliding down Christopher's cheeks startled him. With that realization, the floodgates opened, and Christopher leaned against his horse's neck, his body shaking from the sobs. At least a minute passed. Then, he straightened up in the saddle and slapped himself across the face. "Shut up. Shut up," he hissed. "Stupid baby. Crying like a stupid baby." No amount of chastising could stop the tears, though. Finally, someone actually cared whether he lived or died.

*   *   *

The ride to Staley's provided Christopher with ample time to repress his emotions. He had never ridden there from Lorenz's, but like the path between most any two points in Kansas, it was literally a straight line, with no trees or rivers to divert him. He pointed Thor in a general direction and rode until he saw the outline of a farmhouse, and his estimate turned out to be off by only a few hundred yards.

Christopher pulled Thor to a stop about half a mile from Staley's house and dismounted. All he wanted was a glimpse of the pasture, and then he would turn and head back to town. He wrapped the reigns around the saddle horn and stalked toward the sheep pasture, not at all worried about leaving Thor alone in the open. He was a smart, even-tempered horse. He didn't need to be hitched to anything to remain in the general area.

The spring had provided plentiful rain, making the grass a little taller than usual, and for whatever reason, this particular patch had grown almost to Christopher's head. He could hardly see anything and had to clear a path with his hands as he walked. A vague plan of action had already taken shape in his mind, the entirety of which involved circling around the fenced-in sheep pasture to the furthest point from the house. From there, he would stay as low as possible coming over the slight rise and get a good look at the hole in the ground.

He was no master tactician, but it seemed like a good strategy: simple and cautious, yet direct. More than anything, he wanted to stay as far away as possible from that house. There were many things wrong with the situation, but Old Man Staley's appearance took the prize for most disturbing of all. Not only that, the last time Christopher visited the house, along with the bigot, the rapist, and his father, Old Man Staley had stood there, waiting. Even though he could not have had any idea that the party was on its way, even though he might not have entertained any guests other than Doc Ferguson in the last year, he still anticipated their arrival. If he could help it, Christopher wasn't going anywhere near that house.

Christopher stepped gingerly through the grass, parting the blades with the wedge formed with his arms. Would Staley spy the tips of grass parting and know he was coming? Or would the work of the healthy breeze disguise his movement? It would probably take a little over a minute to reach the fence from his current position at his current pace. His sense of direction rarely failed in this environment. It took years to develop an internal compass like that, and people that grew up in the city and moved west could rarely do it, but Christopher was a child of the plains, so it was all he knew.

His hands pushed through yet another identical cluster of grass and Christopher nearly walked into a shoe that hovered at eye level. His internal tension gradually had been ratcheting up since he left Deklan's, such a high level that the sight of the shoe nearly caused him to wet himself, run for home, and drop dead from heart failure all at the same time. He did none of those, however, and instead, slowly rotated his head skyward. A scarecrow hung from the pole, and Christopher's abdomen unclenched and his lungs began to work again. Just a scarecrow. A short, almost hysterical burst of laughter escaped his lips. Thank the Lord no one was there to see his initial reaction; that was the sort of thing that persistent nicknames are made of.

He took a momentary rest from his reconnaissance mission to admire the workmanship of the scarecrow. In contrast to the shoddily constructed strawmen with which Christopher was familiar, someone had gone to great pains in putting this one together. The clothes were almost new, as was the broad, felt hat, the sewing looked nearly seamless, and very little straw stuck out from its fabric casing. The creator even went so far as to equip this one with shoes and gloves.

Mrs. Staley must have made it, he decided. Her sewing skills were beyond reproach and she had more time on her hands than her husband. An image from his last visit, the filthy sheet blowing on the line, stuck in his mind. At least she had that kind of free time prior to the past few days. He shook his head. Something that well-constructed could scare a lot more than crows, obviously. Such a shame that her creation hung in such an isolated location.

He rose up on his tiptoes and scanned the top of the sea of swaying grass. He had traveled further away from the fence than he thought, overshooting the north end by a dozen yards or so. Taking a hard left, Christopher grew slightly more concerned about his time restrictions with each passing second. He would really have to push Thor to make it back home at a decent time. He shrugged, dipping his shoulder through a curtain of green. He would just have to give Thor a carrot with his dinner and clean out his water bucket with a fresh towel to compensate him for his trouble. If his return ended up exceptionally delayed, he could tell his father that a horsefly stung Thor after he had dismounted and it took a while to catch up to him. The excuse sounded plausible enough; Christopher had thought of the lie some time ago and saved for a special occasion.

Doing his best not to rush, he crept toward what he hoped was the fence line, and noticed that, dead ahead, a fifteen- to twenty-foot-wide swath of grass stood a good deal shorter than the rest. He crept forward, realizing that his head and shoulders were now visible from the sheep pasture. Upon further examination, he realized that the top of the grass had been singed fairly recently. Stepping amidst the shorter cluster, the Staley's fence became visible and he could see into the pasture. The slight rise blocked any view of him from the front porch. The sight held him transfixed.

A single, charred rift marred the picturesque, emerald pasture. Something burned its way into the earth about twenty feet from the fence line and continued toward the rise. As it traveled away from the fence, the path dug deeply into the rising earth, taking a sizable chunk out of the hill, a feature Christopher somehow failed to see from his perspective two days prior.

Christopher could make no sense of the sight; it seemed so unlike anything he had ever seen or heard of. The ground had obviously been burned. Something big enough to make a moderately sized hole had struck the pasture with tremendous force. The best explanation his fourteen-year-old mind could manage involved a shooting star cutting the path. The question then became: why would Old Man Staley want to hide a shooting star?

Christopher stepped toward the fence. His thoughts quickly jumped to another question, one that in no way followed his previous train of thought. It happened from time to time; Christopher would encounter something perplexing and then forget about it, only to have it randomly pop back into his head with greater clarity minutes or hours later. His father called it "being a scatterbrain." In this case, the thought was a question: why would anyone in their right mind put a scarecrow in the middle of an acre of nothing but grass? A shadow fell across his face as the scarecrow shuffled forward.

Christopher screamed, but it came out more like a sigh. The scarecrow ambled forward in quick, spastic motions, in other words, exactly how one would expect a scarecrow to move. Christopher stood with his back to the fence, paralyzed, not only from fear, but also from disbelief. This was far beyond anything he'd ever seen, heard of, or even read about in the Bible. The fear must have provided a significant influence, though, because he lost control of his bodily functions and let go of what little water his body had retained on this hot summer day. Christopher didn't notice; damp trousers were not a primary concern at this point, not even close.

Christopher cringed and pulled his arms in to his chest as the scarecrow flailed a gloved fist and struck him in the midsection. His forearms absorbed the brunt of the attack, but the right-handed strike sent him sailing over the top of the fence into the sheep pasture beyond. At the end of his twelve-foot flight, he hit the ground and rolled into a reverse somersault, which may be all that prevented him from breaking his neck.

Christopher's momentum carried him into a crouch. His left foot slid in some sheep droppings on his first attempt to stand, but he scrambled to his feet cleanly on his second attempt. The clicking sound behind him sent him bolting across the open space of the pasture, a second before the scarecrow crashed through the fence. The sturdy, wooden fence boards failed to even slow it down. A dozen sheep lethargically staggered toward Christopher, emitting sickly bleats and coughs. They were dirty and thin, and dozens of flies swarmed around each of their gray faces, but those passing observations were all he cared to notice as he zigzagged his way through them. His superior speed across open spaces should have distanced him from his pursuer, but a second slip on sheep excrement nearly finished both him and his hypothesis.

He reached the opposite side of the field maybe two seconds ahead of the clicking scarecrow. He grabbed hold of the rough wood of the top board and attempted to scramble over, but his pursuer took the direct route and blasted through the solid, wooden construction. The scarecrow slammed into the back of Christopher, cleaning his legs out from under him and shattering the section of fence.

He hit the ground, hard, again, this time landing on his shoulders and reverse-somersaulting onto on his side. Christopher's hands clawed at the ground, trying to pull himself to his feet and away from the scarecrow, but something clamped down on his left ankle. He glanced back and saw that, at some point during their chase, the scarecrow had lost its shoes, leaving in their place a pair of narrow, red feet with two long, talon-like toes at their tips and a single, opposable toe at their heel. They certainly were not human feet, and more importantly, one had latched onto Christopher's ankle.

The scarecrows gloves had also disappeared, Christopher noticed as his eyes traveled up its body, and the lone two fingers of the hands were in the positions corresponding with the toes of the feet, complete with a sharp, opposable thumb adjoined just below the palm. One of these grotesque hands lashed out and grabbed hold of his shirt collar as Christopher groped about the immediate ground for something to hold on to. His right hand fell upon a large piece of the broken fence, and his fingers wrapped around the jagged hunk of wood before the red "hand" ripped him to his feet. Christopher focused on the three digits clutching his shirt collar. Anything was better than looking at the head, with the cloth draped over its face and the blankness staring from behind the two wide eyeholes.

Ants ran across Christopher's chest and shocked him out of his fear-induced stupor. He slapped at them with his free left hand, then realized that they were rushing out from the scarecrow's sleeve. He pounded his chest with his free hand and twisted, but the scarecrow seemed content merely to hold him in place. Christopher reached his right arm back as far as he could and swung the length of wood in an upward arch, toward the scarecrow's head. He grasped his brittle, makeshift weapon with only one hand, and he was only fourteen, but with the amount of force his panic stricken body generated, he might as well have been the veteran of twenty-five summers and swinging an axe handle with both hands. The makeshift club cracked against the side of the creature's head.

The hat flew off.

The mask tore away.

The scarecrow's grip broke, and Christopher began running the moment his feet touched the ground, running as he had never run before toward the original section of fence the scarecrow had broken through, running for his life. He sprinted through the grass, his feet almost traveling too fast for the rest of him, expecting to smash headfirst into another scarecrow, thinking that the scarecrow's head looked just like an ant's when the mask came off. Just like an ant's head, complete with inky black eyes and huge mandibles, perfect for eating the faces off of fourteen-year-old boys.

The smaller ants bit his flesh as they scurried up to his neck. He flailed his hands wildly at them as he ran, slapping, clawing, and in all other ways, shedding them. Dashing through the tall grass scraped some of them off, but there seemed to be a million of them crawling and biting his shoulders and nipples and neck.

Find Thor! his brain intermittently screamed amid the tiny sparks of pain that erupted over the surface of his body. *Find Thor and you will be safe!* This remained his only coherent thought, even though he felt like he could run all the way to Liberty, or Kansas City, for that matter. He considered trying to find his original path through the grass but quickly gave up on that. He leapt blindly through the mass of green and yellow blades, at the mercy of his internal compass.

The sea of grass did not end, and Christopher's pulse rhythmically thudded all the way through his body, from his temples to the tips of his fingers and toes. What if he was running in circles? Had he run within a few feet of Thor and not noticed? What if the scarecrow had discovered Thor and torn him apart? Christopher's internal compass had failed and he was going to die. He burst from a thicket of grass and almost collided with Thor's right flank. He threw out his hands in a defensive embrace, causing the uncomfortable animal to lurch forward. Some euphoric, incoherent verbalization burst from his lips when Christopher saw his horse and felt the coarse hair of the creature's mane under his fingertips. His legs experienced the relief first and buckled a bit too early, leaving him to literally crawl his way up Thor into the saddle. The instant he was secure, without waiting for any urging, the brilliant, wonderful horse began to gallop back to town.

A few seconds later, after he had shifted around into a correct riding position, Christopher slumped forward and hugged his horse's neck. Carrot for dinner? By God, he was prepared to erect a life-sized monument in Thor's honor. After what seemed like an hour, but was probably closer to thirty seconds, he untethered the reigns from the saddle horn, clutching them in a death-grip, and chanced a look behind them. Nothing followed in their wake, only grass tips swaying in the breeze. Christopher wiped his eyes dry and checked again. Still nothing. He relaxed enough to notice that tears were streaming from his eyes.

Something crawled up Christopher's right earlobe. His last reserves of adrenaline surged through his body, propelling his hand upward and snatching the ant that dashed toward his inner ear. He brought the ant in front of him and crushed it between his thumb and forefinger as forcefully as one can.

His middle finger curled back as he prepared to flick the insect corpse away, but stopped when he noticed a few peculiar characteristics about the latest casualty of this excursion: the ant had two body segments, instead of the usual three, and four legs, instead of the usual six. The most obvious abnormality about this creature, though, involved its crushed innards and the fact that they glowed a bright green, much like a firefly's.

At this time, without daring to so much as slow down, Christopher leaned over and in one mighty heave, regurgitated the heavily salted corned beef, hard cheese, and dry bread that Deklan had generously prepared for lunch.

*   *   *

CHAPTER SEVEN

Christopher rode east until the steeple of Liberty's church came into view. Only then did he feel secure enough to tug on the reigns and slow Thor to a walk. The horse immediately unleashed a body-rattling sigh, and after a few steps, Christopher leaned forward and patted the animal's sweaty, gray neck. Leaving too early or leaving too late could have been the end of both of them. The gesture did not seem like thanks enough.

As the setting sun cast long shadows of the irregularly spaced homes into the street, Thor carried Christopher across town to the Rutlage home without incident. The boy's pants had dried, and the taste of vomit in his mouth had largely disappeared, but if he was tempted to attribute the day's events to his imagination, Christopher merely had to check the constellation of ant bites lining his torso. Within the cluster of familiar houses and businesses, the ordeal, it seemed, had finally ended. Structure can have that effect, and whatever other characteristics Liberty possessed, it possessed structure. Once inside the barn, Christopher unsaddled Thor as quickly as he could, brushed down his sweaty coat, and gave him a final embrace about the neck. After hanging the saddle on the wall, he remembered his silent promise of the carrot and walked inside the house to retrieve one.

When Christopher pushed the front door open and stepped onto the wooden floor, the last vestiges of adrenaline dried up, and he felt the kind of security that can only come from returning home. Even in the aftermath of his brush with death, he did not forget that he had suffered more abuse within that building than in all the pastures of Kansas combined. At the same time, though, the greater danger lurked outside those walls. The beatings and bruises that his father had inflicted upon him were known evils that he had survived many times. Father would protect him from the creature in the field, if for no other reason than because he could not stand the thought of a foreign hand striking his children.

Christopher stepped into the kitchen to see if his mother had picked any of the finger-sized carrots from the garden that morning. Both his parents were present that evening, acting completely out of character by sitting at adjacent ends of the table, talking. Christopher performed a double-take, because he only needed one hand to count the number of times he had seen them engage in an actual, private conversation, but that was indeed what they were doing. It must have been a fairly important topic, too, because they both stopped when he entered.

His parents turned and stared at him with gaping mouths, and Christopher froze, wondering why. Amid the wash of relief, he had nearly forgotten about the disheveled appearance he had gained from getting thrown through a fence and sliding across every inch of the Staley's sheep pasture. Swellings and minor lacerations also dotted his body, evidence of the inhuman beating he had absorbed. God only knew what those bug bites looked like.

Lewis Rutlage sat on the opposite side of the table in his hard, inflexible chair, and Christopher could not remember ever being so glad to see that soot-stained face and chicken neck. He actually had to suppress an urge to embrace the craggy-faced man. This burgeoning fantasy lasted until Lewis opened his mouth. "Where you been, boy?" he demanded.

"I went out to Staley's — ," Christopher began, without even considering the impact those first words would have. He had the audacity to think that his father would let him rattle off at least one sentence.

"Staley's?" the elder Rutlage repeated, shaking his head, unable to believe his son's words. Agatha Rutlage's frail hands flew to her mouth. Lewis's eyes narrowed, and his lips barely moved as he asked, "Did you have any deliveries out there?"

Christopher swallowed hard. Out of the corner of his eye, he saw the precursor of things to come: his mother slowly rising from her chair and easing toward the back door. It seemed a statistical impossibility to avoid beatings after his mother disappeared on consecutive nights, and his entire body began to ache and throb in synchrony with the beating of his heart.

Lewis knew the answer to his own question, but he asked it again. "Well, did you?" he demanded, his voice even sharper.

Tears clouded Christopher's vision and clogged his throat. He was too tired to be panicked, having sweated out all of his adrenaline during the ride home. If he was going to get whipped, at least, he needed to explain himself; this whole ordeal seemed kind of important. "No, sir, but — "

"But? But what?" Lewis barked. His longish fingernails raked across the surface of the table. "Why were you out there botherin' those folks?"

Christopher's incisors dug into his lower lip. His father was going to hit him, but if he wept openly, it would convey a lack of dignity, and the beating would double in severity. After all he had endured in the past couple hours, he honestly wasn't certain he would survive. He had to risk it, though. He had to tell his father, to warn him of a danger of

Biblical proportions lurking on the outskirts of town. "I wasn't botherin' them," he explained with admirable composure, for any age. "I went to see that hole I tried to look at the other day."

Lewis stood up. The legs of the chair squeaked a few inches over the floorboards. He glowered at his son as he stepped closer, on the verge of bursting like an over-stoked furnace. "You were trespassing on someone else's property." Property was sacred. It made the Rutlage family the respectable family that it was. Lewis looked away. His back shoulder dipped. Christopher braced himself. "You little... bastard!"

Christopher had not expected a closed fist.

The blow hit him squarely on the left cheekbone and sent Christopher reeling backwards, over a chair. He landed on his shoulder and slid against the wall. Fortunately, the assault left him too dazed to cry. He thought that lying still on the floor might end it, but when he could see again, the blurred form of his father stood over him. The first punch had landed against the side of his face and avoided his nose. To his knowledge, Christopher had not bled on the nice, clean floor... So, why was Father so angry? "You breakin' chairs, boy?" he growled. "I bring you into this world. I feed you and cloth you, and all you can do is disobey me at every turn and go breakin' my chairs!"

"Daddy! No!" Marry yelled. Christopher hadn't the slightest idea what direction her yell came from. He hadn't even seen or heard her come in. Actually, he neither saw nor heard anything very well at that point, but when a pint-sized form ran between him and their father, it couldn't have belonged to anyone else.

Lewis grabbed a handful of his daughter's long, curly hair and dragged her out of the way. Mary squealed. Christopher could not hear much of what his father yelled at Mary, it all reached his ears in a garbled slur, but it was lengthy, so it probably involved a quote from the Bible. He did see his father slap her, though, and heard her shriek. Despite a loss of equilibrium, Christopher managed to climb to his feet.

"Don't you touch her!" he yelled, launching a pathetic moan in the general direction of his father's back. Christopher took a lethargic step forward, and Lewis caught him with an elbow. The taste of blood filled his mouth as a jagged bit of tooth bounced onto the floor, but somehow Christopher remained standing. This proved unfortunate, because Lewis momentarily let his hands drop, and a glimmer of hope made Christopher's instinct take over. He cocked his left arm and threw a punch at his father.

On the continuum of punishable offences, attempting to strike his father probably resided on the same level as if Christopher had attempted to rape his mother. It was like breaking five Commandments at once. The punch he threw with his lead-like left arm missed badly, but Lewis saw. His son had tried to hit him. He looked over his shoulder with one dark eye, and Christopher's arms contracted toward his chest, instinctively protecting his vital organs. For the third time that day, he started to weep.

Rutlage grabbed his son by the back of the neck and threw him to the floor with one arm. Christopher curled up into a tight ball and did his best to protect his head from the flurry of kicks and punches and kicks and kicks.

Your mind travels to strange places when someone is beating you senseless. While fighting, you tend to maintain an almost superhuman focus, but after the outcome becomes inevitable and you have lost, your mind tries to escape without the body. Christopher tried to think of another time and place to take his mind off the pain. In this instance, he thought about the time, just after he had turned thirteen years old, when he visited Reverend Skidmore.

It occurred about a year-and-a-half ago, so he remembered it well. Christopher's father had beaten him earlier that day for not straightening the shop after Lewis had left him a note telling him to. Christopher visited to the Reverend at home to complain about this, to find out if he, or anyone, could do anything to help. Skidmore sat Christopher down at his dining room table, gave him a glass of cool water, and proceeded to tell the story of the Hebrews wandering through the desert after the Exodus from Egypt and about how this was a test and that Christopher's reward would be in the next life. Christopher started crying at this point, and continued to cry as Skidmore ushered him out the door, patting his shoulder and telling him that everything would be fine.

That evening, Christopher wandered around town for close to an hour, thinking that maybe Reverend Skidmore was right, and that maybe the fault lay with him for not straightening the shop like Father had instructed. It was possible, after all, that he was a weak and sinful child, and that he was making excuses for his shortcomings. Maybe he should stick to worrying about being a good son and leave the rest to God. He actually felt better when he got home. Later that day, however, Reverend Skidmore had a talk with Lewis. Later that night, Christopher received another beating. Christopher never sought out Reverend Skidmore or anyone else for help after that.

*   *   *

Christopher woke that night in his bed, having no idea how he had gotten there. Excruciating pain of every flavor consumed most of his body. The dull ach of his upper back. The throbbing of his ear and mouth. The sharp, searing pain in his wrist, where his father had kicked him. The taste of old blood filled his mouth. His mind didn't work very well, either, and he barely remembered what had happened that day. In the middle of the night, though, he fought his way out of bed, wincing the entire time and consoling himself with the knowledge that the longer he waited, the harder it would be. He shuffled out the side door, walked through his mother's carefully tilled garden, and unearthed a carrot for his horse. He fed it to Thor that night, and although it was probably his imagination, Christopher sensed gratitude in the brave animal. He owed Thor his life, even though he wasn't sure what that was worth.

Christopher stood out in the barn, his back pressed against the wall, not caring if his father found him and beat him again. By his estimation, after what he saw out at Staley's earlier that day, everyone in town would die very soon.

He was almost right.

*   *   *

July 6, 1877:

The following morning, Christopher forced himself out of bed, one inch at a time, as the rays of dawn snuck across the floor. Soreness and stiffness had overtaken his body in his sleep, and he could hardly take two slow steps in succession without having to hold back tears. He was amazed that he had any tears to hold back. It would not have surprised him if he had used up all the tears allotted to him for the entire year in that one hellish night.

Christopher methodically shuffled his way into the dining room, where Mrs. Rutlage had already spooned out his breakfast into a bowl and set it on the table. His tiny mother wore her usual shapeless, black dress and wrinkled scowl. Christopher gingerly eased his aching body into the hard, wooden chair, picked up a spoon with a shaking hand, and prepared to dig into a steaming bowl of plain oatmeal. Plain oatmeal always constituted his post-punishment breakfast. His parents sent him to bed without supper countless times, but he always received breakfast the next morning. Probably to give him energy for the workday ahead.

The first spoonful did not taste like much, but that had less to do with the quality of food, and more to do with the fact that his tongue had swelled to the size of a steak during the night. Like a flash of lightning, the memory burst in front of him of the uppercut that slammed against his jaw and nearly caused him to bite off the tip of his tongue. Christopher closed his eyes and waited for the image to disappear before taking another bite. The second tasted sweet upon his tongue, too sweet to be accounted for by oats or blood or delirium. His mother had included brown sugar to his oatmeal. The sensation would not have been more overwhelming had the substance been frankincense.

From his mother, who during their fourteen-year, mutually non-communicative relationship in which indifference constituted the deepest emotion felt toward one another, the brown sugar in the oatmeal seemed to be her way of saying, "I love you," or at the very least, "I wish you hadn't been beaten quite so badly last night." Further evidence that he might not be the evil creature his father accused him of being. Agatha did not look at her son while he ate, and her complete lack of lack of affect made him consider that perhaps this gift from heaven was an absent-minded mistake on her part. After all, she wasn't there to witness the brutality.

When Christopher had finished scraping the bowl clean, he took it over to the dirty dish bucket that his mother stood beside. He set his left hand on his thigh for support and gently lowered the bowl and spoon into the bucket with his shaking right hand, saying, "Thank you for the breakfast," although the girth of his tongue nearly mangled his solemn thanks into something unintelligible.

His mother responded with, "Your father wants you to chop some wood and haul it over behind the shop." Perhaps she could have summoned a more tender response, but her callousness failed to dampen the glow of affection that pulsed within Christopher.

"Oh," she added as Christopher shambled toward the front door at an old-man gate, "your father said not to go out into public until after dark. He doesn't want the neighbors seeing your face."

Christopher started to nod, but his neck hurt too badly.

Chopping and hauling wood proved harder than usual. The overcast sky kept the temperature down, but his body had suffered greatly since the last time Christopher had to pick up an axe. The tool felt twice as heavy in his hands, and the slightest bend sent an arc of pain shooting through his middle back. Each successive swing of the axe extracted a wince from his face, and Christopher realized that one more beating in the near future stood a very real possibility of crippling him permanently. His fragile condition demanded that he rest as much as possible and remain unconditionally obedient over the next couple of days. This sounded like an easy enough task... at least until the eighteen-hour-old memory of the altercation with a giant insect invaded his thoughts.

When the logs were (somehow) chopped, Christopher set the axe against the stump and ran his tender wrist across his dirty forehead. He still had to transport it to the shop, located all the way over on the other side of the house. This proved an equally taxing activity, with all the bending and lifting, but thankfully, during the few occasions that Christopher passed the shop's open door and came into his father's line of vision, Lewis Rutlage showed no indication of seeing him. Christopher doubted he could have endured his father's distinctive look of disappointment without some kind of emotional outburst.

Such a look a disgust, coming from such a man, contained a difficult-to-describe power. Lewis Rutlage was not just some cretin whose opinion the son could dismiss: the man was the boy's father, and Christopher had been taught his whole life that your father was someone you respect and obey or else you suffered the wrath of God. After each beating ended, no matter how much he believed otherwise, in the back of his mind, a persistent, impossible to ignore voice told him that the blame lay upon his head. Punishment was not a choice made by the punisher; it was a neutral force, like gravity, that fell on the heads of bad sons.

Christopher had his own original sin to contend with, as well: he was born, and his father abandoned a prosperous business in Kansas City because he didn't want to raise children in the Godless den of iniquity that was the modern city. He left the business and the relative wealth, and came out here to Liberty, where sometimes it seemed like there was nothing but dirt and grass. He knew early on that he owed his father for this chance at salvation, but he could never seem to repay the man with anything but aggravation.

He had to stave off the dizzying fog of unconsciousness more than a few times, but Christopher finished loading the firewood. With the last split log stacked, he walked over to the water pump to for a well-deserved drink. His swollen tongue made the act of swallowing difficult but hardly impossible. It seemed as though his senses were slowly departing. He had already become deaf in one ear, his right eye had almost totally swelled shut (which complicated the act of accurately swinging an axe like he would not have believed), and his swollen tongue prevented him from tasting much of anything.

Hopefully, he wouldn't see Emma for a while. He could not very well seek her out in the immediate future for fear of being beaten, and she probably would not contact him for similar reasons. Even if they encountered one another in the next few days, though, his puffy, misshapen appearance would no doubt destroy her lust for sex. Still, he might have to leave soon, and if he left, he might try taking her with him.

Ever since his mother's warning about traveling in daylight, Christopher had successfully managed to avoid mirrors, but every time he wiped the sweat from his face, he got an idea of just how swollen his features had become. The only way intercourse would be available to someone in his state was if he were to carry some cash over to the Waits' Tavern and pay for it, Christopher thought with a cryptic chuckle. Not lost on him was the fact that his temporary condition provided him with a window into some of the conditions that Deklan Lorenz lived under every day of his life.

Christopher gingerly walked into the house in attempt to escape the increasing heat of the day, but although the environment inside did not boast quite so high a temperature, the air remained stagnant. He sat at the dining room table, attempting to make a decision as to what he could do, and after that, what he should do. The sun had broken through the thin layer of clouds and hung in its mid-afternoon position, so his mother was probably visiting her church friends or at Harkness's. Mary was similarly absent, although she rarely played inside the house during summer because she wasn't stupid. For the time being, Christopher was alone in the house with his thoughts.

He interlaced his fingers and set them on the tabletop. Before he made any other decisions, Christopher first had to make certain that the events out at Old Man Staley's had actually happened, that they were not part of some elaborate, trauma-induced hallucination. He unbuttoned the top three buttons of his sweat-soaked, gray shirt. Beneath the layer of black and blue flesh, dozens of ant bites dotted his skin above the nipple line. Evidence enough, he supposed.

The next issue: something had to be done about that thing out at Staley's. Given its strength and foul temper, it was incredibly dangerous, even if it was the only one of its kind. At the same time, his initial idea of maintaining complete obedience remained a tempting option. If he waited a few days to heal, it was possible that he could steal a horse during the night and flee town, possibly with Emma, definitely with Mary. Standing out in the barn last night, he realized that the conditions of his life had changed: remaining in town put his life in danger. One more kick could have broken some rips or crushed his windpipe. He did not wish to die at the hands of his father. After last night, this fear had grown to the point that nearly surpassed the fear of the thing haunting Staley's sheep pasture.

It also eliminated many of Christopher's options, especially those that required resources or time, because he vowed to take only minimal chances.

He decided that he would need more information. The moment the sun began to set, he would visit Doc Ferguson.

*   *   *

Christopher bypassed asking his mother for permission to walk down to Doc Ferguson's office, because if the past provided any indication, she would have turned away and said, "Ask your father." Instead, he went directly to his father. Lewis Rutlage had finished most of the heavy work for the evening and was replacing his metal instruments on the wall of the shop when Christopher walked in. He normally saved cleanup detail for Christopher, but maybe today was an exceptionally slow day, or maybe he questioned Christopher's capacity to sufficiently perform that duty. He seemed slightly surprised to see his son; he gave a slight start before deciding to ignore the added presence and continue straightening.

Christopher limped forward, painfully aware that it would mark our first interaction since his father had nearly beat him to death. "Father, may I go to Dr. Ferguson's?" he asked, looking the older man straight in the eye, as not to appear weaker than he was. He treaded a thin line even being there. Hopefully, this act would not be viewed as defiant, but by the same token, Christopher could not accept letting his father feel that he was broken.

"Why?" Lewis asked, the momentary discomfort dispersed by his regular companions: suspicion and rage. He eyed Christopher closely, as though his son planned to sacrifice virgins over at the doctor's office. While Christopher judged this answer superior to a flat "No," his father was no doubt looking for another reason to hit him. For example, if he had stated that he needed medical attention, that would have been an excellent reason.

"I've been worried about Mrs. Staley," Christopher began, quickly remembering to add, "since that day I worked over there, and was wondering how she was doing."

Mr. Rutlage looked through the open doorway to the outside as the long shadows of evening had begun to creep in. He set his jaw and said with obvious reluctance, "Be back before supper, and wear a hat when you go so can't nobody see your face."

"Thank you, sir," Christopher said with a nod, before walking back into the house to retrieve a hat. He wanted to add, *Thank you for letting me go to the doctor to check on someone else's welfare*, but his father's fists hadn't beaten all the sanity from his head just yet. He had two hats to choose from: a brown, floppy felt one and a flat, black, wide-brimmed hat Mr. Dickens once remarked looked like a Quaker's hat. Christopher picked up the black one and realized that it looked remarkably similar to the hat Deklan Lorenz wore. He placed it on his head, secure in the first-hand knowledge that such a hat effectively could shield one's face from prying eyes.

Christopher walked out to the barn, put a bridle on Thor, and led him out of the barn. He did not plan to ride the short distance to Doc Ferguson's, but Thor had stood in his stall the entire day, and Christopher thought that the horse would appreciate the activity. What his horse would or would not appreciate never concerned Christopher before, but he had never owed his life to a horse before, either. Also, to be perfectly honest, he felt infinitely more secure with Thor by his side.

It took Christopher and his horse several minutes to walk across town. Evening had descended, and the cooler air brought in by a northwesterly breeze that made for pleasant walking conditions. Under normal circumstances, Christopher would have walked at a casual pace to enjoy the temperature, but in this case, his lack of speed was due purely to soreness and outright pain. He did his best to move briskly, though because the less time he spent on the street meant a lesser chance someone would see him. He tilted his head so that none of the occasional fellow pedestrians could catch more than a glimpse of his puffy face.

The Liberty Tavern appeared near capacity as Christopher passed through its shadow, and an abundance of wagons littered the front of the building. He had no idea why this much traffic had collected in town. When crowds like that assembled, it was usually a group headed north to Kansas City for some reason, and the only time those reasons involved Christopher was if someone's horse threw a shoe and needed a blacksmith.

Christopher arrived at Dr. Ferguson's two-story office/home without anyone speaking to him. The doctor usually continued to work at this time of day, and even if he was not working, his two-room office connected to the rest of the house. He spent nearly all of his time there. Even when night fell, one could usually see lamplight emanating from the second story, indicating that the doctor was still keeping busy.

The man almost never went out except for work-related reasons, not to drink, not for recreational riding, not for anything except for grocery shopping and sporadic church attendance. He just stayed in the same house that he and his wife lived in before she passed away three or four years prior. Everybody in town feared he would move away to the city when Mrs. Ferguson died. Even the faction of people who disliked him still shuddered at the thought of spending even a short time without a competent doctor residing in town. Instead, he stayed in Liberty and became more dedicated to his craft than ever.

So far as Christopher knew, Doc Ferguson's sole leisure activity involved reading books. He had more books in that house than resided in the rest of the town, including Bibles. That Dr. Ferguson had such an impressive library actually caused many to view him in a negative light, mostly because in a town with more than its share of borderline illiterates and alcoholics, a man that stayed home and read at night was viewed almost as a pagan.

Christopher draped Thor's knotted reigns around the corner of the hitching post in front of Doc Ferguson's office, walked up the steps to the door of the office, and knocked. A pair of gruff, burly men that Christopher did not recognize rode up the street, toward the tavern, and almost as an involuntary reflex, he pretended to scratch the side of his face and turned away. When he stood alone again, he stepped down to the ground and extended himself upwards on the tips of his toes to peer in the window nearest the door. No lamps burned inside, but something shifted in the darkness. He reached over and knocked again, louder this time.

Still nothing. Christopher grasped the doorknob, and it turned under his hand. He eased the door halfway open and stepped inside. His long shadow occupied the rectangle of orange sunlight on the floor. "Doc?" he called out. "Dr. Ferguson?" Something large flashed across the sliver of light and again receded into the shadows. A familiar clicking sound echoed in the spacious room, and Christopher's un-swollen eye became painfully wide. The giant insect had come for Doc Ferguson.

Christopher stood frozen in the doorway. It wasn't too late to leave, and part of him demanded that he run, ride off on Thor, do anything to get as far away from that thing as possible. Each individual ant bite dotting his upper body began to itch like crazy, and when he blinked, the hollow, blackness in the eyes of the scarecrow flickered before him. He had to help Doc Ferguson, though. Ferguson was a full-grown man, bigger and more capable of taking care of himself than Christopher, but he did not know what he was dealing with. The insect would rip him apart. Christopher at least had some experience with the creature.

Christopher continued to debate his strategy when the inch-long, ant-like creatures, dozens of them, scurried across the floor toward the open doorway. Goose bumps erupted all over his body, as his eyes reminded his skin its last encounter with the little bloodsuckers. He backed out of the office, failing to close the door the entire way.

He needed help, but would Dr. Ferguson still be alive by the time he got back? No. No he wouldn't. If he wasn't dead already, the thing inside would kill him and shred his corpse with those horrible mandibles. Christopher set his swollen jaw, huffed out a breath, and bent down to grab a stone from the beautiful flower garden that graced the front of the house. It was a fist-sized stone that gradually tapered to a point, perfect for the occasion: small enough for Christopher to wield with one hand, large and sharp enough to inflict damage. Christopher glanced over at Thor, who pressed his ears against his skull but remained motionless. "Get ready for a quick retreat," Christopher muttered.

He crept further down the side of the white house, to the window of the examination room, and peered in. The drawn drapes covered most of the window, but enough of a gap remained in the corner of the left windowpane for him to get a decent look at the interior. Christopher stood on his tiptoes and strained his eyes but had had trouble making out anything beyond vague shapes in the darkness. His eyes swept the room a second time, and this time he saw the three humanoid shapes standing against the far wall… three, vaguely man-sized, motionless shapes. Something moved in front of the gap in the curtain, blocking his view. Christopher recoiled, pulling a few inches away from the window, but not nearly far enough, not nearly fast enough. The sound of glass breaking tightened his grip on the stone.

A pair of claws dug into the boy's shoulders like jagged vices as they ripped him off his feet and into the darkness. Christopher let his body go limp and braced for impact against the hard, wooden floor. His tender shoulder crashed against the floorboards, but being the expert on getting thrown around a room that he was, Christopher bounced off the wooden boards and rolled to his feet without losing a second.

He didn't have a second. The giant insect launched itself on top of him in a heartbeat. The visibility within the house had improved, courtesy of his limp body tearing the drapes from their normal position and allowing the days remaining sunlight to puncture the gloom, and Christopher had just enough time to make a couple of panicked observations as images swirled about him. The wetness on his neck indicated a laceration from a piece of broken glass. The people "standing" against the wall were Harold Riley, Margarette Snellenbarger, and Lucy Sheets. It would be more accurate to say they were "propped" against the wall, encased as they were in a sticky-looking, amber substance that looked like shiny mucous. Christopher also noted that the giant insect wore a different set of clothes. This time it had dressed itself in Dr. Ferguson's black vest and pants and white shirt. None of it made sense in the half second he had to process the tornado of information, and Christopher's enemy gave him no time for a more detailed observation. Given the circumstances, it was rather remarkable that he noticed that much.

The boisterous, half-drunk cowboy noises emanating from the Liberty Tavern would mask the sound of breaking glass, so no one would be coming to Christopher's rescue. When preparing to be assaulted, wash of panic normally seized his body. This time, however, an odd calm swept over him when the giant insect launched its attack. Stressful, painful events had quickly become the norm for Christopher, and perhaps, just a little bit, he might have gradually begun to overcome his fear of death. Really, what was the worst, the absolute worst thing that could happen to him? Certainly nothing he hadn't already considered. He deftly ducked under the creature's swinging arm, but when it kicked a leg out, Christopher rolled over the offending appendage and slid across the floor.

When his momentum stopped, Christopher sat up, rock in hand, coiled, waiting to strike anything that touched him. The insect quickly obliged, grabbing the young human about the waist with its right "hand," and Christopher brought the sharp, pointed end of the rock down to his hip in a smooth, stabbing motion. The moment he heard the sound he was waiting for, the unmistakable crunch of an exoskeleton being breached (although the term "exoskeleton" would remain out of his vocabulary for years, he was still familiar with what happened to ants when someone steps on them), he prepared to move.

The snap reverberated through the spacious room and sounded louder than Christopher had anticipated, as did the ear-splitting shriek the monster emitted. The effect, though, coincided with his prediction: the creature loosened its grip enough for Christopher to shake free and dash toward the front door. The adrenaline surging through him more than compensated for his previous soreness.

If he had closed the front door during his initial examination, Christopher's two-second head start would not have been enough. The creature would have caught him at the edge of the waiting room, thrown him to the ground, and done whatever it did to helpless victims. The door was open, though, and Christopher slid into the dry July evening. His good ear barely registered the sound of his feet trampling the dozens of pseudo-ants in the pair of footsteps it took to traverse the waiting room.

He leapt from the doorway to where his trusty steed waited. Following an awkward landing in the dry dirt, Christopher slid the reigns off the corner of the hitching post and threw himself over Thor's bare back. The animal knew the routine and started to move. Sharp pain on his back and neck awakened Christopher to the fact that strange ants had once again infested his person. His bare hands slapped and scrubbed with a life of their own.

After dispatching of the half dozen vicious little wretches warring against his flesh, he glanced up and noticed that Thor had enacted a rather leisurely escape. The animal casually sagged from one side to the other as it lurched forward. Christopher pulled his horse to a stop and looked back. The door to Dr. Ferguson's office again stood closed. Nothing was running after him or even standing in the doorway. A broken window remained the only visible evidence that the altercation had ever taken place.

Christopher urged Thor down the street until they were a safe distance away and dismounted. The street was still, almost silent, save for the wind and the shouting and piano playing coming from Waits' tavern. His fingers absently reached upward and ran themselves through his hair, allowing him to note that his hat was missing. Returning for it did not cross his mind. The flat, black hat might as well have simply burst into flame and disintegrated. He grasped Thor's reigns in one hand and reached up to touch the cut on his neck with the other. The injury appeared less serious than he had first thought, as the blood had already begun to clot. Survival, once again, was the order of the day.

A loud crash echoed in the street, causing the piano music to stop and nearly causing Christopher to swallow his own tongue. Another, similar crash sounded. Both came from the Waits' place. *Someone got drunk enough to start breaking tables*, he thought, starting to breathe again, *maybe chairs.* Shooting a glance back toward Dr. Ferguson's silent, looming house, Christopher prepared to swing back into the saddle and dig his heels into Thor's flanks at a moment's notice. There remained, however, the question of where to ride.

The sun had nearly disappeared below the horizon, injecting a bloody hue into the clouds. Christopher stood alone in the street, accompanied only by his horse and noise from the rabble in the tavern. He was fourteen years old and facing a decision more important than any he had ever made or would ever make again. Something threatened his town, his world, and he needed to decide how to stop it.

He first needed to tell someone, that much seemed obvious. He was certainly no match for the creature. Informing someone that Dr. Ferguson was in danger and making up a believable story as to why presented itself as one option. He had become a good liar over the years, after all. He could tell this story to Sheriff Townsend, and Townsend would investigate in good faith and, in all likelihood, leave his wife a widow.

Christopher had survived two encounters with this creature, but had been lucky the first time and prepared the second. More importantly, at least three other, equally competent people had not been as fortunate. He could not, in good conscience, lie to the person he expected help from. They must know what they were facing.

Who would believe him? He did not know. Dr. Ferguson might have, were he still a viable option. Even if Emma were accessible, he doubted she was the handiest person in the world to carry into a fight. Approaching Father was... well, that wasn't even funny. He wasn't even sure he would ever return home again.

The red-gold sun continued to fall into the earth, and while Christopher busied himself exhausting every conceivable option, people were dying. He turned Thor to the northwest and rode out of Liberty. From the beginning, he knew he had only one option. He just thought Deklan Lorenz deserved better than to be dragged into this.

*   *   *

CHAPTER EIGHT

Christopher fashioned himself a makeshift scarf from his left sleeve of his store-bought shirt. His father would not have approved of his son destroying clothing he paid for, even torn and bloodstained clothing, but with the reopening of his neck wound, Christopher decided to utilize the ruined garment for a final purpose. Bandaging the cut minimized the health risk, rather than hoping that it closed and didn't become infected. Besides, his father's opinions were fast becoming tertiary concerns at best, as Christopher did not plan to have much connection with the man going forward.

Thor trotted out of town in a matter of moments, and after pointing the horse in the right direction, Christopher positioned his arms on either side of Thor's neck and slumped forward, trusting the horse to take him to Lorenz's without incident. A terrible faint closed over him, perhaps from blood loss, physical exhaustion, or some combination of the two. Riding a horse over uneven ground wasn't the best prescription for Christopher's already battered body, each step sent a jolt through him, but the thick coat of hair on the horse's saddleless back felt softer and more inviting than a quilt.

Christopher closed his eyes for a moment during the methodical ride through the grass. It drove away the dizziness for a few seconds, but before long, the image Harold Riley, Margarette Snellenbarger, and Lucy

Sheets stuck to the wall of Dr. Ferguson's office flared in the darkness and forced his eyelids open. Stray rays of purple sunlight still clung to the horizon over his left shoulder, and the tall grass seemed to stretch endlessly toward the shadowy distance. They still appeared to be headed in the correct direction.

With the town's buildings slowly sinking into the ground behind him, Christopher forced himself upright, pushed his shoulders back, and strained his eyelids to their widest point. Splashing water on his face probably would have shocked him into a more alert state, but this journey had started off as a cross-town ride, and he had brought no water. During a mid-day ride, he probably could have seen the cluster of trees surrounding Lorenz's distant house from his current position. This was not mid-day, though, and far away images melted together. After a particularly stormy spring, it had not rained in the region for over two weeks, and while a continued drought posed a danger to the crops, the lack of humidity made for a lovely night. Lovely, that is, except for people slowly bleeding to death.

Wind blew through the grass, shifting the shadows, breaking apart the silence with a rasp or a rustle. The strain from turning at every movement, at every noise that he perceived as being out of the ordinary, quickly began to take its toll on Christopher's mind. A choice between being paranoid and being dead, though, was really no choice at all. It did not help matters that his hearing problems made it difficult to pinpoint the source of sounds. At any given second, he anticipated some sub-human monstrosity to spring from a cluster of grass, grab him, and drag him into Hell with it.

Thor calmly plodded through the terrain, and Christopher felt perfectly defenseless sitting atop the relentless animal. His father, probably out of a sense of self-preservation, had never taken time to make Christopher proficient in the use of any weapon except for the axe, and that instrument would only prove useful if a legion of logs attacked the boy. His heels remained poised, ready to spur Thor on at a moment's notice.

Behind Christopher, only the ghostly white church steeple remained above the horizon. *Father will wonder where I am*, he thought. Would he go down to Dr. Ferguson's looking for his troublemaker of an offspring? He might. Ferguson and Christopher's father were never particularly friendly toward one another, so his father would not feel especially awkward about intruding on the man's night. Would the three bodies that lined the wall of the office, bodies that Christopher could not stop seeing, would they remain in the same position when Lewis Rutlage arrived? Probably not. Any creature intelligent enough to execute the scarecrow ruse it performed out at Old Man Staley's was intelligent enough to hide a few bodies. It would know that Dr. Ferguson's shattered window and the bloodstains dotting the windowsill were obvious to all but the most casual passerby; they practically screamed out for further investigation... but not until morning. No one would discover the bodies. Given the strength of the giant insect, it would require no more than a minute or two to move the three bodies to a less conspicuous locale.

Thor's hoof landed in a small hole, and he stumbled through a step. For an instant, Christopher thought the animal was about to break into a run. After his body unclenched, inch-by-inch, he reached forward and patted the animal's neck. "Can't lose you now," Christopher said to the horse. "You're about the only thing keeping me alive." The only thing keeping him from knowing how it felt to be trapped, like the three people at Doc Ferguson's were trapped.

Christopher shifted atop Thor's bare back, badly wanting to banish the thought. Why did the creature need the bodies? That answer was obvious: food. Like a spider, it was storing the townsfolk in those cocoons to be later used as food. Why it chose to wear its victim's clothing, on the other hand, continued to baffle Christopher. Perhaps it preferred clothing to nudity, just like humans did, or perhaps it used clothing as a simple camouflage, so that it looked human from a distance. He shook his head. The truth was, he didn't have a clue.

Christopher rode on, feeling every bit the frightened fourteen-year-old.

The once brooding tree line now welcomed the young man into security, and the sound of a barking dog swept over him like a warm hug. By the time he reached the house, Lorenz stood on the porch, fully clothed, looking alert despite the lateness of the hour. In the darkness, he looked like a normal human. *I probably do, too,* Christopher reasoned. "What's wrong?" Lorenz asked, evenly.

Christopher sat on the back of his horse, dumbstruck, suddenly aware that, in all the time he spent on his paranoid ride out here, he probably should have developed a strategy for explaining the farfetched story to Lorenz. He must have been quite a sight: a blood-soaked shirt with one sleeve, a sleeve-scarf, face beaten to a pulp. "I, uh, I need help," he began, stating the obvious as he desperately searched for the right words.

"Is it an emergency?" Lorenz asked in the same calm, even voice. Christopher could not come up with an immediate answer to even that question. Yes, yes it was an emergency, but an emergency that took a great deal of explanation and even more faith. When no answer came, Lorenz nodded. He took a step toward his front door and motioned for Christopher to follow. "Hitch up Thor and come inside."

Christopher did as instructed, grateful that someone finally made a decision for him. He hitched Thor to the fence and scratched behind the horse's ear. On his way inside, Dante nuzzled his limp, dangling hand. Christopher absently returned the gesture with a pat on the head before continuing up the steps. His arrival apparently interrupted Lorenz from reading *Paradise Lost*, because the book and a lit gas lamp sat on the kitchen table.

Lorenz had no vision problems that Christopher was aware of, so he must have noticed the boy's malformed face but he gave no indication of this. Christopher gingerly eased into the chair opposite the one with the book in front of it. "You want anything to eat?" Lorenz asked. "I fixed some grits about an hour ago. They're still warm." Christopher had yet to sup that night, so he nodded silently. Within a minute, he was spooning lukewarm clumps of grits into his swollen mouth.

Lorenz waited patiently for his young visitor to finish shoveling half the bowl down his throat before speaking. "You mind if I look at your neck?" Christopher shrugged and paused from eating long enough to untie the shirtsleeve bandage. It took a several seconds longer than he had expected because the blood had soaked into the cloth and congealed. The cloth gave a light rasp as he pulled it free.

Lorenz bent down and examined the wound before cleaning it with a soapy sponge and redressing it with one of the gauze bandage that he kept in his kitchen cabinets. When the cut was clean and covered, Lorenz sat down in his chair and asked, "So what's happened that is so bad that you'd risk riding out here in the middle of the night?"

Christopher nudged the empty bowl away toward the middle of the circular wooden table and took a deep breath. "Remember yesterday, when I left here and told you I was going over to Old Man Staley's?" he began. Lorenz nodded, and Christopher proceeded to recount his life's story over the past thirty hours. He omitted some of the speculation, but none of the pertinent details. With his arms folded across his chest, Lorenz sat stoically and listened, not interrupting once. Christopher could not read the man's limited facial expression and could not discern whether Lorenz believed the tale or was simply being polite.

At the completion of the story, Lorenz remained silent, apparently digesting the finer details. He sat, pensive and motionless, for an inordinately long time, so long that Christopher felt as though he would burst if a response did not come soon. "Do you believe me?" he asked hopefully.

Lorenz raised his eyebrows, or at least the area above his eyes where eyebrows once grew, and gave a brief, unnerving chuckle. "Of course I believe you, Christopher."

Christopher exhaled a gust of air that he felt his lungs had been clutching for a month. *Thank God thank God thank God.* His overwhelming sense of relief only lasted a few seconds, though, when he considered the answer. "But why?" he asked. As he was telling it, he felt as though he was conjuring the strangest children's fairy tale ever told; he couldn't imagine how stupid it must have sounded to someone who hadn't lived it. "Isn't it the strangest story you've ever heard? Isn't it, you know… unbelievable?"

Lorenz licked his gray, shriveled lips. "Christopher, I have no idea how to explain what you saw, no more than you do, but I believe you when you say you saw it. You have no reason to lie to me, none that I know of, at any rate. More importantly, only something as serious as the truth would cause you to put yourself in the position to receive the severe beating coming to you the moment you return home." Christopher shook his head on reflex, feeling a bit ashamed that, at some point, his family situation had been divulged. "There is one thing I must know, however, before I intervene."

"What's that?" Christopher asked, fearing that he might not be able to answer correctly and that his titanic effort he expended that day had been for nothing.

Lorenz raised his chin. "Why did you choose to come to me?" he asked, perhaps amused.

Christopher took no time in admitting, "Because I didn't know where else to go. Doc Ferguson's probably dead, and I figured you might believe me, because you've always treated me with respect."

"You do realize that no one is going to believe me, either?" Lorenz said. "You and I are going to be the ones to handle this situation."

Christopher shrugged, still thinking about how final it had sounded when he uttered the words, "Doc Ferguson's probably dead." "Like I said: I don't know who else I could have gone to... and I thought you could handle it... because you've always sure seemed like a... dangerous man." He looked up quickly, unsure of whether or not Lorenz would take offense to this statement. The older man showed no reaction one way or another, so Christopher continued. "You were also the only person I knew that I wasn't sure couldn't do it, if that makes any sense."

"It makes perfect sense," Lorenz assured his guest. He let out a slight grunt as he shifted out of his seated position and rose to his feet. "You made a good choice," he added, his eyes falling on Christopher, "because I am, indeed, a dangerous man." He wasn't boasting; he said it like someone stating the time of day.

Lorenz's boots thudded across the smooth, even floorboards and into the bedroom. Moments later, he emerged with a small, burlap bag. Unknown equipment bulged from it. It almost seemed to Christopher that Lorenz had somehow prepared for this eventuality and was merely waiting for the right moment to act. "I'm going into town. I'll lay out a clean shirt for you. Get some sleep."

Christopher's face tightened. "Wh—What?"

"Don't worry about it," he said, shaking his head. "Dante will watch over you. We'll talk in the morning."

Lorenz drifted toward the front door. Before he could push his way into the night, Christopher stood up from the table. "I want to go with you."

"No, you need to rest; I won't need you tonight," he explained from the doorway. "I'll let you know when I do." Lorenz continued outside, and Christopher replaced him in the doorway, watching Lorenz saddle his horse and climb on. He gave no wave, no farewell, and Christopher continued to stare until the trees swallowed the master of the house. Lorenz acted as though it was a leisurely ride into town, but for Christopher the scene conjured feelings similar to when Doc Ferguson galloped into the setting sun the final time Christopher saw him. Would Lorenz make it back alive? The thought chilled him.

He never did relax during his lone night at the Lorenz house. Sleep came only once weariness prevented Christopher from keeping his eyes open. Before he reached this point, of course, it was an anxious night. For the first time since childhood, Christopher had to spend the night in a bed other than his own, under a roof not built by his father's calloused, soot-stained hands. More than foreign surroundings made his stay an anxious one, though. The main reason Christopher did not feel safe in the house had to do with the fact that he knew he was not safe in the house.

Dante was a good dog, but only a good dog that stood as tall as a horse and had the temperament of a wolverine could stand up against the giant insect effectively. Fortune had smiled upon Christopher to allow him to escape the creature's grasp not once, but twice. Neither occasion would have been possible without Thor. Thor now stood alone, outside, tied to a post, with the crickets and God only knew what else. Thor would certainly die first; the creature would rip out his throat with its three-fingered claw-hand. After it dispatched Christopher's beloved horse, the giant insect would snap Dante's neck like a twig before the dog could do anything more than emit a few barks. It would come for the human next.

Lying in the unfamiliar bed, Christopher had ample time to run through the scenario in his head. Each time a sound drifted in from the outside that was louder than the wind brushing against the leaves and less regular than the chirping crickets, anytime Dante barked or moved, Christopher imagined the giant insect clicking across the front porch in its black britches and vest. Or maybe it had intercepted Deklan on his ride into town and donned his clothes instead...

Regardless of its attire, it would first smash through the screen door like paper. Assuming his fear did not cause paralysis, that sound would send Christopher out of bed and running for the bedroom door. It would reach the hallway right behind him, trampling over the chair and lamps and whatever else Christopher frantically tossed behind him in a feeble attempt to slow its progress. With any luck, he would reach the outside before it overtook him. From that position, the creature would throw Christopher to the ground and treat him to the sound of his own bones breaking. That was the best of the fates he envisioned.

There he lay, shivering despite the hot summer air blanketing him. Cold and alone...

*   *   *

The sound of a barking dog awakened Christopher shortly after daybreak. He sprang to his feet and staggered lethargically out into the hallway to the window. Still wearing his bloody shirt, he stretched his suspenders over his shoulders while his eyes began to focus. Had anything other than a man on a horse approached the house, Christopher would have run out the back door as fast as his legs could manage. When the unmistakable, hulking outline of Deklan Lorenz in his flat brimmed hat rode into view, the tension left Christopher's body in a sigh.

The relief only lasted a few seconds, before a brand new tide of fear surged through him. Out there. On the horse. It might be the giant insect in Lorenz's clothes. Just like with Old Man Staley. Just like with Doc Ferguson. Before this possibility sent him screaming out the back door, Christopher reasoned that it was highly improbable that Deklan's horse would let a giant insect ride him, regardless of what clothing the insect wore. When the rider dismounted and Christopher counted five fingers on its hands, the panic began to subside.

Lorenz walked through the front door and regarded his guest with a brief nod. "Good, you're awake," he said and motioned toward the table. "Take a seat, we need to talk." Christopher obeyed the instruction quickly and folded his slightly perspiring hands atop the table. He watched Lorenz closely, perhaps to see whether it was really him, perhaps to see if he had found anything to confirm Christopher's story. If the search turned up nothing, Christopher worried that he might launch into another bout of weeping.

Lorenz must have noticed the young man's apprehension, because his scar-encrusted face shifted into its version of a smile. "Relax," he told Christopher while sitting down at the end of the table that still sported a battered copy of *Paradise Lost*, along with a clean, folded, grey cotton shirt. "I still believe you, more than ever."

Christopher vigorously rubbed his forehead. "What'd you find?" he blurted out.

Lorenz removed his hat with both hands, gingerly set it on the tabletop, and cleared his throat. "Well, I never did see the giant insect you encountered, but there were plenty of people around town looking for you, Doc Ferguson, and the others, the ones you said were in Doc Ferguson's office. There were a few dozen people in the town square. If I didn't know any better, I'd say the crowd had the makings of a lynch mob." He leaned back and crossed his legs. "This being the case, I didn't get a chance to ask anybody questions, or look around the Ferguson place for that matter."

Christopher looked across the table, quizzically. "A lynch mob? That's good, isn't it? I mean, at least they're starting to organize some kind of defense, right?"

Lorenz might have winced. "Christopher, assuming there is no giant insect, which to everybody in town, there isn't, don't you think one of the first people on their lynching list would be a man that supposedly burned down a schoolhouse full of children and murdered his own wife?"

Christopher's eyes fell to his lap, and he nodded, feeling like the perfect idiot. "Do you think they'll be coming out here?"

"Yes, yes I do. Soon, too. They might be riding out as we speak. You'll have to be gone by the time they get here."

"But where will I go?" Christopher protested. One night of relative security must have been too much to ask for. "If I go home, Father will kill me. I mean that, too. He may beat me to death." The thought made his stomach churn.

"Don't worry," Lorenz assured him. While his subdued manner lacked empathy, Lorenz never roused any unnecessary panic nor gave the impression of leading one on. "I'm not going to send you home. You'll just need to ride around for a couple hours, then meet me over at Old Man Staley's."

Christopher blinked hard, sure that his hearing had malfunctioned again. "I'm sorry; did you just say we were meeting over at Old Man Staley's?"

Lorenz nodded, explaining quickly that: "It's obvious that the creature's in town right now. I went out to Staley's last night and didn't see it." Christopher remained silent, telling himself to sit and listen, that what the man said made sense. Lorenz continued, "What I did find out there, though, was a lot of carcasses: sheep stripped to the bone... Hell, Staley's horse looked like it'd been torn apart. What I didn't find, though, were Mr. and Mrs. Staley's bodies."

Christopher shrugged. "Maybe it buried 'em."

Lorenz shook his head. "It wouldn't do that and leave the animal corpses laying all over the place."

Christopher shifted in his seat and absently picked at the corner of his neck bandage. "Why do you need to go back if you've already been out there?"

"I want to look in the house and get another look at that hole you were talking about. I gave it a once over last night, but I want to see it in daylight."

Christopher shook his head. "I... I don't know —"

Without warning, Lorenz slammed his fist down on the wobbly tabletop. The whole room seemed to rattle, nearly causing Christopher to tip over backward in his seat. "Look, I don't like ordering you around, but if you want my help, we're going to do this my way. Remember: you came to me, and it's your town that needs saving, not mine." He fell silent for a moment, then took a breath. When he again spoke, his tone softened, marginally. "Look, I know you're scared, but fear can be overcome, death can't, and this is life or death, so we need to stop wasting time and you need to get moving."

Lorenz stood up and stalked over to his kitchen counter, trying to disguise the fact that he was fuming. Christopher appreciated the effort; his father usually did his utmost to magnify his rage for effect. After a few seconds, the younger man rose from his seat and walked slowly across the creaking wooden floor toward the door, his fear temporarily in remission. Before pushing through to the outside, he turned back. "What if the lynch mob comes while I'm gone?"

Lorenz stretched his arm behind him and grabbed a large hunk of bread from off the counter top. He tossed it to Christopher, who caught it before remembering that he had not eaten breakfast. "Christopher," Lorenz said patiently, shaking his head. He really did have a nice voice when he wasn't adding the hard, rasping edge to it. "It would take fifty men to get me here. Now, change your shirt and go, but don't go straight there. Ride around for three hours, then head over to the Staley's. Oh, and trust no one."

*   *   *

CHAPTER NINE

July 7, 1877:

Before the sun had risen above the tree line, Christopher sat atop Thor, riding westward, consuming a hunk of stale, but not altogether tasteless, bread. The shirt Deklan had given him was comfortable but would not fit him properly for several years. Three hours of paranoia loomed ahead. Three hours can seem like an eternity to someone convinced that his killer lies in wait behind every blade of grass. Christopher briefly considered his other options, but when he realized he didn't have any, he rode on.

He rode with his shoulders slumped, more from shame than weariness or soreness. Christopher didn't like getting yelled at, but he deserved it. He could be stupid and weak sometimes, and he knew it better than anyone. It felt different than when Father yelled at him. For one thing, he didn't sense that Lorenz enjoyed yelling. For another, he didn't anticipate that Lorenz was going to backhand him. As different as it was, though, it still made him feel like dirt. He had been trained to respect his father, but he chose to respect Lorenz... and maybe he expected more. At least he expected the yelling and chastising from his father.

Christopher bounced along on the bare back of his horse, scanning the countryside as the sun climbed higher and higher into the sky. In that area of the country, with its abundance of financially disadvantaged people, pocket watches were usually a family heirloom entrusted to the eldest male, so everyone else had to learn to gauge time using the sun. Under ideal circumstances, this was an imperfect science at best. It was a cool morning, and Christopher's meandering ride over the gently rolling countryside proved unexpectedly pleasant, so much so that he nearly let the time slip away. Had he ridden in a more scenic region of the country... say, Iowa... he might have truly lost himself in the ride and arrived at Staley's late.

Thor still managed to carry his master on to Old Man Staley's property before Lorenz made his appearance. During the tail end of the ride, Christopher hoped and prayed that he would not arrive first and get stuck standing like a stationary target poking out from the high grass. The way his life had been shaping up the past several days, though, he seemed destined to confront wave upon wave of anxiety at every turn.

He pulled Thor to a stop within clear view of the squat, wooden house. It was a tight, contained building with uniform shingles and intact windows, but filtered through Christopher's current state of mind, it resembled a sleeping badger. He scanned the area. Virgil was not visible, so either his timing was grossly off or Lorenz must have faced some sort of delay. He hoped that either of those was the case, at least. There was no point even contemplating the alternative; Lorenz was essentially an unknown commodity, but he was Christopher's last hope.

Christopher shifted his weight toward his horse's haunches, but his eyes continued to dart toward any movement. He slowly moved Thor a couple hundred feet to the north, over to an area where the grass was only about knee-high. He felt a little more conspicuous and helpless than an injured bird. The tall grass would not have provided him with a greater degree of protection, though, and at least by staying in the open, he could spot potential attackers. Guns. Could the creature use guns? It had those long, jointed fingers, so, yes, it probably could.

Beneath Christopher's legs, Thor let out a few heaving sighs, punctuated by a shudder that rippled through his body. "Save your strength," Christopher whispered as he reached forward and stroked the creature's neck, but that only released another shudder. Probing the recesses of his equine mind, Thor probably remembered his last trip to this locality and wondered why in the world his master had brought him back to this evil, violent place. On the other hand, the shaking may have come from Christopher.

He did not know how long he sat atop his horse in that open field, flinching at every strange noise, telling himself that the giant insect posed no threat to him because it was currently skulking through the streets of Liberty. The wait took an hour in his head, but in all likelihood amounted to less than ten minutes.

The brightening sun failed to warm his clammy skin. Christopher's face tightened, as though sucking on a sourball. He thought Lorenz would be more punctual. He certainly put on airs about being some kind of —

Something squeaked through the grass on his left. Too small to be the giant insect. And it made the wrong sound, too. The insect clicked. This squeaked. Probably a rodent. Lorenz was dead. He wasn't late, he was dead. Oh god...

The dull thud of horse hooves approached from the east. Christopher whipped his head toward a bulky, shadowy figure in a flat hat that bounced above the grass line. That silhouette, one that would have caused a full-body shudder to ripple through him a week ago, now allowed him to take a deep breath and let his posture and eyelids go slack. Only then did he notice the pungent odor of rotting flesh blanketing the area and forcing itself up his nostrils via the southeastward blowing wind.

Finally, Virgil, the chestnut brown horse, emerged into the expanse of short grass, and the unmistakable, yet comforting visage of

Deklan Lorenz greeted his young partner. He wore a leather strap across his chest that looked like a bandolier, except that it held the six throwing knives Christopher's father had forged less than a week ago. "I'm a little late," Lorenz admitted. "I apologize. I'm sure this is just about the last place on earth you wanted to be left waiting, considering what happened the last time you were here."

"I'm fine," Christopher lied with a shrug. He noticed that his white-knuckled hands were squeezing the reigns with all their might and forced his fingers to relax. "You ready to take a look at that hole?"

Lorenz nodded, and the pair cantered their mounts up to the fence line. A ghastly sight awaited: a legion of slaughtered, half-consumed sheep lay strewn about the pasture. Some of the carcasses were torn in two distinct sections. Some were mangled so badly that it would have been hard for an unfamiliar observer to tell what the bloody collection of legs and guts had once been. The few sheep that still lived and had not fled through the broken section of fence did their best to keep the stubby blades of grass down. Deklan and Christopher dismounted and cautiously climbed the short wooden fence.

The instant Christopher's shoes hit the ground, it was as though he had stepped onto the surface of a strange planet. He had wanted to see this crater since the day he rode out with his father and the others, and a nervous energy surged through him as he strode up the slope behind Deklan. Lorenz only broke his determined gate when having to sidestep the sheep droppings and sheep corpses that dotted the landscape.

At the approximate center of the rectangular pasture, they found both the crater and its probable source: a large (about three feet in diameter), mostly spherical, jaggedly surfaced rock. A "rock" is what it most closely resembled, but Christopher had never seen its like before. Tiny holes dotted its surface, holes too small to peer into, but perhaps, big enough for ants to crawl from. Even more interesting, a slight, three-inch long rift ran across the section of the rock that faced the sky. A dull blue light emanated from this crack, radiating clearly, even in the daylight. Even to Christopher, it seemed rather unbelievable, but he reminded himself that after a giant, man-eating insect accosts one, one should recalibrate one's definition of "unbelievable."

Christopher squatted down on his haunches to get a better look at the bizarre hunk of rock and maybe to feel its surface, but Lorenz's fingers dug into the younger man's right shoulder, halting the examination. "Don't get close, and absolutely do not touch it." His voice belied the fact that he had no more of an idea what the rock was than did Christopher.

"Why not?" Christopher asked and rose to his feet.

"Because it might be dangerous," Lorenz answered, absently, refusing to detach his gaze from the rock.

Christopher huffed. Having already endured several panic-filled minutes at the scene of the most terrifying experience of his life, he was determined to glean something from it. "Why are we even here then if we aren't even going to touch it?" he asked in exasperation.

Lorenz rubbed the fingertips of his gloved hands. "I've got some dynamite in my saddle bags," he said slowly. "I'm going to blow it up."

Christopher's eyes widened in alarm. "Dynamite?" he repeated as Lorenz turned and walked toward the horses. "Where did you get dynamite?" Lorenz either did not hear the question or did not feel inclined to answer it.

Christopher's head rotated toward the other end of the field, the end where his airborne body broke through the fence during his most recent visit. He tracked the proposed flight of the rock from right to left. The scorched grass, the gradual deepening of the hole... his original deduction remained unchanged: the rock fell from a great height at a great speed.

While looking in the direction of the singed grass, he attempted to find the two spots of fence that his body had broken through. He blinked, then rechecked. He had to be looking in the correct location, but there were no gaps in the fence, or even fragmented boards littering the ground. He examined the two sections closely. A few of the boards hung from the posts at slanted angles, as though someone had used loose boards for a patchwork repair job. When Deklan stomped back over the ridge, Christopher pointed out the two sections. "Those are the two places the fence was broken," he said.

Deklan shrugged. "Someone must have wanted to keep the sheep in," he flatly replied. Given the older man's terse mood, Christopher decided that this was probably the best answer he would receive. So, it would have to do.

Christopher had never seen actual dynamite before, and the thin, gray-brown sticks fascinated him. He was familiar with what it could do, had heard the explosion in the distance when Albert Morris tried to rid his field of a persistent tree stump, but it seemed unfathomable that something so small could inflict so much damage. Seeing it chilled him more than the sight of a loaded rifle. As Lorenz held the stick in front of him and dug into his coat pocket, a thought occurred to Christopher. "If we blow it up," he began, "we might not ever find out what it is."

Lorenz looked down at his young partner. "I don't know what it is, so I don't care what it is," he stated, then shifted his gaze from the boy to the rock. Christopher failed to follow the logic, but listened when Lorenz warned, "Get ready to move." A match materialized in his gloved fingertips and he lit it with a flick of his thumb. Christopher's mouth fell open, and he made a mental note to learn how to execute that maneuver. Lorenz ignited the end of the fuse and dropped the explosive stick into the crater.

Christopher's retreat ended with one step. The instant the dynamite touched the rock, several dozen of the four-legged "ants" flooded out of the rock and swarmed over the explosive rod, overtaking it in seconds. Christopher froze, thinking about what would have happened moments earlier, had Deklan allowed him to touch the mysterious rock. Something grabbed the back of Christopher's loose-fitting shirt and nearly pulled him off his feet. It was Lorenz. He all but dragged Christopher to the other side of the rise, moving so fast that the youth's flailing feet could hardly stay under him. Just when Christopher was about to submit and let the man carry him the rest of the distance, Lorenz flung the younger man to the ground and dove on top of him. The awkward formation of their bodies on the clean section of pasture only lasted a second, before the explosion rattled teeth, bones, and everything else between Heaven and Hell. It reminded Christopher of when lightning struck the tree that used to stand next to the shop, the one that now acted as his family's chopping stump.

After the dislodged hunks of airborne sod slapped back to the earth, Deklan and Christopher shakily rose to their feet and surveyed the devastation. The hole had grown by a factor of five in every direction, leaving a strangely circular cavity of dark, rich soil. Apparently, the blast also caught a few unsuspecting sheep grazing on that side of the rise and launched them toward the far recesses of the pasture.

From the edge of the fence closest to the Staley house, two figures made their way through the curtain of dust and dirt, toward the two intruders. Christopher rubbed and blinked the debris from his eyes, but could still see no more than the outlines of the figures. He tapped Lorenz on the shoulder, but Lorenz had already spotted their approach. Their stiff, jerky movements gave away the fact that they were both giant insects.

The un-synchronous clicking turned Christopher's blood cold. The fact that two giant insects existed, though, did not unsettle him nearly as much as what he saw when they drifted through the curtain of dust. One wore Mrs. Staley's distinctive white dress with blue polka dots. The other wore Mr. Staley's brown britches and light blue shirt. Christopher stared while the flicker of illumination began to catch fire in his mind. He was on the threshold of a revelation, but before he could make sense of these new pieces of evidence, the creatures rushed forward in their uneven gait.

The giant insects scurried across the pasture quickly enough to catch Lorenz back on his heels. He fumbled with his weapons, like a man reaching for four things at once. A new thought sprang into Christopher's head: Whatever Lorenz's military history consisted of, he might be horribly out of practice. Maybe... maybe Christopher should have trusted a professional with this job and told Sheriff Townsend, instead.

The creatures stomped forward, legs striding and arms churning mechanically. They split up, the "female" rushing for the smaller target and the "male" advancing on Lorenz. Christopher should have been accustomed to adjusting to bizarre situations by this time, but he stood frozen in his tracks, his eyes transfixed upon his destroyer in a housedress. It closed within five feet, reached its long, clawed hand behind it, but then the wind whistled, and a brief crunch echoed through the sheep pasture. The creature pin-wheeled to the ground beneath the force of one of the Lewis-Rutlage-forged throwing knives.

The creature dropped in front of Christopher like a bag of dirt, but continued to claw blindly at the ground in front of his toes. Horrified, he scampered backward several feet. Its upper body twisted and its arms beat the air with drunken energy, but after several seconds, Christopher realized that the impaled knife had mortally wounded the creature, and these movements were probably involuntary. The creature squirmed for several seconds longer, with Christopher looking on in fascination, before the sounds of battle brought him back to the situation at hand.

Blood, or what he assumed was blood, was everywhere. Splashes of red blood stained the ground, which must have come from the gash on Deklan's chest that had reduced his over-shirt to ribbons. A thick, black substance accounted for the remaining liquid on the ground, probably coming from the hole in the remaining creature's shoulder. The glistening steel hilt of a throwing knife protruded from the useless limb.

Deklan and the creature cautiously circled one another, the insect occasionally taking a swipe at Deklan's head with one of its bone-shredding claws, and Deklan returning the favor with one of the razor sharp knives he clutched in each hand. Deklan's hat lay several feet away, and his stringy strands of black hair fluttered in the wind. Neither combatant blinked: the creature because it did not possess eyelids, Deklan because he could not afford to.

Lorenz's good, gray eye looked hard and cold, like the eye of a wolf, but the animal similarities did not end there. Despite his size, the man moved like a cat. Every movement was measured and balanced... graceful, even. Christopher had not seen many hand-to-hand combats during his short, isolated existence that did not involve a pair of inebriates spilling into the street from Waits' tavern, but he quickly recognized that Lorenz would have easily disemboweled anyone he ever saw fight at the Waits' place, including the professional soldiers that occasionally passed through town.

The insect's mandibles clicked away a couple times every second, and while it only had one speed for its rapid, flinching movements, it doled out its sidesteps in short bursts to match Lorenz. It fought with infinitely more care and strategy than Christopher would have expected, giving further credence to the idea that the intelligence of these creatures rivaled that of human beings. The insect seemed to toy with its human opponent. While one might have seen Deklan as "winning" the fight due to his single, direct hit, he hovered one misstep away from having his head rent from his shoulders.

Christopher clenched and unclenched his hands, helpless. A few steps away, the handle of a perfectly good throwing knife protruded from the round head of the felled creature. He licked his lips, knowing that he couldn't let Lorenz die, and that was all there was to it. Christopher bent down and grabbed hold of the knife handle. Four-legged ants swarmed out of the cracked skull and over the knife, forcing him to scrape them off before he could even get a handle on the weapon. His shoe pressed against the monster's head to the left of the entry wound, and with a mighty tug, he wrenched the blade free. The thick, black blood dripped from the metal and carried a few ants earthward with it. Gingerly, Christopher wiped the blade clean in the stubby grass.

A few ants scampered across the fleshy area of Christopher's thumb, but he blocked them out of his mind for a moment, trying to remember the motion Lorenz used when throwing his knives. He held his breath, waiting for the opponents to gain some separation from one another and focusing in on the right side of the insect's bulbous head. He clenched his teeth, drew back his arm, and whipped it forward, elbow first. The knife cut through the air. It missed its desired target by at least a foot high and two feet to the left.

The insect swiveled its head toward Christopher so that he could see his slack-jawed reflection in the inky, emotionless eyes. His heart rate danced higher and higher as his body prepared for yet another flight response. The creature realized its fatal mistake a moment later and turned back toward its real opponent in time to catch a throwing knife full in the face. The blade smashed between the target's eyes and impaled itself up to the hilt. The insect's body went down in sections.

Christopher let out a sigh and pumped a fist in the air at the apparent victory. Lorenz, however, did not bother to celebrate. He strode over to the fallen corpse and stomped on the handle of the throwing knife, driving it so far into the creature's face that the blade nearly to split the skull in half with a sickening squish. Only then did Lorenz reach down and extract his weapon. "Make sure you don't have ants on you," he said evenly.

Christopher nodded and crushed the pair of stray ants that had begun to scurry up his left arm. The bodies of the larger insects lay ten yards apart, one on its stomach, one on its back. "There were two of them," Christopher announced, still feeling a bit numb.

Lorenz picked his hat off the ground and beat it against his thigh a few times to shake the dirt loose. His head rotated toward Christopher, slowly. "I noticed."

Christopher's nodding head turned into a shaking head. "No, I mean, I don't know how to explain it, but I think these used to be people." His head stopped moving and he blinked, and his confidence in the hypothesis grew with each passing second. It *felt* like true statement. "I think these used to be Old Man Staley and his wife."

Deklan walked several paces past the body and pulled the knife Christopher had thrown from the earth. He scraped the mud from the blade and stared hard at the younger man. "Then how in the Seven Hells did they come to look like...," his gravelly voice began as he whipped his arm in a vague, circular motion toward the bodies, searching for the right words, "like big ants?"

Christopher shrugged while his teeth ground together. It really was speculation, but he was so sure he was right... "I don't know," he admitted, frustrated, "but I think it has something to do with the little, four-legged ants." Lorenz continued to stare, demanding either a retraction or a better answer. When none arrived, he started moving again.

"So what difference does that make? They're dead now," Lorenz said with a definitive nod. He finished wiping the refuse from his knives and shoved them back into the slots of the leather knife holder he wore strapped diagonally across his chest.

"The difference is...," Christopher began, but the implausibility of the situation and his limited vocabulary tripped him up. Trying to put words together that made no sense frustrated him to the point of madness. "I think the one I saw at Doc Ferguson's office... was Doc Ferguson, and the three people stuck to the wall of his office were the next people that were going to be changed."

"Four more?" Lorenz said and rubbed his craggy, stubbled chin. No disappointment or frustration marred his voice. Nor did fear rear its ugly head. On the contrary, there might have been a hint of... excitement?

"At least," Christopher answered.

He nodded. "Let's dynamite the bodies."

"Shouldn't we keep 'em for evidence?" Christopher wondered aloud, feeling rather confident since Lorenz received his last idea so well.

Lorenz shook his head, refraining from firing back with a patronizing answer that would have wounded the younger man's ego. "No one would believe us enough to come out here, and those ants, the little ones, make the bodies damn near impossible to carry." He took a final glance at the motionless corpses and started back toward his horse.

Giant, human-insect hybrids and rotting sheep corpses littered the ground surrounding Christopher. He took a final look before breaking into a trot after Lorenz. He waited until he was even with the older man to ask, "What're we going to do, you know, after we blow the bodies up?"

Lorenz shrugged and kept walking. "Go after Doc Ferguson, I suppose." His body bobbed slightly with each step, but his eyes remained focused on the horses, several yards away. "And anyone else who's changed."

"You mean kill him?" Christopher asked, horrified. The instant the words left his mouth, he knew the plan made perfect sense; it was the practical thing to do, especially assuming the creatures could spread their condition. Still, it seemed somehow wrong, and deeply saddening, because they were talking about killing one of the few people he cared about. Doc Ferguson wasn't just another nominal adult occupying a featureless house in Liberty; he was an ally, a kindred spirit. Killing him couldn't be right. According to Christopher's own theory, though, the man had already encountered a fate worse than death.

"I ain't talkin' about surgery," Lorenz said, sliding his foot on top of the lowest fence board and preparing to climb over.

"Is there any way to change them back?" Christopher asked, hopeful that this mysterious man could wave a magic wand and save him from the discomfort of planning the murder of people he grew up amongst.

"Maybe," Lorenz admitted, kicking his leg over the top of the fence, "but we don't have the time or the resources to figure it out." He hopped to the ground. By the time Christopher followed him over the fence, Lorenz was removing two sticks of dynamite from his saddlebags. His gaze, though, was directed toward town. He stood like that for a long moment, his eyes locked eastward in the shadow of his hat brim. "We'll have to go back to the house before we go after him," Lorenz announced. "I'm going to need some guns."

The statement took a moment to sink in, but when it did, Christopher whipped his head in Lorenz's direction. "I thought you said guns were a coward's weapon."

Lorenz shook his head as he pulled himself over the fence yet again. "I said they were a weapon for desperate men," he corrected, "and right now, that's exactly what I am."

On the other side of the fence, Lorenz walked up the rise. Christopher considered following, but the fear of freezing up again and getting caught in the dynamite blast kept him where he was. He had screwed up enough times today. Almost as if hearing Christopher's thoughts, Lorenz stopped walking while still within speaking range and without turning, stated, "Christopher, we're in this together, and you're in just as much danger as me, so I suppose you're going to need to be armed." He shook his head, obviously detesting the idea. "But if you ever pull a stunt like when you threw that goddamn knife... and this is no exaggeration, you fire anywhere in my general direction without my order, and I will gut you like a fish."

Lorenz's long, steady steps resumed, carrying him onward to dispose of the bodies. He left Christopher to decide that, given the inaccuracy of his throw, regardless of the intent, he got off easy.

*   *   *

Hardly a word passed between them on the ride back to the Lorenz stead. On Christopher's part, the silence did not come from fear or animosity. Rather, his mind was too busy contemplating the various scenarios he might run into in the immediate future, as well as compiling a list of people he needed to avoid at all costs.

Lorenz had established himself as someone that rarely asked questions or otherwise fostered conversation himself. This characteristic probably stemmed from spending the better part of the previous decade living in the middle of nowhere with only four-legged mammals and birds to talk to. Under normal circumstances, Christopher may have privately wondered if Lorenz had always been the avoidant sort, but bumping along on the back of his gray horse, his own future occupied too much of his attention to concern himself with someone else's past.

Christopher had no idea what the situation was like in town, or if there was even a town left to go back to. How fast could the insect-things multiply? Were the three people he saw in Ferguson's office sprouting antennae and mandibles already? Was he even right about the ants? Every time he thought about one of these things, instead of answers, he came up with more questions.

Christopher had always led an ordered life, and while it often reeked of painful regularity, a certain comfort accompanied the fact that a minimum of surprises awaited his rise from bed each day. Maybe that buttoned-down lifestyle, in and of itself, served as a reaction to the dangers of frontier life. That life had evaporated, though, and nothing was sure anymore. Even living from one hour to the next was no longer a forgone conclusion. The questions, the nagging uncertainty made him long for some inkling of familiarity to ease his apprehension.

They stood in Deklan's barn when Christopher reached his decision. "I'm going back into town to see my family," he told Lorenz with as much firmness as he could muster. The words came from his mouth, but they sounded like someone else was speaking them, someone a million miles away. Someone who wasn't particularly smart.

Lorenz acknowledged the proclamation with his all-purpose answer: a brief nod. "I don't know what you're going to be running into," he added, "but even if it's your own death, that's your choice and I'm not going to stop you."

Christopher's eyes found the tops of his feet as a palpable disappointment exuded from Lorenz. "Well," Christopher began, trying to salvage his position, "we don't really know what's there, like you said, and I can go find out. It's probably not safe for you to be seen in town before dark anyway."

Lorenz shrugged as he hefted Virgil's saddle over to the wall and hung it on a hook. "Call it what you will, I'd better give you something to take with you."

Lorenz rubbed his dusty hands on his dirt-encrusted pants and led the way into the house. Without breaking stride, he grabbed the unlit lamp that sat atop his kitchen table. Christopher followed him into his bedroom and watched Lorenz lean against the chifforobe positioned across from the foot of the bed. He pushed it across the smooth, wooden floor and revealed a two-foot-by-two-foot, square trapdoor with an iron ring for a handle. Lorenz lit the lamp, pulled the door open, and leaned it against the bedroom wall before descended the steps.

The hidden staircase contained more stairs than Christopher would have imagined, well over a dozen, and when he stepped off the last one, he could see why. The chamber he stood in was more of a cavern than a cellar. Barrels of gunpowder were stacked four high to the ceiling. A total of ten stacks must have lined the wall. Wooden crate after wooden crate of rifles, revolvers, bayonets, and ammunition consumed the majority of the remaining floor and wall space. Lorenz even had a cannon and a stack of cannon balls resting in the far left corner with an enormous section of canvas covering it. Six earthen passages of varying widths trailed off this main chamber (at least, Christopher assumed this was the main chamber), no doubt leading to other strange and amazing rooms. "You've got enough stuff down here to start a war," Christopher stated, wide-eyed.

"Yep," Lorenz answered in his usual monotone, "it's a real pain to maintain, but everything still works." He walked over to a space on the wall reserved for various guns and removed the smallest pistol Christopher had ever seen. It looked roughly the size of a bent spoon. "It's a woman's gun," Lorenz explained, though Christopher had no idea of the differences between the firearms of males and females. "It's already loaded, but it only houses two bullets, so if you have to use it, make your shots count."

Christopher nodded. He took the cold metal pistol in one hand and cupped his other hand to accept the half-dozen loose bullets Lorenz handed him. "Deklan, where did you get all this?" Christopher asked, circling his head to indicate the entire room.

Lorenz looked up. His face contorted into its version of a smile. "Ask me next time you see me."

Christopher nodded, now with an extra reason to stay alive. He gently shook the bullets in his cupped hand as he turned toward the staircase. "Well, thanks for the gun," he said awkwardly and started up the stairs, eager to get back to some semblance of normalcy.

"Christopher," he Lorenz called out, stopping his young accomplice in his tracks. He paused, choosing his words carefully. "If your Pa starts in on you with his fists… remember: it only takes one bullet."

Christopher froze. Instinct called for outrage, to yell and renounce this man and his ways. "Killing doesn't solve all the world's problems," he could have yelled. Any anger he dredged up wasn't for Lorenz, though. It was for his father, for making Lorenz's statement true, and for himself, for not being a better son. Instead, Christopher merely continued to slowly ascend the stairs, knowing that violence might be the only answer to that particular problem. Lorenz had already turned his back and started cleaning his arsenal.

*   *   *

CHAPTER TEN

It was the oddest of things. From the instant his father first struck him in anger, Christopher relished the day that the walls of that square, wooden house would no longer imprison him. He dreamed of waking up to a morning where he would not worry about lousing up something so badly that it warranted a beating. Until that day came, part of him would always remain coiled in a defensive crouch, and he could not be whole. The belief intensified over the years until it became a necessary condition for salvation. It became his lifeline, almost like the concept of life after death is to the very religious, because no matter how severely his state deteriorated, the condition would improve once he walked from that house the last time.

Without warning, that day had arrived. Christopher had safely distanced himself from the house and its builder, and the one man who he knew could successfully defend him from his father guarded the escape. With these factors on his side, what did he decide to do, after less than one day of freedom? Go back, back behind the walls, back where every act and relationship turned evil and violent but contained some kind of horrible, predictable logic.

The irony struck him on the ride back through town. Even Thor acted as though the prospect depressed him, covering the distance in what amounted to a waddle. Christopher did not return solely out of weakness, though. He still had to rescue his sister from that mess, even if it meant enduring a final flogging. His bruised flesh was still tender, and the welts on his back were still days from transforming into inert scar tissue, but part of him may have looked forward to another beating, in some strange way... perhaps to show that he could take it, or perhaps it was an obligatory farewell present for the man that spawned him and fed him and taught him everything he knew.

That constituted the extent of Christopher's strategy: take his obligatory beating, sleep in the familiar comfort of his bed one final time, and the next morning, he would slip away with Mary. If anything caused a major deviation from this course, he could always rely on the miniature gun and its pair of bullets that Lorenz had given him. Christopher used his free hand to touch the lump of metal in his left pants pocket and nodded. By no means a best-case scenario, getting beaten to a pulp, but no doubt the most probable one.

Thor's falling hooves seemed to pound out the mantra: Eh-Ma, Eh-ma. What about Emma? Christopher had avoided thinking about her and her supple thighs for days. If he ventured over to the Waits' place, given the man's past tendencies, her father would probably have her locked up in her upstairs room, and he would most likely try to kill Christopher. Was she worth risking his life over? Shame weighed on Christopher's head as he considered the question. His eyes fell toward Thor's long, black main. *Probably not*, he decided.

If asked two days prior, he might have responded differently, but back then, an adolescent mania for intercourse gripped him. Since then, he had endured a lot of terrible things. Christopher thought he was in love with her for a while, but much as the first rays of dawn creep through one's window and expose the true appearance of one's lover, a short refractory period revealed his feelings for her as nothing more than lust. He had wanted sex, and who else was going to give it to him? Emma probably was counting on him to save her, at least in terms of providing her with passage out of town, but it just wasn't possible. He wished her well, and he hoped she would escape that deathtrap of a town her own way, but unless fate's fickle hand intervened again, their paths were sharply diverging.

Christopher's fingers wrung the reigns as he inaudibly cursed his weakness. So he wasn't in love with her. Was he supposed to leave her there to die instead? He blinked. The thought shocked him. Never before had he entertained the idea that his hometown might not survive this bizarre dilemma. It still seemed unfathomable that this mysterious force could destroy an entire town, but that was the point: he had no idea what the unholy monsters were capable of. Even Lorenz got injured fighting two of them. With at least four more currently or soon-to-be haunting Liberty, what chance did a fat blowhard like Sheriff Townsend stand?

Panic from earlier in the day resurfaced, pushing its way through his pores. Then the flood of speculation really started rolling. What if the town already had been destroyed? What if there was no Mary left alive to save? What if he rode headlong into his own death? His life had always featured a maddening lockstep of regularity, and suddenly not knowing what came next wreaked havoc on his nerves.

The possibilities shot back and forth through his head for several long minutes, until Liberty's church steeple appeared, and the rest of the rest of the roofs pitched at their irregular angled steadily bounced into view. The town looked the same as it did when he left it; it wasn't burned to the ground or turned into a giant ant hill. Christopher could breathe again. His heart continued to slam against his ribcage until he rode close enough to see that people still walked Liberty's streets, albeit a bit more sparsely and briskly than he recalled. Harvard Yokam stooped his shoulders and trudged down the far side of Main Street, and while his movements were soaked in apprehension, they were movements of a human being.

Christopher led Thor behind his parent's house and hitched his reigns near the woodpile. If the plan went sour, he would have to escape as fast as possible. His father had guns, too, and friends. Concealed by the woodpile he had created, Christopher checked to make certain that the gun was still loaded and made a silent prayer that he would not have to use it. He placed the small, silver weapon in his palm and stared at it for a couple seconds, the orange rays from the setting sun bouncing over its shiny surface. Christopher stuffed the weapon into his pocket. When he walked around to the house's front door, he felt prepared.

Christopher pushed through the front door, scanning the room for his father. His mother sat at the kitchen table. Her hands lay on the tabletop, folded so tightly that her knuckles were even whiter than the rest of her pallid form. She rocked back and forth as though in dire need of a toilet. Clearly she had been praying... for something. The dining room remained as dimly lit as ever, but she anxiously looked up when the door opened and her son entered. Her face, devoid of any insectoid distinctions, allowed Christopher a second of relative relaxation. *Well,* he thought, *there went the absolute-worst-case scenario.* His relief passed in a moment, however, because the instant she recognized her prodigal son, her face quickly contorted into a demonic scowl.

"You!" she snarled. "Where in God's name have you been?" Any goodwill leftover from the oatmeal incident of the other morning had evidently left her.

Mother Rutlage rarely raised her voice, and for her to take the Lord's name in vain was nearly unheard of (she would say a second prayer to beg for forgiveness later... and maybe a third). These events were enough to stun Christopher, but fortunately, he fell back on a previously concocted explanation for his absence, one that he had rehearsed on the ride back a satisfactory number of times.

"Mother," he began evenly, though not too evenly, "I meant to come home last night, but when I was over at Dr. Ferguson's office..." Images from the actual event flashed through Christopher's head as he spoke. Images of ants, three-fingered claw-hands, and people cocooned against the bookshelves swirled around him. The darkness and pain that lingered fresh in his mind instilled the proper tremble in his voice as he recounted a fabricated story to his mother.

The tale was simple, direct, and easy to remember: a strange man whom he had never seen before (he emphasized this part, as to not implicate Deklan Lorenz) punched out Doc Ferguson's window and grabbed hold of Christopher. They wrestled for a moment on the floor of the examination room, until Christopher grabbed hold of a doorstop and struck his unfamiliar assailant with it. The blow broke this crazy man's grip, and Christopher was able to run outside, sling himself over Thor, and ride to safety. He concluded the lie by deducing that he must have fainted from all the exertion, and when he later revived, he had no idea where Thor had taken him. He spent the night in the wilderness and had only now managed to make it home. Sure, it was a little unbelievable, but he had enough physical evidence to make it stick for twenty-four hours.

One would never mistake Christopher's mother for an intelligent person, and he anticipated her believing the story. In this respect, she did not disappoint. Unfortunately, he neglected to account for the fact that she, like her husband, firmly believed in the virtue of driving the devil out of a child through regular punishment, and also like Lewis Rutlage, had become especially adept at inventing excuses to invoke said punishment.

"Just now you're getting back, are you?" she screeched. "I'm sure you're very concerned for your father, seein' how he's out lookin' for you!" Christopher let his mouth fall open in a feigned expression of shock.

He even mouthed the words, *Oh no.* "Yes! Yes, that's right! Your sin has put a member of your family in danger again."

His mother's ranting trigged an actual concern. "Mary?" Christopher asked with genuine earnestness. "Is she alright?"

Agatha Rutlage rose from her seat and silently glared at her son, her lower lip quivering. She was a small woman, and growing smaller with each passing year, but at this moment, Christopher actually feared physical confrontation with her. It looked as though every angle of her body could draw blood. "Don't interrupt me again, you ungrateful boy." She stared with eyes so dark and sunken into their sockets that she looked very much like Christopher's personal conception of the Angel of Death. She was always high-strung, but he had never seen his mother quite this distressed. *It's Father,* he thought to himself. *Father was more important to her than even the church. She worried herself sick about Father, because if she isn't Lewis Rutlage's wife, she isn't anything.*

"Your sister is fine," she shook her head and muttered absently, "don't you ever interrupt me again..." Her voice trailed off and her stooped shoulders dropped even lower as she lowered herself into her seat. The superhuman rage drained from her, and she seemed to age ten years in as many seconds. Christopher waited patiently from his position two steps inside the door, not moving a muscle until she waved a hand in a dismissive gesture. "Go to bed, Christopher," she said. "Your father will deal with you in the morning."

Despite the fact that he had been trained since birth to honor his mother, Christopher nearly laughed as he passed her. What a joyless little troll she was. Only moments earlier, he had actually feared this broken, pathetic, hateful creature. "Your father will deal with you in the morning?" That was just fine, because Christopher planned to make himself a memory long before sunrise. It was not beyond his father's ethic to drag him out of bed in the middle of the night to administer a beating, but nevertheless, Christopher liked his chances.

Christopher walked out the house's back door, breathing easy. The orange and violet sky still held some small vestige of daylight, but his mother expected him to go to bed soon. Some punishment. He needed all the rest he could get to prepare for the next day. As long as the world didn't end in the next six hours, things were finally looking up. He took Thor's reigns and let him into the barn, so as not to cause any suspicion. There was no saddle to remove, so he hung the bridal on the wall and dumped a can of grain into Thor's feed bucket. "Eat up," he told his horse. God only knew how far or how fast they would have to ride in a few hours. In the shadow of the barn, he slid the bullets from the gun before walking back inside the house.

When he shut the door behind him, his mother's voice rang out. "Your harlot came by looking for you earlier," she said, staring out the front window in search of approaching shadows.

Christopher merely nodded. He could visualize Emma standing in the doorway, silhouetted by the sunlight, and he could visualize the soft skin of her face sinking into a frown as Mother told her that Christopher had disappeared. He could see her eyes glistening as they found the dusty ground. In his mind, though, he had already left town, and circumstances with Emma stood fully resolved. In his mind, a man-sized bug broke through the door to Emma's bedroom as she screamed and cowered in the corner of her bed. Christopher clamped his eyes shut and forced the image to disappear.

Christopher had ample time to think that evening while he lay in bed, staring at the slanted wooden ceiling. He noticed the seamless construction. His father was a good carpenter. He had to give the man that... and he was one hell of a blacksmith. Lewis Rutlage was good in a lot of utilitarian ways: he worked hard, practiced thrift, provided for his family, went to church on Sunday. He wasn't a seamless man, though. Gaping holes existed, where there was nothing to shore up the structure. No one is perfect, but Lewis Rutlage was grossly imperfect in some fundamental ways.

Christopher folded his hands behind his head. He could leave the house now; just get up and walk out the door. He just had needed to see it one more time, to satisfy the little boy lingering in him that the sting of the belt had yet to drive out. Mary might prove rather difficult to abscond with, he considered, but things were falling into place so wonderfully that he scarcely paid attention to the thought. She would remain quiet as a mouse as they departed, probably become a bit homesick for a couple days, just as he had, but she would recover, steadily growing accustomed to not living in fear. Brother and sister would escape, and Christopher would take care of her like no big brother in the history of civilization had ever taken care of his little sister.

He smiled, something he could rarely do within these walls. What of the insects? It seemed laughable at that point, truly laughable. The insects were a minor concern at best. Deklan Lorenz was catering to them, and with such a man dealing with such a small problem, nothing but good things would happen.

Despite everything that had happened to him during his fourteen years of life, Christopher still believed in happy endings.

*   *   *

Later that night, a nearly full moon hung in the sky as Christopher eased the front door shut behind him. Mary remained half-asleep as he closed his fingers around her tiny hand and led her to the barn. She scarcely made a sound the entire time, doubtlessly confused and more than a little frightened by the darkness and the night sounds. He needed her trust to escape, and Mary had always been the respectful, obedient child that Christopher never was.

The dark, rectangular doorway of the barn loomed before them like the mouth of a great beast. Mary stopped walking about ten feet short. Christopher gently tugged on her arm, but she pulled away and silently shook her head, wet eyes glistening in the moonlight. *Don't cry. Don't cry.* She had a loud, moaning cry when she cared to unleash it. Christopher glanced from the doorway to Mary and back. Inside the barn, horses stamped their hooves and whipped their tails at some nocturnal, flying insects invading the stalls, but from the outside, it all sounded like a series of ominous, inexplicable noises. Maybe this was the first time she ever saw the barn at night; certainly it was the first time she saw it this late at night. Christopher gave a reassuring nod in Mary's direction and proceeded into the blackness alone. The time he ventured past Doc Ferguson's unlocked doorway hung in his mind. Shapes, movements filtered through the shadows, and he felt more confident closing his eyes and letting memory lead him through the void. He tried to step evenly. Four stalls on the left. Four stalls on the right. Thor stood in the second stall on the right.

Christopher's fingers danced over the cool, metal latch. When he drew back the bolt to Thor's stall, a voice in the darkness sent a jolt through him. "What do you think you're doin', boy?" Christopher's lingering hearing problem made it difficult to locate it origin. The voice itself, however, sounded all too familiar.

Christopher turned, and his hands automatically found each other behind his back as his posture became picket fence-straight. "Looking for you?" he offered lamely.

The quip failed to amuse Lewis Rutlage. Rutlage spit on the ground, which allowed Christopher to pinpoint his father's location. It took another long moment, though, before he could even make out a silhouette. Had he been waiting out here? For how long? "I'd like to believe that," Lewis began, sounding insincere, "but I know you too well.

You've always been a damn coward, and you were running away... and taking your sister with you, it looks like. She's just lucky I came back when I did." Mary still stood just outside the doorway, reluctantly observing the confrontation between two most important men in her life.

A small, nearly weightless piece of steel pressed against Christopher's upper thigh. He needed a moment to remember it was a gun and another to realize that he was desperate enough to use it. Dirt ground beneath boots as his father's footsteps grew closer to Christopher. The boy reached in his pocket and fought to free the weapon from its cloth cocoon. He had unloaded the gun before he went to bed, but his father probably wouldn't know that. He'd be too shocked at seeing his son pointing a gun at him to even consider it possible.

Christopher stood closer to the doorway and must have been the more visible of the two, because as he pulled the gun free, Rutlage grabbed his son's right wrist and repeatedly slammed it against a wooden post until Christopher dropped it. It was his sore wrist, the one that the ant creature in Doc Ferguson's nearly crushed the night before, and Christopher cradled it against his chest while his salvation lay in the dirt, gleaming in the moonlight.

"Tryin' to shoot your own father are you? You little ungrateful bastard," he snarled. He pressed his face inches from Christopher and exhaled a rancid breath. His disproportionately large and muscular hands wrung Christopher's shirt collar. Outside, Mary yelped, but Christopher could barely hear her; she stood to his right, the side with the nonfunctioning ear, and their father's leering visage dominated his vision and attention. "Goddammit, boy, if you think I hurt you before... You don't even know what hurt is."

Christopher didn't bother to answer. He felt oddly calm, like the other night at Doc Ferguson's. It struck him as ironic, in a way, that he had twice escaped the clutches of a race of supernatural beings, only to be beaten to death by the hands of his own father. Lewis Rutlage and the insects inspired different flavors of fear in Christopher. While the insects inspired immediate, instinctive action on the most basic levels, his father appealed to a fear he had slavishly worked to instill in his son since before Christopher could remember. It was a paralyzing fear that told Christopher to take his punishment. This "righteous" fear assured him that if his father called him an ungrateful bastard, he must be an ungrateful bastard, and probably deserved whatever he got.

"If you were fixin' to shoot me, boy," Rutlage hissed, the words sliding out of the darkness, "at least you could have used a man's weapon." The darkness prevented Christopher from seeing the punch coming, but the speeding fist burst against the front of his abdomen like a sledgehammer and lifted him off the ground. Those oversized hands, when balled into fists were like mallets. When his feet hit the ground, Christopher sank to his knees, then doubled over. "I thought it over, night after night, but I don't know what your Ma and I done to deserve a pathetic little coward like you."

Lewis Rutlage stood in front of the stall with the saddles and assorted other riding tack. He could easily reach over the gate and pick up a hammer or something else to bludgeon his son to death with. Or he could just start kicking. His father had big feet and, they both knew from experience, legs strong enough that a well-placed kick could lift Christopher's entire body off the ground. Christopher didn't know which option his father would take, only that he was helpless to stop it. Both sets of his eyelids pressed together, or else he might have seen a shadow looming in the doorway.

A muffled crack resonated through the barn. Christopher winced and for a moment, thought his own body made the sound. He lifted his head and opened his eyes in time to see his father's shadowy corpse hit the dirt floor in a heap. In the darkness, his father's vacant eyes gazed out at nothing.

I don't know what your Ma and I done to deserve a pathetic little coward like you... Those had been the last words his father ever said to him.

Sitting on his hands and knees, fighting for breath, Christopher stared at the one-foot section of ground between his dirty thumbs. He knew exactly what had happened: his father was dead, and Deklan Lorenz had killed him. He also knew that the murder weapon was one of those damn throwing knives Deklan thought so highly of, good for killing people in the still of the night, constructed in the victim's shop, not twenty feet away, delivered to the murderer by the victim's own ungrateful bastard of a son.

Christopher was fourteen years old and had no father.

"Are you alright?" Deklan asked, his clipped tone indicating that he wanted a brief status report and nothing more. Before Christopher could answer, Mary yelped again. "Shut her up," Deklan commanded.

"Mary," Christopher wheezed, "Mary, it's okay. Go back to bed now Mary." His voice was little more than a hiss, but she heard him and fell silent. She didn't know exactly what was going on, but she knew it wasn't good, so she just stood in the doorway, taking heavy, deep breaths, ready to scream again at a moment's notice.

Christopher set his hand on one of the lower boards of the nearest stall and pulled himself into a standing position. His abdominal muscles remained tightened like a balled fist and prevented him from standing fully erect, but he could still shuffle over to his sister. "Mary," Christopher said, placing his hands gently on her shoulders to steady her trembling body, "you need to go back inside and go to sleep, okay?"

"What about Father?" she asked, unable to remove her wide-eyed gaze from the prostrate form of their father.

"I'll take care of Father," Christopher assured her, hoping against all hope she did not deduced that the man lay deader than a gutted sow. "Now give me a hug." She complied, throwing her doll arms around his neck. "Now get back to bed." They ended their embrace, and she trotted back up the steps to the house, quietly closing the door behind her.

Numbly, Christopher remained in his crouch. The instant the door closed, his eyes dropped to the ground. He hadn't been beaten *that* badly, but his mind wasn't working properly. An instant later, Deklan snapped his head toward him. "Are you ready to ride?" he asked.

Christopher shook his head. "You just killed my father, Deklan. I'm going to need a moment."

"We don't have a moment," Lorenz shot back in an impossibly even voice. He plucked the empty, silver pistol out of the dirt and thrust it toward Christopher. The boy absently took it and dropped it into his pocket. "You'd better load this."

"It wasn't always bad with him," Christopher said absently as he pressed the tips of his fingers into the soft, dry earth to steady himself. "When I was little, before he started hitting me, I saw how strong he was, how everyone respected him. I wanted to be just like him."

"You didn't know any better," Deklan said, his words taking on a harder edge, "but if you want an apology, you aren't going to get one. He was going to kill you this time."

"You don't know that," Christopher stated, his voice slow and toneless. He did not believe a word that came from his own mouth, but somehow, it seemed like the right thing to say.

"Yes, I do," Deklan insisted, "and so do you. I'm just surprised he didn't do it sooner." He bent over Lewis Rutlage's body and slid the knife free from the man's cleaved-open face. He paused long enough to take another glance down at the still-warm corpse before stating, "A painless death is more than a man like this deserves."

Automatically, Christopher responded, "He was my father." His voice sank in the darkness.

"I know he was your father, but it's still true." Deklan stooped and unceremoniously wiped the soiled knife clean on his victim's shirt. A chill shot down Christopher's spine as he considered what cocktail of substances stuck to the blade. "This may sound cruel, but we have work to do. Your sister will be fine for the time being, so just saddle up your horse and we'll be on our way. I'll take care of the body, and you can ride in front." Lorenz awkwardly set a heavy, gloved hand on Christopher's shoulder. He intended it to comfort, but his comforting skill resided a notch or two below his carpentry skill. "It's hard, but it can be done." He paused, then added, "Believe me, I know."

Christopher stood up and stepped away, letting the hand slide from his shoulder. Lorenz was trying to shame him into action by invalidating his grief, and he both recognized and resented the attempt. Lorenz implied that the grief for his dead wife had been greater than Christopher's grief for his dead father, that Christopher was using it as an excuse for inactivity because he was scared to go on. He implied that Christopher grieved because sons were expected to grieve when their fathers died, not because he felt anything for the bitter, cruel man.

Lorenz might not have meant any of those things. After all, he had all the subtlety of a battering ram. In truth Christopher probably pulled those feelings from somewhere inside himself because he was so confused, and because they did need to get moving. Whatever their source, they shamed him into action.

Christopher walked into the first stall to retrieve Thor's saddle. In the darkness, an image of his father materialized. He was in the shop, hammering away on a red-hot piece of iron, providing for his family. He looked up, in Christopher's direction, and smiled. *Where the hell did that come from?* Christopher wondered, shaking his head as he lifted the saddle off the wall. When had he seen his father smile at him? When did he see his father smile at anything?

Christopher slid Thor's saddle into position and turned in time to see Lorenz enclosing his father's head in a burlap bag to prevent it from dripping. Virgil waited several paces outside the door, and Deklan hefted the corpse over his shoulder as though it were a dead coyote, walked it over to his horse, and tossed it over the horse's back.

Christopher never did get around to thanking Lorenz. It never struck him as the kind of thing you thank someone for, like shooting your horse to prevent someone from stealing it. In fact, he didn't say anything until they were a quarter mile beyond the last of Liberty's houses. "How did you find me?" he asked.

"I heard your sister crying," Lorenz replied. "She has a really loud cry."

They rode the rest of the way to Deklan's house in silence. With Lorenz riding behind him, the shadows and shifting grass no longer startled Christopher, and the time passed quickly. When they arrived at his house amid a chorus of friendly barks, Deklan's deep voice announced, "Go inside, Christopher. I'll take care of the body and will return in an hour or two."

Christopher nodded and dismounted from Thor. His father's bagged head dangled limply less than a foot in front of him. Curled fingers extended from arms that swayed like pendulums. The sight made Christopher think of his grandfather. He never knew the man, but he had once considered that all this might be his fault. Perhaps Lewis Rutlage did not rejoice in the pain he visited on his son. Perhaps it was all he knew. Perhaps he, too, was a victim at some point in his life, afflicted with the wrath of a bitter old man, and he wasn't conjuring the hate he inflicted on Christopher, merely transmitting it.

Christopher reached forward with trembling fingers to touch the body one last time before Deklan carted it away to God only knew where. He wanted to touch the flesh for once without the contact coming in the form of a closed fist to his jaw. His fingers stopped inches from the cold, dead shoulder, though, then fell to his side. It was... too late. Too late for gestures. Too late for regrets. He turned away and let Lorenz ride on. He stood in front of the porch with Dante on one side and Thor on the other, listening to the clop of horse hooves until there was nothing left to listen to. Then he went inside.

Christopher thought about his father that night and included the man in his prayers. He asked God to give the man peace, and told his father that he forgave him. Gestures are often unnecessary, but this one might have served an actual purpose. He had become convinced that God did not visit Liberty, but that the spirits of people like his father were drawn to it. In that way, his prayer might have involved some degree of self-interest.

*   *   *

Chapter Eleven

July 8, 1877:

By the time Lorenz returned from burying the body of Lewis Rutlage, the eastern sky had taken on a pink-orange glow. Christopher stared at it from his seat on the steps of Lorenz's front porch, still wide-awake, still immobilized by shock. He couldn't get the confrontation in the barn out of his mind, the way the sequence of events unfolded, and all the things he could have done differently.

Christopher had no idea what he was doing at Lorenz's house. Why did Deklan ask him to ride out to the house in the first place? What was the point? Riding in front of the limp, bouncing corpse of his father was an arduous, and wholly unnecessary, experience. Unnecessary, just like everything else Christopher had done after informing Lorenz of the menace coming from Staley's pasture. Deklan Lorenz needed help from no man. Christopher felt sure of this, more so than ever before. To Christopher, Lorenz possessed all the qualities of a steel-coated, finely calibrated instrument of violence.

Lorenz dismounted beside the barn and unsaddled his horse using a fluid, precise technique that he developed himself. He once explained that his technique allowed him to have a properly trained horse saddled and bridled in exactly ten seconds. Half the time he did not use a saddle, though. "I like to keep up on the practice of riding bareback," he once told Christopher, "because you never know when a saddle won't be available." It gave Christopher a glimpse into the man's world. Preparation. Preparation. Preparation. For the emergency that might never come. All those guns, all that gunpowder in his cellar, remained functional and ready to go, because he took the time to maintain it. All of his killer's instincts honed to perfection, just in case the end of the world arrived.

Lorenz walked from the barn to the porch, stopping at the foot of the stairs long enough to administer two strokes to the back of Dante's head. While he climbed the porch steps to stand beside his guest, his gaze locked onto the distant sunrise, and Christopher notice a gleam light in the man's good eye. He seemed younger to Christopher now than he did a week ago, his movements sparked like those belonging to a man of thirty, or even twenty. Lorenz was, Christopher realized, enjoying himself. This assumed, of course, that he possessed the capacity to enjoy things. Christopher's thoughts found his voice. "Are you actually enjoying this?" his asked.

Lorenz's gray lips probably moved, but in the pale morning light it looked as though the voice emanated from an inanimate caricature of a face. At least he stood on Christopher's left side and the young man could hear every word. "I... don't know," he said. "That's an interesting question. I haven't enjoyed myself in so long, it's hard to tell." His gloved hand found the porch railing. "I'm good at it, that's all I know." He let out a ghastly chuckle. "It's odd: I've spent every day since my wife died preparing for a situation like this... well, not like this, but something where I'd be needed again. It became necessary to occupy my time. I needed something I could do alone, to make the pain manageable. I'd grown soft since the war, and getting my body and mind back into condition were the only things I could think to do. I prepared for the moment, and now it's here. So, maybe I am enjoying myself, Christopher. Maybe I am."

Christopher looked up at the man, silhouetted against the rising sun. Lorenz stared out toward the east, the same as Christopher, but his eyes focused upon something not visible to anyone else. Christopher wanted to ask another question, and receive the answer that was promised him, but how to begin? Theirs was a vague relationship of friendship, protection, and other things with obscure names. Their statuses shifted back and forth and found them at equals one minute and mentor and protégé the next. Had the scarred man in the flat-brimmed hat become "Deklan," or was he still "Mr. Lorenz?" The former sounded not formal enough, the latter, too much so. Perhaps no form of address was best. "What exactly did you do during the war?"

Lorenz's head tilted earthward as he let out a weary sigh. He betrayed his fatigue for the first time, but the sagging, vulnerable body only remained visible for a second. He merely needed to inhale once more to absorb the weakness and become strong, tall, and impervious. "That's funny," he said in a toneless manner that belied no humor, "not even my wife was privy to that information. It was so long ago now that it doesn't matter..." He cleared his throat, and his fingers drummed uneasily on the porch railing. "I... worked for a private group of wealthy abolitionists in the North who called themselves the Sons of Aaron. Lots of merchants, a few politicians. Most of them were from Boston, New York, Philadelphia. The group was part business guild, part cult. Out east, there are a handful of secret societies, but this was one of the few with real clout. They had their own ceremonies that featured robes and candles, and I really didn't understand much of it. I didn't have to, though. I was what they referred to as 'an earthbound agent of God's heavenly wrath,' or what normal people might call an assassin."

Christopher nodded through most of the information, unable to grasp most of it. The last part caught his attention. "An assassin?" he repeated. He had heard the word before, but this was the first time he had ever used it. It felt exotic; it was like hearing someone proclaim to be a maharaja or a sultan.

Lorenz nodded. "There were several of us. A dozen, to be exact."

"Were you the best?" Christopher asked, feeling almost giddy. It was like the stories of the knights of Christendom. The sorrow and fear of the previous night's tragedy had receded into the background, and the mystery of Deklan Lorenz once again held him in thrall.

Lorenz slid his eyes toward Christopher. "I was very good. We all were."

"An assassin," Christopher said again, tasting the word this time. "In America. Who did they have you kill?"

Lorenz shrugged his massive shoulders. "Whoever. Plantation owners, financiers, gunrunners, Confederate officers. All our operations were run independent of the Union army, for obvious reasons. The army supposedly didn't know the organization even existed, much less what it was funding, but there had to be some level of coordination, and in reality, they probably just didn't care."

"That's how I came to get that arsenal," Lorenz explained, pointing downward with his index finger. "I was in charge of a robbery involving a trainload of explosives, right across the Illinois State Line. We did the job well enough, but then the war ended, and since the army couldn't even admit they knew about us and take blame credit for the robbery, the six survivors of the operation split up the take. I buried my share in a cave and didn't even think to come back to get it until after Cla—," he coughed into his gloved fist, "until after my wife died. It took a wagon or three, but I got it all here in one trip. The gunpowder was useless by then, so I got some more, but everything else was salvageable."

Christopher nodded, not overly surprised. He never expected the story to be this exotic, but the evidence all pointed toward Lorenz leading some sort of pseudo-military existence. "Pseudo-military," because not even soldiers fought the way Lorenz did, and professional soldiers usually didn't have access to the kind of money Lorenz did. His living conditions were not quite lavish, but he was relatively young, leading a life devoid of marketable work, and his home and its furnishings were at least as nice as those of anyone in town.

Christopher licked his lips, hovering on the verge of asking some pointless question regarding the transportation of the cannon when Lorenz interrupted. "I'm sorry, Christopher," he said, his voice tightening, "but we really don't have time for this."

Lorenz proceeded to inform his young protégé that nothing had happened in town the previous day to increase the casualties. The three people that Christopher saw adorning the wall of Dr. Ferguson's office (and could still see every time he closed his eyes) remained missing. "If your theory's correct," Lorenz stated, "that means they've taken on a distinctly more insect-like appearance by now." He also said that the quiet day may merely mean that the creature that used to be Dr. Ferguson might simply be biding its time, waiting for his three victims to make their full transformation.

From Lorenz's initial tone, Christopher expected more. If they were that pressed for time, Lorenz wouldn't have bothered to rattle off a status report that nothing happened, followed by speculation as to why this was so. The pressing issue, he realized, was that Lorenz didn't want to talk about his past anymore.

"You can go home now, if you want," Lorenz said, looking at Christopher fully for the first time since he returned from burying the boy's father. "You don't have to, but you can. Understand, though: it is far more dangerous in town than it is out here, even with your father gone. On the other hand, you could keep better tabs on the situation in town, not to mention the fact that you would be closer to your sister."

Christopher nodded vehemently, nearly forgetting that he had left Mary back in that deathtrap of a town. "What are the people in town going to do when they find out Father disappeared?" he asked.

"If we're lucky," Lorenz replied, "they'll attribute his disappearance to the same cause as the rest. If we're unlucky, the cause they attribute all the disappearances to will be me." He leaned on the porch railing and drummed his fingers. "If that happens, the sheriff'll form a posse and ride it out here. You should be in the clear, though... that is, unless your sister told anyone what she saw."

Christopher shook his head as he looked in the direction of town and the brightening sky. "No, Mary won't tell anybody," he assured Lorenz, even though he wasn't sure at all. No one can make any certainties about the behaviors of five-year-olds. Still, Lorenz's dark tone forced him to say something. He half expected Lorenz to suggest "silencing her permanently." Christopher turned to Lorenz and wondered aloud, "What do I do if they ask me anyway?"

Lorenz shrugged. "What else? Claim total ignorance."

"What if they send a posse after you?"

"Our timetable doesn't allow for me to evade them, so I'll have to kill them." Lorenz spoke very matter-of-factly. Regardless of number, training, or his personal prejudice, he would kill them. Not "try to kill them," but "kill them." He continued, "Assuming this doesn't happen, I'll be in town tonight to do some more investigating." Without saying a farewell, he turned and walked inside. The screen door banged shut, leaving Christopher to find his own way off the man's property.

*   *   *

Christopher's conversation with Lorenz replayed through his head on the ride back to town. These days, it seemed like Christopher had nothing but time to think. He thought while he rode back and forth across the prairie, contemplated while he lay in bed because the pain from the injuries forced him awake, or pondered while he waited around for Lorenz to show up, and these acts now seemed to constitute ninety-nine percent of his waking day. Of course, the other one percent involved fleeing from something trying to kill him. He would have cherished some mindless, monotonous chores for a while, something like adding to the family woodpile, just so he could run from the quite times and the thoughts of terror and death. As it was, though, he could just press on and endure the long stretches of time where he had only worries of the future and regrets of the past to keep him company.

When he arrived back in Liberty, everyone appeared shaken by the recent, mysterious events. Men and women stalked down the dirt streets with darting eyes and hunched shoulders, and these were the few people with the courage to step outside their doors. They were Christopher's neighbors, and three days ago, they likely would have greeted one another with nods or hearty hellos. These people, the visible people, tried to cope with the anxiety by keeping the same routine to their daily lives. People like the Braxtons occupied the other extreme: they literally boarded up their doors and windows about thirty-six hours before Christopher returned to town, and no one had heard from them since.

The eerie paranoia did not emanate from the fact that someone disappeared; on the frontier, people killed one another or died from dozens of "natural" causes all the time. If there was a disappearance, within a day or two, a body would surface with an obvious cause of death. In this case, the panic came from the number of disappearances, the lack of bodies, and the inability to produce a culprit. Nobody knew how to deal with a situation like this, or even how to identify the nature of the threat or its source.

Christopher rode Thor past the church, turning right to get to his house. He knew the reason for the disappearances, of course, but he also knew that no sane person would believe him. He didn't know how to respond to the mood of the town, though. Few people in the course of modern history ever endured a situation similar in its community-wide paranoia. The Ancient Egyptians must have felt the same way, when they faced the wrath of God. The more Christopher saw the sullen faces and hollow eyes, the more he saw their need for answers, even wrong answers. The temptation to blame the town boogeyman already had to be present, steadily growing stronger. The black cloud looming over Liberty threatened to burst in the direction of Deklan Lorenz's stead.

The citizens of Liberty probably had little idea what to make of Christopher. Although he was managing his own anxiety, he rode down Main Street in the early morning hours on his gray horse a little more confident, maybe his bruised head held a little higher, than normal. That made him standout from the rest of the town, and from people whose fathers had recently disappeared. Losing one's only father can affect a person in many ways, but the experience rarely invigorates a person. His neighbors couldn't have known that, unlike them, he was safer today than yesterday. Although few of the pedestrians looked up while they walked, Christopher caught several stares during the short ride from the church to his parents'... to his mother's house.

After returning Thor to the barn, Christopher walked into the gradually building heat of the house. His mother sat at the table, in much the same position as she was the last time he saw her, no doubt too terrified to set foot outdoors. Maybe she had been praying again; she didn't know how to do much else. Agatha Rutlage turned toward the opening door and gazed at her son with white, circular eyes and a pale, drawn face. She had a wild, desperate look about her, the kind that only surfaces when someone's world implodes. Of course she blamed him for his father's death: Christopher received the blame any time anything went wrong. Granted, this time she would have been right, but she was never one to wait for confirming evidence before rendering a decision. He considered for a moment, *Maybe she did know. Maybe she lay awake in bed last night and heard everything that happened out by the barn.* That was impossible, though; she never would have allowed him to take Mary without a reflexive fight. Without speaking, his mother twisted off the chair, scurried across the room, and exited through the back door.

Christopher's eyes tracked her until the door closed. It felt a bit awkward being feared rather than despised in that house, but not wholly unpleasant. To have a presence that induced some level of fear... it made him feel secure. He shrugged and walked to the cupboards on the left-hand side of the house in search of something to eat.

As he set his hand on the handle of the cupboard, the front door burst open. Christopher wheeled, his hands dropping into his pockets in search of the dainty pistol that he still hadn't gotten around to loading. "Christopher!" Mary said, cradling her rag doll under her arm. "I thought I seen you come in." She tromped across the wooden floor with her arms spread. He had to crouch down to embrace her. He could have fit his arms around two of her.

"Hey, how've you been?" he asked, then kissed the mass of curly brown hair atop her head.

"I'm... I'm okay," she answered, a bit winded. She seemed okay. Much better than he expected. Maybe she didn't understand what had happened the night before, or thought it was all a bad dream.

"Have you eaten today?" he asked. She shook her head. Christopher's joints popped as he stood up. A quick perusal of the cupboards yielded only foodstuffs that required cooking. This led him to one conclusion: "Um, I've gotta go down to Harkness's and pick up something to eat," he told his sister. "I'll be back in a few minutes."

He popped the lid off the metal flour tin that set on the back of the kitchen counter and jammed his hand into the soft, white powder. His parents probably never knew he was aware of their little stash of coins, but there clearly were a lot of things his parents never knew about him. He groped for a few seconds before his fingers closed on a metal disk large enough to be a quarter-dollar. "Wait here," he reminded Mary as he cleaned his hand on a kitchen towel and walked toward the door.

She nodded and looked at her brother with large, brown, innocent eyes. "Christopher, I didn't tell nobody what I saw last night," she said, clutching her doll against her chest. "I didn't tell nobody."

"I know," he said and tousled her curly hair. The gesture made her smile. They were in this together.

Christopher remembered to walk to Harkness's with his head down, shoulders slumped forward, and frown fixed in place. It was his disguise, like the times he used a hat to shade his bruised and bloody face (which reminded him: he probably should have worn his other hat). When he walked through the door of the general store, a loud bell announced his presence but failed to interrupt a conversation between Sheriff Townsend and the shop's proprietor. Christopher instinctively drifted to his right, to the furthest aisle from the counter and the conversing adults.

He scanned the nearly empty shelves for some sort of sausage or dried goods hearty enough to provide an instant meal. There wasn't much left after people like the Braxtons stocked up for the long haul. The conversation at the front of the store failed to concern him; he was too focused on finding something that he could actually prepare and that Mary would actually eat. In addition, the front counter was positioned on his deaf side. Cursory bits of discourse and stray syllables floated in his direction, but they were no more meaningful than the echo of his footsteps on the floorboards. Just as he turned to scan the opposite side of the aisle, Harkness's voice stated, "Oh, I agree, I just don't understand why we don't go out there and lynch that freak right now. Ain't nobody gonna give two shits if we blow him to hell, even if he ain't the one who done it."

Christopher froze in mid-step.

The gruff voice of Sheriff Townsend explained, "I already told you, the time isn't right. That maniac is obviously dangerous, and I don't want anybody rushin' in to that killin' box he's got built out there without enough firepower. We gotta pull together enough people so he'll think twice about tryin' to shoot his way out."

The "freak" to which they referred was Deklan. It wasn't the first time Christopher heard someone refer to him as such; in fact, it might have been the only context in which he heard the term used. The "right time" for Sheriff Townsend probably had less to do with availability of manpower than it had to do with his take on the public's state of mind. Public opinion is a delicate matter in a small town, even for a man such as him, who probably thought he had his finger planted firmly on the town's pulse. His ideal situation followed thusly: on one hand, he wanted a public panicked enough to put up with a quick, private lynching. Conversely, he wanted to avoid a public so distraught that the people would start to leave town. Even if Lorenz wasn't the source of the disappearances, Townsend could use him as a scapegoat and buy some valuable time with the townsfolk. Maybe quelling the public hysteria justified the murder of an innocent man in his Townsend's mind; it certainly did in Harkness's.

Christopher carried the loaf of bread and jar of dried beef he had selected to the front counter. The conversation abruptly ceased at his approach. The sheriff hooked a thumb in his extra-large gunbelt, causing the leather to creak, and regarded the fatherless boy from under the brim of his extra-large hat. Christopher and the bald, hawk-nosed shopkeeper acknowledged one another with a nod. "How's your ma holding up, Christopher?" Harkness asked in his sly, rat-voice.

Despite the gathering warmth of the day, the question sent a chill through Christopher. *They don't know,* he reminded himself. Harkness always sounded like he'd just uncovered a plot against the person to whom he spoke. *They don't even know you're with Lorenz.* "Mother?" Christopher repeated, trying to invoke an appropriately sorrowful tone. "She's holding up about as well as can be expected."

Harkness scribbled down some numbers on an inventory sheet, and Christopher pushed the quarter across the counter. Sheriff Townsend shifted so that his ample middle pointed toward Christopher and asked, "Did you hear anything last night, Christopher?" He stroked his black and gray-speckled mustache as the question formed.

Christopher shook his head. "No, sir, nothing out of the ordinary." The sheriff's tone was neither accusatory nor patronizing, but Christopher badly wanted to take the focus off of himself. "Do you think Father's... dead?" he asked the burly lawman, arching his eyebrows as he pressed the corners of his eyes down and calling upon the acting skills developed from years of lying to his father. It was a good delivery. I had to be; both of these men were smarter than his father.

"Well, you know how much folks in this town respect each other's privacy," Townsend said, shifting the brim of his hat so he could scratch his forehead. "Why, it's a damn admirable quality most of the time, but sometimes it sure makes my job difficult. I interviewed just about everybody, but only Mrs. Libby gave me any information at all."

Christopher nodded. Mrs. Libby was a pale, thin woman that most considered the town gossip. She claimed to be a little over thirty, but she looked ten years old. What she didn't know about a situation, she would make up in order to become the center of attention. Someone with Townsend's experience should have known this.

"Yeah, Mrs. Libby lives right down the street from your folks," Townsend continued, "and she says she heard a scream last night, a little girl wailing. Do you know if your little sister... what's her name? Do you know if she saw anything?"

"Mary?" Christopher asked, knitting his brow so to appear shocked. "Gosh, I don't think so. She does cry awful loud, but I seen her a couple times today, and she never said nothing about it."

Townsend's lips slowly twisted into a broad smile that showed both rows of tobacco-rotted teeth and sent a wave of panic through Christopher. "Well, I wonder if I might stop by and talk to her later, just in case?"

"You'd have to talk to Mother about that," Christopher said quickly, no longer able to look at the two men, "but I'm sure she wouldn't care." He scooped up his purchases, ignoring the pennies in change he had coming to him, and started out the door. "You gentlemen—"

Harkness cut Christopher off. "Y'know, Christopher," the man's whine announced, "Sheriff Townsend was telling me before you came in that Mrs. Libby never heard a gunshot last night, nobody did."

"Gosh," Christopher began, not at all sure what the lanky shopkeeper was driving at, "that's good." His upper body tilted further and further toward the door.

"Yeah," Harkness said leaning his gangly frame over the counter, "the thing of it is, I've known your pa damn near twenty years, and I can't believe anybody could've taken him without a gun." If weasels could speak, they would sound like Tom Harkness. He paused, pretending that a thought had just occurred to him. "Tell me, Christopher, did your pa ever do any work for the Mick that lives northwest of town? Lorenz is the name, I think."

"Father usually made and repaired horse shoes for Mr. Lorenz," Christopher stated with genuine conviction. Stating non-fabrications sometimes helped him get his rhythm back. Still, he clutched the bread tight enough against his chest to leave a handprint.

"Is that all?" Harkness asked. If he leaned forward any more, he risked spilling over the counter and falling on his face. When Christopher looked at Harkness, he focused on the bald head instead of the beady, green eyes or the yellow-toothed sneer.

How in the Seven Hells could they know about the throwing knives? Maybe Father blabbed to Harkness about how strange it was. Christopher took another step toward the door. This time, Sheriff Townsend's voice stopped him. "Your face is healing nicely, Christopher," he said, tugging on his gunbelt.

Christopher temporarily had forgotten about the bruises and wondered what he did look like. Maybe the sheriff was experimenting with sarcasm, but Christopher smiled awkwardly and said, "Thank you, sir." He now stood one step from the door.

"What happened to you, if you don't mind my asking?" Townsend asked smugly. "You were pretty banged up a couple days ago?"

"Oh, I got kicked in the face by a horse," Christopher quickly lied as he stepped out the doorway. "Good evening," he called over his shoulder as he legs carried him away from the store. Yes, they knew he was lying, and they knew that he had something to do with his father's disappearance, but it would not matter in the long run. They would go after Deklan before they did anything to Christopher, and so what if they thought Deklan killed Christopher's father, or that Christopher did it, or that Christopher paid Deklan to do it? They operated on a far smaller timetable than they could possibly comprehend. They formed their little posses, called in their reinforcements, while forces beyond their reckoning had already prepared to take it all out of their hands.

*   *   *

The Rutlage house continued to hoard heat as the day progressed. That afternoon, looking for any reason to escape an environment that made his skin stick to his clothes and his clothes stick to the furniture, Christopher walked out to the barn to brush down the horses. *Is Emma still locked up in her second-floor prison?* he wondered. Not that he wanted to see her, in particular. On the contrary, the last thing he needed right now was another person to show up that needed saving.

He ran a brush over Thor for a few strokes before his peripheral vision picked up the tall, broad-shouldered figure looming in the doorway. Deklan only remained in the daylight long enough for Christopher to recognize him, then slipped into the shadows of the barn. Despite his size, cloaked in his standard black and dark gray clothing, Deklan could melt into the darkness. He only required a bit of shade, and maybe not even that; Christopher imagined a scenario where Lorenz could lie down on the ground and effectively pretend to be a shorter man's early afternoon shadow. In this case, the only reason Christopher could see him at all was because a fine, powdery dirt clung to him from his hat to his boots.

"They were talking about you today at Harkness's," Christopher announced while his arm mechanically ran the brush across Thor's gray back.

"I'm not surprised...," Lorenz said, then quickly asked, "Who's 'they'?"

"Harkness and the Sheriff. They'll probably be riding out to your house soon, maybe tomorrow."

Lorenz remained silent for a moment. "That won't be a problem. In fact, I'm surprised that it's taken them this long. Did you find out anything else today?"

Without turning, Christopher relayed his other two bits of related news: Mary claimed that she did not tell her mother what she saw out in the barn and Sheriff Townsend alluded to a possible future interview with her. Christopher considered telling Lorenz about Townsend's remarks about the bruises "healing nicely," but that probably constituted personal business. "That's it," Christopher concluded. "Things are so tense around here, it's hard to talk with anybody."

"They won't interrogate your sister," Lorenz assured the younger man. "Why would they? They've already made up their mind that I'm the one they want."

"You find out anything?" Christopher asked, adjusting the path of the brush to cover the course, dirty hair of Thor's neck.

"I finally got a look at Dr. Ferguson's house," Lorenz replied, folding his arms. Folding his arms amounted to Deklan's version of relaxing. He proceeded to explain that he searched the house and discovered the means by which the creatures removed the three bodies from the house undetected: a jagged, three-foot diameter hole in the corner of the cellar. Once Deklan removed the crate that covered it, he saw that the hole dropped about ten feet and became a tunnel heading west.

"I crawled into the hole," Deklan said, "and followed it for about a hundred feet, but I didn't have a light and eventually, a pile of dirt blocked the path."

Christopher gulped, visualizing the cramped, dark, hot tunnel, and hearing the echo of the clicking sounds. A shudder rippled through him, all the way to the tips of his brushing fingers. Thor must have felt it, because the horse turned toward his master and regarded him with his large, brown eyes.

"Truly amazing, the digging ability those things must have," Lorenz marveled, "although, the fact that our enemies would dig to escape is something I should have already considered."

Christopher stopped brushing and turned to directly look at the ghostlike man in the corner of the barn for the first time. He should have anticipated this happening sooner, but when Lorenz referred to the giant insects as "enemies," it meant that he considered this a war. Christopher didn't know the ramifications of that mentality, but it didn't seem like a good thing. "What are you going to do now?" he asked.

Lorenz unfolded his dusty arms and placed his hands on his hips, indicating that time for relaxation had ended. "Go home. Prepare for tomorrow. I need to find some of the live ants, the small ones. There were dead ones all over Ferguson's floor, but I need some live ones to find out how long they live."

Christopher's brow wrinkled. *The little ones were easy to kill*, he wanted to remind Lorenz, *just like real ants*. Squeeze them, and they pop. Lorenz probably had his reasons for wanting to know the lifespan of the little creatures, though, some strategic reason that Christopher might not understand. There were more important questions to ask. "Do you think they'll send a posse after you?"

The wide brim of Lorenz's hat rose and fell. "Eventually, after outrage overcomes fear. They'll bring numbers, too, as a show of force. I don't think they're quite there yet, but it's only a matter of time before something sparks and ignites the pile of tinder that's been laid down... In any case, I'm a big believer in preparation." He paused. Silences rarely felt awkward around Deklan, simply because they were the norm. This one stood out as an exception. Christopher could almost hear the dust settling to the ground. Finally, one of the horses sighed. "Be careful, Christopher," Lorenz warned. "The insects may decide to come after you. After all, they seem intelligent, and they know you know about them." Another pause, shorter this time. "I'll see you tomorrow."

Lorenz stepped out of the barn and disappeared into the lengthening shadows of the early evening, leaving Christopher chilled by the cryptic farewell. After a few moments in the barn without his capable protector, Christopher could feel the absence. The other horses, the ones without names, didn't need brushing, he decided. Somehow it seemed safer inside, with a layer of solid floorboards between him and the ground, than standing alone in the barn after dark.

The front door rattled shut behind him. His mother sat at the kitchen table, again. That was fast becoming her roost. She appeared deep in prayer, again; the flesh of her knuckles shown white from her wringing her hands so tightly, and tears seeped through her closed eyelids and trickled into the wrinkles dug into her face. With Lewis missing, she leaned on religion, the other pillar of her life, for support. Christopher walked toward the countertop on his left. "I'm going to make myself a sandwich," he announced, opening the cupboard to retrieve the dried beef he had purchased earlier. "Would you like one?"

"No," she said, coldly. She may have opened her eyes, but he didn't turn to find out. "Thank you."

Her refusal may have come from the fear that her son might poison her, a lack of appetite, or an attempt to commune with God through fasting. Christopher did not care what her reason was. He had enough to worry about, what with the looming threat to his sister, his town, and his life. He never respected Mother in the same way he had respected his father. Lewis may have been a demon, but at least he was his own demon. Agatha was content to let him decide right and wrong for her, blissfully following along the path he cut. She may not have been worthy of hate, but neither was she worthy of respect. Besides, she never comforted Christopher while he lay in bed with a flayed back and swollen jaw. She never wiped away his salty, stinging tears. Maybe he would drop some brown sugar in her oatmeal tomorrow and call it even.

Christopher gnawed on his sandwich while the golden sun dropped toward the horizon. Except for the scene at Harkness's, the day proved wonderfully restful. His attempt to play the dutiful son and mourn the passing of his abusive father had evolved into a mechanical ritual by mid-day, and he resigned himself to the fact that he did not care that Lewis Rutlage no longer walked on the Earth. Sitting on the fourth rung of the ladder to his loft, Christopher pressed his shoulders back. They felt lighter, unburdened by the weight of unwanted duty.

The masticated bread and sausage inched down his throat. He hoped that the next day would prove equally uneventful. Deklan himself had said the town's outrage had yet to overtake its fear. It seemed possible that things might calm down and sanity may yet prevail. He continued to hold onto this hope for another ten hours, until the screams started coming from the Braxton house.

*   *   *

Chapter Twelve

July 9, 1877:

Unlike the previous night, the cries for help that pierced the early morning hours evoked a sense of community spirit. Michael Jacobs heard the shrill screams coming from the Braxton house and reached the house before anyone else, but apparently, he forgot that Mr. Braxton had nailed plywood panels over the doors and windows. Jacobs banged on the front door while the screams continued to reverberate from the inside, until Joseph Cook showed up with an axe. It took the two men less than a minute to hack their way through the front door, but by then, the screaming had stopped and the four members of the Braxton family became the latest additions to the ranks of the disappeared.

The low rumble that had been building over the previous few days finally broke into the inevitable storm. The bulk of the sun had barely finished clearing the horizon when the town became a flurry of activity. Barricading themselves into their home had proven fatal for the Braxtons, so the rest of Liberty's populace, much like a cornered animal, saw immediate, violent action as their only remaining option. Men strode through the street, toting their long-barreled hunting rifles over their shoulders, speaking to one another in sharp, angry voices. Women herded their children into the church, and with the help of Reverend Skidmore, took to praying for the safe return of the posse that formed in the long shadow of Harkness's general store.

Christopher observed the action from his seat on the front steps of his mother's house. Harkness stood at the periphery of the group, locking up his store. He still looked like a grocer, even without his white apron. Were he not dead and buried, Christopher's father would have been there, too, probably standing in the middle of the cluster of people, organizing the rabble, like the pillar of the community that he was. Christopher's half-closed eyes perceived the hazy forms that scurried about in the streets, but his thoughts were slow to develop. The gravity of the situation finally registered when the overly gruff voice of Nelson Burns shouted, "I'm gonna kill that son of a bitch." At this, Christopher scrambled to his feet and ducked inside the house. He had only a short time to act.

Christopher rubbed the corners of his eyes as the door banged shut behind him. Mary sat at the table, fully awake, her legs dangling over the side of one of the oversized kitchen chair. Strands of steam rose up from the bowl of oatmeal in front of her. Even though she must have awoken the same time as Christopher, her eyes were bright and movements quick.

"Where's mother?" Christopher asked.

Mary carefully wedged a spoonful of oatmeal into her mouth at an agonizingly slow pace before answering. "She fixed me breakfast and left and went to the church with a bunch of other people."

Christopher nodded as he snapped his suspenders over his shoulders. This left him with a difficult, but ultimately resolvable situation: he would have to carry Mary into the middle of the hornet's nest. As dangerous as it undoubtedly was, he preferred that plan to leaving her at the house by herself. "Get dressed as fast as you can," he told her. "Then, meet me out at the barn."

Perhaps it was the tone he used, or the prospect of returning to the shadowy barn and its manifold horrors, but Mary shook her head, shifted her mouth into a frown, and started silently crying. The sniffling and the low whine grated on Christopher like a fork on a metal skillet, and he had to take a deep breath to compose himself. He slowed down his movements so that he could gently rest his hand on Mary's shoulder and say with as much serenity as he could muster, "Mary, I know you're scared, but you're going to have to be a brave girl if we're gonna get out of this. Now, you finish your oatmeal, throw some clothes on, and come out the front door." She looked up at him with her large, dewy eyes when he said this. "That's right," he continued, "you don't have to go out in the barn. Just come out front, and I'll be waiting. Okay?"

Mary nodded slowly, blinking a couple times every second. Her crying subsided into a few random sniffles by the time it took Christopher's heart to thud against his ribcage a few dozen times. Satisfied, Christopher dashed over to his chest of clothes and pulled on his remaining clean shirt. He would have to trust her word. If she failed to stay true to it, they would never make it to Lorenz's before the posse.

Christopher sprinted out the front door so fast that he was inside the barn before the front door banked shut. He threw a saddle onto Thor's back, deliberately mimicking Deklan Lorenz's efficient movements. When he reached for the bridle hanging from a nail on one of the supporting posts, Christopher paused. A minute splash of brown blood stained one of the lower boards of the middle horse stall. It was a small stain, a few drops worth, but it sent the sounds of a cracking skull and a lifeless body collapsing into the dust ricocheting through his brain. With a shake of his head, his senses returned, and he finished equipping Thor.

Christopher trotted to the front door with his horse in tow. Mary stood waiting at the top of the steps. Despite everything, she looked cute as a button in her favorite, daisy blue dress and white bonnet. She smiled so broadly that her brother had to look closely to see her fear. She was a brave child, he realized, more brave than he was at her age, maybe more brave than he was at fourteen. He placed his hands under her armpits, preparing to lift her onto the horse. Then, he paused for a moment as he peered into her red-rimmed eyes. "I won't let anything happen to you, Mary," he said. "You can count on that." Without waiting for a reply, he hoisted her onto Thor's back.

Thor kept an easy pace as he carried the Rutlage children out of town. Onlookers who bothered to notice them might momentarily have wondered where they were going, but so long as they did not appear panicked or run into their mother, Christopher anticipated a swift, safe exit. In the middle of town, the cluster of humanity that formed the posse had grown incrementally since he last saw it, like flies on a corpse. Sheriff Townsend had finally appeared and was in the process of deputizing the most recent additions to the bloodthirsty mob and telling them his master plan. For a second, Christopher thought he saw his father out there, but with a second glance, realized that it was just some cruel-looking out-of-towner.

Christopher made a quick count of heads as he passed. Twenty-five men assembled in front of Harkness's, each with so much iron strapped to his body that he jingled when he walked. "Guns are the weapons of desperate men," Deklan had said, or something like it. If that was the case, the light clink they made created a chorus of desperation. Some of the men, he did not recognize: temporary residents of The Liberty Tavern, no doubt, either moved to join up by the bountiful community spirit, or by the desire to go shoot something. They were not bad men, he reminded himself, just ignorant. Looking at them churned his stomach the same way the sight of Horace Buttice dangling from a noose did, back during the summer of '75 when the man's horse-stealing escapades came to an end. All those men, even Harkness, were not necessarily the worst kind of human, but they were rushing to their deaths, just the same. He had no idea how Deklan would kill them, but kill them he would.

Christopher glanced a final time before the corner of Reverend Skidmore's house obstructed his view of the mob. Emma's father was not amid the collection of grim-faced men, he realized. That's a shame; Christopher probably would have taken the time to rejoice in James Waits' death. It also struck him as odd. Waits always seemed exactly the sort of man who would lead a charge when he had his opponent outnumbered twenty-five to one. Maybe teenage girls were the sternest opposition he could face. Maybe Waits suspected something about Deklan Lorenz the others did not.

With the town at his back, Christopher dug his heels into Thor's flanks. Soon, Thor's powerful legs churned forward in a mechanical stride, fast enough that Christopher had to wrap his free arm around Mary to prevent her from bouncing off the saddle.

Twenty-five men. It would not be nearly enough.

*   *   *

Several times during the ride, Christopher had to check Thor's speed because the practice of holding the reigns with one hand and Mary with the other threw off his balance. However miniscule this lost time, it weighed heavily upon his mind. He checked over his shoulders constantly, expecting to see the hats of the advancing men bobbing over the horizon. Even if the posse had departed right after Thor left town, of course, it probably still lagged a mile or two behind. Christopher told himself this every time he looked, but it would not stop him from checking again a minute later.

Mary remained silent and motionless for most of the ride. Fear, not discipline, may have frozen her atop the saddle, but whatever it was, it made Christopher's job easier. He wasn't sure how many times she'd ridden on the back of a horse or left town and half-expected her to start calling for Mother at any moment, but the moment never arrived. She remained a life-sized doll in his arms. *Should I ask her how she is doing?* he wondered. *No, that might start her crying again.*

At last, like a latter-day oasis, the cluster of trees that surrounded Deklan's house came into view. Christopher leaned forward. "We're almost there," he whispered into Mary's ear. She gave no reaction one way or another, probably because she didn't know where "there" was. She didn't know Lorenz. She didn't know anything but that her brother said that everything was going to be okay. However convenient, her silence struck him as a bit eerie. Christopher made a mental note to talk with her when they weren't running away or getting shot at.

Amid the tall, thin trees, Thor trotted down the dirt path that led to Lorenz's single-story abode. Oh God... what if he isn't home? He could be out at Staley's... or crawling around in some tunnel under the town... or... Christopher pulled the horse to a stop in front of the porch. Lorenz emerged from the front door while his guests dismounted. Resting a gloved hand on the railing, his alert eyes scanned Christopher, then the surrounding area. Christopher lowered his sister to the ground beside him, suddenly feeling a bit like Paul Revere, one hundred years too late. "What's wrong?" Deklan asked.

"Posse's coming," Christopher said breathlessly, as if he had carried Thor from town and not the other way around.

Lorenz remained unfazed. His fingers drummed themselves against the railing. "How many?" he asked without looking at Christopher.

"I counted twenty-five while we were leaving town," Christopher reported. "I think we got maybe a two mile head start of 'em."

Lorenz nodded. "Take your horse to the barn," he instructed and disappeared into the house.

While Mary looked up at him with doe eyes, Christopher shrugged and led Thor toward the barn. This was no time to argue. He had decided days earlier to place his life in Lorenz's hands, and the time had passed for changing his mind. Mary proved equally obedient and followed in silence. When they reached the barn, Lorenz stood in the doorway. Christopher blinked and pointed back at the porch. "How'd you get—"

"I'll show you," he said and grabbed Thor's reigns from the boy's hands. Christopher's other hand wrapped around Mary's small, sweaty digits as he led her inside. The barn was roughly the size of the Rutlage family's, but its open window faced the still rising sun and bathed the interior in brightness. Somewhat surprisingly, Virgil did not stand inside the barn.

Lorenz half-dragged the reluctant, gray horse into position on a small, wooden platform. "Get on," he instructed the Rutlage children, and they stepped into position. They stood on either end of Thor when Deklan pushed aside a bale of hay, revealing an oversized hand crank. He stepped off the platform, and with a mighty heave, he rotated the handle counterclockwise and the platform began to lower. Christopher placed his free hand on Thor's back to steady him, and the horse replied with little more than a quiver.

The slow, mechanical descent ended after only seven feet and left them in a narrow, dimly lit passageway. Christopher shuffled off the platform, taking his charges with him, before Deklan dropped into the hole. Using an identical set of controls located on the tunnel wall, he rotated the handle clockwise and cranked the platform back into its original position.

Lorenz ushered them down the tunnel until they stood in the larger chamber, the one Christopher had visited earlier, although it seemed distinctly less crowded than it had the first time. The cannon was still there, and most of the boxes of guns, but several barrels of gunpowder were missing. In the center of the room, Virgil stood fully saddled and ready. Dante walked under the horse's stomach and barked and wagged his tail at Christopher's approach. The scene made Christopher wonder how much his warning actually accomplished. He also wondered how long Lorenz had been waiting for the attack.

Deklan turned toward Christopher with one of those fluid, rabbit-like movements. "Stay here until I come for you." He raised an index finger in the direction of a narrow tunnel Christopher had never traveled down. "Point your horse down that run and be prepared to move out. Once this starts, everything is going to happen very, very fast."

Mary could not stop staring at Deklan's face while they stood beside one another in the lantern-lit chamber. Christopher privately hoped his host did not notice, but supposed that Lorenz noticed everything. Although he never would have thought it possible, by now, Christopher had almost become accustomed to the sight, but looking through Mary's eyes, he once again appreciated Lorenz's fascinatingly ugly appearance. Of the entire crater that had once been a face, the most disturbing aspect had to be the beady, bloodshot, possibly useless eye. It stared out from its socket with an agenda of its own.

He stopped staring when Lorenz's glower smacked him fully in the face. Lorenz shook his head, turned his back to Christopher, and began to climb the steps that led up to the house. "What are you going to do?" Christopher asked, confident for once that his inquiry came at an appropriate time.

"I'm going to engage them, make 'em think they've got me in a stand-off." With that, he disappeared up the stairs, leaving Christopher alone with his five-year-old sister, two horses, a big dog, and a whole Hell of a lot of explosives. It seemed as appropriate a time as any to have that talk with Mary.

"So," Christopher began, squatting on one of the stacks of gun crates to bring him closer to Mary's eyelevel, "how're you feeling?"

Mary pushed some dirt around with the tip of her right foot and shrugged. "I'm fine," she answered, unconvincingly. Perhaps she lacked the understanding to experience the requisite emotion, or the vocabulary to describe a state beyond "scared."

Christopher waited for her to say something else, to finish the thought, but nothing else came. "It's okay to be scared," he assured her. "It's perfectly natural, but remember what I told you." He stared at her, hoping that she would look up and they could make eye contact, but she kept her head down. He finished the thought anyway, "I won't let anything happen to you."

"'Kay," she said, continuing to smear the dirt with her foot.

"You're just going to have to trust me, Mary."

"'Kay."

Christopher sighed, deciding to stop before the question of who actually needed the reassurance germinated in his mind. "I'm glad we had this talk," he told her and sagged backward against a larger stack of crates.

"Christopher?" she said, temporarily giving the dirt a respite.

"Yeah?" he said, quickly leaning forward. A storm swirled about him, and he needed to feel some control, to fulfill *some* function.

"Is Father dead?" she asked, staring at her brother with her big, brown eyes that had already taken on a sheen.

Christopher swallowed. He could have lied. It might not have worked, though, and it was important for her to trust him. She probably didn't want the "happy" answer, either. She just needed confirmation of something she already knew to be true. Christopher nodded. "Yeah... yeah, he is. I'm sorry you had to see it."

"I'm okay," she assured him, sounding more like his little sister at that moment than she had since the night in the barn. "I know he used to hurt you so bad and I thought you was going to die, and I miss him, but I'm glad he won't hurt you anymore."

She closed half of his waist in her arms, and Christopher patted her back. Even as the tears threatened to creep out of his own eyes, he could not help but smile. He had begun to fear for Mary's sanity. He was no doctor, but he knew of far less traumatic events that had unhinged people, and he knew that scars formed in childhood were the hardest to get rid of. Their embrace consumed a couple seconds before the shooting from aboveground interrupted it.

The first shots came from the inside of the house, exactly four in regular sequence, and were quickly followed by a deafening volley of shots from the outside. Glass shattered inside, and people shouted outside. It continued like that for several minutes, with the lone man trading shots with the small army. Christopher sat amid Deklan's honeycomb of tunnels, helplessly squeezing his sister against his chest, hoping to God that Deklan had some idea how to use a firearm.

Gradually, the sound of enemy shots grew closer and closer. Wave after wave of shivers ran through Christopher's body corresponding with each rifle report, and his bladder begged for relief, but he found some solace in watching the animals. Their only movement came from Dante's lolling tongue and the swishing tails of the horses. Still, Christopher's ego was not coddled by the fact that a five-year-old girl, a dog, and two horses showed more spine than him. During a rare moment of silence, the trap door flew open and hit the wall with a thump. Deklan scampered down the steps a second later, closing the door behind him. "Mount up!" he announced.

Christopher sprang to his feet and grabbed Mary under the arms. The adrenaline rush nearly caused him to toss her over the top of Thor's back. He quickly followed her up onto the saddle, managing to catch his foot in the stirrup on the first frantic stab. Once seated securely in the saddle and prepared to move, he glanced over his shoulder, where Lorenz stood bent over, lighting a length of white wire. A fuse. He was lighting a fuse. A rather short fuse, one that led directly into one of the barrels of gunpowder.

Lorenz saw Christopher staring at him with a look of slack-jawed ignorance pasted on his face, and after jumping onto the back of Virgil, he growled in exasperation, "Ride! We've got thirty seconds!"

Christopher dug his heels into Thor's sides, and the horse reared up high enough to scrape Christopher's head on one of the wooden beams running across the ceiling. His hooves hit the dirt an instant before he bolted forward. This passage proved a good deal wider than the one leading from the barn lift, and Thor accelerated into a gallop without mangling Christopher's kneecaps on the rocky walls. Christopher leaned forward and clutched Mary almost as tightly as he clutched the reigns. With a trickle of lantern light shining down the tunnel, all he could do was squeeze and worry. Would it be fast enough? Was the tunnel free of debris that might cause a speeding horse to misstep? How long was the tunnel? Thoughts like these kept him from considering the number of people that he knew who were about to be blown apart.

The light grew dim as Christopher used his thighs to squeeze his mount's midsection. If they did not exit the tunnel by the time the powder blew, a fireball would come roaring after them. And what about that thirty seconds? Thirty seconds from when he lit the fuse or thirty seconds from when Lorenz yelled, "Ride!"? Pulling Mary tightly against his chest, Christopher tried to count the seconds in his head but lost track after "five."

Another couple horse-lengths and the tunnel fell into complete darkness, but only for a second. The tunnel floor shifted into an upward slope, and the sunlight shining in from the other end of the passage acted like a beacon for the horse and its passengers. Thor dashed across the hundred-yard stretch and broke into the daylight, running full tilt across a flat stretch of grass. Christopher's eyes canvassed the scenery, and only after he was absolutely certain that an armed militia did not lie in wait did his breathing return to normal.

Virgil shot from the tunnel an instant later, carrying his black-cloaked rider. Christopher glanced over his shoulder, refusing to pull Thor to a stop until Deklan did so. Lorenz gave a fierce pull on Virgil's reigns, causing the horse to rear on its hind legs a good fifty yards from the exit. The mouth of the tunnel turned out to be a hole dug in the side of a hill, recently cleared of the scraps of foliage that had camouflaged it. Virgil's forelegs tapped the ground a few times as he turned to face the tunnel, issuing a mighty sigh in the process. The instant the puff of air left his nostrils, a cacophonous explosion shook the earth.

Dirt, wood, and bone were all indiscriminately engulfed by the fireball that blasted skyward from the former patch of trees that belonged to Deklan Lorenz. It might have been visible for ten miles in any direction. Gone was his expensive furniture. The chickens. The barn. Gone was the recently repaired fence. Gone was the only existing picture of his wife.

The magnitude of the blast held Christopher spellbound. It was like a pocket of thunder had erupted from the earth. At first, he thought Deklan stared at the man-made cloud as well, but then realized that the former assassin instead gazed toward the darkened exit. After a few long seconds, Dante raced out of the hole with a steaming cloud of dust and soot at his heels. The dog veered left in time to narrowly avoid the gray jet of hot, dirty air.

Thor and Virgil, however, were not quite far enough away to avoid the jetting cloud that bellowed from the subterranean tunnel and engulfed everything in the area. The steaming air wrapped itself around the spectators, leaving them slightly singed and covered in a thin layer of ash. When the cloud dispersed to the point where Christopher could safely open his eyes, Deklan was again covered in a ghostlike gray, just as he had after crawling under Doc Ferguson's house. Twenty, maybe twenty-five more feet to the north, and they would have avoided the cloud altogether. It remained Deklan's only miscalculation of the day. He had brought everyone safely out of a life-or-death siege, with the exceptions of a few chickens and a pig.

Similarly, Sheriff Townsend and his all-too-eager posse made a single mistake on that day, but it proved to be their last. Simply put, they should never have engaged Deklan Lorenz in a life-or-death siege.

*   *   *

"Why did you bring your sister?" Deklan asked as the dusty trio eased its way toward town.

Mary glanced up at Lorenz when he referred to her, but remained silent. The leather creaked as Christopher shifted in his saddle. "Well, Mother was gone, and I didn't have a lot of time. I also figured she'd be safer here, with you protecting her against a bunch of normal humans, than back in town with nobody to look after her, and... God knows how many insects crawling around underground."

Lorenz grunted. "It was a wise choice," he admitted off-handedly, "but remember this: I am not responsible for her, or for you, for that matter. I am an attacker, not a protector, and, circumstances being what they are, making the kill is always my top priority."

Christopher nodded. A morbid announcement, to be sure, but it allowed him to ask the question he had wanted to put forth ever since the dust settled over the crater where Lorenz's house once stood. Christopher licked his lips that still tasted like ash. "What happened up in the house when you were shooting at the posse?"

Lorenz took a deep breath and proceeded to recount the progression of the shootout from what he could see out the shattered windows. The invaders first tried to fan out and use the semi-dense foliage surrounding his house as cover. Before they traversed half the wooded area, four horses and their riders had fallen into separate, camouflaged, ten-foot-deep holes. Undoubtedly, the fall mortally wounded the horses and, at the very least, seriously injured the men. Deklan had dug the holes years ago in anticipation of an attack. Only days ago, he had set the snares that incapacitated three more riders.

Lorenz took the moment to break from the story. "Understand, Christopher: I hate breaking the legs of horses as much as I hate blowing them up, and if I could have conceived of a way of separating the horses from their riders, I would have done so. Losses like those are… unfortunate, but acceptable. In a situation like this, you really can't lose sight of the big picture." Christopher nodded, even though use of the term "situations" implied that there were other circumstances that resembled the one they were in.

Deklan's voice lost its detached monotone as he resumed the story, telling of how the remaining riders converged upon the main path, quickly giving up on the disastrous notion of a multi-front attack. He likened the shooting the men as they came down the path in single file to shooting fish in a barrel (even though Christopher didn't know why one would shoot fish, much less when they are packed into a barrel, he got the point). He gave names, too, in his cold, unwavering monotone. Names of men etched into Christopher's past: Abe Harrington, who used to walk around town humming "Old Dan Tucker." Lorenz shot him in the face. Lukey Byrer, who, a couple Christmases ago, started the habit of buying enough lollypops for every child in town and leaving them in a jar on Harkness's front counter for them to pick up. Lorenz's bullet carved his throat open.

Before Byrer's still-warm body choked out its last breath, the remaining men started emptying their weapons into Deklan's house. Most had dismounted by this point and were inching forward on their hands and knees. Deklan did not know how many of these men fell prey to his remaining booby traps because he never looked. By this point, he knew that he would have to use the gunpowder, so he no longer cared if the bullets he fired actually struck anything. He simply kept his head down, extended the barrels of his revolvers out the window, and blindly fired. With his chambers empty, he checked their position a final time, deemed it close enough, and dashed for the cellar. He finished by saying, "Even though we didn't check the blast sight for survivors, anyone caught on my property is either a casualty by now or well on his way."

In front of Christopher, Mary was staring at the passing ground. "Sorry you had to blow up the house," Christopher said, "what with the furniture... and the photographs being in there and all."

Lorenz's craggy face flinched as he deduced the implication of the statement. "I don't need photographs to keep her face fresh in my mind," he said. He looked down at Dante, who diligently pranced along beside Virgil. "I got my dog out, that's all that matters." The dog, as if knowing he was being spoken of, glanced up at his master, reverently.

"So what now?" Christopher asked, trying to keep up with Lorenz's evolving strategy. They were not equal partners, but they were partners nonetheless, and an exchange of information is never a bad thing between partners, especially when your partner has proven himself capable of reducing a considerable chunk of perfectly good acreage to rubble.

"Our jobs've been made easier," Lorenz announced, even though he meant "my job." "Not only did we significantly decrease the number of armed males in Liberty, we've also decreased the number of potential insects..." His voice trailed off, and he got a strange, distant look in his eyes, as if spying the town already.

"Wait a minute," Christopher began, not sure whether his partner was even listening. "I'm confused. Isn't the town more defenseless against the insects now more than ever?"

Deklan scoffed (it sounded forced, because he wasn't a natural scoffer), but his sight remained on something not present. "Those ignorant cowards wouldn't have stood a chance. You could have laid out the Staley's corpses and told them your entire story, and they still wouldn't have believed or understood what was going on. If they didn't kill you, they probably would've packed up and left town by sundown today, and that's something we just can't have."

Christopher bit his lip, trying to follow the thought, tired of sounding like an idiot. Finally, he gave up and shook his head. "Why not?"

Lorenz sighed, pulling his gaze away from the invisible town and looking like a non-drugged version of himself again. "Think about it, Christopher: we're isolated out here, but what if the bugs reached Kansas City? You mentioned that you saw Edgar Staley in Ferguson's office suffering from the symptoms before he totally changed. That means they need a day or two to incubate, just like a regular infection. Even if the people that fled weren't infected, they could be carrying the smaller ants in their belongings. If those things reached the city, they would have thousands… thousands of people to infect and there is no way they could be stopped." Lorenz looked down at Christopher, maybe in attempt to detect whether or not his fourteen-year-old brain properly appreciated the gravity of the situation.

"So what can we do?" Christopher asked, his voice jumping up an octave. He could only conjure vague images in his head. A city of thousands, where the citizens were covered in sticky, amber cocoons. A city where the deafening clicking sounds echoed through the barren streets. What if it didn't stop with one city... Christopher shut down the thought. He had only recently accepted responsibility for determining his little sister's fate; he wasn't ready to determine the fate of the world.

"I know the solution," Lorenz assured Christopher, scratching his dirty, angular chin with his gloved right hand, "but first... first I'm going to have to find me some ants."

*   *   *

Chapter Thirteen

They spent most of the day in a tree-lined area next to Niles Creek, waiting for the sun to begin its downward descent. They only had a little bit of water and hardtack to subsist on, and Mary complained like a five-year-old about the lack of selection. Christopher probably exchanged more words with his little sister during that time than he did with Lorenz, although Deklan did take a few minutes to explain to Christopher about Thor, the God of Thunder, and the basics of Norse mythology.

Finally, under a darkening sky, the pair of horses approached the squat outline of Liberty when Lorenz announced, "We're going to split up, rendezvous at the Braxton house." Anticipating a "why" from Christopher, he added, "You said Harkness had his suspicions, but he's dead, and I highly doubt anyone is convinced that we're working together. So, you can make it there safely in the open, and it's easier for me to make it there undetected alone." He waited for Christopher to nod before pulling on the left-hand reign and spurring his horse in that direction. Dante followed.

When Lorenz's shadowy form bounded out of earshot, Christopher tilted his head toward Mary. "How are you feeling?"

Her face was drawn, but it was not a terrified expression. It was the same expression she wore the time Christopher explained where beef came from, one tinged with disgust and confusion. "Why did Mr. Lorenz say those things about Mr. Byrer?" she asked in her squeaky child's voice. "He bought peppermint sticks for me one time."

"It's complicated," Christopher told her, then decided that she deserved at least some elaboration. "Mr. Byrer and some other people in town blamed Mr. Lorenz for some things he didn't do, and they were going to hurt him." She responded with a tight-lipped nod, but Christopher decided that, until Lorenz presented her with some candy, Mary would continue to privately champion the late Lukey Byrer over him.

When Christopher rode away that morning, the main street of town had been a flurry of pacing and shouting vigilantes. On his return, the only person visible from the street was the silent sentry posted outside the church's front door. Most of the town probably sat crowded into the enormous white building, but because it stood over a hundred yards away, Christopher decided against investigating. On either side of Main Street, stationary covered wagons stood in front of a few of the dwellings. None were hitched to animals, but that alone kept them from being travel-worthy. Some were fully loaded, their owners waiting for word from Sheriff Townsend before fleeing in one direction or another. As Lorenz predicted, Mary and Christopher reached the Braxton house unimpeded; at that point, a circus could have paraded through the center of town because no one was there to stop it.

Christopher pulled Thor to a stop behind the silent, mostly boarded-up house. Deklan had already arrived, somehow, and stood lurking in the thick shadows between the house and the barn, standing between his trusty horse and dog. Christopher did not bother to ask how he had arrived so quickly, because when dealing with Lorenz, he learned to take the small impossibilities for granted.

Holding Mary's hand, Christopher wordlessly followed Lorenz around to the front of the two-story house. A gigantic, jagged hole hovered in the middle of the door. Even though Joseph Cook had chopped the hole into creation with an axe earlier that morning, to Christopher's eyes, it looked just like a dark mouth inscribed with jagged teeth. Lorenz stabbed a leg into the hole and ducked inside without disturbing his hat. In the darkness, he motioned for Mary and Christopher to follow. Christopher checked the sky, where steely gray thunderheads had begun to gather. The eerie silence, combined with the increasing wind, chased his sister indoors, toward her proven protector. Thankfully, she remained oblivious to the fact that a family of six had lost their lives hours earlier in the very building she sought refuge.

Hot, stagnant air pressed against Christopher's skin as he stepped through the gaping hole in the door, a product of the lack of ventilation. Sweat began to leak from his pores almost immediately. The Braxtons' first-story rooms were modestly furnished, but Deklan gave them no more than a cursory glance. He spent a couple minutes slowly creeping across the main room, listening for the sound his boots made on the wooden flooring, before straightening up. "They don't have a cellar," he announced. "Check under the beds for holes. If you find one, tell me immediately." He disappeared into the kitchen, which lay adjacent to the mangled front door.

Christopher nodded, doubting he would have opted for any other strategy. His legs carried him to the far side of the house, toward the parlor. If an open prairie provided an abundance of imaginary hiding places, this gloomy den created even more. Benches, closets, cabinets... the bugs could be anywhere. Mary took short, choppy steps to keep up with him. It was a flattering gesture, but if there were any bugs lurking in the house, he'd be about as much protection as a bed sheet in a tornado. He stopped in front of what appeared to be a walk-in closet. "Keep still," he told Mary and slowly pulled the door open. The inside was choked with coats on hangers. The far side of the closet stood only two feet away.

Christopher crouched and started to crawl forward when Deklan's low, flat voice stopped him. "Christopher," he announced. "Come here."

Christopher found Lorenz standing hatless in the kitchen, staring down at a gaping hole at the base of one of the floor-level cabinets. The hole looked narrower than the one Deklan had described at Doc Ferguson's but left plenty of room for a grown man to squeeze through. It was eerily symmetrical, though, especially compared to the jagged, man-made hole in the front door. The only thing that kept it from being a perfect circle were the edges, which sported uneven ridges, as though pairs of large, strong mandibles had chewed them into shape.

Deklan silently pointed over Christopher's shoulder. Christopher turned to find a hand-held lamp on the table behind him, in front of a row of empty, glass canning jars. He fetched the lamp and extended it toward Lorenz. "Hand me one of those mason jars, too," Lorenz instructed, while receiving the lamp, "and a lid." Christopher handed the items over and backed against the counter. His eyes widened. Where was... Mary brushed against his thigh as she inched closer. Christopher's eyelids relaxed, but he still roundly cursed himself for losing track of her.

Lorenz set his hat on the countertop and gingerly set his fragile, glass objects by the rim of the hole, and without word or hesitation, lowered himself into the darkness. When he had disappeared completely, his gloved hands extended over the rim and brought both lamp and jar into the hole with him.

Loose dirt ground beneath Deklan's boots as he grunted and shifted himself into a suitable position. The grunts came every few seconds and did not sound frantic or pain-induced, so Christopher held his position against the Braxton's kitchen counter. The air seemed twice as thick as the air outside. Sweat that his recently laundered shirt failed to absorb trickled down the length of Christopher's arms. He had never set foot in this house before. Even if he had, though, he wouldn't have recognized it; this wasn't a human dwelling anymore. He didn't feel like a trespasser so much as he did an undertaker, rifling through the belongings of the dead. His eyes shifted from the hole to Mary to the kitchen doorway every few seconds. So much could go wrong. So much...

Mary's oversized eyes turned toward him while he was in mid-gaze, and he forced a smile.

Lorenz finally returned after a minute that seemed like an hour. He pulled himself out of the hole, crawled out of the cabinet opening, and stood up, not bothering to dust himself off. Empty jar in hand, he gave a status report. "The hole goes about seven-feet-deep before it heads east," he explained. "It gets narrow awfully quick. I think that's where they tried to collapse the tunnel... maybe when the locals started chopping through the door. They must have run out of time, though, because the job was only half finished. I couldn't possibly squeeze through, but..." His voice trailed off.

Christopher stopped staring at the empty jar and looked up. "You want me to go through?" he asked in disbelief. Just standing in the stuffy kitchen made him feel like he was inhaling a pound of sand with every breath. Just the thought of wedging himself into a dirty tunnel threatened to cause his lungs to collapse.

"Not you," he said, cutting short Christopher's panicked thoughts. He set the empty jar on the counter. "You're not a lot smaller than me."

Christopher breathed a sigh of relief. *Thank God... wait a minute.* Lorenz's eyes had locked onto the smallest member of their group. "Oh no," Christopher said firmly and stepped in front of Mary. "Can't you just dig out the blockage?"

Lorenz shook his head, shifting his stare to Christopher. His eyes lacked any semblance of amusement or patience. His stare was like a colder version of Lewis Rutlage's. "To get it out of the tunnel, we'd have to bring it up to the kitchen. That would take hours," Lorenz informed his young partner. "I don't know how long we have, but we don't have hours."

"I don't care," Christopher told him, somehow refusing to break eye contact with the former assassin. "You are not going to send my five-year-old sister into that tunnel."

Lorenz's uneven eyes refused to blink. He seemed reluctant to say this next part, but he did. "I could make her go, you know."

Christopher swallowed, feeling the familiar sensation of the abyss opening up before him. "Then you're going to have to," he returned.

Mary's small sweaty hand squeezed his own, and Christopher broke his ocular standoff with Lorenz long enough to regard her. "Christopher," she said, almost whispering, "I'll do it. It's just ants."

Christopher's head whipped back toward Lorenz. He started to mouth word "no," but Lorenz cut him off. "She'll be down there for less than a minute, just long enough to get some of those ants," Lorenz assured him, with all the confidence of a man explaining that the sun would rise tomorrow. "I'll go after her and shoot anything that comes."

"That's a terrible plan," Christopher insisted.

"But it will work," Lorenz countered.

Mary released Christopher's hand and stepped out from behind the human shield he had formed. She giggled, a genuine-sounding laugh that her brother had not heard her utter in what seemed like a year. While it did provide a much-needed break in the tension, Christopher found the laugher a bit unsettling. Either the stress had unhinged her, or she trusted Lorenz more than he did at this point... more than she should have.

Mary continued to giggle when she told Lorenz, "You can't shoot ants, silly!" It was the first time she had spoken directly to the frightening man.

His face twisted into its version of a smile, threatening to crack the mass of scar tissue that formed his face. "Ah, but you've never seen me shoot, sweat heart." He let out an awful, hoarse laugh and extended a gloved hand to Mary. Still giggling light-heartedly, she walked the rest of the way around Christopher and took Lorenz's hand. Christopher's mouth had fallen open, but he stood frozen in the gloom, helpless as a kitten. Maybe Lorenz could shoot the ants; Christopher could actually believe that... What he had come to question, though, was whether Lorenz would bother wasting the bullets to do so.

Lorenz grabbed a dishtowel from the counter, shook it out, and wrapped it around Mary's head like a turban, making certain to cover her ears. He wrapped it tightly, but not so tight that she cried out. His manner seemed almost playful, but it was so obviously contrived. It reminded Christopher of his father: only showing affection when he could use it as a tool. The man's gigantic hands gently patted Mary on the top of her head. By the time this sight registered in Christopher's numbed mind, Lorenz was steering her toward the hole. The empty jar still sat on the counter top. Seeing it granted Christopher the ability to move.

Lorenz dropped into the hole, holding the lamp. Mary crept her way toward it until the gloved hands appeared and lifted her into the void.

"You forgot the jar," Christopher called toward the hole.

Some grinding, shifting sound reverberated up to the surface. So did Lorenz's voice. "Just crawl down and back," he instructed Mary.

"You forgot the jar," Christopher repeated. He went to the edge of the hole and looked over the rim. Lamplight filtered around the top of Lorenz's misshapen head, but he never looked up. "You forgot the jar," Christopher snapped for a third time.

"Keep it ready," Lorenz replied in a low, even voice.

Christopher shifted into a squatting position. In the hole, a revolver slid from its holster. Seconds later, Mary shrieked and nearly sent Christopher's heart through his chest. He fought off the urge to jump into the hole or start digging at the floorboards. Instead, he dropped to the edge of the hole and yelled, "Get her out of there!"

Lorenz desperately tried to do just that. He wedged his massive frame as far down the tunnel as he could, almost crushing the lit oil lamp in the process, as he reached into the crevice where Mary had disappeared. "Just crawl to my hand," he firmly instructed. "Don't touch the towel. Just crawl to my hand." His flat, even voice wormed its way through Christopher's throbbing head. How could he be this calm sending a five-year-old to her death? How could he be this calm unless he didn't care?

Christopher's instincts urged him toward the hole, maybe to jump down and try to pull her out himself. It was useless, as useless as the instinct that told him to dig through the floor, but it would have felt better than sitting by the edge of the hole, clawing at his face or his forearm or whatever other section of flesh presented itself. Diving in was worse than doing nothing, though, because diving in ruined Mary's only chance for survival. Only Deklan could get her out now. Christopher just had to sit, and stare at the light dancing up from the hole, and hope that when he emerged, Lorenz would not shoot them both.

At the bottom of the hole, Lorenz slowly retracted his right arm from the tunnel. Mary's screams sounded different, quieter. Her panting breaths echoed up to him, and Christopher stuck his head so far into the hole that he nearly tumbled in. When he righted himself, he could see Deklan's hand dragging Mary's leg behind it, along with the rest of her. He pulled her from the tunnel like she was a flailing cat held by the scruff of the neck. Even while she tried to cling to her savior, Lorenz extended his arms and sent Mary up to the surface, to where Christopher could pull her to the Braxton kitchen. After Christopher hoisted her onto the floorboards, brother and sister acted in direct opposition to one another. She frantically stretched her arms toward him, trying to latch onto an available part of his body like a drowning victim, while he slapped and scraped at the ants dotting her arms and neck with equal conviction.

With a grunt, Lorenz hefted himself out of the hole, but instead of joining Christopher's assault on the unholy invaders, he contentedly used his gloved hands to sweep stray ants toward the mouth of the hole and into the lidless glass jar. His manner was gentle, as gentle as it had been when he coaxed Mary into the hole. Christopher barely took notice, though. Any dark fleck of dirt, mole, or scab on his little sister's person was met with a pinch or a swat. After lifting up her long, curly hair and examining her neck a second time, Christopher's breathing began to return to normal. His chest still heaved as Mary threw her arms around his neck and sobbed. He tried not to embrace her too tightly but found it difficult.

Amid a chorus of creaking floorboards, Lorenz pulled himself to his feet, immediately replaced his hat atop his head, and walked around the kitchen, crushing the remaining ants under his boots. His back faced the brother and sister when Christopher noticed that, at some point during the commotion, the towel covering Mary's head had shifted upward an inch or two, exposing her right ear. His left hand snapped upward and readjusted the towel, then continued to hold the shaking, sobbing five-year-old against his chest.

"We need to get out of here," Lorenz announced, looking down at the frightened pair with his perpetual glower.

Christopher nodded, and this welcome news seemed to calm Mary enough to stand. She wrapped all ten stubby fingers around Christopher's left hand as they walked to the front door. "Where are we going?" Christopher asked from the fractured doorway as a bolt of lightning split the distant sky. It had yet to begin raining, but the air had the cool, energized feeling about it as though the moisture collected in those steely gray clouds would break loose at any moment. Christopher reached his free hand toward a set of hooks to the right of the door and removed a pair of raincoats for his sister and himself. The Braxtons would no longer need them.

"The school house," Lorenz answered as he stepped through the jagged hole to the outside. "I need some time to observe the ants."

Christopher paused from sliding his arm into the raincoat. The mention of the building conjured images of one of his sexual encounters with Emma, images of legs and breasts and soft, soft skin. He shook his head and forced the picture from his mind. "I thought you said we didn't have hours?"

Lorenz glanced over his shoulder, his stark form outlined by the violent, cloud-choked sky. "We didn't have hours to spend getting the ants because I might have to spend hours observing them. Besides, we have time to kill now, at least until the worst of this storm blows over."

Christopher swallowed the lump in his throat at Lorenz's choice of words. "Time to kill..." That was one thing Lorenz always seemed to have time for... and Christopher was the one who invited him to this particular party. "Why can't we just stay here?" he asked, his weary voice coming out in a whine.

"Jesus Christ, Christopher!" Lorenz uttered in exasperation as his hands wrung themselves. *So it is human...* "Do you really want to have this conversation right now? We're in the middle of town, and if you didn't notice, the bugs don't seem to have a problem getting in!"

Christopher nodded, aware that Lorenz would not wait for his approval, and guided Mary through the cavity in the door and into the outside. The gusting wind plastered Christopher's hair back as he made the few steps out to his horse, and another blast threw him off balance during his initial attempt to mount Thor. Once he sat atop his horse and they were moving, Mary huddled against his chest for protection against the elements, and whatever else awaited her.

*   *   *

Lorenz led them into Main Street at a fast walk as the sky continued to spit. Mary still had that dishtowel wrapped around her head, somehow making them look more conspicuous than they already were. Fortunately, the streets remained empty. Just to be safe, Christopher gingerly pulled the towel free and tossed it to one side, allowing the wind to fling it down the street. Thor dropped his head and trudged ceaselessly through the stiff wind until they had reached their destination.

A pair of squat, wooden buildings comprised the schoolhouse. The smaller of the two was used as a stable with room enough for five horses, to accommodate the teacher and children who were old enough to ride but who lived too far away to walk. Lorenz and Christopher dismounted and entrusted the welfare of their mounts to the watchful eyes of Dante as they forced the stable doors closed and rushed toward the schoolhouse. With a deafening clap of thunder, the downpour commenced before they made it halfway.

A lock barricaded the schoolhouse doors, but a bullet from Deklan's revolver made short work of it. Once inside, Lorenz removed his soaked, gray overcoat, threw it on the second row of benches, sat down in the first row, and began staring at his jar of a dozen or so ants, seemingly oblivious to anything else. Christopher helped Mary extract her arms from the raincoat. He had nothing dry to cover her with, but despite this, by the time Christopher had slid out of his own coat, Mary already had stretched out atop one of the hard, wooden pews against the wall and shut her eyes. Within a minute, she was issuing long, regular sighs. Christopher stood over her, shivering, as her tiny chest rose and fell. The stress of the day had nearly overwhelmed him at times; he could only imagine what it must have felt like to a five-year-old girl.

Christopher slumped into the first row of benches behind Lorenz's raincoat. A chalkboard sat on wheels at the front of the building, the same one that was there when he and Emma... Emma again. He should really –

"I saw you replace the towel," Lorenz said from across the schoolhouse. His voice remained even, normal.

Christopher expelled a weary sigh, lacking the energy to formulate a lie. "You don't know when it came off."

"True," Lorenz conceded, his eyes fixed on the jar, "but neither do you. As long as there is a possibility they got to her, I'll keep my eyes open."

"You won't touch her," Christopher told him.

Lorenz finally turned and looked across the darkened room at his young accomplice. "I already told you, Christopher: the mission always comes first. I've got a war to wage, and every war has casualties."

Casualties. Christopher barely knew the word. "I'll kill you first." The second the words left his mouth, he wished he could take them back.

Lorenz gently pushed the jar of crawling, four-legged ants a few inches further down the bench and stood up. He took three even strides toward Christopher before stopping. A nearby thunderclap caused Christopher to flinch, but Lorenz stood still as a statue. He removed one of his two Colt Peacemakers from his gun belt, turned it so that its handle faced Christopher, and extended his arm. "It's loaded," Lorenz informed him. "I don't carry unloaded guns."

Christopher stood up, and reluctantly reached out and took the weapon into his hand. He had not expected the weight and nearly dropped it. If he squeezed the trigger, the recoil would probably send him through the wall. Still, he summoned the strength to stand and, with elbows bent, pointed the gun at the former assassin's chest. "I don't want to kill you," Christopher lamely offered. The barrel twitched and trembled as though a palsied hand held it.

From the moment he had threatened Lorenz, Christopher second-guessed his every word and action from the last few days. The evening he had ridden to Deklan's and told him a story about giant, mutant insect wearing human clothing, he not only expected Lorenz to be a hard man, he had counted on it. The job required someone that was brave, calculating, ruthless even... someone that would do whatever it took to emerge from this situation victorious. Deklan Lorenz, though, turned out to be a completely different form of human. He was willing to sacrifice morality and basic human decency in his adoptive quest.

"You might as well do it now instead of later," Lorenz said with a shrug. "It's really very simple: if one of them survives, they all survive. If she got infected, she's one of them." Christopher's head turned to his right, to the pew where Mary slept. *Please, God, let her stay asleep.* Standing with his chest exposed, Lorenz continued, "If she's one of them, I'm going to kill her. So make your choice."

The sting of forming tears stabbed Christopher's eyes, but he pushed the sensation away. He had cried in front of his father, but he refused to cry in front of this man. *God... damn it,* he thought, covering his face with his cold, empty hand. *Be a man, you little baby! You stupid, weak son of a bitch!* Handing the gun back to Lorenz butt first, Christopher's incisors sunk into his lower lip to stop it from quivering. "I can't do this without you," he admitted, feeling as though he had aligned himself with the Devil.

Lorenz pulled the revolver back as if wielding a feather and dropped it into his holster. "You're right, Christopher," Lorenz told the exhausted youth. "And that's why you shouldn't feel guilty for involving me: because I'm the only one who can win this war."

Lorenz turned his back to Christopher and sat down to continue his ant-watching vigil. Christopher lifted his head. "Why'd you have to send her into that hole?" he asked in a shaky voice.

"Why'd you have to bring her along?" Lorenz returned.

Christopher had never felt more helpless than when Mary was screaming down under the Braxton floorboards. She was out now, but the feeling did not go away. In some ways, she was still crawling around down in that hell, and no one could pull her out. The sensation of drowning overcame Christopher, and he didn't know what to do about it. Lorenz was right. He was always right, but Mary was... he had to take care of Mary. She couldn't be infected. She couldn't be, because if she was, whether he decided to... end her life or let her live, Christopher could never live with himself.

On the other side of the windowpane, storm clouds glided across the sky, ushering in a premature midnight. Why couldn't a bolt of lightning make its way into the schoolhouse, Christopher wondered, and strike him down where he stood? Why couldn't an army of lightning bolts reach down and like fingers of God and destroy this entire, accursed town?

A final statement continued to ring in Christopher's ears long after Lorenz finished speaking it. Seated on the other side of the pew, intently watching his miniature army swarm over one another, Lorenz's voice cut through the silence. "Don't be weak, Christopher," he said. "Don't be like the rest of them."

*   *   *

CHAPTER FOURTEEN

Built shortly after the first school burned down, Liberty's schoolhouse stood a touch over two hundred yards from the main cluster of buildings that comprised the town. An empty, pancake-flat stretch of land separated the two points. The squat building's distance from the center of town was the primary reason Lorenz had decided upon it as the most secure place for the damp trio to catch their collective breath.

He deduced that since the bugs mainly traveled underground, it would take them hours, if not days, to expand their tunnel network this far away from the center of town. The plan was not foolproof, however, as one soon realizes that the bugs were not confined to their subterranean lifestyle, it merely constituted a preference. Their locomotor capabilities easily allowed them to traverse the distance from the middle of town to the schoolhouse, as Deklan and Christopher should have known from their deadly confrontation Old Man Staley's sheep pasture. At some point during the dark, rain-soaked evening, several of them must have crawled out from a hole in the ground and shambled toward the tiny pair of buildings on the eastern edge of town.

Shortly before the attack, Christopher lay flat on his back atop one of the pews that lined the wall, staring at the gently pitched ceiling. Mary lay silently on her side several feet from his head. Her chest rose and fell with the rhythm of the rain on the roof, which had eased from a monsoon to a mere torrential downpour. She had not moved since the first minute of their arrival. Deklan had not spoken in at least two hours, and a light hiss of breath made Christopher realized that at some point, the older man had fallen asleep sitting upright.

Christopher kept his eyelids peeled back. If the thoughts of ants and their larger brethren were not enough to keep him awake, the thoughts of what Lorenz might do to Mary on the offhand chance she had been infected kept him on the verge of shaking. All things considered, though, he felt safe in the building, and the time spent there ultimately proved restful, from a physiological standpoint, at least.

Christopher rubbed his numb face with an equally numb hand. He had to stay awake. Lorenz might do away with both of them if he dozed off. He might not be able to do much to stop Lorenz, but at least he had to try, dammit. The small-caliber gun still rested in his pocket. He could remove it right now and shoot Lorenz in the head. The thought disappeared just as quickly as it had materialized. Christopher didn't have it in him to kill another human being. Lorenz had already proved that tonight. Maybe someday he would "mature" to that point, when time and circumstance would warp him into something unrecognizable. Life has a way of –

A muffled, scratching sound interrupted Christopher's silent desperation, and sent him bolting upright. The pew creaked under his weight as he swung his legs off it and onto the floor. The scratching continued as Christopher crept toward the center of the schoolhouse in attempt to isolate its source. Directly in the middle of the room, he stood above the probable source of the sound. He eased to one knee and lowered his head, almost to the point where his ear grazed the wooden floor, when the front door smashed open.

Splinters of wood flew in every direction, as if someone had driven a train into the school. Christopher sprung to his feet and wheeled. A creature that used to be Joshua Tyler, widowed father of two, stared at him with glossy black eyes. Christopher had not yet even counted him among those missing. Still dressed in a pair of tattered overalls, Tyler stood in the doorway amid the downpour long enough for Christopher to get a good look at him. The last stages of the metamorphosis had set in. Only stray strands of hair remained atop his head. His skin still wore a flesh color but had begun to take on a hard, armored look. Most unsettling of all, small mandibles had punctured his skin and sprouted from either side of his mouth.

Tyler stared with a pair of large, opaque eyes as his waxy chest heaved like a pair of bellows, but he made no move. Two feet to Christopher's left, the section of the floor that had produced the scratching sound exploded upward and outward, and one of the fully-formed bugs popped its head out of the hole. At that point, the shooting started.

Christopher stood frozen in his tracks. Not because he was terrified, but because he knew that if he stayed in one spot, none of the bullets would hit him. The eerie calmness that he had become familiar with over the past several days settled over him again. After all, he had Deklan Lorenz with him, and when it came to killing in the service of his all-important mission, Deklan did not make mistakes. Christopher still believed this. Certainly, he questioned the moral implications of some of the man's actions from time to time, but not whether they were effective. Had Lorenz taken the Rutlage children to the schoolhouse in expectation of finding a safe haven, that would have constituted a mistake. However, he had taken them to that location because he deemed it safe merely in comparison to the other locations in town. Much like his country home: the school wasn't siege-proof, just siege-impaired.

Lorenz probably anticipated an attack and formulated a strategy the instant he stepped through the schoolhouse doors. He probably went through his day-to-day existence expecting to be attacked, having developed the habit long before he saw the first of the giant insects. As detrimental to his emotional health as that might have been, it aided his cause and those around him: nothing ever caught him off-guard because he never let his guard down. His unhesitant reaction to this well-engineered sneak attack stood as a testament to this.

The bugs might have had as many as three full seconds to kill Deklan. The crack of the splitting wood that signaled the breach of the front door roused him from his light slumber (Christopher assumed that he must have slept light; people that constantly anticipate ambush probably don't allow themselves to drift into the deepest recesses of sleep). He awoke fully aware of his surroundings. By the end of the second second, Deklan had launched himself to his feet and spun toward the front door, although the appearance of a second target in the middle of the floor must have slowed him fractionally. During the third second, Deklan took a short hop backwards, presumably to bring both targets into the scope of his peripheral vision, as his hands shot toward his holsters.

Lorenz wore his two gun belts in a backward, crisscrossed fashion. Christopher had rarely seen this done, and deemed it an inefficient style. In this instance at least, Lorenz proved him wrong. Deklan crossed his arms as he reached for his guns and kept them crossed at the forearm, with his left hand gun pointing at the right target and vice versa. This technique kept his arms in front of him gave him a more effective kill-radius than extending his arms away from his body. By the time the third second ticked off the imaginary clock, whether Lorenz's opponents knew it or not, the fight had nearly finished.

Thunder echoed through the spacious schoolhouse and smoked rolled from the hot gun barrels. Christopher covered his face with his arm but kept his feet welded to the floor and trusted his protector not to miss. Not satisfied with shooting each target once in the face, Deklan proceeded to empty half his chambers into the bugs before uncrossing his arms and emptying the rest of the chambers into their midsections. In the time it would have taken most men to line up a shot, Lorenz had blasted six holes into his opponents. Some may have called it overkill; he called it "being thorough."

When each weapon clicked to an empty chamber, the only visible movement in the room belonged to the smoke curling out of the muzzles of his Peacemakers. Christopher turned toward Mary. She was awake, probably from the time the door broke. She also was still alive, but remained motionless, breathing slowly from her upright position. Her eyes locked onto something on the floor, next to Christopher's feet. Without looking down, he knew what held her attention: ants, crawling out of the bullet holes in the exoskeleton of the fully formed bug that burst through the floorboards. The instant she started to scream, Christopher hurried over to her. Out of curiosity, he stopped several feet away and checked the body of Joshua Tyler. Only streams of dark, red blood ran out of the holes Deklan had blown through him. The sight reminded him of the limp form of his father, dangling over the rump of Deklan's horse with a bag on his head. All Christopher could think was: *You got lucky, Father.*

Christopher turned to comfort Mary and left himself blind to the attack of the bug dashing through the front doorway. So far to Christopher's left that it was barely visible, the tail of Deklan's coat flipped back. The results of his movements were becoming all too predictable: a familiar whistle, then a crack split the air, and the bug crashed lifelessly into a bench directly in front of Christopher. The only surprise lay in the fact that not one, but two throwing knives jutted from the side of the horror's skull. Lorenz's quick action managed to stun Mary into silence.

The late Joshua Tyler's appearance initially shocked Christopher, and one minute later, he remained dazed. He actually had to perform a quick count of the corpses to fully register what had just happened. The clink of metal hitting the floor made him turn toward the door, only to find Deklan relieving his guns of their spent shells and dropping the brass cylinders to the floor.

Christopher scanned the corners of the darkened building. He actually wanted more action at this point. Out in the open, Deklan dispatched of the man-sized creatures as fast as Christopher dealt with the ant-sized ones. The former assassin had succeeded in dropping their number by three in the time it took Mary to awaken from her nap, and Christopher hoped the rest would rush in the front door so that they could finish the whole dastardly ordeal in a matter of minutes. Unfortunately, General George Armstrong Custer was a human, and after a couple seconds, Christopher accepted that no more bugs were coming. He turned back toward Mary, who remained silent atop her bench as she stared at the ants swarming across the floorboards in spellbound horror.

Lorenz stepped to the door and gazed into the driving rain as his nimble fingers automatically fed bullets into the chambers. Christopher took one more look over at Mary's drawn face before following his gaze. Barely visible in the distance, half a dozen hazy forms ran toward town in a rigid, marionette gate. No humans moved like that, even if they wanted to. They were nearly out of sight by this time and definitely out of pistol range. "Are we going after them?" Christopher asked. His voice seemed to ricochet around the schoolhouse for several seconds.

Lorenz shook his head and flicked his wrists so that his revolvers snapped closed. "Never catch them on foot," he said, re-holstering his weapons, "and they'd disappear by the time we got to the horses." He pointed back at Mary without actually looking at her. "Get your sister and let's go."

Christopher crushed innumerable insects under his shoes as he took long strides toward Mary. The crunching sound brought him some degree of satisfaction, but it was a small degree. After all, it only took one intruder to make it past a person's defenses, and they had thousands. Some of the ants had begun to climb the legs of the bench, and when Christopher gently lifted his little sister up to his shoulder and marched over to the door, it could not have been soon enough for her taste.

In the doorway, close enough to the sheets of falling rain that they received some splash-back, Lorenz started to walk outside until Christopher tapped him on the arm. The assassin stopped and looked down at him, slightly annoyed, and Christopher hooked a thumb over his shoulder. "What about your jar of ants?" he asked.

"They're all dead," Lorenz stated matter-of-factly, leaving Christopher to discern whether this was a good or a bad thing.

Christopher remembered the raincoats and grabbed them from off the first pew. "So?" he asked. "That's good, right?" Deklan Lorenz had shown himself to be a man of many talents, but clear communication did not number among them.

"After an hour in the jar, they started dying," he explained, curtly. "By ninety minutes, they were all dead, and there was enough air in that jar to last them days." Clearly, he wanted to move. He did not even take the time to remove the throwing knives that jutted from the fallen insect's head.

"They could've been in the tunnel longer than that," Christopher offered, practically begging for a glimpse at the larger picture for once.

Lorenz shrugged off the statement. "Only five or six hours. No rider from this town could make it to another town in less than eight hours."

Christopher blinked. Mary remained motionless as a sack of potatoes against his right shoulder. "Another town?" he asked. "What does that have to do with anything?"

"Plenty," Lorenz assured the younger man and stepped into the rain. The rain fell with enough force to bend the brim of his hat. "I'll explain later." With no other options available and eager to wash any remaining ants off his person, Christopher shifted Mary onto his left shoulder and followed him into the wetness.

*   *   *

The horses trudged their way through the downpour, back to the Braxton house. The dirt street had transformed into mud almost instantly, and the horses' hooves made a chorus of suck-plops as they shoved into and pulled out of the oozing ground. Christopher shielded his eyes from the rain and scanned the ground for insect footprints but found nothing; with all the mud, he might as well have been staring at an unplowed field. When the horses lumbered into the Braxton's watertight barn, a wave of relief passed through him and he felt a bit more optimistic. It took him several moments to identify the feeling as absurd. Circumstances were almost exactly as deadly and hopeless as when they left, but... at least they were out of the rain? While tethering their mounts, Christopher turned to Lorenz. "What are we doing back here?"

"We aren't safe anywhere," he replied, "but at least here we don't have to worry about any of the townspeople interfering."

Christopher nodded as he approached the doorway and the numbing rain. The logic seemed sound enough to his tired mind, but a dormant idea again dawned on him: why not simply tell the citizens of Liberty what they were up against?

The raindrops pelted the three figures as they stalked back from the barn. The notion of warning the town continued to preoccupy Christopher, but he waited to ask until they had climbed through the hole in the door and were shaking the water from our raincoats. Lorenz stared in silence as Christopher spoke and continued to stare when the boy had finished. Christopher's eyes shifted around, anywhere but at Lorenz. "Look," Christopher explained, "between the holes and the bodies in the schoolhouse, we have all the evidence we need, so the blame won't fall on you. Plus, think how much easier it would be to flush out the bugs if the town was evacuated."

Lorenz sighed, but it sounded more like a hiss. "You've got a good heart, Christopher," he said, wearily, "but it makes you naive." He held up the palm of his gloved right hand. "Show them the bodies of the insects, and they'll think I conjured the bugs through black magic. Humanity as a whole is superstitious and cowardly. And let us also not forget that we blew two dozen of their husbands and fathers into oblivion earlier today."

We, Christopher thought. *So now it's "we."*

"As for evacuating the town," Lorenz shook his misshapen head. "No one leaves until the bugs are dead, because we don't know who's infected and who's not." Deklan clenched his right fist tightly. "If even a single ant reaches Kansas City alive, they can't be stopped, and I will not allow that to happen."

"But how do we even know who's been infected and who hasn't?" Christopher protested, noticing that Lorenz continued to eye his sister like a wolf stalking a lamed lamb. She still seemed fine to Christopher, but it's possible that he wanted to believe it so badly that he forced himself to not notice any subtle changes. Besides, Lorenz probably noticed things normal humans didn't. "With everyone shutting themselves up inside their houses, we don't even know who's missing."

"That's part of the problem," Lorenz agreed, rubbing the back of his neck, "and a part I intend to rectify quickly." He scanned the dining room, then marched over to the mantle and with one hand, snatched the shotgun that hung above it. "Take this," he instructed and handed Christopher the over-sized weapon. The shotgun's weight nearly carried Christopher to the floor with it. "There are some old shells in the top right drawer of the bureau over there," he said, pointing to a set of drawers in the corner. "Load the gun and take it and your sister upstairs. I'll return for you in two hours. If anything moves up those stairs that isn't me, shoot it." He took a step toward the front door.

"Where are you going?" Christopher asked, holding the shotgun like it was an animal carcass. He clearly remembered his less than auspicious first attempt to use a lethal weapon against a living being, as well as the grim warning that followed it. This particular firearm could do ten times the damage of a throwing knife, and he could barely lift the barrel to point it at anything.

Lorenz paused in front of the hole in the Braxton's front door. "I don't have time to explain now. I need to get everything in position before the rain stops." Christopher set his jaw. The frustration must have shown, because Lorenz set a heavy hand on his shoulder and stated, "You're just going to have to trust me, Christopher." He waited for Christopher to reply with a lame nod before stretching one leg through the hole and adding, "I need to use your father's horses and wagon. He has a cover for it, doesn't he?"

Christopher nodded, unable to look at him. "Yeah, go ahead, he doesn't need it anymore." Lorenz paused for a moment, his massive frame half-inside and half-outside, and Christopher thought he might say something else, maybe some additional words of comfort. Instead, he nodded in agreement and disappeared into the curtain of falling water. No matter; Lorenz's attempts to comfort tended to leave a greater hollowness behind them than the empty air.

Boots stomped down the front steps and splashed once when they landed in the muddy street. After that, the only sound came from the raindrops drumming on the roof. Alone in the house, the shadows expanded and began to suffocate Christopher. "C'mon," he said to Mary and let her take his hand. He led her toward the steps that ascended to the second story, and with his free hand, Christopher dragged the gun behind him as they climbed the stairs.

The second story of the Braxton house consisted of two bedrooms, one on either side of a short landing at the top of the stairs. The room on the left contained three beds, obviously the room of the three boys. Christopher attended school with the eldest of the Braxton boys for a year, but he was several years older than the late Kenneth Braxton and barely knew him. Still, it struck him as almost sacrilege, fortifying a position inside the sparsely furnished room that once housed three boys and now only held their three beds and three dressers. It was like desecrating a mausoleum.

Mr. and Mrs. Braxton must have once occupied the room on the right. It consisted of a pair of single beds and contained slightly more ornate furnishing than the boys' room. The additional accoutrements consisted of a large mirror above one of the squat dressers, a gas lamp on the other dresser, and an ornate, silver crucifix on the wall overlooking the beds.

Standing in the small, square hallway, Christopher checked both rooms a second time. He dragged Mary and the gun to his right, into the parents' room, for the simple reason that if it got any darker outside, the gas lamp might prove useful in protecting them from enemies, both real and imagined. Mary followed him over to the window on the far wall. The Braxtons had neglected to board up either of the second-story windows, perhaps deducing that whatever the mysterious menace threatening them was, it couldn't make it through half an inch of plywood or climb eight feet up the side of the house. *Oh, well*, thought Christopher.

So much the better. If worse came to worse, he and Mary could escape out the parents' bedroom window.

First, they had to get situated. Christopher set the shotgun on the floor and planted his feet against the wall and his back against the bedpost. Mary provided token support, but he still had to lean into the solid wood bedframe with every ounce of his body weight to budge it. After nearly thirty seconds of struggle, the bed lay far enough away from the wall to allow about three feet of clearance. "C'mon back here," he said to Mary, breathlessly nodding toward the gap between the bed and the wall. Mary obediently scampered into this fortified area as Christopher situated the shotgun atop the mattress. The heavy barrel sagged downward into the feather cushion, so he stuffed a pair of pillows under it to keep it propped up and pointed at the open doorway. They weren't *safe*... because the bugs could crawl under the area where the barrel was pointed and kill them, or tear through the wall and kill them, or rush in with overwhelming numbers and kill them... but they were *safer*.

Christopher removed a match from the box next to the lamp. After a few attempts, he lit the lamp and placed it on the nightstand next to the bed. Then, he leaned against the wall and wearily slid down it until his backside hit the floor. It took almost two minutes of still silence before Mary started to shift about uneasily. "How long do we have to sit here?" she whispered.

"A couple hours," he assured her in a normal speaking voice, even though he didn't believe his own words. Lorenz said two hours, but something was bound to happen that would alter the timetable. His gaze remained fixed on the empty doorway. "Go to sleep if you can."

"Christopher," she said, still whispering, "I was just asleep, remember?"

"Then don't," he told her. *Don't be terse with her,* he reminded himself. *She's been through a lot.* Volunteering to enter that hole was heroic, even if she didn't know all the dangers it involved. Hopefully it wasn't for nothing. The fact remained, though, that Christopher was now solely responsible for both of their lives. Even though they did not plan to stay in the house long, he took his task very seriously. Even though he never slept during their two hours in the schoolhouse, his alertness reached new heights while in the Braxton bedroom. He sat with his eyes locked onto the empty doorway, his ear searching for any sound other than raindrops and breathing.

While silence may have been Christopher's ally, it was not Mary's. Her age may have prevented her from fully grasping the situation or from summoning the patience to deal with it. All she knew was that talking made her feel less scared, so that became her sole ambition. "Do you think we'll ever see Mother again?" she asked from her cross-legged seat on the floor.

To his credit, Christopher remained patient with her. One has to prioritize resources in an emergency, however, and he could not spare the effort needed to humor her. "I don't know," he told her tonelessly. "It's hard to tell. I hope so... but I would probably guess not."

Mary did not cry when she heard this. Though she did not possess Christopher's desire to rid herself of their parents, only limited affection existed between Mary and the elder Rutlages. She may have felt similar to a prisoner informed that the guard that had fed her for the last five years had received a sudden transfer. Mary simply nodded at the prospect of never again seeing the only maternal figure she had ever known, probably agreeing with her brother's assessment. Her next question, though, disturbed Christopher far worse. "Is Mr. Lorenz going to kill me?" she asked.

Christopher blinked and finally detached his gaze from the doorway. His eyebrows drooped and his lips opened, but no words came out. Five-year-old children should never have to ask a question like that, and he felt like he had utterly failed to instill any sense of security in her. Mary looked up at him with wide, glistening eyes that made Christopher want to pull her close and tell her that nothing would ever happen to her as long as he lived. This statement would be a lie, of course. If Lorenz deemed his little sister a threat, he could break Christopher in half and put a bullet in her head without breaking a sweat. Mary stared up at her brother for several seconds, until he slid an arm around her and gave her a gentle squeeze. "Nothing's going to happen to you, not as long as I'm alive," he swore to her. She returned his embrace, and her tiny body did not tremble in his arms.

A bolt of lightning split the sky, and Mary flinched and looked out the window an instant before the thunder arrived. The rigid movement looked almost natural, barely worthy noting had one not seen its like before. Christopher had seen such a movement, though. He saw it several days ago, when Old Man Staley twitched his way out of Dr. Ferguson's office.

*   *   *

She's one of them, said a voice in his head.

No. Your mind is playing tricks on you, replied another.

That went on for a while.

No time pieces adorned the walls of the Braxton bedroom, but something close to thirty minutes passed from the moment Christopher noticed his sister twitch to the moment when he recognized a critical flaw in their defense: he had neglected to load the shotgun. A cold sweat erupted on his upper back and trickled between his shoulder blades. On the positive side, it was the first time in half an hour that he had thought of anything but that his little sister was going to die a horrible death. Christopher eased to his feet, trying his best to keep his face serene and his manner nonchalant while his heart hammered against the front of his ribcage. "Mary," he said, concentrating on breathing normally despite the weight of her bewildered stare falling on him, "wait here, I'm going to check on something downstairs."

"But Mr. Lorenz said –"

"I know what he said," Christopher mumbled in reply. He floated toward the doorway like a man in an opium-induced trance, preparing to step from his world into the unknown. The profound numbness permeating his bones prevented Christopher from engaging in the name-calling and self-berating that normally would have accompanied such a potentially fatal mistake. Nausea crept through the entirety of his being and settled in his stomach and throat. His body demanded nothing less than a total retreat into the corner where it could curl up into the fetal position, but his brain had a different idea. *Get those shotgun shells*, it instructed, *as fast as you possibly can*. Christopher compromised between the two messages, and walked slowly and deliberately toward the staircase.

His soaked clothing still clung to his damp skin as he stopped at the top of the stair. He could tell how much he could blame the rain for his chills, though. The blackness hovering below him might as well have been the pits of Hades. His eyes attempted to convince his mind that something moved down in the darkness, waiting to kill him the instant he left the bottom step, but Christopher willed himself down one creaking step after another.

He knew he must have looked like a zombified idiot stiffly marching into the gloom, but he had more pressing concerns than maintaining a socially acceptable appearance. Halfway down the staircase, the weight of his bladder seemed to increase by forty pounds and blasted lesser thoughts from his mind.

His eyes gradually adjusted to the diminished light, and when his foot drifted off that last step and slammed against the floor, Christopher realized that the darkness of the lower level was not as absolute as he had expected. Every time lightning flashed, the light would penetrate cracks in the window barriers and the hole in the door and illuminate slivers of the downstairs. The shadows would regroup instantly, though, and his eyes would require another second or two of adjustment. Each time a section of wet clothing bunched up on his clammy skin, he imagined a three-fingered hand were closing around his wrist or ankle, or calf muscle, gently pressing before clamping down with the vice-like grip he had felt on two occasions. Christopher kept his feet moving forward only by telling myself that if he went forward, he might die, but if he gave in to his fears and ran back upstairs empty-handed, both he and Mary would certainly die.

The motivational strategy worked well enough, because Christopher soon found himself standing on the other side of the room, rummaging through the desk Deklan had indicated earlier. He plunged his hands into the nearly vacant desk drawers, and after a pair of blind stabs, his fingers danced over the surface of the box of shotgun shells. If the drawers had been littered with more items, the search may have used up several more precious seconds, and the delay may have proved lethal. Judging from the bedroom furnishings, though, the Braxtons appear to have been minimalists. Christopher wrapped his hands around the box as though it was the Holy Grail, turned, and marched back toward the staircase and his sister.

Halfway to the staircase, a rustling sound bounced around in the darkness behind him. Given his hearing difficulties, Christopher could not pinpoint its origin or even the nature of the sound, but something that wasn't his footsteps and wasn't the thunder definitely made a noise. *Run! Run! Run!* his mind screamed, in the event that its source was something more dangerous than hysteria. His feet would not move, though. They had rooted themselves to the wooden steps while his lungs slowly closed off the available air. He remained perfectly motionless, as though snakes and not mutant insects pursued him.

Christopher listened with all the focus he could muster. Neither his imagination nor the echo of his movements caused the sounds. A very real, scraping emanated from under the floorboards. He had heard it slightly over an hour before while standing in the schoolhouse. Fear flooded his brain and sent him sprinting up the final half-dozen stairs. The breath of his phantom pursuer caressed the hair on his neck the entire time.

He flew into the elder Braxtons' bedroom, scrambled over the bed, and all but collapsed against the wall. His shaking hands fumbled the box of shells open as his eyes shifted from the box to the doorway every other second. A few shells bounced out of the box and rolled under the bed. He broke the shotgun open. The metallic click signaled to every human or humanoid within earshot that the idiot inside was armed with an empty weapon. Mary stared, mouth agape. "You forgot to load the gun?" she asked in utter amazement. Christopher nodded and tried to ignore the pale, wide-eyed features that betrayed the fact that his sister's confidence was draining from her.

This is all your fault, the voice in his head yelled. *You idiot! You stupid, stupid, ignorant, incompetent moron!*

Christopher tried unsuccessfully to load the first of the barrels, but the shell slipped out of his clammy, sweat-layered hand and dropped onto the mattress. He took a deep breath, eyes flitting from gun to door and back, and made a second attempt. This time, he got it right. He used his thumb to jam shells into both barrels, snapped the gun closed, and cocked it before repositioning it on the pair of pillows. No signs of life immediately appeared, and Christopher began to wonder if his imagination had played tricks on him. He needed only wait a matter of seconds for confirmation.

Sweat crept into his eyes by the time the first of the giant insects stuck its head around the corner. The red, black-eyed head remained visible for only an instant before disappearing again. It must have been a former citizen of Liberty, but since it had no clothes, Christopher could not hazard a guess as to even its sexuality. *Just assume its James Waits*, he told himself, *that'll make it easier to shoot.*

Christopher rotated the gun barrel a few inches to the right of the door. The skin of his index finger pressed lightly on the metal trigger. He badly wanted to fire through the wall. It might not be the best strategy, but blasting something would give him some feeling or release, no matter how small. Only two shots resided in the gun, though, and given how long it took him to load the weapon the first time, those were probably the only two shots he would get. The bugs probably knew this. They probably knew enough about shotguns and teenage boys to try to get him to waste one or both of the shots. Christopher slowly lifted his quivering finger off the trigger and vowed not to shoot until they stepped fully into the room.

Mary knew enough to not speak or move to touch her brother. Had she done either, he might have wasted a shot. Instead, she remained huddled in the corner with her hands clutching her knees, a terrified, porcelain statue.

The marionette dance at the top of the stair picked up speed. Two or three of the insects roamed the hallway. Christopher could not determine their exact number because they continuously scuttled from one side of the doorway to the other, taunting him with their stiff, macabre contortions. Sometimes a single insect traversed the space, firelight from the lamp reflecting off of its opaque eyes. Sometimes, they went in a pair. Christopher tracked them with the barrel of the gun but kept himself from pulling the trigger. The standoff persisted for several agonizing minutes, with the bugs refusing to enter and Christopher refusing to fire. He secretly held onto the hope that Deklan would return to the scene at any second and kill the whole cowardly lot of them.

Ultimately, the bugs broke the stalemate. The cavorting in the hallway apparently had a twofold purpose: to get Christopher to waste a shot, or failing that, to lull him into relaxing. He did neither.

The invading bug was in the process of prancing across the space of the doorway, like it and its brethren had done a dozen times before, when it made its move. It braced its back leg and launched itself one step inside Christopher's sanctuary before a single thunderclap flung it back into the hallway. The force of the shot sent the gun leaping off the mattress and shoved Christopher against the bedroom wall.

After recovering his senses, Christopher slung the weapon back into position atop the pair of pillows and shifted himself back into an uncomfortable crouch. Only then did he realize that his initial shot had struck his intended target squarely in its midsection (thorax?). The creature lay sprawled on its back, spread-eagle in the little square of hallway, at the edge of the lamplight. It looked as though jackals had chewed on the corpse for a week. Shotguns, it seemed, took little more than general aiming to be effective. If guns were the tools of desperate men that Deklan had claimed, Christopher decided that shotguns were tools of the desperately unskilled.

Christopher basked in his success for a brief moment before realizing that he and Mary's dilemma had worsened, not improved. By blasting open the creature's exoskeleton, he had released a legion of ants that were rapidly advancing on the bed. Christopher stood up. The odds of surviving an escape through the window were bad. The odds of surviving an exit down the stairs were nonexistent. He picked up the shotgun and rammed the barrel through the windowpane.

Most of the glass sprayed out onto the roof. Some fragments tinkled to the floor. Christopher ran the metal barrel around the rim of the window to clear it of the largest remaining pieces and turned to his little sister. Mary gawked at the approaching ants. "Go out the window," Christopher told her, and actually might have seen a wave of relief sweep over her. She gingerly scrambled out the window and into the downpour. Keeping the gun leveled at the doorway, Christopher squatted down and extended a leg out onto the roof. He paused, half-in, half-out of the house, hoping one of the remaining bugs would make a run into the room so he could take a last shot and thin their ranks further, but they failed to cooperate.

Once out on the roof, Christopher squinted through the torrent of rain at the hazy outline of the roof. The tilted surface shot earthward at a sharp angle, but from the edge of the roof, the drop looked to be only ten or twelve feet. It could be worse, he thought, a lot worse. In seconds, his clothes clung to his body like a second skin. The rain-soaked shingles provide slippery footing, and his first step out of the house nearly became his last. He put a hand on the roof and steadied himself despite the driving rain and the enormous shotgun he still clutched. Mary had latched onto the windowsill and did not move a muscle.

Christopher glanced inside. One of the bugs had crept into the bedroom. Christopher righted himself and hoisted the gun into a firing position. Before he could take aim, though, the bug scampered back into the hallway. Christopher pushed a clump of soaked hair out of his face and realized how fortunate he was; pulling the trigger from his position might have landed him on the ground with a broken neck.

He turned back to Mary, but kept one eye on the doorway. "On the count of three, take my hand," he instructed. He had to yell to force his voice through the cacophony of beating raindrops. "We'll slide down to the edge and I'll lower you to the ground." She hesitated, but ultimately gave him the nod he sought.

After he counted "three," Christopher heaved the cocked shotgun through the broken window with all his might. The gun sailed, barrel-first, past Mary and through the window, like a dying, metallic eagle. Christopher hoped the shotgun would strike an object and fire its last shell, and it did exactly that. The report of the gun echoed through the room like a thunderclap. Whether the blast hit anything could not have meant less to Christopher; he just wanted a two-second head start. Sister-in-hand, he started down the side of the roof.

Amid the deluge, they descended in a controlled slide. Trust is a wonderful thing; it allows five-year-old girls to perform acts they never thought possible, even when their big brother has no clue what he is doing. Christopher's foot hit the ridge running around the edge of the roof, and he almost pitched forward onto his head.

Nothing clicked or crawled its way to the window, so Christopher eased down to his backside. He grasped the ridge and gave Mary a little tug, nodding in the direction of the ground below. She lowered herself down on her hand and knees and crept to the edge, but then stopped and looked at her hand. "There's glass down here," her barely audible voice announced. "I think it cut me." Christopher clenched his teeth. A second, more forceful tug sent her over the side.

Mary gave a shriek of surprise but did not fight her brother. The weight of her petite body nearly tore Christopher's arm out of socket, and her wet hand nearly slipped from his wet hand, but he held fast until her fall stopped. Her momentum carried her to Christopher's left and back to the center before he released her hand. She dropped a few feet, plopping softly in a mud puddle. Her hands and knees were cut and her already soiled dress became even filthier, but she was alive.

Christopher paused at the edge of the roof. Was that the sound of the front door opening? With his hearing and all the extraneous noise, it could have been nothing more than his imagination, but it was enough to send him over the edge without a second thought. Only the shotgun kept him alive back in the Braxton bedroom, and as far as he was concerned, the ground could not meet him nearly fast enough.

His feet hit the muddy ground and slid out from under him. Christopher rolled on his shoulder and sprung to a standing position if he had merely tripped during a Sunday stroll. The moment his hand closed around Mary's, however, there was nothing leisurely about the way they sprinted away from that house. He had decided on their destination from the moment he broke out the glass of the bedroom window, so in the direction of the church they ran.

When the shotgun blast perforated that bug in the upstairs of the Braxtons' house, Christopher realized just how vulnerable the invaders truly were. Though only fourteen years of age, he had not only survived encounters with the creatures on three separate occasions, but also killed one of them using a weapon with which he was hardly proficient. Maybe twenty-five of Liberty's best fighting men had gone to a fiery grave, but surely the rest of the men in town could match the efforts of a young boy. Only their lack of information held them back, and Christopher vowed to rectify that problem.

Warm candlelight streamed from the church windows, beckoning Mary and Christopher as they slogged through the mud. He needed to get to the church before anymore of the citizens of Liberty were infected, and before Deklan Lorenz did anything rash.

*   *   *

CHAPTER FIFTEEN

Christopher banged the butt of his fist half-a-dozen times on the locked double doors of the church. "Open up," he yelled, just in case the people inside decided to shoot through the door. The right-hand door shuttered as someone unbolted it, then opened. The cautious faces of Davey Fredrikson and Stewart Korschot peered out and glanced over the two Rutlage children. Both men carried revolvers that they pointed at the ceiling. Both had been left behind by the posse that morning. Davey was excluded due to his youth (only eighteen months Christopher's senior) and Stewart because he was an admitted atheist and could not be trusted, until now, apparently.   The two amateur guards looked at one another, uncertain as to how to proceed. Finally, Davey, with his skeletal shoulders and wispy mustache, nodded toward Stewart's balding head and thick jaw, and they stepped aside to allow Mary and Christopher's rain-soaked forms to enter the building without a question. Reverend Skidmore stood at his lectern and droned his way through one of the cheerier passages of the Old Testament, but now, even as he continued, every pair of eyes in the building fixed on Christopher's mud-caked visage. The church was barely half-full, he noticed, and it wasn't just because the explosion out at Lorenz's had incinerated a healthy portion of the town's adult male population. There were a lot of people missing. Some had no doubt fled early on or lived far enough away from the town proper that the troubles missed them altogether. Many others, however, must have been lurking in a tunnel somewhere under the ground, changed, or stuck to the tunnel wall, waiting to change. It was hard to say how many.

Dozens of people still occupied the pews, though, constituting a larger audience than Christopher had ever spoken to. The architecture of the church involved raised platforms in both the front and back of the church, giving him a nice speaking elevation with which to address the assembly. He took a deep breath. It was his chance to speak, and humiliation be damned, he would take advantage of the situation. "Ladies and Gentlemen," Christopher began, his voice trembling only slightly, as everyone in the church cast their eyes upon him. Maybe he should have started with "Citizens of Liberty," or something less formal. Undaunted, he continued, "I have seen with my own eyes the forces threatening our town." He searched for a euphemism suitable for what he had to say next, but none came to mind. "They are inhuman creatures, monsters that look like giant insects."

Dead silence followed. Not even the expected ripple of whispers made its way through the crowd. The words sounded incredibly stupid to his ears, a mockery to the recently deceased, and Christopher could only imagine how they must have sounded to the frightened, angry congregation. An idea dawned on him: blame bandits, get someone to view the insect corpse he had left at the Braxtons', and only *then* tell them the truth. Unfortunately, the best ideas tend to arrive far too late. The confused, hard faces stared up at him as if he had just told the worst joke in the history of mankind.

Christopher stood at the back of the church, shivering and alone. Even Mary took a half step away from him. No one knew what to say at that point, least of all, him. Any sort of outburst would have provided a welcome respite from the wall of silence bearing down on him. Maybe Reverend Skidmore could use it as an allegory. An "Oh yeah? Prove it!"

would have been nice, even. When someone finally did speak out, though, he began to miss the wordless glares.

"You are the monster!" the person screeched in a voice so shrill that one could scarcely tell if the voice belonged to a male, female, or human. "You and your devil-spawned master, Lorenz!" Christopher searched the see of wide-eyed faces, expecting to see Mrs. Dean, the biggest religious zealot in town, but instead discovered that the voice belonged to his own mother, the second biggest religious zealot in town. She wore an entirely black outfit that made her look like some variety of mythical witch. It also succeeded in turning the drawn flesh of her face several shades paler.

Christopher bit his lower lip. She probably didn't have a solid foundation to work with. She probably just adopted the popular demonization of Lorenz and threw Christopher on the pyre for good measure. Still... publicly denounced by his own mother. What was the point in saying anything else? Granted, he could have delivered the news more skillfully than he did, but Deklan was right from the start: they couldn't accept any truth that didn't conform to what they wanted to hear. While Christopher came to this unfortunate realization, his mother continued to rant. She pointed a bony finger at her son and hissed, "He gave his soul to the Beastmaster and sealed the pact with his father's own blood!" This proclamation received the gasps that it sought to elicit. This was a crowd ready to hear about all-powerful cosmic entities and their agents on Earth, even if they did find the concept of giant insects absurd.

Christopher eased a step closer to the door, but stopped when Davey Fredrikson slid behind him. Korschot was a cooler head, but Davey probably wanted to prove his metal now that he'd jumped up twenty-five or so rungs in the alpha male pecking order. He was groping for a reason to shoot Christopher in the back of the head. If someone in the front row had not shouted, "Ants!" as loud as they did, Davey might have done just that.

Christopher never could divine the exact principle the bugs utilized to generate the four-legged ants that he encountered so many times. Was it voluntary? Could they increase the rate of production? It was clear, however, that somehow, when they reached their final state of metamorphosis, the bugs generated the tiny creatures internally. By whatever means they accomplished the feat, however, it must have taken several bugs working a long time and with great diligence to produce the sheer volume of ants that invaded the church. The assault did not hit like a wave; no solid mass poured out of any one section of the church. Instead, the church itself resembled a sinking boat, and the ants acted as the water spraying through innumerable cracks and fissures in the floors and walls.

The writhing mass of blackness seeped in from everywhere at once, including the back of the church where Mary and Christopher stood. Even while he and his sister attempted to stomp the invaders into oblivion, Christopher could not help but notice Mary make the twitchy, mechanical movements with her head as she looked from her left to her right and back to her left again. *It's nothing*, he told himself. Half a dozen ants chomped into the flesh of his leg with near synchrony and reminded him that he had more immediate concerns.

Cold, damp air swept in and around from behind him. Christopher never heard the church's doors open, nor did he see the pair of large, gloved hands grasp Mary and him by the necks of their clothing. He felt as though he was flying backwards as the powerful hands swept him outside and away from the screeching maelstrom with one swift movement. His momentum carried him down the steps almost too fast for his legs to keep up. When he cleared the bottom of the steps and the hands released him, Christopher careened onward for several steps and took a headfirst slide into yard-long mud puddle. Dripping with muddy water, he twisted his head around toward the church.

During the few minutes he spent inside, the rain had lightened to a weak, but steady, drizzle. Light from the church's lamps and candles streamed through the open doors, silhouetting the figure in the black raincoat and flat, broad-brimmed hat. A person only had to see Deklan once to never confuse him with another. He had apparently whisked Christopher and his sister to safety while amateur guardsmen Davey Fredrikson and Stewart Korschot busily slapped their necks and torsos. It looked like a clean escape; Lorenz merely had to close the door and run away. So why did he remain standing in the open doorway? Christopher blinked, and Lorenz's revolvers materialized in his hands.

Insects, being an age-old enemy of man, bring about a rather primal instinct in him. If ants crawl over your skin, you slap them off, purely on instinct. When the attacker washes over you with overwhelming force, however, another instinct takes over, telling you to flee. The remaining citizens of Liberty who were crammed into that church reacted in a similar manner at roughly the same time. When they turned toward their escape route at the back of the church, however, before they could begin to claw past their friends and neighbors in effort to escape the madness, a sight gave them pause. A man stood in the doorway, with two revolvers and an impossibly misshapen face. He stood underneath the flapping coat and squat hat, living evidence that the Devil himself had invaded Liberty. The pause proved brief, and the crowd surged forward.

A double-thunderclap resonated above the human keening and Fredrikson and Korschot both fell in a heap. They were armed, and therefore, the most immediate threat. Again the mob swayed to a stop, but this time for less than a second. When a swarm of insects invades one's orifices, the prospect of death by bullets creates only a momentary pause.

The crowd surged forward again, and the gunshots echoed like a violent chorus.

Rising from his knees, staring through the evening drizzle, Christopher had an excellent view of the sordid affair. People he had known his entire life, had eaten with, had prayed with, fell in sequence as a volley of slugs carved their faces open. The bullets didn't hit anything but faces, and the people in the front were always the first to go. The slug that slammed through Old Mary Huggins' forehead was powerful enough to send her sprawling backward. A hole the size of a baby's fist appeared in the neck of young Peter Sterling before the life left his legs. He wore a glassy expression as he twirled around and fell on his face. Lorenz fired his guns with sickening efficiency, at times putting two people down with a single shot.

The people churning toward the main exit all wore the same wild look in their eyes as they scrambled for what they mistook as their only way out. It was like a church full of Mrs. Deans. Those parishioners who still kept their wits about them began to use chairs and their own fists to break out the side windows and climb through to the outside. The wave of desperate citizens stopped their futile slapping and acted as if they had forgotten about the ants crawling all over them.

Deklan did not have enough bullets to shoot everyone in the building, but the blockage caused by the dozen fallen bodies slowed the rush enough for him to launch the next phase of his plan. The instant the twelfth bullet left its smoking barrel, Lorenz grabbed the edge of the doors and flung them closed behind him. Guns still in hand, he leapt from the flight of steps, landed, and sprinted toward Mary and Christopher. He splashed through a puddle about ten feet from them when the church erupted in a blossom of flame.

The blast knocked them all flat, but Christopher managed to lunge to his left and tackle Mary in time to use his body to shelter her from the flying debris. A wave of dry heat coaxed its way around him, reminding him of standing in his father's shop. Bits of wood bounced off his back before something more substantial slammed into the base of his spine. When he deemed the worst to be over, Christopher uncovered Mary and glanced around to find the large object that had struck him. It was the remains of some unidentifiable man's arm, blown off at the shoulder. Had he eaten anything recently, Christopher would undoubtedly have lost it at the sight of the limb.

His eyes passed over the lonely limb and refocused on the church. The blast that made a crater of Deklan's home involved a larger explosive charge, but this one didn't have a few feet of earth to muffle the effect. Also, Christopher's proximity to this one and the darkness of the sky made for a far more spectacular sight. The world became crimson, as if Surtr, the dreaded Fire Giant of Norse myth, had thrust his sword into the earth and set the night aflame. A tongue of flame arched from where the church steeple once stood and took a lick at the night sky. Yellow firelight danced on the surface of dozens of puddles and dozens of windowpanes.

Christopher lay still for a moment, making certain that both he and his sister were alive and that neither had caught fire nor had visible ants on their persons. Somewhere, someone was wailing. Christopher could barely hear it, though, as the pieces of the remedial puzzle began to fall into place: Deklan had taken Lewis Rutlage's horses and covered wagon to retrieve the gunpowder he had not used in destroying his home and placed it in back of the church. His precise timing allowed him to remove Mary and Christopher without any real danger of the explosion consuming them.

Lorenz must have somehow known the ants would attack. Maybe he found another tunnel leading in that direction, decided that the people insider were doomed, and parked the wagon in the back. Christopher would have asked that pressing question, as well as several others, had Lorenz not already recovered from the shock of the explosion… recovered and reloaded. He had silently slipped into the shadows and stalked amongst the flaming wreckage, greeting stunned survivors with a single, thunderous bullet to the head.

The shootings in the doorway of the church unnerved Christopher more than any other sight he had witnessed in his short life, but Lorenz's ensuing systematic, execution of the helpless townspeople surpassed it by a wide margin. Instead of foaming at the mouth, these victims wore slack, dazed expressions. In some cases, fresh tears hung in their eyes. Instead of trampling their friends and family in vain attempt to claw their way outside, these either lay still or writhed in pathetic agony. He never saw Lorenz shoot any children, but Christopher did the math… In a certain light, one could view the first set of shootings as acts of self-defense. It takes a great deal of embellishment to move the second set of shootings beyond the scope of slaughtering the wounded and unconscious.

With his back to Christopher, Lorenz surveyed the blast site. Even in a morass of mud, his footsteps made no more noise than a cat's. He kept his walking pace brisk, pausing only long enough to discharge one of his firearms at point-blank range. Squirming bodies that lay prone on the ground convulsed when a bullet blasted through their skulls, then they lay still. His movements contained no trace of hesitation or remorse. Christopher could not help but stare in horrified fascination. How could a human do something like that so easily? Thankfully, the long shadows prevented Christopher from seeing the victims' faces. He couldn't see Lorenz's face, other than the orange embers of the lit cigar that Christopher originally mistook for the man's bloodshot eye. Mary must have caught at least a glimpse of the massacre, and he hoped that she failed to fully understand what she saw.

A part of Christopher demanded that he at least *try* to stop Lorenz, but he had too many reasons to ignore this voice. First and foremost, he did not want to die, which he surely would have had he crossed the assassin. He also did not want his sister to die, and Christopher's staying alive amounted to Mary's best chance of doing the same. The overwhelming reason, though, for not interfering involved a solid belief that Lorenz had a good reason for what he did. The sheer volume of ants swarming through that building guaranteed that every person there probably received multiple infections.

When the carnage ceased (although with Deklan Lorenz, the carnage never ended; it temporarily subsided), Lorenz returned to where Mary and Christopher stood. The misting rain tried in vain to remove the mud caked onto the two Rutlage children. Mary pressed against her brother's side while Christopher and Lorenz regarded one another in the flickering firelight. Christopher felt the need to say something, even if he could not lift his eyes above Lorenz's black-clad shoulders. Before he could speak, Lorenz exhaled a line of cigar smoke and asked, "You told them everything, didn't you?"

Christopher reluctantly nodded. Maybe he didn't tell them everything, but their reaction to the main points made it pointless to tell them the rest. His head hurt so badly that nodding created the sensation of his brain bouncing around inside his skull. "Yes, sir," he admitted.

Lorenz flicked one of his revolvers open and allowed the spent shell casings to fall to the ground. "Mistake," he stated in a tone he had never used toward Christopher before. Partly it was because he held the cigar in his teeth when he said it, but the statement definitely contained a hint of disgust, as well. "Nearly a fatal one." His fingers flicked bullets into the empty chambers with the dexterity of a card cheat.

Christopher again nodded. The shame he felt momentarily engulfed the lingering horror. "Did any bugs die in the blast?" he asked, hoping to alter the direction of the conversation so that it gravitated more toward Lorenz's triumphs and less toward Christopher's failures.

"Probably," Lorenz said and looked over his shoulder at the flaming, gutted husk of a church. "Hopefully." He snapped the revolvers closed.

Christopher remembered his question from earlier and asked it. "How did you know they'd attack the church?"

Lorenz continued to stare at the flames, perhaps searching for more crawling bodies he could annihilate. The flames danced off the shiny surface of his eyes, making them both appear red. "I didn't," he stated, flatly. "I was eliminating potential recruits. I guess I just got lucky." He turned and marched toward the flames a second time.

Christopher ran his tongue across his wet lower lip and tasted his own blood. His innocent mind processed the new information slowly: Lorenz planned to kill the people in the church to prevent them from becoming a future enemy. Although such an action makes sense tactically, a thinking, feeling human does not behave in such a manner. No man is God. Babies are not jailed for crimes they might commit. Justice does not work that way. Lorenz was not right, not this time, but he was still Christopher's protection, and he was leaving. Despite his throbbing skull, Christopher staggered after him for several paces, leaving Mary standing alone amid the puddles and the kindling. "Where are you going?" Christopher asked.

"Shoot horses," Lorenz replied without breaking stride. The guns stuck out from his coat sleeves like extensions of his hands. "Can't have people escaping."

Christopher hesitated, unsure of what to do, before turning and jogging back to Mary. She still needed him. Maybe more than ever. He took her tiny hand and led her across the broadest stretch of Main Street, over to the overhang of Harkness's store. They sat down under the awning as the light rain dripped around them. They sat on those steps for a long time, watching the church burn, listening to the sporadic report of guns.

*   *   *

Chapter Sixteen

Christopher's anxiety metastasized as the shock of the evening wore off. In an adult, hopelessness might have replaced the shock, as the fires began to dim and the circumstances changed from bleak to bleaker. Christopher was still young, though, young enough to hope and to be devastated when that which is hoped for does not materialize. Sitting in front of Harkness's amid the fire and the rain, he held Mary's twitching form, trying not to notice the small bumps sprouting from her forehead, bumps that would eventually become antennae. As he sat there, the anxiety seemed to ooze out from his stomach and permeate his bones. He knew how to cope with fear, though. If the previous few days had not inoculated him against the effects of fear, the previous fourteen years had. He had become so used to living in constant fear that some degree of anxiety had become the norm.

Christopher's anxious state stemmed from the fact that he had begun to fear death again. He wasn't certain when that happened, exactly. Most boys in their early teens do not overcome their fear of death, but he had started along that nihilistic path many years before. During the times that his father flogged him to the point of collapse and told him what a terrible son he was, Christopher would have welcomed death's merciful embrace. In recent days, however, he had endured so much to keep both he and Mary alive. The thought of ultimately surviving this hell served as his main source of both motivation and anxiety: something to hold onto and something to lose.

The smell of smoke and burning things reminded Christopher of his father. Lewis Rutlage had stood next to soot and flame for so long that he rarely emanated normal, human stink; it all smelled like charcoal. It was a comforting smell, by far the most comforting thing about the man, because it smelled like the shop. The shop was the source of the man's competence, and he never beat Christopher while in the shop. *Is Father watching me right now?* Christopher glanced up at the dark sky. He hoped not. He was dealing with enough pressure as it was. Allowing for life after death, he wondered whether his father resided above him or below. Despite his juvenile desire for revenge, he hoped that the man was in a better place, a place that could cleanse him of his hate.

Amid the light, steady precipitation, flaming bits of church formed constellations in the streets of his hometown and illuminated the rain and blood-soaked corpses in the night. He considered walking around in the rubble, seeing if he could find anything left of his mother. What was there to find, though? Hunks of obliterated flesh, or maybe a fully intact body with skin pricked by a thousand ant bites and half of a skull? Neither possibility was better than the other. If he found anything that used to be her, what would he do? Nod and walk away probably. He knew she was dead, though. They were all dead. And Mary… he couldn't leave Mary.

He shouldn't have been worried about Mary. He should have resigned himself to her death the instant he saw her twitch up in the Braxton house. She was infected, and Lorenz would kill her. Christopher nodded to himself and pulled her close against him. He was still responsible for her in the time he had left… until she tried to kill him, maybe. She shivered and twitched under his embrace.

Lorenz would kill him; he had to. He probably wouldn't do Christopher the courtesy of telling him, either. Just creep up behind Christopher, the same way he did the first day Christopher visited his house and shove a gun against the back of the younger man's head. This time, though, he'd pull the trigger without saying a word. All signs thus far pointed to that invariable conclusion. Survivors of Lorenz's one-man war were quickly becoming latent enemies. If blowing up the posse out at his house had not carried Lorenz past the point of no return, than destroying the church certainly had. Yes, the posse would have killed him in their desperate search for a scapegoat, and, yes, the ants would have consumed everyone in that church, but to the few people in the surrounding area who knew anything about Liberty, he was now the obvious person to blame for the devastation.

Lorenz had made himself a target to anyone with a gun, which included every still-living person in town. In accordance with his way of thinking, everyone now had to die, because nothing could be allowed stop him from carrying out his brutal mission. A single person left alive meant that all the sacrifice was for nothing. Christopher may end up being the last to die, Lorenz may keep him around for a while, just for company or for unskilled backup, but die he would, of that he had no doubt.

So, his long moments of thought under the awning had yielded these invariable conclusions: Christopher finally wanted to live, and Lorenz was going to kill him. Christopher nodded again. He had to do it, he had to kill Lorenz first. He clearly couldn't do it in a fair fight, so he probably would have to shoot him in the back. That was unfortunate. Even his father believed that was an underhanded tactic. This was survival, though, not ethics. Lorenz himself taught Christopher the difference.

Mary continued to quiver between his arm and chest. He gave her a gentle squeeze. Hopefully, his body heat was making her descent into hell a little more pleasant. A low-grade furnace, he could play that role well. It was all he could do. He was her brother and he promised to save her, but it was all he could do. Reflections of the flickering firelight danced over her vacant eyes.

This would end soon. It had to.

The click of a pistol being cocked behind his good ear caused Christopher to turn. He expected Lorenz, all grim and silent, but a floppy brown hat and a familiar, yellow-toothed sneer told Christopher that James Waits was pointing a gun at him. He held an enormous revolver against Christopher's temple. This had become a sadly familiar position for Christopher, and the sight barely raised his pulse rate. Besides, if Waits wanted him dead, he would have fired immediately.

Although Christopher never asked for an explanation, Waits provided one. "All I wanted," he began, "was to get the Hell out of this town with my family, but that damn lunatic went and shot all our horses. Now, I seen him pull you out of the church before it went up... I was watching upstairs and I seen him pull you out... so maybe he'll give me some horses if I got you."

Christopher's eyebrows arched. Well, at least Emma was still alive. Good for her.

Waits flipped the gun barrel upward, and Christopher rose to his feet, pulling Mary up with him. She moved rigidly. By this point, nothing short of a drawing and quartering would have coaxed a response from her. What were her last words? A shriek? "You forgot to load it," maybe?

"You're making a mistake," Christopher informed Waits as they walked toward the flaming husk of a church, presumably following the chorus of gunshots that echoed through the night. "Lorenz was planning on killing me anyway."

"Shut up, you little bastard," he snarled. Of course Waits didn't want to hear that; this half-assed plan marked his last chance of surviving the night. "I've got my own reasons for seeing you dead. Christ almighty! After what you did, I'm surprised your daddy didn't kill you hisself."

"He tried," Christopher wistfully assured Waits. "Lorenz threw a knife into his face." Christopher's lips warped into a weary smile as he glanced over his shoulder at his temporary captor. Here stood a man, a normal human... at best, preparing to test the resolve of the most ruthless man Christopher had ever seen or heard of. With his own death pending, at least he could see Waits meet his end first.

In their search for Lorenz, they passed over a dozen slaughtered horses of various ages, sizes, and breeds lying in their various pens, barns, and enclosures. Some of the kills were fresh enough that blood still ran out of the bullet holes. In some ways, it was worse than the human carnage; at least most of that meat was cooked. Toward the north end of town, almost near Doc Ferguson's place, Deklan strode from one of the last barns on his itinerary. He walked with the casual purpose of a surveyor. Mary and Christopher shuffled in front of their captor, but in the firelight, Waits' gnarled shadow flinched when Deklan appeared. He cowered behind the Rutlage children, using their bodies as a human shield.

Waits must have considered taking a shot at Deklan's back before the former assassin turned his attention toward the trio, but the target was dark, far away, and distorted by the firelight... and then the moment passed and he lost his nerve. "What do you want, Waits?" Deklan asked, sullenly. He removed the nub of remaining cigar from his lips and tossed it into the street. Christopher frowned, disappointed. He had expected Lorenz to skip the conversation and blast James Waits to hell.

"Nothing much," Waits assured him in a quivering voice. This was fast becoming the defining moment of his long, misanthropic life, and he was failing miserably. "I just want a couple horses so I can get my family out of here."

Lorenz froze. "All right," he said, voice nearly breaking, "whatever you want." He shakily placed the gun he was holding on the ground, looking and sounding every bit like a scared man. Christopher's mouth fell open. Lorenz had displayed emotion in front of him before, but it mostly fluctuated between hate and remorse. He was not totally convinced that the man could be frightened, having never witnessed it. And frightened by James Waits, no less. That was like being frightened of a small dog with mange. *No*, Christopher decided. *This is an act.* No one who faced down a posse of two dozen men and an army of mutant insects could be afraid of a pathetic worm like Waits.

Waits, conversely, found Deklan's shameless show of vulnerability most heartening. He apparently felt so good, that he forgot that Deklan carried two guns on his person (at least). He should have kept quiet. It probably wouldn't have saved him, but Christopher winced the moment he heard Waits utter the words, "Not so tough now, are you? Can't shoot people in the back or blow up buildings they're standing in? Whimper like a little girl when it's somebody you care about. You ain't shit." He spoke in a contemptuous tone reserved for subordinates: children, half-wits, freaks, etc.

After placing his only visible gun on the ground, Deklan slowly rose to, a standing position. It was an abbreviated version of his full, imposing height. Christopher fully could see through the mock fear now. Being an expert at feigning submission, he judged that it wasn't even that good of an act, but one that Waits badly wanted to believe. "Whatever you do," Lorenz said, "I beg you, don't hurt the girl."

Christopher's eye flew open. He turned to Waits, ready to warn him that Lorenz was lying, but Waits smacked him in the head with the barrel of his gun before Christopher could utter a word. Christopher fell to the ground, stunned; he'd never been hit in the head with steel before. Both hands drunkenly reached upward to cover the cut that crossed his forehead. "Don't tempt me, boy," Waits growled. He shoved the gun against Mary's temple. She stood twitching worse than ever, probably not even registering the gun pressing against her skull. "Okay, boy," Waits said to Deklan, "get moving. We're goin' to get some horses."

Deklan did not move. His spine straightened. His shoulders pressed back. His chin lifted, and he stared at Waits. When he spoke, though, the words were directed at his teenage accomplice. "Mary looks bad, doesn't she, Christopher?"

Squinting through the blood and rain, Christopher did not know how to respond. Yes, she certainly did look bad, not like his sister at all, but he did not want her to die; he just wanted the thing inside her dead. "Please" was all he could manage.

"She got infected in the hole," Lorenz stated, evenly, as if her crawling down there had been her idea. "I figured as much. Probably not a lot of your sister left inside. The children probably don't last as long. Another hour. Maybe two."

Watching his control slip away unnerved Waits. He shoved the revolver against Mary's head with even more force. Her head tilted to the left at an awkward angle, but Mary remained silent as a rag doll. "What the Hell are you talking about?" Waits demanded. Whatever James Waits saw when he looked into his opponent's eyes, it caused him to wilt.

Christopher never actually saw Deklan draw or fire his weapon. His eyes stayed with Waits as the man ducked behind Mary's frail body. The runty, evil man probably forgot that he even held a loaded gun. Hiding behind a hostage might be a decent strategy, but that assumes that the person you are hiding behind is actually a hostage. To put it simply, Lorenz shot through her.

The bullets tore through both of them like paper, five shots in all. The slugs ripped through Mary, four in the chest and one in the head, and she was dead before her pulverized body hit the ground. It finally stopped her twitching. Christopher managed to yell, "No!" after the first bullet struck, but it was more of a token gesture than anything.

The bullets that hit Waits tore through his torso as well, but they must have missed his vital organs, because he writhed in the mud like a half of a snake. His hat had fallen off, and his face pressed into the muddy street. The gun had fallen from his hand and sat only inches away, but his eyes clamped shut, and it might as well have been in Omaha. Lorenz stepped over the wheezing man and extended his gun with its final, filled chamber. "He that hides a dark soul and foul thoughts," Lorenz whispered, "benighted walks under the mid-day sun; himself his own dungeon." Waits didn't react. The final shot seemed louder than the others as it obliterated Waits' face.

Christopher scrambled to his feet and took a step toward Mary's body, but the dime-sized entry wound in the center of her forehead oozed dark blood, forcing his eyes to avert themselves. His gaze shifted over to Deklan for a moment as the man's nimble fingers slid bullets into the gun's chambers with practiced efficiency, but that sight proved equally repulsive.

Lorenz picked up his discarded gun, wiped it on his trousers, and marched past Christopher's flaccid form, off to add to his equine death count. Abruptly, he stopped. "I'm sorry about that, Christopher. I know you loved her." His comments probably were meant to be tender, but he spoke as though reading a letter from a stranger.

"Why do you even say that?" Christopher asked as Lorenz took another step. He knew his voice sounded like that of a pouting child, but Good Lord, assuming his mother was either incinerated or struck down by a bullet, Lorenz was responsible for killing his entire family. "I know you don't mean it."

Lorenz again stopped walking. "I do mean it," he assured me. "I just can't afford to let any of this affect me, that's all. She was hours away from becoming one of them, body and soul. I'm sure that I did her a favor." This time, he waited for a response.

"You're worse than my father," Christopher snorted. It was the most severe insult he could come up with.

Lorenz replied with a characteristic response. "If you want her buried," he called behind him, "just take her into one of the buildings. I'll be dynamiting them shortly."

*   *   *

The nearest house belonged to Davey Fredrikson's parents. Christopher picked up Mary's corpse and carried it through the front door. Her body was lighter when it was limp. He set her gently on the floor, face up so that he did not have to see the ferocity of the exit wounds, and started to brush the matted, curly hair out of her face. His fingers ran across one of the bumps on her forehead. His hand recoiled and he stood up. He should have said goodbye. After all, she was the only human he had ever loved. Maybe he took some satisfaction in the fact that she died quickly and died human. Maybe he thought that he would be joining her shortly. Whatever the reason, Christopher wordlessly pulled the door closed behind him and hurried onward to find Lorenz.

Deklan proved easy to find because his shadowy, stalking form was the only thing moving in the street. Several townspeople still must have been alive at that point. The two explosions killed close to a hundred people. About a dozen more were now bugs, not counting the Staleys, who were not technically part of the town's populace. That left a couple dozen people huddling in their houses, confused and frightened. They would all be dead before the sun rose the next day, either blown up by the assassin or dragged into hell by his inhuman enemies.

Deklan stood in front of the tavern belonging to the late James Waits. His back faced Christopher, who still carried the gun that Lorenz had given him with two bullets in it. "What's on your mind, Christopher?" he asked without turning.

"Nothing," Christopher answered automatically. "What are you thinking about?"

Lorenz ignored the question, and to be honest, Christopher doubted he wanted to know the man's thoughts. "Don't lie, Christopher," he said. "You just watched me shoot and kill your little sister. I know how much you cared about her, and on some level, I'm sure you want to kill me."

"No, I don't," Christopher insisted, defensively. Lorenz could turn, draw both weapons, and empty them into Christopher before Christopher could extricate the tiny gun from his pocket. Even if he did pull the gun free in time, bullets probably didn't hurt Lorenz.

Lorenz continued to stare into the darkened tavern as if waiting for it to do something. "Be that as it may, you think that I was overly brutal."

This seemed safe enough ground to tread upon. "Weren't you?"

"It had to be done. Who else was going to do it? You?" His voice contained a bit of a spark, but his eyes never left the building. Christopher wondered if the prostitutes that worked upstairs had been welcomed into the church and doubted it. Perhaps Lorenz wondered the same thing.

"I would've... gotten around to it," Christopher said absently, hoping that it did not sound as lame out loud as it did in his head.

"Yes," he agreed, "I image you would have, after she tried to kill you." Christopher did not respond, so Lorenz continued. "I did your sister a favor because I could. You don't have to like it, just accept it."

"Why do you care if I accept it or not?" Christopher demanded, not at all happy with Mary's killer instructing him on how to cope with her death. "Why do you care anything about me? Why not kill me like you did everybody else?" He was yelling now, which he found surprisingly difficult to do when facing someone's back.

"You're hysterical," Lorenz informed him, flatly.

"What do you care?" Christopher growled. "You just shoot people that don't mean anything to you! You don't have children! You don't have a family! These people are my life!"

Lorenz remained silent for a long moment, which provided Christopher with some small smoldering of satisfaction. "We'll talk later," he assured the younger man. "This fight isn't over yet. Right now, I need to check this building."

"How do you even know there'll be a later for either of us?" Christopher demanded. "Or are you so god damn omnipotent you know what's going to happen?" It was the first time he ever took the Lord's name in vain aloud, with another person present.

At last, Lorenz turned and regarded Christopher. "There will be a later," he stated. That was it, just a flat assurance. He again faced forward and climbed the steps. Instinctively, Christopher reached his hand behind him and glanced back for Mary. No one was there, though, and he took a few seconds to relive the image of the bullets blasting apart her five-year-old body. He followed Lorenz into the tavern.

The barroom appeared open for business, with the exception the extinguished lamps and a few broken bottles on the floor, no doubt dislodged by the church explosion. Even with the light of the still-blazing church shining through the windows, the darkness inside proved nearly as absolute as the downstairs of the Braxton house when Christopher went to retrieve the shotgun shells. Unlike the incident in the Braxton house, though, Lorenz was present, and that made all the difference.

Lorenz scanned the barroom for a moment before creeping toward the staircase. Eyes weighed on Christopher the instant he stepped through the doorway, and he constantly felt compelled to look behind him. This compulsion nearly caused him to walk into a gaping hole in the floorboards. God only knows what would have happened had he fallen down the shaft, but Lorenz kept him from finding out by throwing a hand behind him and halting Christopher's forward movement with inches to spare. "Be careful," he warned before skirting the round hole and ascending the stairs.

Christopher followed him up the staircase and paused to look back into the black void of the bug hole. This location of this entry point lacked the stealth of their previous efforts. This one lay directly at the bottom of the stairs. The bugs had come back for the few living recruits they could get. James Waits could not have come down these steps and not noticed a hole of that size. That means it wasn't present when he came to abduct Mary and Christopher. Maybe the insects extinguished the lights. Maybe the rest of the Waits family rushed down the stairs in a panic and…

Christopher turned to his left, then to his right, and found himself alone in the darkness. He bounded up the stairs in a series of uneven stomps, taking them two or three at a time in attempt to rectify the situation. By the time he breathlessly caught up with Deklan, the man was exiting from a room on Christopher's left where something had ripped the door from its hinges. From Christopher's limited experience inside the tavern, he knew that Lorenz exited from the part of the building where the Waits family had resided.

Briskly stepping past the younger man, Deklan announced, "It's empty," before continuing across the walkway overlooking the barroom. Christopher glanced inside. In the darkness, he could make out the outline of the chairs and piano that stood in the Waits' parlor. In the darkness, it wasn't hard to imagine a bug dragging Emma cross the floor by her hair, her choking on the ants that ran down her throat.

Christopher pulled his eyes away. Lorenz had moved on, down the hall, toward the door that led to the four rooms constituting the town brothel. Christopher inched forward, but did not follow Deklan all the way in. He was careful not to let Lorenz's bulky outline out of his darkness-inhibited sight, but at the same time, standing inside a brothel made his skin crawl. Saying "God Damn" was enough of a giant leap for one night; he wasn't quite ready to parade through a whorehouse without feeling like a sodomite.

Lorenz's footsteps trailed off toward the back of the apartment, then approached the doorway. "Entire place is empty," he said upon emerging. "Rest of the town is, too, I'm willing to bet, or soon will be."

"Bugs?" Christopher asked in a tone that one normally reserves for people who did not gun-down one's family.

Lorenz nodded. "We have to assume that," he said. "Looks like they've decided to—"

Christopher interrupted. "Um," he began, "is it alright if we continue this outside. This place is making me uneasy."

"Oh," Lorenz said, almost apologetically. In the darkness, he gave an understanding nod. His voice softened, and he asked, "Do you know what I do when I get scared?"

"What?" Christopher asked, buoyantly. He never knew Lorenz even felt fear, and he found that fact slightly heartening.

"I fight through it," Lorenz stated coldly. He took a moment to make sure his words sunk in before continuing. "Now, as I was saying, the bugs must have figured out what I was doing and got as many living people infected as they could find and took them underground."

"What're we going to do?" Christopher asked. Being one of two living humans in an entire town cannot help but bring out the spirit of comradery in a person. As much as he hated to admit it, Lorenz's verbal lambasting of his weakness nearly erased Christopher's fear. It was ridiculous, after all; standing next to Lorenz and his two loaded guns was the safest spot he'd occupied in days.

"I'll think up something by morning," Lorenz assured the young man. "I want them to have as little darkness to work with as possible." He seemed more animated at that moment than he had in the streets, perhaps spurred on by the challenge presented by this latest turn of events. He spoke more to himself than to Christopher. "They think they're safe underground; they'll stay down there and make sure the infection takes hold, build up their numbers, before they do anything else," he said, clasping his gloved hands in front of him. "Well, I'll just have to take the fight to them."

*   *   *

CHAPTER SEVENTEEN

Only twenty-four hours earlier, Christopher had viewed Deklan Lorenz as a savior. Granted, he recently had thrown a knife through Christopher's father's skull, but the act was forgivable. The grief Christopher experienced following his father's passing proved mostly a fabrication: him feeling the way he thought he should feel. In reality, Deklan probably saved his life and completed an act that, deep down, Christopher had considered performing himself many, many times. Christopher never considered igniting multiple barrels of gunpowder under a church full of people, however, nor had he considered shooting his little sister five times in the face and chest. These acts were wrong, regardless of the results. What good are results when they cost a man his humanity?

Christopher did not hate Lorenz, because, despite everything, the man's ultimate intentions were beyond reproach. There was no doubt that he fought for the greater good, not because he was some sort of bloodthirsty misanthrope. He had killed Mary, though, first by taking her down into that hole, then by firing a volley of bullets through her fragile, little body, and Christopher could not forgive him for this. After all, if one sacrifices his humanity by spilling the blood of innocents, logic dictates that the same holds true for someone that condones these acts. No human should be able to be so good at performing acts that were so inherently bad, and Christopher could no longer consider Lorenz a human being, so much as a brutal-but-necessary machine.

Lorenz told Christopher to wait for him at the Braxton house, a location no more or less safe than any other, while he went to fetch dynamite that he had squirreled away in some secret location. Standing in front of the hole in the front door, Christopher removed the small gun from his pocket, hoping that he would not require more than two bullets. Inside the stuffy house, he found an unlit candle wedged into a candleholder in the Braxton's parlor, lit it, and used it to light the way to the staircase. The downstairs of the house was quite, but it was a dead quite, not the creeping, organic kind of quiet it had been before. The bugs were unlikely to have held their position, given everything that had happened outside.

Walking back up the creaky stairs amid his small circle of light, Christopher found the trusty shotgun lying in the middle of the bedroom floor, at a right angle to the doorway. Hunks of shot were imbedded in the left-hand wall, a souvenir from when Christopher tossed the cocked gun through the broken window. The box of shells still sat open atop the bed. It had only been two hours... maybe less, since he sat up here with Mary. He set the candle holder on the nightstand, next to the spent lamp. Then, he picked the shotgun off the floor, reloaded it, and re-fortified his position against the wall. He went through the movements deliberately, mechanically, just like he used to chop wood, back when he had a real life. Only a black, tarry bloodstain remained on the floorboards of the Braxton bedroom as evidence of Christopher's kill. The body had disappeared.

The wind conjured strange noises as it blew through the shattered window to his left. Sometimes it sounded like the wail of dead souls. Outside, the smaller fires had burned themselves out with the help of the gentle rain, and only the flaming corpse of the church remained. While he waited, Christopher thought mostly about Mary. This was the place where she started to die, after all. Did she feel any pain when the bullets ripped through her? The mental image of what her body would look like in the morning would not go away. He knew what dead animals looked like the day after, but he'd never seen a decaying human.

He leaned his head back until his skull thumped against the sturdy wooden wall. The thought of the bugs coming for him failed to concern Christopher. Deklan had said they would not, and he did not make mistakes when it came to killing. Christopher corrected the angle of the gun two inches to his right and checked the flickering candle on the nightstand, just in case.

The hour passed quickly, even though Christopher had to shake himself awake on a pair of occasions. When Lorenz returned, he returned the way he had departed, on foot. Christopher had no idea where he kept the horses, and he doubted it was a coincidence; Lorenz was not going to allow any of the infected to escape. Deklan's boots clomped up the stairs, a deliberate indicator of his approach. When stepped into doorway of the upstairs bedroom, he acknowledged Christopher with a grim nod that was returned. He carried of a bundle of something, slightly larger than a baby, swaddled in a red blanket.

Christopher sat on the floor against the far wall, in the same position he had sat with Mary. His position, crammed behind the former bed of either Mr. or Mrs. Braxton, had become his temporary home. Lorenz slid down against the opposite wall, setting his bundle behind him. Propped on the folded pillows, the barrel of the shotgun already pointed in his general direction. It was hard to miss with a shotgun…

The silence that followed Deklan's entry became uncomfortable, too uncomfortable to last. All this would be over by the next day, so any conversation between the two men on this night might be their last. It seemed much longer than the few days that had passed since Christopher conversed with Lorenz while they repaired his fence. Shady trees, warm breeze, and good conversation. Christopher still considered those couple days some of the best times of his life. That was before the holy war started, though. The house was obliterated at this point, along with any desire to delve into Lorenz's warped thoughts.

Lorenz must have sensed the approaching finality in their relationship (whatever relationship it was), because he went so far as to initiate the conversation. "Christopher, we need to talk," he announced, smashing through the silence with his usual blunt monotone.

Christopher nodded. Had Lorenz not said anything, Christopher probably would have, eventually, if for no other reason than to gain some sort of closure. With Lorenz speaking first, though, it allowed Christopher to drop back into the role he seldom occupied, that of reluctant conversationalist. "What's on your mind?" he asked.

Lorenz fell silent for a moment. Letting his guard down, even a little bit, was like cutting off his hand. "I... want you to understand why... I've done what it is I've done," he said, the words coming out in clumps. Christopher wanted to tell him to save his breath, that maybe when the world had worn him down the point it had Lorenz, the twisted logic might make sense. His lingering respect stopped the words before they left his lips.

The way Lorenz spoke reminded Christopher of the way he sounded the first time they met back in the glow of the blacksmith shop. Back then, he was little more than a recluse, and Christopher was a boy who had encountered sexual intercourse less than an hour before and who had yet to encounter real, world-altering violence. "I don't expect you to understand me," he continued, "even if you were old enough, I don't know if understanding me is possible." Lorenz, the black-clad, hulking man-demon, seemed to shrink. He sat with his back pressed against the far wall, his forearms propped up on his knees, looking exhausted to the point of fragility. "I don't expect you to condone what I've done, either. You shouldn't. You're too good for that."

His rambling left Christopher confused. Every word that came from him seemed to contradict all his anti-weakness posturing. "You aren't making any sense," Christopher told him during a long pause.

Lorenz laughed at the statement, actually laughed that eerie, coarse laugh of his, and the sound churned up yet another flavor of fear, one of the few that Christopher had yet to experience that night. Laughter might indicate a breakdown, a complete, mental schism. A chill slid down Christopher's spine. He half-expected Lorenz to draw a gun and blow his own head off. "No," Lorenz agreed, "I'm probably not making much sense. It's just that," he blinked hard, and when he opened his eyes, they seemed to look through Christopher, "I'm doing things the way I'm doing them because it's the only way I can be sure. Whether you or the bugs or anybody knows it or not, we're winning, and we're going to win. It's come at a terrible cost, but we can't afford to lose this war. That's what it comes down to: we cannot afford to lose, so no cost is too high."

He exhaled, and Christopher thought that he was done, but he wasn't. "I've done terrible things," he continued, "and I don't say this as if I'm going to be retroactively exonerated. It would be a disgusting world if my actions were acceptable. They aren't; they're monstrous. But I am alright with that: I'll be the monster that they always thought I was, and people can safely judge me for generations to come."

"Why couldn't you just tell somebody about the bugs?" Christopher asked, privately continuing to insist that this time Lorenz was wrong. It *felt* wrong. They had covered that ground before, but Christopher desperately wanted to believe that better, non-lethal alternatives always exist.

"You tried it, you tell me," Lorenz stated, effectively silencing his partner. "If I'd tried doing the same thing, they'd have strung me up." He sighed and looked down at his big, black boots. It's hard to believe he could move like a silent shadow wearing boots that big. "They're too weak to believe, because it would mess up the delicate order of their lives." He coughed a wet cough into his fist. "God-fearing Christian societies don't have demons from other worlds. They don't even have fathers that beat their sons." Christopher glanced up right as Lorenz's eyes fell. "You were just lucky you were at Staley's the day you saw the bug. If not, you would've been in the church with all the others."

Christopher gulped, having never thought himself "lucky" having taken part in the nightmarish scene in the sheep pasture. Even though this declaration implied that Lorenz would have somehow gotten involved without being told, it remained a sobering thought. If he had become involved, Christopher would have died in a fiery explosion, after clawing his way past half his friends and loved ones. If Lorenz had not gotten involved at all, Christopher would have... the ants would have... The thought made him ill: dozens, hundreds of ants crawling over his, into his hair, his mouth, his ears. And that was only the beginning. What was it like, to be in that amber cocoon? The three people in Doc Ferguson's office knew, as did the doctor himself. Emma knew, too, by now. He shuddered, but the sensations lingered.

"For a sane person, it takes strength to inflict pain," Lorenz continued, "and I was the only one strong enough to do what had to be done. You knew as much, or else you wouldn't have come to me. You just didn't know how far I would go." He shook his head. "Neither did the bugs. To beat them, I've had to be ruthless enough to do whatever it took, and I will continue to do so. I will prevail, Christopher," he announced, his eyes once again coming into focus on his conversation partner, "and I want you to know that I've done all those things... all those terrible things, because I'm the only one who could."

The silence begged for a reply, but Christopher had no idea what an adequate response would be. If he lived to be two hundred years old, he would still not know how to respond to that. "Thanks," was all he said.

Christopher had never seen Lorenz caught off-guard. Human-insect hybrids exploding through the floor of a schoolhouse, waking him from a nap, did not take him off-guard. The single-word response, however, did just that. He expected Lorenz to reply with something like, "Don't thank me yet; we've got a big day ahead of us." A lesser man might have responded that way to avoid acknowledging the word of gratitude. Christopher might have given such a response in a similar situation (as if a similar situation were possible). Deklan Lorenz simply said, "You're welcome." He looked down at his feet. "Y'know," he began, awkwardly, "back at the tavern... the Waits' place, you noted that I didn't know what it was like to have children... to have people to care about..."

Christopher shut his eyes. "Look, I didn't mean—"

"No," Lorenz insisted. "You were right. I haven't cared about anything in a long time. When my wife died, everything I cared about went into the ground with her." He took off his hat and set it on the floor next to him. His gigantic right hand ran its way through his wispy scraps of hair. "Clarice was never able to have children, so I stopped wanting them. I just want you to know that... if we'd ever had any... I would've wanted a son that was a lot like you." He glanced up from his boots, only for a second.

Christopher exhaled, and his body sagged, as if fourteen years of tension had just run out of it. He'd been waiting his whole life for someone to tell him he was worthy of drawing breath, to really say it and not just leave him to interpret hugs or sex or sugar in oatmeal. He just hadn't known he needed it until then. He started to say something, something like, "That's the nicest thing anyone has ever said to me," but he already was blinking back tears and didn't want to start sobbing.

Instead, he asked, "What was that you said to Waits, before you shot him? 'Benighted something something?'"

"'He that hides a dark soul and foul thoughts,'" Lorenz said, his composure having returned in seconds, "'benighted walks under the midday sun; himself his own dungeon.' It's from John Milton."

Christopher nodded. The name sounded only vaguely familiar. It wasn't a book of the Bible, so he hadn't read it. "Why did you say it?"

"Over the years, I've gone to town a lot more than people think," Lorenz said as he leaned his head back against the wall. "I usually went at night, when no one could see me. I saw and heard a lot of things. Lately, in the last year, I heard some things coming from the upstairs of the Waits' place that made me consider shooting James Waits earlier than I did." His frozen lips tried to form a smile. "I think I said it as a reminder, that he was a man trapped in his own weakness and that I was doing him a favor."

"Do you think he understood it?"

"No," Lorenz said, "but the reminder was for me."

What good are results when they cost a man his humanity? Christopher thought again. This time, he had an answer. *The results are useless to the man... but they might be useful to everyone else.* After that, the conversation remained light. They talked about likes and dislikes and took turns telling some amusing stories from their pasts. Lorenz laughed several more times, but the sound never disturbed Christopher again.

The little details from that night would stand out in Christopher's memory, like realizing that Lorenz's favorite city was Cincinnati, Ohio, and that the man actually could smile. It was a memorable snatch of time, but not for the usual reasons. Christopher had similar experiences (with people whom Lorenz had blown apart). Not many, given his lack of peers and strict upbringing, but there were times in his life when he had sat on a hard, wooden floor, back to the wall telling stories until the early hours of the morning. Lorenz never had, though. This was a first, and Christopher was there to see it. Deklan seemed genuinely entertained, genuinely happy for the first time since his wife died those many years ago. For this reason, the night remained a special one for Christopher, because as they sat in Braxtons' bedroom, he got a good, long look at the man inside the machine and appreciated the strength it took for him to do the things he did.

Christopher slept soundly after snuffing out the nub of a candle on the nightstand. He crept into one of the Braxtons' beds and fell asleep in less than a minute. It was easy to relax that night. Deklan had informed him that nothing would happen to him and stayed awake the entire night to ensure it.

*   *   *

CHAPTER EIGHTEEN

July 10, 1877:

Scrape. Scrape. Scrape.

Scraaaaape.

Christopher's eyes flew open. A pitched ceiling hung above him, far higher than the one above his bed at home. It took him another half a second to realize that he wasn't at home; he was in the Braxton's home. He turned and saw Lorenz leaning against the wall next to the doorway, diligently cleaning his revolvers. The grim manner in which he performed the task led Christopher to wonder whether the conversation they had shared the previous night had actually taken place. He felt terribly sluggish but after shaking his head a pair of times, the memory became even more solid and clear. The man he had spoken to hours earlier, though, had laughed multiple times, while the man sitting before him seemed incapable of such an action.

Something sat bundled in a dull yellow oilcloth near the doorway. Christopher saw Lorenz carry it in last night but never got around to asking what it was. "What've you got wrapped in the blanket?" Christopher asked, easing himself into a seated position atop the bed. His entire body radiated soreness due to the various explosions, beatings, and other abuses it had endured the previous days, but soreness was no novelty. He was fully capable of hopping out of bed and reducing a pile of wood to quartered logs with only minimal delay. Yet another incidental gift from his father.

"Dynamite," Lorenz explained with his typical bluntness. "We're going to blow up the perimeter of town. I don't know how elaborate their tunnel network is, but I can't imagine it extending outside of town; it wouldn't serve any purpose. If all the buildings on the edge of town get blown, it'll drive them toward the middle. I've got enough dynamite for most of the buildings, but I'm going to leave this house standing so I can go in the tunnel. When the dynamite goes off, they'll come running from every direction, and I'll be waiting for them." He held up one of his Peacemakers and peered through the empty chamber. "We're only a couple hours away from winning."

Christopher nodded as if the plan sounded like a good one, as if he had any input into the scheming. It did not sound feasible, sending a lone man into a subterranean tunnel against killers indigenous to that environment, but most of what Deklan had done to this point would not have been wise had normal humans performed the tasks. And "winning." What did that mean, anyway? Those things effectively had killed an entire town. They had already destroyed everything in Christopher's life. To some extent, if the last few days had been a contest between his "team" and the bugs "team," the bugs had already won. At best, at the end of the day, he and Deklan could hope to have not lost quite as badly as they could have. Maybe they would "win" as representatives of humanity, but that, too, rang hollow. "What do you want me to do?" Christopher asked, stretching his arms and yawning.

Deklan continued to run a long, pencil-thin file through a chamber of one of his revolvers. "If you have to do anything," he explained, "that means something has gone wrong. You need to watch, and if anything does go wrong, fix it."

Christopher nodded, wondering whether Lorenz could have given a more vague set of instructions. Nothing would go wrong, though. Ever since he involved Lorenz, Christopher had merely been along for the ride. All of Lorenz's plans and predictions had come true, so far (with the glaring exception of Mary getting infected...). This plan would work perfectly, too. Christopher would not have to do anything.

The file disappeared somewhere into the folds of Lorenz's coat as he rose to his feet, wincing as he stretched the stiffness from his joints. The movement wasn't graceful at all. He looked shaky, almost like an old man. Lorenz didn't have an expressive face, so it was hard to read fatigue, but Christopher wondered how much he'd slept in the last three days. "Are you ready to go?" he asked while mechanically dropping bullets into the chambers of one of his guns.

Christopher had yet to fully awaken, but if he claimed to need more time, Lorenz might leave without him. "Yeah," Christopher said and swung his legs onto the floor. He probably slept three hours the previous night and hadn't eaten in almost a day, but it would have to do. Standing, he tucked in his shirttail into his pants and pulled his suspenders over his shoulders.

Lorenz flicked his wrist and the chamber of his pistol snapped shut. He deposited his gun into its holster, joining its twin, and announced, "Then let's finish this."

*   *   *

When Christopher exited the Braxton house into the infinitely more dangerous world Liberty had become, the first assault came from the stench. The overpowering odor of decay clung to the air, thanks to the damp, open-air graveyard Liberty had become. He took two steps out the door before gagging. Lorenz stopped at the porch rail, ran a match over it, and used it to light another cigar. Once armed, he strode through the street, seemingly oblivious to the debilitating smell, and the sight gave

Christopher the strength to march onward. He would just have to get used to putrescence and breathe through his mouth. The air had a taste to it, too, a thick, meaty taste, but it was nothing compared to the smell.

Christopher walked with oversized strides to remain in Lorenz's shadow. Lorenz was human, he'd learned that last night, so it stood to reason that Deklan must have noticed the smell, even through the cigar odor. His focus, though, allowed him to push intrusive sensations away so he could perform his necessary tasks. It was easy for him to adapt, almost to the point of being automatic. After all, if one cannot block out something as small as a gross smell, how could one hope to block out things like ethics and fear? Christopher shrugged. Then again, maybe the school fire just damaged his olfactory sensation.

Bodies from the previous night's handiwork littered the ground. In the light of day, the carnage gleamed in such shocking, luminous detail that it was almost too much to believe. It reminded him of the Staley's pasture, except with people instead of sheep. Limbs that were still attached twisted in unnatural ways. Slugs or the explosion had carved apart most of the bodies, and they looked more like unidentifiable hunks of meat than former humans. Christopher didn't try to identify the bodies, but Reverend Skidmore was hard to miss with his brown suit that he always preached in. His face was bloody with insect bites. His legs were missing.

Christopher didn't see his mother.

The thick, humid air clung to Christopher's skin, a lingering aftereffect of last night's storm. They emerged from the hole in the Braxtons' front door a bit past dawn, but all the early signs indicated that the heat of the day would reach unbearable heights. Christopher sweat a lot, always had, and he should have been used to operating with a thin layer of sweat and grime caked to him. Yet, the prospect of enduring an entire day in such conditions without so much as a quick bath made his skin crawl. How odd. He could follow around a dynamite-toting mass-murderer like a trained dog, yet couldn't handle putting up with his own stench.

Deklan wasted no time, marching around the town at the same, relentless pace he had the previous night in the light of the church fire. While Christopher slept, he had cut the fuses on the large sticks of dynamite to various lengths, with the longest one expected to burn in at a little over five minutes and shortest under one minute. He planned to light each fuse with a torch he had fashioned last night from a chair leg and a scrap of tablecloth from the Braxtons' house. Lorenz carried the twenty-five sticks of dynamite in a woman's wicker handbasket. The sight struck Christopher as surreal: the enormous, deformed man stalking about town, carrying the most destructive substance mankind had ever produced in the sort of reticule a flower girl might use in a wedding. It would have been an absurd picture, indeed, had anyone survived to witness it.

About the time when Christopher's nasal passages began to grow accustomed to the stench, he witnessed a sight nearly as vominous as the smell had been. Sheriff Townsend's brown German Shepard, Rusty, lay on its stomach in front of May Carter's two-story, whitewashed house, contentedly chewing on an object. Christopher peered closer and found that the object was someone's denim-swaddled leg, no doubt torn off in the explosion. He grimaced and recoiled, hoping that he had remembered to close the door of Davey Fredrikson's home so that a similar fate did not befall Mary's body.

Deklan reacted differently to the hungry German Shepard. Without breaking stride, he handed Christopher the torch, pulled a gun from its holster, and blasted a single bullet through the dog's cranium. The dog flipped over onto its head and lay still. Lorenz shoved the weapon back into its holster as the animal's tail slapped the ground a final time. "We don't know if they can infect dogs," he explained without stopping or looking back. He flipped the revolver around and deposited it into his holster, then continued walking.

Lorenz maintained his brisk pace, only pausing long enough to push a door open or break a window and toss a freshly lit stick of dynamite into someone's home. Deklan began using his cigar to light the fuses and let Christopher keep the torch to light a few of his own. Christopher completed the task even faster than the assassin, the fear of dynamite spurring him on to speeds he never thought himself capable of. They bypassed only those buildings that they felt sure the bugs had not violated (for example, if all of the homes occupants had been at the church, the bugs probably had no reason to invade it). Davey Fredrikson's parents' house stood toward the end of their route. The door had remained closed and no dogs were visible, so Christopher took some small comfort in that. Still, he hung back while Lorenz proceeded to cross that house off the list. By the time they had snaked around to every building in town and returned to the Braxton house, Christopher's mental count put them at thirty seconds before detonation.

Lorenz tossed the empty basket into the middle of the street. As they hustled past the Braxton's barn, they passed a feeding trough filled with rainwater from the previous night's deluge. Lorenz dropped his cigar into it and motioned for Christopher to do the same with the torch. As the resulting steam hissed upward, the former assassin hastily led the way through the hole in the Braxtons' boarded-up front door. Once inside, he knocked his hat from his head and began to tie a large, blue bandanna tightly around his scalp, making sure to fully cover his ears. He shook off his raincoat on his way into the kitchen and stepped up to the hole. He gave a silent nod in Christopher's direction, drew a gun with his right hand and plucked a second torch off the countertop with his left, and dropped into the hole. He disappeared before Christopher even had a chance to return the nod.

Christopher continued to stare at the hole that had swallowed Lorenz when his mental count reached five and the first building exploded. The earth trembled, but his experience with far larger explosions kept Christopher from unraveling. Seconds later, however, when houses all over town started going up in rapid succession and taking whatever cats, dogs, bugs, or still surviving humans with them, the ground shook so hard that Christopher fell to one knee and covered his head.

Plates rattled in the Braxtons' china cabinet, and the family's few wall decorations fell from their perches. Upstairs, the bedroom mirror shattered. The horrendous sequence of explosions outside made Christopher glad that he had only one working ear. Twenty long seconds after it started, the dynamite eradicated the last small, wooden house, and silence re-asserted itself. Christopher remained in his cautious crouch for several seconds, though; the ringing in his ear kept him from noticing that the ordeal had ended.

His hands still shook badly as he eased his body out of its coiled position and cautiously rose to his feet, fully anticipating another explosion to rattle the foundation of the house. None arrived, and after a brief moment of unease, Christopher knew that the last of the dynamite sticks had detonated. With a final look toward the oddly symmetrical hole in the floorboards, he stepped outside to survey the damage.

While in school, Christopher once saw a photograph of a Liberty-sized town that a mid-summer tornado had leveled. Climbing through the Braxtons' front door was like looking at the same photograph, except in color and with three dimensions. Buildings that had served as landmarks of his childhood were now little more than a testament to both the destructive capacity of dynamite and flatness of the Kansas landscape.

The stench of rotting flesh had been replaced by the only slightly less offensive stench of cooking flesh mixed with sulfur. Small fires burned themselves out everywhere he looked, lacking anything substantial to consume.

Christopher scanned the area, noting the handful of houses that, whether from lack of time or resources, Deklan proved unable to dynamite. The Rutlage stead still stood, as did their barn, where Deklan had thrown a knife through Christopher's father's head, where the night before he had no doubt shot all of the family's horses. Only a few other buildings were left intact. Christopher's eyes quickly swept over them: the Lawsons' place, Sheriff Townsend's house, Harkness's store... Christopher paused.

The green awning of Harkness's showed through the smoky haze, taunting Christopher. The building should have gone up with the rest of them. He had watched Lorenz break a windowpane with the barrel of his revolver and toss a lit stick of dynamite inside. Christopher remembered that distinctly. Then Lorenz had said, "I don't know what those things eat, but if we blow this up, we might cut off a food source." What other building would he have made that comment about? Yet there it stood, perfectly solid, like a tombstone poking out of the earth. Something had gone wrong, which meant that fixing it became Christopher's responsibility.

Christopher peered back into the shadowy interior of the Braxton house. Hopefully, Deklan's head would come poking out of the hole in the kitchen to inform Christopher that it was all over. Any second now.... any second now... Christopher rubbed his eyes, which had become irritated by the fumes in the air. Lorenz wasn't coming. Someone needed to investigate, and that someone was him. Having no other options, Christopher jumped off the porch and raced across the middle of town, dodging smoldering piles of rubble and the occasional body part, until he arrived breathlessly at the front steps of Harkness's store.

The front door remained closed, so Christopher gingerly, breathlessly stepped inside through the broken window with more than a passing consideration as to what might await him. A building full of ants might have lingered in the early morning shadows, or perhaps the fuse just took a little longer than the rest to detonate. Whatever lay waiting, his job description involved correcting things that went wrong, and that building should not have been standing.

The interior of Harkness's looked as though a giant had picked up the building and turned it upside down. Harkness was always fastidious about keeping the smallest crumb from marring the shelves or the floors, and he probably would have wept openly at the state of his store (were he not already a smoldering husk blasted across the Kansas prairie). Most of the shelves lay at awkward angles, torn from their brackets, and their contents littered the floor. One might have been tempted to attribute this to the explosions, but the destruction appeared too selective to come from an indiscriminate shaking of the earth. For instance, despite residing in glass jars, none of the pickles had been violated, while none of the bags of sugar were left intact. The sheer quantity of white crystals that lined the floor and collected in the cracks of the floorboards looked as though a snowstorm had blown through the store.

Christopher spent a frantic couple of minutes tossing the displaced contents of the store left and right, searching for the missing stick of dynamite. By the time he gave up, his hands and most of the rest of his clothes were covered in jam, sugar, and assorted other dry goods. The only thing useful he found was a familiar, symmetrical, gaping hole in the floorboards behind the counter. The darkened pit led straight down.

The now unmistakable sound of exploding dynamite shook the ground and halted his search. Christopher sprung to his feet and rushed to the window in time to witness the fiery bits of the Braxton house hitting the ground like spray from a flaming fountain. Something else was moving on Main Street, about a hundred feet away from the building Lorenz had disappeared under. One of the bugs displayed its mechanical running motion on its way back to Harkness's ransacked store.

Those bastards killed Deklan was the only thought racing through Christopher's mind as he reached into his pocket and removed the miniature gun Lorenz had given him. They had won. They had now taken everything from Christopher, and the world was theirs. It was all over, but at least Christopher could kill the cowardly insect that had killed Deklan Lorenz.

Christopher crouched to the right of the door as the creature waddled toward the entrance. As it pulled on the door handle, Christopher leapt to his feet and leveled the gun. The creature's head was roughly the size of a pumpkin, so it would be hard to miss. In the shade of the store's green awning, the bug froze.

Christopher had a significant size advantage of on the bug. In its previous life, it might have been one of the Braxton boys. Mary would have been even smaller as a bug. The thought shifted Christopher's face into snarl, which reflected in the creature's bulbous black eyes. It stood still long enough to catch a pair of bullets in the face, from a distance of about two feet. The body careened backwards and smashed against the wooden porch. Christopher stood with his gun hand still stretched out in front of him, temporarily mesmerized by his second kill in two days.

A satisfying warmth traveled through him as he looked at the prone body of his enemy, but it didn't have long to radiate. As usual, the ants running out of the holes in the bug's face shocked him back to reality. He instinctively slammed the door and jumped back, but they easily crept under the half-inch gap between the door and the floor, ignored the mounds of white, granulated sugar, and raced toward Christopher. He stood contemplating a course of action until one of the four-legged terrors scampered within an inch of his feet. With his first step forward, he ended half a dozen of the ants' pathetic lives. He opened the door, and with a second step, he escaped the store. A strategy had begun to form.

Deklan may have survived the blast. Christopher considered this possibility as he hopped off the wooden steps and sprinted into toward the center of the leveled town. It was the only possibility to consider, because if Lorenz was dead, Christopher's only chance at a human life involved finding a deserted island to inhabit. Assuming Lorenz still lived, he sat trapped underground, not knowing which exits were blocked. Trapped... down there... with the bugs.

Christopher dashed through the streets in a drunken trot, trying to visualize Liberty with all its buildings intact. He ran west from the church, down to the third pile of rubble, which he estimated was the Fredricksons' house. He stopped stared at the rubble, chest heaving. Mary was under there. He shook his head. Nothing to do now. The spray of rubble made it difficult to discern where the wreckage ended and the street began, but Christopher got down on his hands and knees and began picking through the wreckage. Maybe a minute later, he located the faceless corpse of James Waits. Several seconds after that, he found Waits' revolver. It was a newer model Colt single-action, probably never been fired. More importantly, it was small enough for a teenage boy to fire without the recoil knocking him unconscious. Even more importantly still, when Deklan killed Waits, the man had fallen onto his back, so the gun hadn't lain underneath him, marinating in a mud puddle all night. Clutching the weapon in his right hand, Christopher dashed back toward Harkness's.

When he arrived back at the store, hundreds of ants milled about amid the sugar-dusted floor. It seemed like more ants than the late bug's tiny body could hold. Christopher needed two long steps to get past them, ignoring the chills that riffled down his spine at the sound of a dozen simultaneous crunches, and continued to the back of the store. There, just in a short hallway that receded into the storeroom, sat a hot-blast kerosene lantern on a shelf. He grabbed it and returned to the front of the store.

Already sweating profusely from all the running and the morning heat, Christopher set the gun on a countertop, then unbuttoned and removed his shirt before tightly wrapping it about his head. Harkness probably had some clean aprons lying around, but he had already wasted enough time. His chest would be raw tomorrow, assuming there was a tomorrow, but it was better than leaving his ears exposed. He picked up the gun and stuffed it into the front of his britches. The ants had shifted course and locked onto his current location when Christopher grabbed the lamp and a box of matches lying nearby and marched around to the back of the counter.

For once, the ants were proving helpful. Had they not stayed a step behind Christopher, forcing a snap decision for every problem, someone might have found him days later, sulking at the mouth of the hole, still waiting for Deklan to emerge.

Looking into the hole soaked up any of the confidence he had gained from his latest kill. The thought of jumping in made him shiver despite the building heat of the day. This hole was identical to the one that had initiated Mary's slow death and swallowed Deklan, and despite having seen them half a dozen times, Christopher had never ventured down there. The downstairs of the Braxton house during the thunderstorm marked his closest approach to Hell. Frightening as the experience seemed at the time, he never forgot that he still stood in a man's house, in a man's world. The bugs had been the interlopers. The world inside the hole, though, belonged to them, and their world functioned in an altogether different manner. It was less of a hole than it was a gateway.

Christopher took a deep breath to collect himself, crouched down, and jumped in with both feet. He was lucky to not break his leg during the foolhardy leap into the darkness, but going down slowly involved contact with the ants. Luck was with him, though, he scraped the side the tunnel on his way down, slowing his plummet, and landed in soft, freshly dug dirt. His right ankle wouldn't be forgiving him any time soon, but he managed to keep from damaging the lantern.

The hole dropped nearly ten feet. Jumping in was an irreversible act. He was now in it until the end.

*   *   *

CHAPTER NINETEEN

Fear is a fascinating beast. It wells up inside us and overrides our more rational impulses. It can be an obstacle to overcome, infusing our muscles with a rigor that freezes us in our tracks, or it can be an effective motivator, electrifying every fiber of our being and prodding us away from a known threat and into the unknown at maximum velocity. Christopher encountered both its incarnations after plummeting into darkness.

The instant his fingertips contacted the soft dirt on the tunnel floor, every bodily fiber told Christopher to get out, go back, do anything to scramble back into the light. He fought down that urge like a rising tide of bile. *You're safe down here in the tunnel*, he told himself, *at least safer than you are up there.* If he even tried to scale the sheer sides of the pit and make the ten-foot climb to the surface, the ants would swarm over him while he helplessly clung to the side of the pit, and he might die just like Mary. Nothing could be worse than that, nothing in the tunnel, anyway. Christopher dropped to his knees, unlit lantern and matches in his hands, and crawled toward where the Braxton house once stood.

Christopher inched forward unabated. The expansive tunnel network probably connected most of the strategically important buildings of the town, but the bugs had only a few days to build it and had to keep travel simple. They also must not have anticipated visitors after the church explosion killed a majority of the town, because they ceased to block the tunnels at entry points, as they had in the tunnel under the Braxtons' house.

The paths ran level and straight, much more so than a child's tunnel through a snowdrift, except on the occasion that the bugs had to avoid a cellar or well. The diameter of the tunnels stood at about three to three-and-a-half feet and stayed uniform throughout the sections Christopher visited, and he soon learned why.

The bugs possessed an anatomical feature characteristic Christopher had never noticed in his repeated encounters with them (although, to be fair, most of his "encounters" involved either fighting or running from them, and it's hard to notice nuance in such circumstances). They had extended "arms," which allowed them to run on all fours faster than they could upright. This meant that, while invading humans shuffled through the three-foot-high passages holding a lantern in one hand and a revolver in the other, the bugs might as well have been dashing through an open field.

Christopher crept forward blindly for about twenty feet before remembering to light the lantern. It was an oversight, one that Lorenz never would have made. "Idiot," he muttered to himself as he set the lantern in the dirt. He raised the globe and took a few tense moments to fumble around with one of the matches before he ignited the wick. The lit lamp cast an arc of light that extended only about five or six feet in either direction. He looked up and expected to see a tunnel full of bug faces staring at him with their glossy, black eyes. Only dirt and darkness surrounded him, though. This time, the mistake was not lethal, but he knew fully that was a pilgrim in an unholy land. He tried to take a deep breath, and it was at this point that Christopher discovered that he was claustrophobic.

Living in rural Kansas, a fear of tight spaces never came up.
Riding in a buggy was probably the closest Christopher ever came to an
"enclosed area." Just the same, the timing could not have been worse. The
grainy brown walls appeared to sag in toward him, as if the entire tunnel
stood on the verge of collapse. *Go back*, something inside him screamed. *If
you're lucky, you might have just enough time to make it before the ceiling gives
out and you're buried alive.* He pressed against the floor of the earthen
esophagus, fighting the urge while an icy fist closed around his
midsection. Hissing sounds marked his every inhalation, and he
wondered if the thin air had, in fact, resulted from a collapse of one end of
the tunnel.

Christopher lay in the dirt, clutching his lantern, breathing like a
grounded fish. What was it Deklan had told him? "When I'm afraid, I
deal with it." Something like that. Christopher had no idea how to
alleviate these sensations of impending doom, so he would have to get
used to them, just like Lorenz had gotten used to the corpse stench on the
surface world. *You are fine*, he chided himself. *The tunnel is not going to
collapse. You are not going to die…well, not of a collapsing tunnel, anyway.* He
winced. It almost worked. He slid his lantern-hand a few inches in front
of him, dug his elbow into the dirt, and resumed his forward crawling at a
fraction of his initial speed. He was moving forward, though, and that
was an improvement.

Christopher advanced about twenty feet farther before he
remembered to remove the revolver from the front of his pants. Another
mistake. He was running out of chances. Although the iron barrel no
longer poked him in the thigh every time he moved, his choices now were
limited to traveling either on his knees or on his knees and elbows. After
attempting each for a few feet, he elected to stick with walking on his
knees.

It wasn't a natural motion for him, and his knees became extraordinarily sore after he hobbled forward another twenty feet. Nervous sweat oozed from his pours, especially around his hairline, and mingled with the abundant dirt to form a moderately thick layer of grime about his neck and bare chest. On the positive side, the hysteria had subsided, and Christopher began to entertain the idea that he may see the sun again.

A third possibility existed, between life and death, and he considered it while taking a moment to stretch his legs behind. A satisfying pop sprung from his right hip joint and resounded through the tunnel. He could live, or he could be killed. An equally likely chance, though, involved the ants getting to him. What if they came down the tunnel in a wave, like they did in the church? What would he do then? Christopher stared at the stretch of loose dirt between his knees. *You really should decide on an answer before you move another inch*, he thought.

James Waits' revolver almost gleamed in the lantern light. Shooting himself would not pose a problem. While not ranking among his favorite ideas that ever crossed his mind, it placed well ahead of letting ants crawl through his skull and lay eggs, or whatever they did in there. Unless all the bugs were dead, though, his death would not stop them. Fighting on, conversely, could lead to capture and imprisonment in one of those amber cocoons, which seemed as bad as not committing suicide. He set the revolver on the ground and wiped some sweaty dirt out of his stinging eyes. If he had a chance of completing the mission, he would fight on. If capture became imminent, and he had the opportunity, he would shoot himself. *Great plan. Now get moving.* The progress resumed.

Christopher's arms pumped away like cranks on a locomotive as he slid forward. Where was the best place to shoot one's self? It was a valid question; whatever his sins, he deserved better than to slowly bleed to death in an earthen tunnel. Through the mouth, maybe? That might leave an exit wound in the back of the throat and fail to kill him quickly enough. In the temple, then? Waits' gun wasn't the monstrosity that one of Deklan's Peacemakers was, but it would do the job from the temple.

A few dozen feet further, the circle of sunlight beaming down from Harkness's had long since vanished behind him, and Christopher became disoriented. His first turn lay in front of him, a short jog to his right. He was somewhere under Main Street, but he had no idea how far away the Braxton house stood, or in what direction. He had no idea how far he had even moved. The only direction to move was forward, so he pressed on, this time crawling on his knees and elbows. The long curve further restricted his already limited vision. *There's nothing there*, he told himself. *If they were here, you'd hear them clicking.*

After the tunnel straightened out again, it split into two identical paths. At the edge of the circle of light, one branch trailed to Christopher's left, the other to his right. The one that bent to the right seemed to continue in roughly the direction he traveled. Unfortunately, he had neglected to notice that from his moment of entry, the tunnel that he crawled down gradually had drifted to the right.

Christopher dropped down to his elbows and crawled about sixty or seventy feet before the tunnel began to show signs of a recent collapse. First, his elbows sunk a few inches into a layer of loose dirt built up on the path. He pressed onward another dozen feet, until the circle of lantern light grazed the landslide of earth and floorboards that made the path completely impassable. It must have resulted from a dynamite blast.

"Damn," Christopher muttered. Despite not ingesting liquids all morning, he continued to work up a formidable lather over every inch of his body and did not relish the prospect of spending any longer underground than necessary. The tunnel provided him with about three feet to perform a one-hundred-and-eighty-degree turn. It should have been enough room, and with a little practice, he could have performed the feat with ease, but his experience in tunnels had only recently progressed to mastering forward motion. By either luck or divine intervention, as Christopher struggled to readjust himself in the opposite direction, his functional left ear faced the open end of the tunnel, the same direction from which the bug attacked.

As mentioned earlier, the bugs could literally sprint through the three-foot-diameter tunnels. Had Christopher not heard the distinct clicking sound that announced this one's approach, it would have crushed his skull like an over-ripe melon before he even noticed it enter his circle of light. When the clicking sound registered, his eyelids spread to their widest point, and he raised Waits' pistol with his right hand, his elbow planted in the earth. He still grossly underestimated the speed of his opponent. It nearly sprung when Christopher first caught a glimpse of the lantern light reflecting off of the creature's shiny eyes. He pulled the trigger. In the confined space, the pistol's report sounded like a roar, and the recoil sent the barrel of the gun smacking against his chin.

The bullet struck the bug squarely and blasted a thumb-sized hole in its gigantic face, ending its charge inches short of Christopher's right foot. Immediately, he forced himself the rest of the way around in the tunnel and scrambled over the bug's body and back the way he came so fast that he nearly pitched forward on two occasions. Still, he was not fast enough to elude the escaping ants.

The stinging bites erupted on his chest and legs, several times a second. He crawled a dozen feet away before setting the revolver and lantern on the ground and proceeding to slap the creatures off of his person. It took ten seconds before he had killed all the ants advancing over his bare torso, and it might have been the most anxious ten seconds of his life. He shimmied forward another half-dozen feet before examining his lower half. While wiping his pants down, Christopher's index finger sank several inches into the bullet hole marring the outer portion of his left thigh. He felt the back of his thigh, where an identical hole marked the exit wound. Apparently, on its path to the bug's face, the killing bullet first traveled through the meaty part of Christopher's leg.

He had been moving fine before discovering the self-inflicted wound, but from that moment onward, his right leg became a lead weight that he had to drag through the tunnels. The shock prevented the pain from overwhelming him. He had heard of shock, and knew that it could become a dangerous state, but had no idea how to deal with it. Given a choice between stopping and continuing, Christopher slithered onward, mostly using his elbows and shoving with his good, right leg. This latter tactic increased his pace, but it also dumped handfuls of dirt into the profusely bleeding wound every time he moved.

He was losing blood. He considered removing his shirt from his head and using it as a bandage, but leaving his cranium uncovered seemed like the greater of two evils. The wound was well on its way to carrying an infection. Lorenz was nowhere in sight, but now more than ever, finding him was Christopher's only hope. Deklan would know exactly what to do. Granted, Christopher had never seen him get shot or administer all but the most rudimentary first aid, but he seemed like some sort of world-class scholar when it came to matters of violence and death.

Christopher clawed at the loose earth as he dragged himself down the dark, sweltering tunnel. Thoughts of survival only carried him so far. It would have been so easy to curl up in the dirt and die, or turn the gun on himself to save his soul from the bugs. Yes, suicide was a sin, but there had to be exemptions; God would have understood the situation. It's presumed He forgave Sampson for toppling the pillars to save himself from the Philistines. Christopher pushed on, though, because of a task entrusted to him that was more vital than any Biblical commandment. "If anything does go wrong," Deklan had told him, "fix it." His father never gave him a responsibility like that. No one did. It was the most important task anyone had ever trusted him with (and, in all likelihood, ever would), and he would be damned if he was going to give up.

The motivation to satisfy Deklan's order burned out after about five minutes of dragging his blood-soaked leg through the dirt. Christopher did his best, after all. What the hell was Lorenz thinking, expecting a fourteen-year-old to save the day? He stopped moving and lay the side of his head in the dirt. His chest heaved. His tongue ran around the front of his filmed-over teeth. If he closed his eyes, he probably could have drifted off into unconsciousness. The image of Mary came into his mind. Her screaming and clutching for him with her doll-like hands when she came out of the tunnel. Her twitching when the bolt of lightning split the purple sky. Deklan didn't do that to her: they did. Christopher coiled his good leg under him, used the tip of his left shoe to dig a ridge into the soft ground, and shoved forward. Again. And again. And again.

He pushed onward, lantern and gun stretched in front of him. Sometimes he could move over a foot with a single, solid push. Sometimes he would hit a snag and only covered a few inches. Time ceased to mean anything; he would either find Lorenz or die trying. The flame had nearly consumed the wick when the word, "Christopher?" echoed down the tunnel. It was Deklan's voice. Who else could it possibly be, unless the Devil had tracked him down already? Relief passed over Christopher like a warm hug, almost causing him to pass out prematurely. *Don't cry... at least hold it off until you see that beautiful, malformed face.*

Christopher reached his elbows out as far as he could, then dragged his lower half forward. A terrible premonition haunted him: the instant the lamplight fell upon Lorenz, he would stare back with glazed-over eyes, twitching like a marionette with tangled strings. Christopher looked up, squinting toward the edge of the circle of luminance, at Lorenz and his steady form and mismatched eyes. The only thing amiss about the reassuring image was a blue bandana sat where his flat, black hat should have been. Lorenz reached out and grabbed Christopher by his sweaty armpits and dragged him closer. It was a protective gesture rather than one of affection, but it saved Christopher a few feet of crawling, and allowed him to feel a flicker of security. More than anything else, he no longer lay alone in the darkness.

Lorenz propped Christopher against the far side of the tunnel and eased down to his backside. Wordlessly, he looked Christopher over, then pulled the lantern out of the younger man's coiled fingers. He raised the globe, and blew a puff of air to choke off the flame. "What went wrong?" he asked under the veil of absolute darkness. The question tacitly implied that he trusted Christopher to follow orders.

Christopher pressed his eyes closed and kept his breathing to a low hiss. "They took the dynamite… out of Harkness's and blew up the Braxton place. I came through the floor… of Harkness's and came looking for you." He winced. "One of the bugs… it came from behind me. I shot it… but the bullet took a hunk out of my leg." He drew in a slow breath, somewhat surprised at how brief his summary turned out to be. "That's pretty much… what happened."

Lorenz may have nodded. "Yeah," he began, shifting around above Christopher, "I thought something was amiss. I haven't encountered anything the entire time I've been down here. I was just sitting down here in the dark, listening, when you showed up." A sound of cloth tearing cut through the darkness. "They've smelled the blood by now," Deklan said as he wound the remnants of his shirt around Christopher's wounded leg, "and should be coming soon."

"What if they don't?" Christopher asked weakly. He had promised his body a rest as soon as he found Deklan, and it now attempted to take him up on the offer.

Lorenz never had a chance to answer. Instead, his body shifted into a crouch, and he hissed, "Don't move." The clicking sounds re-energized Christopher. He didn't know which end of the tunnel the sounds came from. Probably both. It was a constant series of uneven clicks, more than he'd ever heard before. Metal rubbed on leather as Deklan's Peacemakers slid out of their holsters. An instant later, a deafening screech bounced through the tunnel, before a rapid succession of shots drown out all other sound.

Boom-boom-boom-boom... The powder flashes that sent bullets in both directions illuminated Lorenz for brief instants as he loomed above Christopher, eyes closed, arms extended... *boom-boom-boom-boom....* The charging bugs hiccupped in the midst of their assault and thudded into the earth a few feet before reaching the pair of trespassing humans... *boom-boom-boom-boom-click-click.*

When the spent chambers clicked, Christopher let go of the clutch of air in his lungs, mistakenly thinking that their ordeal was over. A different clicking sound broke the silence. Instead of pistol hammers smacking against spent changers, this one reverberated from many sets of mandibles snapping together. The remaining bugs pushed past the corpses that blocked the tunnel. Apparently, the passage was a bit too narrow, and Deklan had blindly fired his valuable bullets into dead bodies.

Deklan's impossibly even voice came down to Christopher. "Christopher," he said, "give me your gun."

Christopher fumbled with the revolver he had picked from James Waits' rotting corpse before gripping it cleanly. The bug corpses shifted over the dirt; the others were nearly through. Christopher's shaking hands extended the weapon forward, muzzle first. He could not see anything in the blackness, and blood and sweat made the handle slick, so no one can really lay blame on anyone, but whatever the reason, the gun slid out of someone's hand during the exchange, and hit the ground.

Christopher cringed.

*   *   *

Later, in his shock-induced haze, Christopher would estimate that ten insect bodies lay dead in the tunnel. The bullets probably took six of them down. That left four for Deklan to dispatch after Christopher dropped Waits' gun. Two caught throwing knives in the face immediately, because he heard a crunch on two separate occasions as the blades breached the creatures' skulls. Another knife toss into the darkness followed, and it felled the ninth bug. He can prove this because the slain bug landed on Christopher's chest and it took every vestige of strength left in his body to shove the corpse off of him before it started leaking ants.

While he could never prove it, he suspected that Lorenz killed the last of the giant insects with his bare hands. He had exhausted his supply of throwing knives, and if he had another gun on his person, he never fired it. There is an excellent chance that Lorenz might have carried another dagger somewhere on his person; after all, what's one more knife to a walking arsenal. Regardless of the specifics, the last bug and Deklan grappled with one another at some point. Grunts and hisses intermingled with the constant clicking. Glass shattered after one of the combatants stepped on or kicked the lantern. Ten seconds after they locked up, a sickening crunch split the air and the bug fell. So, at worst, he defeated a creature with super-human strength in absolute darkness with a small knife. Either way, it was an impressive feat.

The moment the last of the bugs hit the ground, Deklan set to work protecting them against the rapidly mobilizing ants. Christopher could see nothing, but could easily hear Lorenz panting as he labored in the darkness. Lorenz plucked the remains of the lantern from the dirt and dashed its contents to the left and right.

Lorenz struck a match, and his pulverized face flickered into being. To either side of them, blackness was oozing forward. When Lorenz tossed the match on the kerosene-drenched bodies, the tunnel turned crimson. Deklan's doubled-over form hovered above Christopher. The melee with the bugs had turned Lorenz's body into a mass of lacerations and blood, with his scar-choked, bare chest taking the brunt of the damage. His left cheekbone may have been crushed. A deep, diagonal cut ran the length of his forehead and caused him to constantly wipe the blood from his eyes. The bandana that covered his ears was still in place, though, and that made everything else irrelevant.

Squinting against the brightness, Christopher shifted to his left, toward the body of the last of the bugs. The flame sprouted from both its crushed head and shoulders, which lay about three feet from one another. Apparently, Lorenz had cut or torn its head off during the climactic fray. Those ants that had not yet cleared the pile of bodies issued forth a collective shriek as the fire consumed them. The near-human squeal seemed to come from a thousand different directions. Christopher never knew they could scream. *Good*, he thought as he slapped at those that had escaped the inferno and scurried up his neck, *I hope they suffer*. Lorenz did not seem to notice; shifting into a crouch, he produced an unbloodied hunting knife from somewhere and began to chop at the tunnel ceiling.

While one would have a difficult time ever describing his actions as "frantic," Lorenz's animated digging on this occasion came close. His face still held the expression of a granite formation, but his right hand stabbed at the earth again and again, the trickle of dirt never falling fast enough for his taste. When his right arm wearied from the constant assault on the tunnel, he switched to his left.

Several seconds passed without him having to kill an ant crawling across his person, so Christopher shimmied up the side of the tunnel and attempted to help Lorenz dig. His fingers raked across the loose dirt several times before he started to cough. The upper half of the tunnel began to fill with pungent, black smoke, and Deklan set a hand on Christopher's shoulder and pushed him back down to the bottom of the tunnel. Christopher didn't have the strength to resist, or to do anything other than draw in another lungful of thinning air. "Stay down there," Lorenz said, his voice sounding high and strained. He was holding his breath.

Christopher's eyes fluttered closed and his thoughts began to drift.

*   *   *

A hand slapped Christopher's face. Christopher blinked in the darkness, disoriented. The cascading dirt must have extinguished the fire, but while the situation lacked visibility, at least breathing was no longer such a chore. "They're all over you," Lorenz's disembodied voice said. "Keep them off your face and neck."

Christopher's hands patted down every inch of his person in search of invaders, while above him, the chop of the knife and the trickle of dirt resumed their mechanical resonance. Lorenz must have stood at his full height at that point, as sounds of slapping reigned down amid the falling dirt. Chop and slap. Chop and slap. When tiny legs no longer caressed the surface of Christopher's skin, he tried to stand again and succeeded only in passing out for the second time.

*   *   *

Hands gripped Christopher under the armpits and pulled him out from under a blanket of dirt. Christopher knew better than to try to stand. Instead, he lay like a rag doll, trusting Lorenz to do all the work. Ant legs tickled their way up Christopher's right forearm, but he had to wait until Lorenz set him down again to dispose of it. *Maybe it's a real ant*, his weary mind offered. *Better to not take the chance.* He lethargically slapped it as it attempted to traverse his bare shoulder, sending it back to hell. He didn't feel any ants scurrying through his auditory canal, but he had no idea what that sensation consisted of in the first place. How long had he been unconscious? How far was Lorenz from the surface? Christopher remained propped against the wall atop the cushion of dirt, vigilant of anything crawling over him.

Several feet above, Lorenz's breaths came in short gasps. He must have wedged himself into the vertical tunnel he was constructing. The chopping sounds came slower, but still steady. For a moment, the sounds stopped, and only wheezing broke the silence. The pause only lasted a second, though, and the chopping became more furious than ever.

Unable to tell if his eyes were opened or closed, Christopher smiled. He could almost hear Deklan's voice echoing in his head: *Do you know what I do when I become exhausted to the point of collapse? I fight through it.* While focusing on the flecks of dirt hitting his skin, Christopher passed out again.

*   *   *

When next he awoke, something dragged Christopher skyward. It wasn't hands this time, but a rope that encircled his torso, directly under his arms. It jerked him skyward a foot at a time. He bounced against the side of the earthen tunnel every few seconds, but the sensation could barely penetrate his layer of numbness. The afternoon sunlight streamed down on his face, stabbing at his unprepared eyes like needles. The ninety-five-degree air felt cool against his filth encrusted, ant-ravaged skin. Christopher closed his eyes and gave into the will of the rope.

When he lay stretched out on the ground beneath the spacious, blue sky, the first wholly coherent image Christopher's eye slits provided belonged to Deklan. His over-sized, misshapen head blocked the sun as he bent over Christopher. His chest expanded and contracted like overworked bellows and he wasn't smiling, but then again, he rarely smiled. Light streamed around the outline of Lorenz's person, creating a halo.

Lorenz still possessed the same features as he had when Christopher saw him brooding in the corner of the blacksmith's shop those many days ago. If anything, his appearance had regressed due to fatigue, filth, and battle scars. He no longer looked like a demon, though. On the contrary, illuminated by the sun before the backdrop of the open sky, he looked positively angelic... an avenging angel, perhaps, but an angel nonetheless.

*   *   *

CHAPTER TWENTY

The pain in Christopher's upper thigh shifted from a dull throb to a sharp burst once Deklan emptied half a bottle of whiskey into the wound. His teeth had bitten into the leather strap Lorenz had handed him, but the instant the alcohol hit and his leg felt like it was on fire, he spit it out and began wailing. Between wails, he slammed his palm into the dirt like a baby having a tantrum. Why not? There was no one left alive to complain about the noise. They were in the shadow of Waits' tavern or would have been had the explosion from earlier not obliterated the structure, destroying practically everything except the half-full whiskey bottle. The job required twice as much dynamite (i.e., two sticks) than most of the other buildings, but it went up just the same.

Deklan glanced at Christopher when the younger man started keening, but refrained from wasting time with reassurances or reprimands, instead focusing on activity. Even though his left shoulder sagged at an awkward angle and he had to force his eyes open, he cleaned and dressed the young man's wound at nearly the rate he had dug them to freedom. He finished the sterilization of the bullet hole in a matter of minutes.

With his usual terseness shining through, Deklan motioned for Christopher to give him his hand. Christopher complied, wincing all the way as Lorenz pulled him into a standing position. Christopher hopped on the leg a couple of times, but was still amazed that when Lorenz released his hand and took a step away, he could stand under his own power. "Wow, thanks," Christopher said as he massaged the bandage over the entry wound and waited for the light-headedness to subside. Walking would still be a chore, but that now had more to do with his sprained right ankle than his perforated left thigh.

"Don't mention it," Lorenz said gruffly, pressing his gloved hand against the injured side of his face. "You're stable enough to travel by yourself now."

Christopher stopped picking at his leg wound. "Travel?" he repeated, surprised. "Where am I travelling to?"

Lorenz pointed north. "Kansas City," he explained laconically. "I know it's a couple days ride, but that leg's probably infected. We're out of whiskey, and you'll need some professional medical attention soon."

"Aren't you coming?" Christopher asked, already knowing the answer. He dreaded the notion of leaving. The town didn't provide security, because there was no town. People make a town and, to a lesser extent, so do buildings. Both were gone now, blown apart. What he did dread was leaving the side of the man that saved him from getting blown apart, too... or worse. It would have been easy for Lorenz to abandon him or use him as bait, then simply blown Christopher's head off in the aftermath, but he didn't.

"I would," Lorenz said. He bowed his head slightly, letting stringy locks of black hair hang in his face, and shook it. "I've got some business to attend to here yet, though. Should take me another day, at the most. I think I got most of the fully formed ones, but the Waits family is underground, somewhere. So are some others, most likely." He flicked a limp hand in Christopher's direction. "You... you've gotta get that leg looked at, though."

Christopher barely heard the end of Lorenz's statement; he was still stuck on the words "Waits." Thinking at Emma sent a bolt of regret through him and made him wince. He had nearly forgotten about the poor girl to whom he would have pledged his eternal devotion only days earlier. Had it only been days? Even with chronically abusive parents, he felt like he'd endured more stress in the few dozen hours that followed the incident in Old Man Staley's field than he had during his previous fourteen years. Emma... When he closed his eyes, he could see the sunlight glint off her hair the day he made awkward teenage love to her for the first time. If the bugs had dragged her and her family underground last night, the ants were probably incubating in their bodies. His eyelids flew open and he shuddered.

His eyes refocused on his partner. "Do you think I can make it in my condition?" Christopher asked, unable to shake the feeling that something terrible would happen the second he left Lorenz.

"You'll make it," Lorenz assured him, staring at the ground. "I loaded Waits' gun and put it in your saddlebag."

Christopher nodded. "So... I've graduated to six-shooters?"

"Yeah, try not to shoot yourself in the other leg," Lorenz said, and Christopher wasn't sure whether he was joking. "I put some extra ammunition in there, too, and enough food and water for a couple days." He finally looked up and met Christopher's gaze. His lips shifted, slightly, forming an uncomfortable smile. "You'll make it. I'll catch up with you."

Lorenz had never deliberately lied to Christopher before, probably, in part, because he was an inept liar. Whether or not Christopher made it to Kansas City alive would prove irrelevant in comparison to the job Lorenz still had to do. They both knew it, but Lorenz was the only one that could deal with it. Religion never took root very deeply with Christopher, but he had to wonder whether it meant something that the rock in Staley's pasture happened to land in one of the few places on the planet occupied by someone capable of stopping the madness it unleashed. Everyone had their job to do... even Mary. In the big picture, neither of their lives was worth any more than any of the townspeople that had been shot, or blown apart, or stabbed. Lorenz probably would have preferred to go to Kansas City with Christopher, but he was a firm believer in the job taking precedence over personal interests.

"Are you at least going to get some sleep?" Christopher asked, trying to mentally tally how much sleep Lorenz had accrued over the last few days. Since yesterday morning, he can only remember the half hour Lorenz dozed in the schoolhouse. The grand total couldn't have been much more.

"Sure," Lorenz returned, wearily. Another lie; he pulled his eyes away at the last second. He wasn't even trying that hard to hide his lies, because they both knew Christopher couldn't do a damn thing about it. He wanted rid of Christopher, and probably had his reasons.

Christopher nodded. "Yeah, well, where are the horses?"

"The schoolhouse barn," he replied. "Dante's watching them." His head lolled forward involuntarily, betraying his weariness.

Christopher nodded again. What the hell was going on? Theirs always had been a partnership of convenience, but why was it no longer convenient? There was *nothing* Christopher could do at this point to help? That seemed unlikely. He didn't know the answers, but he wasn't going to ask. He owed Lorenz more than his life, and he could show some respect for the man's wishes one final time. There had been moments in the past when he wasn't sure he wanted to know what Lorenz was thinking. This was one of those times. He should have said something, though, something better than, "I'll see you later."

Christopher turned toward the schoolhouse, which was now clearly visible from the middle of town, thanks to the flattened buildings. On some level, he knew those were the last words he would ever speak to

Lorenz. The last words Deklan spoke to him, though, would remain steeped in profundity for the remainder of his days. As Christopher limped away, Lorenz called out, "Christopher." The only surviving Rutlage used several small steps to gingerly turn himself to face the tattered man. "Don't tell them what happened," Lorenz said, "but always remember." His voice held a soft quality to it, and came out more a plea than a demand.

Deklan looked at across the dirty street for a long second, his stringy hair blowing in the light breeze. Then, he turned away from Christopher and walked toward a covered wagon that lay on its side. It might have been Lewis Rutlage's but he couldn't be certain from that angle. Nothing Christopher could think to say seemed to be enough, so he, turned and resumed his trek toward the distant schoolhouse. After a few paces, he looked over his shoulder, but Lorenz had vanished. "Thank you," Christopher called to the empty air.

Walking to the barn, an image replayed in Christopher's mind. Fatigue numbed him almost to the point of falling over, but the image still disturbed him worse than one of those demonic ants crawling across his neck. Perhaps Christopher's weary mind spawned the whole thing, or maybe he saw it clearly and couldn't accept it because of its sheer magnitude, but after making his final request, Deklan turned way, and his entire body performed a brief, familiar convulsion.

*   *   *

Christopher reached the schoolhouse barn safely, and the sight of two horses and a dog greeted him when he opened the door. Dante let out a bark at the sight of Christopher, then seemed oddly disappointed that Christopher was alone. Christopher reached down and stroked the back of the dog's head for nearly a minute. Part of him wanted to inch down to his backside, sit and run his hand across Dante's soft scalp until Lorenz returned. Another part of him feared ever seeing Lorenz again. He straightened up and concentrated all his energies on saddling Thor.

Christopher gingerly swung his punctured leg over Thor's back. Dante and Virgil both looked at him, imploringly, perhaps. Should he take them with him? He bit his lip and glanced back toward the middle of town. No, they would be alright; Deklan would see to them, even if that meant a bullet in each of their heads. He turned Thor and slapped the reigns. Dante's intermittent barking followed him as he Thor galloped away from the barn, but Christopher could only muster a final turn. Dante stood at the doorway, wagging his tail, barking, smiling the innocent smile of a dog. He probably continued on until Christopher had disappeared from sight.

Christopher rode about one-half-mile out of town before stopping to take a final look at the only home he had ever known. He looked, but could hardly recognize what he saw. His town was gone, melted into the Kansas prairie, leveled by a firestorm of fate and a tidal wave of circumstance. In some ways, the citizens of Liberty deserved it, first for accusing, than for not believing. A few buildings still stuck out of the earth, here and there, but they were not homes anymore; they were tombstones.

The house his father built still stood, but it didn't look the least bit menacing. It was just wood and nails. Ghosts still lived there, but from this far away, for good or ill, they couldn't ever touch him again.

His home was gone, and he was alone.

*   *   *

After riding north for two hours, the dust of the approaching cavalry mushroomed in the distance. Thor had kept a moderate pace the entire ride, as if knowing the distance he would have to travel. Christopher sagged in the saddle, doing his best to not think about the events that historians would later refer to as "The Liberty Massacre," and failing horribly. His initial thought upon spotting the fifty men riding toward him were that he had never seen a cavalry before.

Neither Christopher nor Thor made any attempt to evade the men, and the mass of mounted humanity eventually consumed their path. The blond-bearded, blue-uniformed captain in the front of the group raised a gauntleted hand and signaled for the troops to stop. Four-dozen armed men looked at Christopher as though he were missing his head. Besides the single bullet hole, his pants and shirt were caked in some combination of sweat and blood and whatever black bodily substance the bugs produced. His visible flesh was covered in bruises and cuts from the numerous beatings and assaults he had endured over the last several days. The captain kept his composure and started in with the questions immediately. Who are you? Are you from the town of Liberty? What happened there? The last one the most forcefully asked.

Christopher remained polite and answered their questions to the best of his ability. When asked to explain what had happened in Liberty, Christopher raised his hollow eyes and stated, "The wrath of God," and left it at that. He let his appearance do the talking for him. Besides his youth, the soldiers could see that the filthy, bloody, wounded young man had suffered greatly. The captain gave a tight-lipped nod.

Christopher expelled a sickly cough into his fist. "Where did you.... how did you know about the...?"

"Gabriel Spencer," the captain answered, sitting high in his saddle, "your town's barber informed us. As soon as the church exploded, he fled town with his family. He stopped off at Fort Harrison on his way to Kansas City and told his story."

Christopher nodded. If Spencer made it to Fort Harrison and the captain didn't mention any insectoid characteristics, he and his family must have escaped the contagion. After a brief examination, the company's medical officer informed Christopher that the wound had not become infected, but he should have it re-examined upon reaching Kansas City. With little more than a cursory glance through his saddlebags, the regiment departed toward the wreckage of Liberty in a cloud of dust.

Christopher rode on until the mid-afternoon, stopping under a cluster of trees to eat. While digging through the provisions Deklan left for him, the bottom of the saddlebag shifted. He wedged his fingers around the edge of the false bottom and lifted. A mass of green paper filled the bottom of the saddlebag. Christopher had never seen so much money in his life. He removed stack after stack and sat down in the grass to count it. Three thousand dollars. To him, that was little more than a number.

Christopher stared in the direction the dusty cavalry had departed. Deklan would not be following him to Kansas City. He would never see the man again. In the shade of a twisted oak, Christopher wept for the loss of his friend.

*   *   *

EPILOGUE

July 12, 1877

The floorboard's creaked under Captain Lankford's boot as he stepped into Colonel Harris's office. He still wore a thin layer of dust like a cloak as he gave a salute. The Colonel, though, always reminded his officers that he wasn't hosting a cotillion ball, and giving a report took precedence over polishing your boots. The tanned, gaunt commanding officer motioned for the captain to sit in one of the hard, wooden chairs across from his desk. The office itself was a moderately furnished affair. In Lankford's experience, lots of these veterans from the War Between the States that had been jettisoned to these backwater positions often felt the need to strew their ribbons and medals all over the walls, but Harris was the efficient, down-to-earth sort, and most of the time, that made him a pleasure to serve under.

"So," Harris said, leaning back in his chair and folding his hands, "was there any basis to Mr. Spencer's story?"

Lankford gave an elaborate nod. "Oh, absolutely, sir. I've never seen anything like it. Every building in town was blown to bits except the schoolhouse. I sent teams out riding two miles in every direction, and we couldn't find a single survivor." He shook his head and watched as the colonel leaned in. "There was a boy we intercepted that was fleeing the town, but he seemed to be in shock and was even less helpful than Spencer in the way of details."

"Blown to bits?" Harris repeated, running his fingers over his thick, white mustache. "You mean with explosives?"

"Exactly, sir," Lankford said, scratching his blond beard. "I would say whoever did it used dynamite. There were a couple dozen bodies lying in the street that had been shot in the head, but it looks like a bunch were sitting in the church when it blew up. I left a dozen men behind to investigate the site, but I don't think they're going to turn up any survivors, either. It was just a massacre."

Harris stared out the window as sunlight streamed into the room. "That's a damn shame," he said, then regarded Lankford. "You ever been out to Liberty?"

"No, sir."

"I'd passed through there a couple times going back and forth from Fort Sill. Pretty little town. Little slice of Paradise," he noted as he shook his head. "A damn shame." Harris put his closed hands to his mouth, thinking. "You say the schoolhouse was standing?"

"Well," Lankford began, "The schoolhouse itself wasn't standing; it'd been blown up and the wreckage was still burning, but the barn next to it was intact."

"Anything there?"

Lankford squinted, thinking back to the scene. "It was a little strange, sir. The barn was empty, but there were some horse and dog droppings that were a couple hours old. The rider must've left just before we got there." When Harris didn't interrupt, Lankford scratched his chin and continued. "The droppings were from a single horse, but there was no way one person could have done all that damage. What I'm guessing is, whoever owned the horse must've been the last one to ride out."

Harris nodded, grimly, still staring out the window. "That's a shame, Captain. A damn shame." He arched a bushy, white eyebrow. "Predictable, though, I suppose. I've been on this earth fifty-two years, and I've seen my share of injustices. I think that you'll find that as you look through the history of humanity, seldom does a man get what he deserves."

"Amen to that, sir. Amen."

THE END